All My Tomorrows

OTHER BOOKS BY AL LACY

Angel of Mercy series:
A Promise for Breanna (Book One)
Faithful Heart (Book Two)
Captive Set Free (Book Three)
A Dream Fulfilled (Book Four)
Suffer the Little Children (Book Five)
Whither Thou Goest (Book Six)
Final Justice (Book Seven)
Not by Might (Book Eight)
Things Not Seen (Book Nine)
Far Above Rubies (Book Ten)

Journeys of the Stranger series:
Legacy (Book One)
Silent Abduction (Book Two)
Blizzard (Book Three)
Tears of the Sun (Book Four)
Circle of Fire (Book Five)
Quiet Thunder (Book Six)
Snow Ghost (Book Seven)

Battles of Destiny (Civil War series):
Beloved Enemy (Battle of First Bull Run)
A Heart Divided (Battle of Mobile Bay)
A Promise Unbroken (Battle of Rich Mountain)
Shadowed Memories (Battle of Shiloh)
Joy from Ashes (Battle of Fredericksburg)
Season of Valor (Battle of Gettysburg)
Wings of the Wind (Battle of Antietam)
Turn of Glory (Battle of Chancellorsville)

Hannah of Fort Bridger series (coauthored with JoAnna Lacy):
Under the Distant Sky (Book One)
Consider the Lilies (Book Two)
No Place for Fear (Book Three)
Pillow of Stone (Book Four)
The Perfect Gift (Book Five)
Touch of Compassion (Book Six)
Beyond the Valley (Book Seven)
Damascus Journey (Book Eight)

Mail Order Bride series (coauthored with JoAnna Lacy):
Secrets of the Heart (Book One)
A Time to Love (Book Two)
Tender Flame (Book Three)
Blessed Are the Merciful (Book Four)
Ransom of Love (Book Five)
Until the Daybreak (Book Six)
Sincerely Yours (Book Seven)
A Measure of Grace (Book Eight)
So Little Time (Book Nine)
Let There Be Light (Book Ten)

All My Tomorrows

THE ORPHAN TRAINS TRILOGY

BOOK TWO

Al & JoAnna Lacy

Multnomah Publishers
Sisters, Oregon

ALL MY TOMORROWS
© 2003 by ALJO PRODUCTIONS, INC.
published by Multnomah Publishers, Inc.

International Standard Book Number: 1-59052-130-7

Cover design by Kirk DouPonce/UDG|DesignWorks
Cover images by Robert Papp/Shannon Associates
Image of orphans by Getty Images

Printed in the United States of America

Multnomah is a trademark of Multnomah Publishers, Inc., and is
registered in the U.S. Patent and Trademark Office.
The colophon is a trademark of Multnomah Publishers, Inc.

For information:
Multnomah Publishers, Inc. • Post Office Box 1720 • Sisters, Oregon 97759

Library of Congress Cataloging-in-Publication Data

Lacy, Al.
    All my tomorrows / by Al and JoAnna Lacy.
        p. cm. -- (The orphan trains trilogy ; bk. 2)
    ISBN 1-59052-130-7 (pbk.)
    1. Homeless children--Fiction. 2. New York (N.Y.)--Fiction.
3. Orphan trains--Fiction. 4. Orphans--Fiction. I. Lacy, Joanna. II. Title.

PS3562.A256A78 2003

813'.54--dc21

                                                                2003001336

03 04 05 06 07 08 09 — 10 9 8 7 6 5 4 3 2 1 0

This book is lovingly dedicated to
our faithful friends, neighbors, and fans,
Nick and Donna Bieber.
God bless you. We love you!

EPHESIANS 1:2

Prologue

In mid-nineteenth-century New York City, which had grown by leaps and bounds with immigrants from all over Europe coming by the thousands into the city, the streets were filled with destitute, vagrant children. They were anywhere from two years of age up to fifteen or sixteen.

The city's politicians termed them "orphans," though a great number had living parents, or at least one living parent. The city's newspapers called them orphans, half-orphans, foundlings, street Arabs, waifs, and street urchins.

Many of these children resorted to begging or stealing while a few found jobs selling newspapers; sweeping stores, restaurants, and sidewalks; and peddling apples, oranges, and flowers on the street corners. Others sold matches and toothpicks. Still others shined shoes. A few rummaged through trash cans for rags, boxes, or refuse paper to sell.

In 1852, New York City's mayor was quoted as saying there were some 30,000 of these orphans on the city's streets. Most of those thousands who wandered the streets were ill-clad, unwashed, and half-starved. Some actually died of starvation. They slept in boxes and trash bins in the alleys, and many froze to death during the winter. In warm weather, some slept on park benches or on the grass in Central Park.

Some of the children still had both parents, but were merely turned loose by the parents because the family had grown too large and they could not care for all their children. Many of the street waifs were runaways from parental abuse, parental immorality, and parental drunkenness.

In 1848, a young man named Charles Loring Brace, a native of Hartford, Connecticut, and graduate of Yale University, had come to New York to study for the ministry at Union Theological Seminary. He was also an author, and spent a great deal of time working on his books, which slowed his work at the seminary. He still had not graduated by the spring of 1852, but something else was beginning to occupy his mind. He was horrified both by the hordes of vagrant children he saw on the streets daily and by the way the civil authorities treated them. The city's solution for years had been to sweep the wayfaring children into jails or run-down almshouses.

Brace believed the children should not be punished for their predicament, but should be given a positive environment in which to live and grow up. In January 1853, after finishing the manuscript for a new book and submitting it to his New York publisher, Brace dropped out of seminary and met with a group of pastors, bankers, businessmen, and lawyers—all who professed to be born-again Christians—and began the groundwork to establish an organization that would do something in a positive way to help New York City's poor, homeless children.

Because Brace was clearly a dedicated young man—all of twenty-seven—and because he was a rising literary figure on the New York scene, these men backed him in his desire, and by March 1853, the Children's Aid Society was established. Brace was its leader, and the men who backed him helped raise funds from many kinds of businesses and people of wealth who believed in what they were doing. Brace took over the former Italian Opera House at the corner of Astor Place and Lafayette Street in downtown Manhattan.

From the beginning, Brace and his colleagues attempted to find homes for individual children, but it was soon evident that the growing numbers of street waifs would have to be placed elsewhere. Brace came upon the idea of taking groups of these orphans in wagons to the rural areas in upstate New York and allowing farmers to simply pick out the ones they wanted for themselves and become their foster parents.

This plan indeed provided some homes for the street waifs, but not enough to meet the demand. By June 1854, Brace came to the conclusion that the children would have to be taken westward where there were larger rural areas. One of his colleagues in the Children's Aid Society had friends in Dowagiac, Michigan, who had learned of the Society's work and wrote to tell him they thought people of their area would be interested in taking some of the children into their homes under the foster plan.

Thus came the first orphan train. In mid-September 1854, under Charles Brace's instructions, Dowagiac's local newspaper carried an ad every day for two weeks, announcing that forty-five homeless boys and girls from the streets of New York City would arrive by train on October 1. The morning of October 2 they could be seen at the town's meetinghouse. Bills were posted at the general store, cafés, restaurants, and the railroad station, asking families to provide foster homes for these orphans.

One of Brace's paid associates, E. P. Smith, was assigned to take the children on the train to Dowagiac. Smith's wife accompanied him, to chaperone the girls.

The meetinghouse was fairly packed as the children stood behind Smith on the platform while he spoke to the crowd. He explained the program, saying these unfortunate children were

Christ's little ones, who needed a chance in life. He told the crowd that kind men and women who opened their homes to one or more of this ragged regiment would be expected to raise them as they would their own children, providing them with decent food and clothing, and a good education.

There would be no loss in their charity, Smith assured his audience. The boys would do whatever farmwork or other kind that was expected of them, and the girls would do all types of housework.

As the children stood in line to be inspected, the applicants moved past them slowly, looking them over with care and engaging them in conversation. At the same time, E. P. Smith and his wife looked at the quality and cleanness of the prospective foster parents and asked them about their financial condition, property, vocation, and church attendance. If they were satisfied with what they heard, they let them choose the child or children they desired.

When the applicants had chosen the children, thirty-seven had homes. The remaining eight were taken back to New York and placed in already overcrowded orphanages. Charles Brace was so encouraged by the high percentage of the children who had been taken into the homes, that he soon launched into a campaign to take children both from off the streets and from the orphanages, put them on trains, and take them west where there were farms and ranches aplenty.

When the railroad companies saw what Brace's Children's Aid Society was doing, they contacted him and offered generous discounts on tickets, and each railroad company offered special coaches, which would carry only the orphans and their chaperones.

For the next seventy-five years—until the last orphan train carried the waifs to Texas in 1929—the Children's Aid Society had placed some 250,000 children in homes in every western state and territory except Arizona. Upon Brace's death in 1890, his son, Charles Loring Brace Jr. took over the Society.

In 1910, a survey concluded that eighty-seven percent of the children shipped to the West on the orphan trains up to that time had grown into credible members of western society. Eight percent had been returned to New York City, and five percent had either disappeared, were imprisoned for crimes committed, or had died.

It is to the credit of Charles Loring Brace's dream, labor, and leadership in the orphan train system that two of the orphans grew up to become state governors, several became mayors, one became a Supreme Court justice, two became congressmen, thirty-five became lawyers, and nineteen became physicians. Others became successful gospel preachers, lawmen, farmers, ranchers, businessmen, wives, and mothers—those who made up a great part of society in the West.

Until well into the twentieth century, Brace's influence was felt by virtually every program established to help homeless and needy children. Even today, the philosophical foundations he forged have left him—in the minds of many—the preeminent figure in American child welfare history.

Chapter One

It was early March 1876. It had been snowing off and on in New York City for four days, and several inches of snow had accumulated on the ground. At the 38th Street Cemetery on Manhattan Island, a small group had gathered at an open grave where a simple pine coffin rested on a cart. A polar breeze was coming down out of the north, and it was snowing lightly beneath a somber gray sky. All of them felt the ice of the breeze and turned their heads into their upturned collars while the minister spoke in a solemn tone.

Ten-year-old Teddy Hansen stared through his tears at the crude wooden box that held his mother's body. It had already been sealed shut by the undertaker, who stood nearby, blinking at the snowflakes that kept settling on his eyelashes.

Teddy was standing between his Uncle George and Aunt Eva Pitts, and his Uncle Henry and Aunt Lois Eades. The stiff breeze was knifing its cold blades through his thin, tattered coat. He was quivering both from the cold and from the grief that was tearing at his heart.

The boy had never seen the minister before, who was speaking in a dead monotone, and was paying little attention to what he was saying. He sniffed and absently wiped his tearstained cheeks and nose with the sleeve of his threadbare coat.

While the minister droned on, Teddy looked up at his relatives, who were also staring at the coffin. Uncle George was his mother's brother and Aunt Lois was his mother's sister.

Teddy's mind ran to his father as he gazed once again on the coffin. *Why did Mama have to die? It was bad enough when Papa left us. I was only eight then, and poor Mama had to find a way to provide for us.*

At that moment, Teddy relived the horror of the day his father told his mother he was leaving and would never be back. He stormed out of the apartment, slamming the door behind him. He remembered how his mother wept as she held him in her arms and told him that they would make it somehow. Three days later, after walking the streets looking for a job, she was hired as a waitress at a café near the tenement where they lived. They had to move into a one-bedroom apartment in the tenement, and his mother had insisted that Teddy have the bedroom. She slept on the lumpy couch in the parlor.

From the start, Claire Hansen had worked a double shift at the café, seven days a week. It was the only way she could earn enough money to provide for her son and her to live on. The pace she kept steadily wore her down, and after keeping it up for nearly two years, her health began to fail. She caught a severe cold this past January, and by mid-February, she came down with pneumonia and had to be hospitalized. After two weeks in the hospital, she died.

The Pittses and the Eadeses had traded off keeping Teddy in their homes since his mother had first become ill. He was hoping that Uncle George and Aunt Eva would let him live with them, rather than having to switch back and forth between them and Uncle Henry and Aunt Lois every few days like they had been doing since his mother got sick.

Teddy knew Uncle Henry and Aunt Lois really didn't want him. And for that matter, neither did Uncle George. But Aunt Eva really loved him, and he was hoping she would be able to persuade Uncle George to let him live with them permanently.

Teddy's gaze was still fastened on the coffin. A shiver slid down his backbone. *Oh, Mama, why did you go off and leave me?*

His mind was almost as numb as his cold feet as he lifted his eyes toward the dour gray sky as though his answer would come from there. The falling snowflakes quickly attached to his eyelashes. He wiped them away and brushed at the flakes that covered his knitted cap. Lowering his head, Teddy looked at the snow on his shoes. His heart was as cold as the ground where he stood.

Oh, Mama, I miss you so much. You always made sure I knew I was loved and wanted. Even though you worked so many hours, you still had time for me. I was left alone a lot, but I always knew you would hurry home as soon as your shifts were over.

Teddy thought about how it affected him when he first noticed that his mother was losing weight and her face was so pale. He was worried about her, and when he voiced it, she smiled and told him she would be fine. From that moment on, whenever she came home from work and opened the door, she had a smile on her wan face, and they enjoyed the moments they had with each other.

The minister's hollow voice was still riding the frigid air as a sob escaped Teddy's tightly compressed lips. He quickly clasped a mittened hand to his mouth, looking up at his relatives. Aunt Eva was observing him with soft, sympathetic eyes. She laid a gloved hand on his shoulder, gave it an assuring squeeze, then let go.

Teddy lowered his head and let the tears course down his reddened cheeks and drip off his quivering chin. He sleeved away the tears and focused on the coffin. *I've been good while staying with my aunts and uncles, Mama. I didn't make any noise or cause any trouble. And I didn't eat too much. I hope Aunt Eva and Uncle George will take me.*

So lost in his thoughts and grief, Teddy was not aware that the minister was closing in prayer. He was unaware that the dreadful funeral was over until he felt a strong hand clamp down on his shoulder.

"Time to go, Teddy," said Uncle Henry.

Teddy nodded. "I want to tell Mama good-bye."

"All right. We'll give you a few seconds to do that."

The aunts and uncles watched as Teddy moved up to the coffin, patted it, and choked as he said, "I love you, Mama, and I will miss you always. Good-bye."

When they arrived at the Eades house where Teddy had stayed the last two nights, Henry said, "Teddy, you go on upstairs to your room. We adults need to talk. We'll let you know when you can come down."

Teddy nodded. "Yes, Uncle Henry."

The heavyhearted ten-year-old mounted the stairs, walked down the hall, and entered his room. More tears were flowing. He closed the door and flung himself on the bed. "Mama! Mama! I need you! I need you!"

After a few minutes, Teddy dried his tears. He thought about the conversation that was going on in the parlor downstairs. He knew what his aunts and uncles were talking about: their orphaned nephew.

Teddy slipped out of his room and moved quietly down the hall. He descended the stairs, crept up close to the open parlor door, and flattened his back against the wall where he couldn't be seen.

Uncle George and Uncle Henry were arguing, each giving the

reason why the other couple should take their nephew.

"I can't let this responsibility fall on Eva!" George said flatly. "The kid will just be more of a problem and a nuisance than he's already been since Claire got sick."

In the hall, Teddy swallowed hard and bit down on his lower lip.

Henry cleared his throat. "Well, I'm telling you right now, George, I'm not letting this responsibility fall on Lois, either! Having that kid around is just too much of a bother."

"Right," said Lois. "Henry and I didn't bring him into the world, and there's no reason for us to be stuck with raising him. And as far as I'm concerned, you and Eva shouldn't have to put up with him, either. Let's put him in an orphanage."

Teddy couldn't see Eva's face, but he could hear the break in her voice as she said, "An orphanage? You know as well as I do that the orphanages in this city are already so overcrowded that they can't take any more children. That's why the streets are so full of them. They have nowhere else to go. And you also know that year round many starve to death; in the winter, great numbers of them freeze to death. We can't put that poor child on the streets."

There was silence for a moment, then Eva said, "George, I want us to keep Teddy and take care of him."

"No!" snapped George. "Like I said, I can't let this responsibility fall on you and for that matter, me, either. Why should we have to feed, house, and clothe him for the next ten years? We're not going to do it."

Eva was crying now. "But, George, we can't just put him out on the streets. We must—"

"That's the end of it, Eva!" George said. "That kid's not living in our house!"

In the hall, Teddy's hand went to his mouth. There was a sudden wave of anxiety that flowed across his mind like a cold wave. He wheeled, ran quietly to the stairs, and mounted them quickly. When he entered his room, he closed the door and leaned his back against it.

"Only Aunt Eva wants me," he whispered, breathing hard, "but Uncle George won't let her have me. I'll go live on the streets with other kids who have no parents. At least they'll understand my problem and show me how to make it."

Quickly, Teddy put on his tattered coat, mittens, and knitted cap. He picked up the small cloth bag that contained some of his clothes and hurried to the stairs. He could hear his aunts and uncles still discussing him as he made his way down the stairs. So that no one would know he was leaving, he darted on tiptoe to the rear of the house and hurried out the back door. "Only Aunt Eva will miss me, but the rest of them won't. Uncle George, Uncle Henry, and Aunt Lois will make sure nobody looks for me. They'll just be glad I'm gone."

It was still snowing and a bitter wind whipped the snow in circles around him as he trudged down the street toward downtown, where the street urchins lived. He had seen them many times, begging for money on the streets. The newspapers called the groups of children who lived in the alleys "colonies." Teddy Hansen would find a colony who would take him in.

By the time Teddy reached the downtown area, it was late afternoon and the snow had stopped falling. The wind, however, was knifing along the streets in hard, hissing gusts, hurling clouds of snow and needle-sharp particles of ice against him.

As he drew up to the mouth of an alley, he spotted a group of boys about a hundred feet away, who were gathered around a fire they had built in a metal barrel. When he turned into the alley and headed toward them, one of the boys called the attention of the others to him, and all eleven of them set dubious eyes on him. He could see that they were all in their teens.

Teddy put a smile on his face as he drew up. "Hi. I'm Teddy Hansen. Could I warm myself by your fire?"

The largest of the boys scowled. He appeared to be about fifteen. "No, you can't, twerp. On your way. Ain't no room for you, here."

"I wouldn't take up much space. I'm really cold. Couldn't I just get warm?"

Another boy took a step toward him. "What is it, kid? You deaf? Rocky just told you there ain't no room for you. If you don't disappear real quick, I'm gonna beat you to a pulp."

"You won't have to, Chip," said Rocky. "If he ain't outta sight in thirty seconds, I'll pound him myself."

Teddy started backtracking, eyes wide, then pivoted and ran. He could hear the boys laughing fiendishly. When he reached the sidewalk, he headed on down the street, cold and discouraged. Soon he approached another alley and saw a colony comprised of both boys and girls about halfway down the block. They too had a fire going in a barrel.

He moved down the alley, and when he drew up, every eye in the group was on him. A husky boy of about sixteen glared at him. "Whattya want, kid?"

Teddy swallowed hard. "I—I'm an orphan. My name is Teddy Hansen. Could I get warm by your fire?"

"No, you can't. Get outta here."

One of the girls said, "Aw, c'mon, Slug. He's just a little guy. He isn't going to soak up much heat."

Teddy smiled at her.

"You shut up, Sally!" yelled another husky teenage boy. "We ain't got no room for nobody else. Next thing, he'll want to eat some of our food. On your way, kid."

Sally glared at him. "What's your problem, Garth? You were his age once. Somebody was kind to you, weren't they?"

Garth shook his shoulders. "Not always." He turned to Teddy. "What you got in that bag, kid?"

"Just some socks and underwear and a couple of shirts."

"Well, take your socks, underwear, and shirts somewhere else before you get hurt."

Tears moistened Teddy's eyes. "I'm really cold. Please? Just a few minutes by the fire?"

Garth leaped up and smashed Teddy on the jaw. Teddy staggered back, and as he gained his balance without falling, Slug hastened past Garth, anger flaming in his eyes. "What is it, punk? You don't understand English?"

The cold in Teddy's bones was greater than his fear. "Please, Slug. As the girl said, I won't soak up much heat."

Teddy noticed the big ring on Slug's right hand just before it lashed out and cracked him on the left cheek. He felt himself sail through the air, and the ground rose up and hit him on the back. There was fierce pain in his cheek and the alley seemed to be swirling around him. Slug and Garth were out of focus as they stood over him.

"Get outta here, kid," said Slug, "or you'll get more of the same."

Teddy shook his head in an attempt to clear it and rolled onto his knees, still clutching the cloth bag. There was something wet on his left cheek. When he put a hand to it, he felt the warmth of the blood and looked at it on his mitten. The ring had cut his cheek, and the cut was burning like fire. He worked his way to his feet, put the mitten to the bleeding cut, and staggered toward the end of the alley. He could hear Sally reprimanding the bullies for what they had done.

When he reached the sidewalk, Teddy made his way slowly past door after door, tears bubbling from his eyes. People he met along the way looked at him, but passed on by. Soon he came upon a dark, recessed doorway of a building that was closed up. He sat down on the step, scooting as close to the door as he could. This took him out of the path of the cold wind.

He opened the cloth bag and pulled out one of his socks. Folding it a couple of times, he pressed it to the cut on his cheek. "Oh, Mama, I need you! I need you!"

Teddy pulled his bony knees up close to his chest, leaned his head against them, and wept. He held the sock tight against the cut. Tears of frustration and pain streamed down his face.

He stayed in this position for several minutes, eyes closed. Then suddenly, he was aware of a hand on his shoulder. "Hey, little fella, what are you doing out here in this freezing weather?"

Teddy lifted his head and looked up at the tall man in dark blue with a badge on his chest.

The policeman saw the blood on the sock. "You're hurt, son. Where do you live?"

Teddy sniffed. "I don't have a home, sir. I'm an orphan. My mother died a few days ago, and I just came downtown to find a colony of street urchins to live with. In one of the alleys, I got punched. The big boy who hit me was wearing a ring. It was the ring that cut me."

The officer hunkered down to Teddy's level. He took hold of the hand that held the sock and turned it so he could see the cut. "You mean you don't have any relatives to live with?"

"I have an aunt and two uncles who don't want me."

The officer looked at him compassionately. "What's your name, son?"

"Teddy Hansen. Well, really, it's Theodore Hansen."

"My name is Officer Justin Smith, Teddy," the policeman said, rising to his feet and taking hold of the boy's arm. "Come along with me."

The boy frowned and stiffened his body, still pressing the sock to his cut. "Where are you taking me? I won't go back to my aunt and uncles who don't want me. I certainly sure won't!"

Smith smiled. "It's all right, laddy, I'm not taking you to them. I'm going to take you to Park West Hospital, just down the street a couple of blocks. That cut needs a doctor's attention. You're losing a lot of blood. Come along. I won't let anything bad happen to you."

Smith laid his hand on Teddy's shoulder again, and Teddy could feel the warmth of it through his shabby coat. "Well-l-l-l…"

"Don't you trust me?"

"Uh…yes, sir. It's just that—"

"Someone you have trusted in the past let you down. Is that it?"

Teddy nodded and rose to his feet, clutching the cloth bag in his free hand.

"Here, let me carry that. You keep the sock pressed to the cut."

They left the protective doorway, and while they walked the two blocks to the hospital, Teddy told Officer Smith his whole story at Smith's request. The officer's heart went out to the boy, realizing that Teddy had already suffered severely in his young life. His father had deserted him two years before, and today, he had seen his mother buried.

When they reached the hospital, Justin Smith led Teddy into the brightly lit lobby. He took him to a small waiting room just off the lobby. Teddy had never been in a hospital before and quickly noticed the strange odors in the air—not all of them pleasant.

Seeing the fear in Teddy's eyes, Smith sat him on a wooden chair and laid a hand on his thin shoulder. "You stay right here. I'll go find a doctor. Promise me you won't move from this chair."

"I will stay right here, sir."

Smith smiled and patted the top of Teddy's head. "Good boy. I'll be right back."

Teddy watched the officer take his long strides as he left the room and headed down the hall.

Ten minutes had passed when the policeman and a silver-haired man in a white frock entered the waiting room. True to his word, the boy was still on the chair. He looked up at both men, still pressing the sock to his cheek.

"Teddy," said Officer Smith, "this is Dr. Randall Martin. He is going to take care of your cut."

The doctor smiled and bent down. "May I see the cut, son?"

Teddy relaxed his hand as the doctor took hold of it and moved it so he could get a look at the bleeding gash. He studied it a moment, then placed the small hand and sock over the cut. "Officer Smith told me your story, Teddy. Come with me, now. We'll get you fixed up."

Teddy looked up at the officer.

Smith laid a hand on his head again. "Dr. Martin and the nurses will take good care of you, Teddy. I have to get back on my beat. How long has it been since you had something to eat?"

"I had a little bit of breakfast this morning, sir. I...I really didn't feel like eating, since I was going to Mama's funeral."

"Are you hungry now?"

"Yes, sir."

Dr. Martin looked at the policeman. "We'll take good care of him, Officer Smith. When I've stitched him up, we'll give him a good supper and a warm bed for the night. You can pick him up in the morning if that's convenient for you."

The thought of a meal and a warm bed sounded heavenly to Teddy.

"I'll be here about nine o'clock in the morning, Doctor," said Smith.

Martin nodded, then extended his hand to Teddy. "Let's go, son."

Teddy slipped off the chair, bent down, picked up his cloth bag, and took hold of the doctor's hand. He looked up at the policeman with his sad little eyes. "Thank you, Officer Smith, for taking care of me."

Smith touched the boy's shoulder. "My pleasure, Teddy. See you tomorrow morning."

The tall man in blue watched as the silver-haired doctor led the boy down the hall. When they stopped at a door and Dr. Martin opened it, Teddy looked back and smiled at him. Smith smiled back, and doctor and patient disappeared through the door.

Chapter Two

The next morning at 8:40, Dr. Randall Martin was at his desk in his office at Park West Hospital, studying a medical report on an elderly patient, when there was a tap on his door.

He looked up. "Yes?"

The door opened, and one of the nurses said, "Dr. Martin, Officer Justin Smith is here. He says you are expecting him."

"Yes. Please show him in."

Seconds later, Officer Justin Smith's tall frame filled the door. Dr. Martin smiled and waved him in. "Come sit down, please."

Smith eased his lanky frame onto a chair in front of the desk. "How is Teddy doing, Doctor?"

"Teddy's fine. I had to put four stitches in his cheek. He's got quite a black and blue mark around the cut, all the way to his eye. The bandage doesn't hide it all. I'll need to see him in a week to make sure he's healing all right. If everything's okay in ten or eleven days, I'll take the stitches out."

Smith eased back in the chair and sighed. "I'm glad he's all right. Such a special little fella."

"That he is. So what are you planning to do with him?"

"Well, I was going to investigate the situation with his aunts and uncles that I told you about when I related Teddy's story to you."

"Uh-huh?"

"When my shift was over and I reported in at precinct headquarters yesterday, I talked to Chief Masterson and told him Teddy's story. The chief agreed that we should make contact with the Pittses and the Eadeses, and see if they really didn't want Teddy as he told me."

Martin nodded.

"The chief told me he would send a couple of night shift officers to talk to the aunts and uncles. When I arrived at the precinct this morning, Chief Masterson gave me the report. The officers said that Henry and Lois Eades flat said they were in no position to take Teddy in and raise him. At the Pitts home, Mrs. Pitts wept and said she really wanted to take Teddy in, but Mr. Pitts vehemently objected, saying he was not going to let it happen. Teddy cannot look to his only relatives to give him a home. I'm sure you know, Doctor, that there is no law to force them to take Teddy in, even though he is their nephew."

"Yes. We hear all the time that the orphanages in all five boroughs are more than full, so what are you going to do?"

"I have a close friend who is on the staff at the Thirty-second Street Orphanage. His name is Bill Waters. Bill has told me many times that the orphanage's superintendent, Wayne Stanfill, is a very compassionate man. I'm going to take Teddy over there and see if I can talk Mr. Stanfill into adding one more little orphan boy to his overflow."

Dr. Martin smiled. "Well, it can't hurt to try."

"That's the way I look at it. And if Mr. Stanfill has the compassion Bill says he does, I believe when he takes a look at Teddy and hears his story, he'll make a place for him in the orphanage."

"Well, if you're right, they have a doctor at the orphanage. He can look after Teddy's cut and take the stitches out when it's time."

Smith rose from the chair. "I'll see that he does, Doctor. I know you're busy, so I'll get out of here and let you go back to what you were doing."

Dr. Martin stood up and smiled. "Let me know what happens to the little guy, won't you?"

"Sure will. And thank you for what you've done for him."

"That's what I'm in this business for."

The sun was shining brightly on the dazzling snow outside as Teddy Hansen sat on the edge of the bed in his room, gazing at its beauty with squinted eyes. He was dressed and ready to go, with his cap, coat, and the cloth bag lying next to him on the bed.

The fear he was feeling was a cold ball in his stomach. He put fingertips to his bandage and scratched at the adhesive tape that held it. "I wonder what will happen to me today. What will Officer Smith do with me?"

Suddenly the door swung open, and Officer Justin Smith stepped in, a broad grin on his face. "Good morning, Teddy."

The boy tried to smile back. "Good morning, sir."

"Dr. Martin told me about the stitches and the black-and-blue mark. But you look better than I expected. Did you sleep well?"

"Yes, sir. I slept real good, and just finished a big breakfast. They have been very nice to me here."

"Good." Smith chuckled. "I hope your face doesn't hurt as bad as it looks."

"No, sir. I know it's there, but it really doesn't hurt at all."

"I'm glad," said Smith, pulling up a wooden chair. "Before we go, I need to explain some things to you."

Teddy nodded.

Smith told the boy about his talk with police Chief Walt Masterson last evening, of the two police officers who visited his aunts and uncles, and what happened in both homes.

Teddy looked down at the floor. "It's like I told you, sir…the only one who wants me is Aunt Eva. But Uncle George doesn't, so it can't happen." He looked back up at Smith. "What are you going to do with me?"

"I have a good friend who works at the Thirty-second Street Orphanage."

Teddy's back arched. "Orphanage? But all the orphanages are full, sir. I've heard that many times."

"I know, but my friend Bill Waters has told me many times how tenderhearted the superintendent is. I believe he will take you, once he meets you and hears your story. I've been to the orphanage a few times, Teddy. The people there really love children. They are very kind. The children I've seen there seem happy. It sure would be better than living on the streets, as you saw yesterday."

"Yes, sir," said Teddy. "It's for certain sure I don't want to go through that again. Let's try it."

The two of them walked through the snow with Officer Smith carrying the cloth bag. When they arrived at the orphanage, Teddy stared up at the two-storied red brick building. Sunlight glinted off the sparkling windows and smoke rose skyward from its four chimneys.

"It looks like an all right place, sir."

"Well, let's go in and see what happens."

Together, the man in blue and the boy in the tattered coat mounted the steps and moved through the double doors. When they approached the middle-aged woman who sat at the desk,

Smith said, "Good morning, ma'am. I'm Officer Justin Smith. Is Bill Waters on the premises?"

"Yes, he is," she said, rising from her chair. "I'll fetch him for you." Her soft eyes went to Teddy. "And who is this young gentleman?"

"His name is Teddy Hansen, ma'am. He's an orphan."

"What happened to your face, honey?"

"I got beat up in an alley, ma'am."

"Oh. I'm so sorry." She headed for the door. "I'll be right back with Mr. Waters."

No more than three minutes had passed when Waters and the receptionist entered the room.

Bill Waters was a husky man with a receding hairline, and he was dressed in a suit and tie. He extended his hand to his friend, then Waters looked at the boy. "What happened to you, son?"

"He got beat up in an alley when he was trying to join a colony," Smith answered for Teddy. "He just became an orphan this week. He's ten years old."

Waters met Smith's gaze. "And you—"

"Yes. You've often told me of Mr. Stanfill's compassion. Now, I need to put it to the test. Teddy needs a home."

Bill nodded. "I'll take you and Teddy in to see him."

Waters guided the officer and orphan a short distance down the hall and tapped on the door that had a sign on it which read: *Wayne D. Stanfill, Superintendent*. He tapped on the door and a deep masculine voice from inside called, "Come in."

Bill Waters led them into the office and introduced Officer Justin Smith, saying they were close friends. Stanfill, who was even a larger man than Waters, shook Smith's hand, then set his eyes on the boy. "What happened to you, young man?"

Smith answered for Teddy again, using the same words he had spoken to Bill Waters a few minutes before. Stanfill invited them to sit down, and Waters excused himself and left.

The superintendent smiled at the boy. "What's your name, son?"

"Teddy Hansen, sir."

Stanfill looked at the officer. "You're looking for a home for Teddy, I assume."

"Yes, sir," said Smith. "Let me tell you Teddy's story."

When the officer finished the sad story, there were tears in Wayne Stanfill's eyes. "Teddy, we are indeed very crowded here, as you will see. But we will make a place for you. I'll call for Mr. Waters, and he'll take you to your room."

Teddy made a nervous smile. "Thank you, sir."

Stanfill went to the door and asked the receptionist to find Waters and tell him to come to his office. He returned to his desk and took out a printed form. He asked Teddy for his full name, and Teddy told him it was Theodore Ambrose Hansen. Ambrose was his mother's maiden name. Stanfill wrote it down, then as he wrote on another line, he told Justin Smith he was putting him down as Teddy's outside contact.

Smith told him that would be fine, then talked to him about the stitches in Teddy's cheek. Stanfill assured him that the orphanage's doctor would take care of Teddy's wound.

Bill Waters came in while Stanfill was writing something else. The superintendent looked up and said, "Bill, I'm putting Teddy in room twelve. He'll have to sleep on the floor as two other boys are. Make sure he gets an extra blanket."

Waters smiled. "Sure will, Mr. Stanfill."

Stanfill set his kind eyes on Teddy. "There are eight boys in the room, son, but only six bunks. Two of the newest boys to come to us are sleeping on the floor, so you can join them. Sorry we don't have a bunk for you, but as I told you, we are very crowded."

"It's all right, Mr. Stanfill," Teddy said politely. "It's still a whole lot better than being out there on the streets."

Officer Smith rose from his chair. "Well, Teddy, now that you're situated here in the orphanage, I've got to get back to headquarters."

Teddy slid off the chair and looked up at his friend. He felt reluctance about Officer Smith leaving him and the look in his eyes showed it.

Smith laid a hand on the boy's shoulder. "You'll be fine here, Teddy. You'll soon make new friends. I'll come back as often as I can and check on you."

"You'll really come to see me, sir? Is that a certain sure promise?"

Smith grinned. He squeezed the slender shoulder. "Yes, Teddy, that's a certain sure promise."

"Thank you, sir, for being so kind to me."

"I have a son just a little older than you, Teddy. He's twelve. His name is Johnny. His mother died just over a year ago with cancer. If something happened to me, and Johnny became an orphan, I would want someone to treat him well. I'm glad I could be of help to you."

Wayne Stanfill's face showed the compassion he suddenly felt for Justin Smith. "I'm sorry to hear of your wife's death, Officer Smith. You haven't remarried?"

"No, sir. There is a widow in her late sixties who lives in our tenement, on the same floor. She keeps Johnny in her apartment when he's not in school and looks after him when I'm on duty."

"I see. Well, I'm glad you have her."

"So is Johnny." He patted Teddy's shoulder. "See you later, pal."

Teddy watched the man leave, then Wayne Stanfill said, "All right, Bill, take Teddy to room twelve and introduce him to his new roommates."

"Okay, Teddy," said Waters. "Let's go."

Teddy picked up his bag and followed Waters out of the office. They moved down the hall, and when they came to room number twelve, the door was open and the boys were laughing. They looked up as Bill Waters stepped in with Teddy on his heels. Their eyes went to Teddy, then back to Waters. "Boys, this is Teddy Hansen. He's ten years old. Mr. Stanfill has assigned him to your room. Teddy knows he will have to sleep on the floor, as two of you do. I'll send his blankets and pillow in a little later." He turned to Teddy. "I'll let the boys introduce themselves to you."

When Waters had gone, the boys gathered around Teddy and welcomed him. Each one gave his name and age. He was treated especially kind by the other two boys who slept on the floor: thirteen-year-old Jerry Varnell and nine-year-old Clint Albright. They assured him they would help make him comfortable on the floor with them at bedtime. After his experiences with the cruel boys in the alleys, Teddy was thankful for the kindness he was being shown and told them so. "This place is for certain sure a lot friendlier than the alleys where the mean boys live."

Later that day when his shift was over, Officer Justin Smith left the precinct station on Thirty-fourth Street in Manhattan and headed for home. Soon he arrived at the tenement where he and his son lived, and before going to his apartment, he knocked on the door across the hall.

There were rapid footsteps inside, then the door came open and Johnny Smith wrapped his arms around his father. "I'm glad you're home safe and sound, Dad. Did you have to use your gun today?"

"No, for which I'm thankful, son," Justin said as Flora Benson came into the parlor, a smile lighting up her wrinkled face.

A wonderful aroma of baked chicken and sage dressing was causing Justin's mouth to water. Flora said, "In case you didn't know it by what you smell, Officer Smith, you and Johnny are not eating at your usual café this evening. You're going to keep a lonely old lady company. I have supper ready, and we're eating together. No arguments."

Justin laughed and looked down into Johnny's eyes. "This lady is really bossy, isn't she, son?"

"Yeah, Dad, and aren't you glad?"

"Don't tell her I said so, but I sure am! It smells awfully good from here."

Johnny made a slurping sound. "I've been smelling it all afternoon! I was sure hoping we would be invited to stay!"

Flora laughed. "Then that makes us all happy! Take your coat off and warm yourself by the fire, Justin. Supper will be on the table in just a few minutes." Flora bustled off toward the kitchen.

Justin stood near the fireplace and glanced about the homey room with his son at his side. A sadness filled his heart as he remembered the warm, cozy home his beloved wife always kept for him and Johnny. Before he had a chance to dwell too long on the past, Flora called them to the table, which was laden with delicious dishes. Both of their mouths were watering in anticipation of the meal.

While they were eating, Johnny said, "Dad, you told Mrs. Benson and me about Teddy Hansen last night. Were you able to get him in the orphanage today?"

"Yes, I sure was."

"How's his gash?" queried Flora.

"Dr. Martin said it will heal up fine inside of a couple of weeks. He had to put four stitches in it. Teddy's got quite a black-and-blue mark where the bully hit him, but that will clear up in time. The doctor at the orphanage will be looking after him.

Poor little guy. He's been through a lot."

Johnny swallowed a mouthful of chicken. "Dad, I sure don't understand why Teddy's aunts and uncles wouldn't want him, but at least in the orphanage, he will have people who care about orphan children and will provide for him. That's a whole lot better than living on the streets."

"After what happened to him on the streets, I'm sure the orphanage will look plenty good to him," said Flora.

Johnny took a drink of milk, set the glass down, and looked at his father. "Thank you for loving me and providing for me, Dad. I miss Mom an awful lot, but I'm so glad I still have you. I know I've said this a lot, but when I grow up, I want to be a policeman, just like you."

Flora chuckled. "Johnny, you've been saying that since you were six years old. I admire you for it, and I hope it works out for you when you grow up."

Justin smiled. "I hope so too. I will be proud to have my son follow in my footsteps."

"Ever since I can remember, I've wanted to wear a badge, Dad. I want to do all I can to stop the crime on New York's streets, but I think the best part of being a police officer will be to do things like you did for Teddy Hansen. It must make you feel good to help somebody like Teddy."

Justin smiled and placed his hand over his heart. "Yes, son. It makes me feel good right here."

In a small, dingy flat in a run-down tenement house on Houston Street near downtown Manhattan, Gerald and Delia Mitchell sat down to supper with their seven children, who ranged in age from the thirteen-year-old identical twin girls to their ten-month-old baby boy. The meals were meager, like all the other meals had been in the Mitchell household for some time.

While they were eating, Gerald ran his gaze over the faces of his children. "Your mother and I have something to tell you. When we went shopping today, we also went to Dr. Baldwin's office. Dr. Baldwin told us that your mother is going to have a baby in October."

The eyes of all the older children were silently fixed on their father, then swung to their mother. Delia Mitchell was little more than thirty years old but looked more like fifty. Her skin was pallid and her thin, lifeless brown hair—streaked with gray—was pulled back in a tight bun on the nape of her neck. She was nothing but skin and bones, except for the small roundness of her middle. A tired sadness pinched her face as she met the dull eyes of her older children and a weary sigh escaped her lips. She looked down at the table, assessing the scanty meal she had put there for her family. And now, there was another one on the way. *Gerald is right. We must let the twins go and find a place for themselves. But how am I ever going to part with them? They're my firstborn and have a special place in my heart. But they'll be better off, and at least maybe they'll have a better chance in life. But I'll miss them so.*

Gerald's voice was tight as he said, "Mama and I had a little talk on the way home from the doctor's office. We're hardly able to keep enough food on the table and clothes on ourselves and you children. As you know, I'm working two jobs. I can't work three. So…Donna and Deena, since you are the oldest, you are going to have to move out. We don't like to have to do this, but there isn't any choice."

Stunned beyond words, the twins stared at each other as though looking in a mirror. The blood drained from their faces. Both were seized by an icy, unreasoning fear.

Finally Donna found her voice. "Wh-where are we supposed

to go? We're only th-thirteen years old and still in school. Papa, please let us stay here with you and Mama."

Tears filled the eyes of both girls as they stared at their father.

Gerald cleared his throat shakily. "We simply can't keep you anymore. There are thousands of children who live on the streets downtown. Some of them do odd jobs for businesses, and others sell different items provided by distributors, such as wooden matches and toothpicks. Others do quite well at begging. They sleep in all kinds of makeshift shelters. Certainly you two are old enough to take care of yourselves as the other teenagers do."

Deena set her tear-filled eyes on her mother. "Mama, is this what you want, too? Who's going to help you with the children? You can barely get out of bed some days because you are so weak."

"I know," Delia replied in a whisper. "I'll just have to do the best I can. Please, girls, look at this as an opportunity. Maybe somehow you can better yourselves. You—" A sob clogged her throat, and she began to cough uncontrollably.

Gerald's face bunched in momentary displeasure. He set hard eyes on Deena. "Now look what you've done. You and Donna will do as you're told, and no sass from either of you. Our situation is desperate. You will have to leave tomorrow morning."

The twins looked at each other, panic tearing at their hearts.

Deena wiped tears from her cheeks and set her gaze on her father. "Why so soon, Papa? The baby won't be born for another seven months."

Gerald's anger increased, but before he could reply, Delia said, "You don't know it, but of late, your papa has had to borrow money from friends on both jobs just to make ends meet. With two less mouths to feed, he will be able to start paying the money back and probably will have the debts paid by the time the baby is born in October."

"So now you know," said Gerald, shoving his chair back and

rising to his feet. He kept his eyes on the twins as he helped Delia from her chair. "You two get the dishes done and the kitchen cleaned up. If you need help, get it from your brothers and sisters, as usual."

Gerald guided Delia into a tiny bedroom. The floor was covered in faded, cracked linoleum. The only pieces of furniture were a battered dresser with sagging drawers and an old scarred bed with a lumpy mattress that was covered with a tattered quilt.

With the help of their three younger sad-faced brothers and sisters—who ranged from six to eleven—the twins cleaned the cramped kitchen. All the while, they discussed what they would do the next day, still in total disbelief.

Once they had done all they could in the kitchen, they readied the younger children for bed in the apartment's only other bedroom, then did the same for themselves. Neither parent had come out of their bedroom, and soon the tiny flat was filled with the sounds of their father's snoring and an occasional sniff from their mother as she wept because of her lot in this miserable life.

When their siblings were asleep, Deena and Donna clung to each other in their narrow bed and wept silently for some time. Then in whispers, they shared their fears of having to go to the streets and alleys. Would they actually be able to provide for themselves, or would they starve to death as hundreds of street children had done? And then there were the great numbers of street children who froze to death every winter. They had read about it in the day-old newspapers their father had brought home, and their schoolteachers had told them about it. Each tried to console the other in an effort to be strong for her twin.

"We'll make it somehow," whispered Donna, with an assurance she didn't really feel.

"Of course we will," responded Deena, with the same secret

doubts assailing her. "We will always have each other."

After a while, they finally cried themselves to sleep.

The next morning at the breakfast table, the twins were unable to swallow more than a few bites past the lumps in their throats while their mother and siblings looked on. Gerald had left for work before any of the children were up.

They helped their mother do the dishes and clean up the kitchen, then went to their bedroom and gathered their scant belongings. They placed a few faded, worn dresses, stockings with holes in the toes, and some ragged underwear in a cloth bag. They also placed a tiny music box in the bag that had been given to them on their eleventh birthday by their maternal grand-mother just before she died.

The twins put on their coats, caps, and mittens, and headed toward the apartment's door, with Deena carrying the cloth bag.

Delia and the children were waiting for them. Their baby brother was in Delia's arms. Tears were streaming down the mother's thin, sallow cheeks. She laid the baby down on the worn-out sofa and gathered the twins in her arms. "I'm so sorry, girls. So very, very sorry. I love you."

"We love you too, Mama," said Donna. "It isn't your fault. We will come by and check on you if we ever can. Try not to worry about us. Just take care of yourself and that new baby."

The other children stood by. When Delia let go of the twins, they gathered close, clung to them, and wept.

As Donna started to open the door, Delia reached into her dress pocket and took out two one-dollar bills. Handing one to each, she said, "I took these from our grocery money. They will help you get started on the streets."

The twins thanked their mother in unison, and while tears

streamed down their cheeks, they stepped out into the hall and closed the door behind them. As they started down the hall, they heard their mother burst into loud sobs. Their brothers and sisters were also crying as if their hearts would break.

Chapter Three

Monday, March 13, was a blustery day in Manhattan, and the wind whistled over the ice and snow on the ground, cutting its way mercilessly along the streets and between buildings. People walking and crossing the streets had their collars pulled up and their heads bent against the wind as they held on to their hats.

Officer Justin Smith was walking his beat on 30th Street, greeting folks along the way. Those who spoke back complained about the cold wind, and Smith agreed. As Smith stopped on one corner, he talked with the owner of a nearby clothing store for a few seconds, then moved on down the block. The howling wind was at his back, and seemed determined to freeze his ears off.

Suddenly the wind's howl rose in pitch and volume. He shuddered as it sharpened itself on his spine. He looked down the street a few doors past the Manhattan Bank and fixed his eyes on the sign that read: *Welch's Delicatessen and Coffee Shop.*

Justin told himself that when he reached Welch's place, he would go inside out of the cold and get himself a nice steaming cup of coffee. That would warm his bones.

As he drew near the bank, he saw a man open the door and start to enter, then stiffen and back away, letting the wind blow the door closed. The man hastened toward the door of the department store, which was the next building after the bank.

Suddenly two masked men bolted out the bank door, carrying revolvers and stuffed cloth moneybags with the bank's name printed on them.

Smith whipped out his gun and aimed it at them. His voice sounded like flint on steel. "Halt! Drop those guns!"

Both of them instantly turned their guns on him and fired. A slug chewed into a light pole beside Smith as he returned fire. One of the robbers went down and hit the sidewalk like a broken doll. People on the street were scattering for cover. Smith saw two women just the other side of the remaining robber, frozen in their tracks. He hesitated to fire for fear of hitting one of the women.

The robber blasted away, and Smith felt a powerful blow as one of the bullets hit his chest. He staggered, but managed to keep his balance. The two women had now darted into the doorway of a shop. Smith saw another flash from the robber's gun and felt the hot breath of the bullet as it hissed passed his right ear. The robber was pulling back the hammer again. Steadying his weakening legs, Smith took careful aim and fired. The slug hit the robber dead center in the heart.

Justin Smith's knees gave way and he collapsed to the sidewalk. He was aware of people gathering around him and one man examining his wound when a black curtain seemed to descend over his brain. He tried to shake it off, but it was impossible.

He could still hear the howling wind around him as he slipped into unconsciousness.

On Thursday morning, March 16, it was another cold, blustery day. Charles Loring Brace, executive secretary of the Children's

Aid Society, was at Manhattan's Grand Central Station to send off another orphan train. His adult sponsors had the sixty-four children boarding the two coaches that were designated by the railroad company to be occupied by the Society's orphans only. Four other coaches were boarding regular passengers.

The orphan coaches were behind the others, with the boys' coach just ahead of the caboose.

Brace, a small, thin man of fifty, thanked the three wagon drivers who had transported the children to the station from the Society's headquarters, and they drove away.

Brace turned and looked back toward the orphan coaches. The last few children were climbing aboard under the directions of the sponsors. When he saw that the girls were all in their coach, he moved toward it and up the platform steps. Upon entering the coach, Brace saw the two women sponsors and the nurse who traveled with them smile at him. The girls, ranging from five years old to sixteen, were chatting among themselves about what lay before them on the western frontier. Their eyes sparkled with anticipation, yet there was also a hint of fear.

The chatting began to wane when they saw Mr. Brace enter. All eyes were fixed on him, then one of the sponsors said, "All right, girls, let's everyone get quiet. Mr. Brace wants to talk to you."

The woodstove had a crackling fire in it, but had not yet warmed up to make the coach comfortable. The girls stayed in their coats and kept their knit caps and mittens on. They huddled close together on the seats.

There was admiration in the eyes of the girls toward the man who had taken them off the streets of New York City, or from the crowded discomfort of the city's orphanages.

Smiling warmly at the curious faces, Brace said, "Young ladies, I usually have this talk with all the orphans in the auditorium at the Society's headquarters on the morning of the day they are to be put on a train, but circumstances kept me from doing it this morning. I want to make sure all of you understand that there will be several stops between here and Kansas City, Missouri. There will not be prospective foster parents waiting to choose orphans until we cross the Missouri River. The first stop where you will have opportunity to be chosen is in Overland Park, Kansas, just across the Missouri–Kansas border.

"I want to caution you not to be discouraged, even if you haven't been chosen after many stops out West. This train is going to San Francisco, and there will be many stops between the Missouri River and the Pacific Ocean. Very few children have had to be returned to New York because they were not chosen by the time they had arrived at the last stop on the west coast. So don't get discouraged if you're not chosen right away, all right?"

Many of the girls were nodding.

"That's good! I'm praying that all of you will be taken into good homes out there and have happy lives. Well, I'll say goodbye now."

A fourteen-year-old girl lifted her hand.

Brace smiled. "Yes, Daisy?"

Daisy stood up. "Mr. Brace, I want to thank you for establishing the Children's Aid Society. Could I thank you with a hug?"

Brace's face beamed. "Of course, honey."

When Daisy left her seat to hug the man who was giving her a new lease on life, the rest of the girls left their seats and got in line. The women sponsors and the nurse looked on with tears in their eyes as the orphan girls hugged the slender little man and thanked him for what he had done for them.

When the last girl had hugged him, Brace wished them all the best, then went to the boys' coach to make the same speech. This was done quickly, for the train was getting ready to pull out.

As the engine hissed steam, the whistle blew and the train began to move out. Charles Loring Brace stood beside the two coaches and waved with a smile as the children looked at him through the windows and waved good-bye.

Many of the faces in the windows were alive with a mixture of fear and excitement. "Take care of each one of them, Lord," he said in a low voice. "They have been through so much heartache and sorrow. They deserve to have happy lives."

Brace turned away and headed for the parking lot where he had left his horse and buggy. "Thank You, Lord, for the thousands of homeless boys and girls the Society has been able to send out West over these many years. And thank You that for the most part, they have found good homes."

It was quiet inside the girls' coach as the train pulled out of Grand Central Station. The girls sat quietly, each one lost in her own thoughts and daydreams. Minutes later, they all started talking at once, going over Mr. Brace's explanations, and the encouraging words he had spoken.

On a seat where a five-year-old sat beside a ten-year-old, little Molly Ann looked up at the older girl with tears shining in her eyes. "Abigail, I'm scared. What if nobody wants a girl as young as me? I'm sort of small for my age, but even though I'm only five, I can be a big help to someone if they'll only take me. I helped my mama a lot before she died."

Abigail took hold of her small hand. "Now don't you worry, little bit. You'll probably be the very first one to be chosen. Any woman would love to have you for her very own little girl. If I was a woman and looking for a girl to choose, I'd take you just for those big brown eyes!"

"Really?" Molly Ann's brown eyes were wide with unshed

tears and wonder.

Abigail put her arm around Molly Ann's shoulder and squeezed her tight. "Really!"

"Well, okay, if you say so."

"I say so."

The sponsors stood at the front of the coach and watched as similar incidents took place. When they looked at each other, one of them said, "What more rewarding work could be found than ours?"

The other smiled. "It doesn't exist."

Forty minutes after he had driven away from the railroad station, Charles Loring Brace pulled his buggy into the Society's parking lot behind the large building on the corner of Astor Place and Lafayette Street in downtown Manhattan, which formerly had accommodated the Italian Opera House.

He released the gelding from his harness and led him past the three wagons that had earlier transported the children to Grand Central Station, put him in the small barn with the other horses, and headed for the back door.

When Brace entered his secretary's office, he smiled at Ivy Daniels. "Well, another precious group of children are on their way west."

"Praise the Lord!"

"Amen to that."

"Mr. Brace, there is someone here to see you—Mr. Wayne Stanfill, superintendent of the Thirty-second Street Orphanage."

"Oh, all right."

"He's in your office."

"Fine. You're new here, Ivy, and you probably don't know that Mr. Stanfill and I are good friends."

"No, sir. I wasn't aware of that."

"I have put many an orphan on our trains from the Thirty-second Street Orphanage. How long has he been here?"

"Nearly two hours. He said it was urgent that he see you, but he was willing to wait. I gave him some coffee."

"Good," said Brace, heading for his office door. "I'm sure he needs more orphans sent west."

When Brace entered his office, Wayne Stanfill jumped to his feet from the chair he was sitting in, and the two men shook hands. "Good to see you, Wayne. I have a feeling this urgent meeting has to do with your crowded quarters at the orphanage."

Stanfill ran fingers through his mustache. "Now, what would make you think that?"

Brace laughed and pointed to the chair where Stanfill had been sitting. "Sit down."

Stanfill settled onto the chair while Brace pulled another one up close and sat down.

Brace smiled. "Tell me about it."

"Well, I need you to take another group on one of your trains as soon as you can. We're really cramped tight."

"I guess Ivy told you I just put a load of orphans on a train this morning."

"Yes."

"There will be another train going in a week, but with the number of children already in our temporary quarters, that train will be full. I think I explained to you that the railroad companies will only donate the use of two coaches on any one train, didn't I?"

"Yes. One for the boys, and one for the girls."

"Right. The next train will go in two weeks: Thursday, March 30. There is still plenty of room on that one as yet. How many do you want to send?"

"I have six boys and eight girls, at the minimum, who need to be on that train. There may be more to schedule on it within a few more days."

"As it stands now, I can easily accommodate that many on the March 30 train. I'll make a note to hold space for six boys and eight girls, and if you have more within a few days, I'm sure I'll have room for them. Tell you what—"

Stanfill raised his eyebrows. "Mm-hmm?"

"Since we just sent sixty-four westward, the Society has some extra room for more children at this moment. You can bring those fourteen over right away if you wish."

Relief showed on Wayne Stanfill's face. "Oh, bless you! I'll have all fourteen brought over tomorrow morning."

"Fine. We'll be expecting them."

When Wayne Stanfill arrived back at the orphanage, he found two police officers sitting beside the receptionist's desk with a dark-headed boy between them. He heard her say, "Here's Mr. Stanfill now, gentlemen."

Both uniformed men rose to their feet and one of them took a step toward him. "Mr. Stanfill, I'm Officer Dan McNally and this is Officer Vince Paddock."

Stanfill shook hands with both men, then set his gaze on the boy, who rose from his chair. "And who is this young man?"

"His name is Johnny Smith, sir," said McNally. "He's twelve years old."

Stanfill shook hands with Johnny, whose eyes were red and swollen. He looked at the officers. "He's been weeping. What's wrong?"

"My dad was killed on Monday, sir," Johnny said. "I know you were acquainted with him. He brought a boy named Teddy Hansen to you recently."

Wayne Stanfill felt as if he had been punched in the stomach.

"Y-your father was killed?"

Johnny choked up. "Yes, sir."

Stanfill turned to the officers. "How?"

McNally drew a suffering breath. "The Manhattan Bank was on his beat. He came upon a bank robbery in progress. There was a shootout. Officer Smith killed both bank robbers, but took a bullet in the chest. He died on the way to the hospital. It was in the newspapers Tuesday."

"I've been so busy the past few days, I haven't had time to read a newspaper."

"Officer Smith was buried this morning at the Thirty-eighth Street Cemetery," said Paddock. "We brought Johnny here after the graveside service. He has no one else to take him. Chief Masterson and his wife have had Johnny in their home the past three nights, and because he is Officer Justin Smith's son they would like to keep him, but they aren't able to do it."

Stanfill nodded, then turned to the boy and looked into his eyes, recalling that Officer Smith's wife had died just a year ago. In those eyes, Stanfill saw the same panic and desperation that he had found in so many homeless, parentless children ever since he opened the orphanage many years ago.

Stanfill laid his hands on the boy's shoulders and gave him a reassuring smile. "Johnny, I know what it's like to be left alone in this big world. I was orphaned when I was nine years old. I was put in an orphanage in Boston and stayed there until I was seventeen. I got wonderful care, and the people who ran the orphanage showed me love and kindness all those years. This is why I chose this business for my life's work."

"We know the kind of care the children get here, Mr. Stanfill," said Dan McNally, "that's why we brought Johnny to you. We've heard you're overcrowded, but we felt sure you would make a place for him."

One hand was still on Johnny's shoulder. Stanfill looked at the officers. "Tell you what, gentlemen. I've just returned from the Children's Aid Society. I made arrangements with Charles Loring Brace to take fourteen of our children on his next available orphan train west, which will be March 30. However, I'm sending them to the Society's headquarters tomorrow morning. They've got room for them, and for a few more, if needed. If Johnny wants to, I can send him and he can go out West and be taken into a foster home."

Johnny looked up at him. "Really? I could go on an orphan train?"

"You sure can. I think it would prove out to be a very good opportunity for you. It will give you far more advantages in life than staying around here. The Wild West sounds really adventurous, don't you think?"

Johnny pondered Stanfill's words for a few seconds, then a smile crossed his face and his eyes lit up. "It sure does!"

"Do you want to go?"

"Yes, sir, Mr. Stanfill! I know I would like the West a lot!"

"Good. That's settled, then. I'll send you to the Children's Aid Society along with the fourteen others in the morning. Mr. Brace will put you on the train with them."

Dan McNally—who had been a close friend of Officer Justin Smith—said, "Johnny, your dad talked a lot about you and your desire to be a policeman when you grow up. He was so proud that you wanted to follow in his footsteps and wear a badge. Hey, if you go out West, someday you can become a town marshal or a county sheriff or a deputy United States marshal."

Johnny bit his lip. "I…ah…well, ah…since Dad got killed Monday, I've been thinking maybe I wouldn't wear a badge someday after all."

Dan nodded. "Well, I can understand why you'd feel that

way. But maybe you'll feel differently once you're over the shock of your father being killed. Don't rule it out completely. Your father was so proud that his son wanted to be a law officer."

Johnny managed a grin. "I won't rule it out completely, sir."

"Good. Justin Smith was an excellent law officer, and I know you would be just like him."

Officer Vince Paddock nodded. "Johnny, I've been out West in Nebraska, Colorado, and Wyoming. The lawmen out there are a breed of their own. Because you're Justin's son, I think you'd fit in and make a great one."

"We'll see what happens, sir."

"Well, Mr. Stanfill," said Dan McNally, "we've got to get back to headquarters."

"Thank you for bringing me here," Johnny said.

The officers wished Johnny their best and left.

Wayne Stanfill said, "Well, let's get you settled into a room. We're very crowded here, so you'll be in a room with nine other boys. There are only six bunks, so you'll have to sleep on the floor with three of them."

"That's all right, sir. I won't mind sleeping on the floor."

"Good. Some of the boys in that room will be going on the train with you. It will give you a chance to get to know them before you board the train together."

"All right. Let's go."

Stanfill guided Johnny down the hall to the room that was occupied by Teddy Hansen, Jerry Varnell, Clint Albright, and the other six boys. They were sitting on the bunks talking when the superintendent stepped in with Johnny on his heels. "Boys, I've got another roommate for you. This is Johnny Smith. I told him he would have to sleep on the floor."

"Hi, Johnny," said Teddy Hansen. "Jerry and Clint, along with me, sleep on the floor. We'll make room for you with us at bedtime. My name's Teddy."

Johnny smiled. "Thank you, Teddy."

Stanfill introduced Johnny to the rest of the boys, then told him he would send blankets and a pillow to him a little later.

When the superintendent was gone, Jerry invited the new roommate to sit between him and Teddy. Johnny thanked him, and when he sat down, Jerry said, "How long have you been an orphan, Johnny?"

"Well, I was a half-orphan for little more than a year, 'cause Mom died. Then my dad was killed just this past Monday."

"Tell us all about it, Johnny," said Clint.

Appreciating their warmth and interest, Johnny said, "How about you guys telling me how you became orphans, then I'll tell you my story."

The boys agreed, and Johnny listened intently as he heard their heartrending stories. The last to tell his story was Teddy Hansen.

Teddy started out by saying, "Johnny, I like the name Smith. It was Officer Justin Smith who rescued me from the streets."

Johnny felt a pang of pain in his heart, and it was all he could do to remain silent and keep from crying while Teddy told his story. Teddy said how his father had deserted him and his mother two years previously, then explained about his mother's recent death and how his one aunt and both uncles didn't want him. All the while Johnny fought the lump that was in his throat.

Teddy ended his story, giving the details of how Officer Justin Smith had rescued him from the streets and brought him to the orphanage. When he finished, he saw tears coursing down Johnny's cheeks. He frowned. "Did I say something that upset you, Johnny?"

Johnny swallowed hard and drew a shaky breath. "Teddy, Officer Justin Smith was my father. He was killed on Monday, shooting it out with bank robbers in front of the Manhattan Bank."

Teddy's eyes widened and his mouth fell open. "Oh, I'm sorry. I didn't realize he was your father. But now I recall. Your father told me he had a boy named Johnny who was twelve years old. Oh, I'm so sorry to hear this about him. He was such a great man."

Teddy's words warmed Johnny's heart, and he told himself that he and Teddy would become good friends. He hoped Teddy would be one of the boys who would go on the orphan train. "Teddy, Dad told me about you. He told me about the cut on your face from that kid punching you and having a ring on his finger. He told me your relatives didn't want you and that he had brought you here."

Teddy thumbed away a tear and sniffed. "Like I said, your father was a great man."

When it was time for the boys to go outside for recreation, Johnny and Teddy walked together. Johnny felt good about the orphanage and the prospect of riding the orphan train out West to a new home.

Chapter Four

That evening, at the Silver Spoon Restaurant next door to the Central Bank and Trust Company some twelve blocks from the Children's Aid Society's headquarters, business was booming as usual.

Cashier Lola Dickens was busy at the counter as satisfied customers paid for the meals. While waiting on the customers, Lola glanced at two auburn-haired teenage girls who were standing by themselves just inside the door. She noted that they were identical twins and quite pretty. Their coats were frayed and worn, and they held their stocking caps in their hands.

Lola's attention was drawn away from them as she finished dealing with a customer. When the next customer—an exceptionally tall, silver-haired man—was moving up to the counter, a closer look at the twins revealed that their faces were pinched from the cold and from something more. She greeted her customer, asking if everything was all right. He smiled and said the meal was excellent.

At the same time the cashier was waiting on the tall man, the twins' stomachs growled from hunger, and the tempting aroma of hot food coming from the nearby kitchen had set their mouths to watering.

"It smells heavenly in here," Donna Mitchell said in an undertone to her twin. "Wouldn't it be wonderful if we could get full simply by smelling the food?"

Deena nodded. "If that were the case, my tummy would be bursting from all of the good smells in here."

At the counter, Lola Dickens had a break between customers and noted that the twins were still there. She headed around the end of the counter, looking straight at them.

Donna whispered, "The cashier's coming over here."

Deena looked at Lola from the corner of her eye. "I hope she's friendly."

Lola drew up and smiled. "Are you girls waiting for someone?"

"No, ma'am," replied Donna. "We just came in out of the cold to get warm."

Lola sensed that there was more to it than stated. "What are your names, and where do you live?"

Deena tried to smile. "I'm Deena Mitchell, ma'am, and this is my sister, Donna."

"And?"

The twins exchanged nervous glances, and Deena said, "We...ah...don't have an address right now, ma'am."

"Oh. I understand. You live on the streets, don't you?"

"Yes, ma'am," said Donna.

Lola gave them a knowing look, which told them she had them figured out. "And you just came into the restaurant to get warm."

Deena cleared her throat gently. "Well, ma'am, we actually came in for two reasons. One was to get out of the cold. The other—the other was to ask if we could wash dishes or do some other kind of work in exchange for some food."

A troubled look came over Lola's pleasant features. "My

employer will not allow any of the street waifs to do any kind of work in the restaurant to earn meals or money. I'm sorry. How long have you girls been on the streets?"

"Just a few days, ma'am," said Donna. "Our parents cannot afford to feed or clothe us anymore, so they sent us out of their apartment. Our mother gave us each a dollar before sending us out on our own, but we spent the last of our money this morning for breakfast."

"So you've had nothing to eat today since breakfast."

"That's right, ma'am."

"And you've been sleeping in a doorway or an alley some-where."

"Yes, ma'am. We've been sleeping in a wooden crate in the alley behind Duggan's Furniture Store over on Westmore Street."

Having come from a very poor family herself, Lola knew what it was like to be hungry and cold. Her heart went out to the twins. "Girls," she said softly, "I'm sorry you have to live like this. You are nice girls and so polite. I want to help you. Wait right here. I'll be back shortly."

Donna and Deena watched as Lola moved toward another female employee who was standing near the counter. They heard her ask the woman to cover for her, saying she would be right back. She passed through a swinging door toward the kitchen, letting it swing shut behind her.

A few minutes later, she returned with hot food in a paper bag and a small jug of water. Smiling, she handed the bag to Deena and the jug to Donna. "Here's your supper."

"Oh, thank you, ma'am," said Donna. "Thank you so very much!"

"Yes, thank you, ma'am," Deena said loudly, her eyes showing excess moisture. "This is very kind of you."

Lola looked over her shoulder toward the kitchen and put a

vertical forefinger to her lips. "Sh-h-h! I could get in trouble with my boss for doing this, but I can't let you go to bed in your wooden furniture crate with empty stomachs. But please understand…I can only take this chance once. I must ask you not to come back. If I get caught doing this I could lose my job, and believe me, I can't afford for that to happen."

Donna furtively patted Lola's hand and said in a low voice, "We understand. We won't come back again."

"But thank you very much," whispered Deena.

Both girls put on their stocking caps and hurried out the door, eager to get to their makeshift home and devour the food that smelled so tempting.

Lola stepped up to the steam-smeared window beside the door and watched the twins disappear into the cold night. She noticed it was starting to sleet, and her heart went out to them.

Deena and Donna walked two blocks to Revere Street and turned into the alley that would lead them to the rear of Duggan's Furniture Store in the next block. They stopped when they saw some other street waifs gathered around a fire about halfway down the alley.

Donna whispered, "I'd like to eat by the warmth of that fire, sis, but they'd probably take this food away from us. Let's go on around the block."

The twins made their way in the driving sleet to the next cross street and headed in the direction of the furniture store. When they reached the alley, they sat on the cold stone doorstep at the back of the furniture store, next to their wooden crate. The door was recessed and offered shelter from the falling sleet. By the light that came from a street lamp at the end of the alley, they took the food out of the paper bag.

While they were eating, Donna said, "Sis, I know we're terribly hungry, but we don't have any idea when we will get more food. We'd better save some of this for tomorrow."

Deena swallowed a mouthful and peered at her sister. "I'm really hungry, sis. Maybe we'll hit it good tomorrow and get more food."

"And maybe we won't. We need to ration this food and make it last as long as we can. Let's measure out how much to eat right now. We'll fill ourselves up with water when we've eaten tonight's ration."

Deena nodded. "I know you're right, sis. I just got tired of my stomach growling at me all day today."

"Well, maybe we'll find jobs and better shelter soon, but for now, let's eat sparingly."

The freezing rain began to fall harder and the wind grew stronger. The twins hurried to finish the food they had allotted themselves, gulped down the rest of the water, then climbed into the furniture crate, dropped the lid, and snuggled close to exchange body heat.

Deena began to sniffle.

"What's wrong, honey?" asked Donna.

"I...I can't understand how Papa and Mama could put us out on the streets. If they love us, how could they do it?"

Donna was quiet for a moment, then said, "In all fairness, sis, we have to agree that Mama loves us. I don't think Papa does, but it's obvious that Mama is afraid of him. She knows if she angers him, he might just walk out and leave her and the children. She would have no way of providing for them."

"Mama has shown her love for us. I shouldn't have included her. It's Papa who doesn't love us. And Mama is definitely afraid of him. We've both seen her cower before him whenever he so much as raises his voice. And besides, she certainly isn't well. She's so thin, and her cough has seemed to worsen since she had that cold back in January."

"Mm-hmm. And maybe she really did figure she was doing us a favor by letting us go. I can't help but worry about her and our brothers and sisters."

Deena sniffed and wiped tears from her cheeks in the dark. "I'm afraid for us too, sis. Surviving isn't going to be easy."

"No, it won't, honey," said Donna, squeezing her tight. "But at least we have each other."

"Yes. I'm so thankful I have you. If you were ever taken from me, I don't know what I'd do."

"That's not going to happen. We'll always be together. And somehow, we're going to survive this ordeal."

"Right. We'll just take it one day at a time. Maybe tomorrow we ought to try another restaurant where we can beg for some food."

"We can try," Donna said, "but there aren't going to be very many people like the lady who fed us tonight. We'd probably be better off to do like so many of the street children do: beg for money from the people who pass by on the sidewalks."

Deena thought on it a moment. "I think you're right, sis. That's what we'll do. I've noticed that most of the street beggars stand on the corners so they can approach people coming from four directions."

"Right. Let's use the corner that's closest to us. We'll start in the morning."

"Okay. I hope this icy rain stops before then."

"Me too. There'll be more people on the streets if—"

Donna's words were cut off by the sound of footsteps in the alley and the low sound of male voices. They gripped each other, and Deena whispered, "I'm scared!"

"Me too!"

The girls clung to each other and listened intently as the footsteps and voices came closer. Soon the footsteps drew up to the crate, and a deep male voice said, "How 'bout thish here crate, Dub?"

A hand took hold of the lid and shook the crate. "I don' know, Ralph. It'sh purdy husky. Without an ax, we wouldn' be able to shplit it up for—" he hiccupped—"the fire."

Ralph's hand took hold of the lid too. "Aw, we could busht it up shomehow."

The hearts of the twins were pounding with terror. These men were obviously drunk. If they were looking for firewood, they also lived on the streets. They could be dangerous.

The girls were trembling, hardly able to breathe.

They jumped when Dub's fist slammed down on the lid. "Le'sh forgit it, Ralph. C'mon. We'll fin' somep'n better than thish ol' crate."

When the footsteps diminished in sound as did the voices, both girls released a sigh of relief.

The wind eased up, and the sound of sleet pelting the lid of the crate lessened. The twins fell asleep, clinging to each other.

Sometime in the middle of the night, Deena was awakened by the sound of her sister whimpering. Reaching out in the darkness, she touched a tear-soaked cheek. "Donna, what's wrong?"

Donna took hold of the hand that was touching her cheek and squeezed it. "I…I had a dream."

"You mean a nightmare?"

"No. It wasn't a nightmare. I dreamed that Mama and Papa had come here into the alley and found us. They were crying and said they were sorry for sending us away as they did, and wanted us to come home. Oh, Deena, it was so wonderful! Papa hugged us and told us he loved us."

Deena made a groaning sound deep in her throat. "That was

a dream, all right. Then what? Did we go home with them?"

"Yes, only it was all different."

"What do you mean?"

"When they took us home, it wasn't to that tiny flat, but to a large, beautiful house on Long Island with a huge yard. The house had several bedrooms. Our brothers and sisters were there to greet us. We had a good time hugging, then Papa and Mama led us into a great big dining room. The table was loaded with food, and—and, well, this is when I woke up."

"Mmm. Well, it was a beautiful dream, sis…but only a dream. We're still in this furniture crate in the alley behind Duggan's Furniture store. And we still have to worry about being able to beg enough money to buy the food we need to keep us alive."

"Yes. I know."

The twins clung to each other, wept together, and finally cried themselves to sleep.

The next morning Charles Loring Brace was at his desk at the Children's Aid Society headquarters when there was a light tap on the office door. "Yes, Ivy?"

Ivy Daniels opened the door and smiled. "Mr. Brace, there's a messenger here from Central Bank and Trust. He says bank president Lee Kottman sent him to give you a message."

Brace rose from his desk chair. "Please bring him in."

Ivy turned and motioned to an unseen person behind her, and presently a thin, silver-haired man appeared. "Mr. Brace, I'm Harold Wiggins, Central Bank's messenger."

"Please come in, Mr. Wiggins. Mrs. Daniels said you have a message from Mr. Kottman."

"Yes, sir. Mr. Kottman asked me to see you personally and

advise you that he wants to see you at his office as soon as possible. He would also like for Mrs. Brace to be with you."

"Well, of course. She's at home, but I can drive over there and pick her up. We'll be there within forty to forty-five minutes."

"Fine, sir. I'll head right back and let Mr. Kottman know."

As Charles Brace helped Letitia into the buggy in front of their modest home, she said, "What do you suppose this is about, darling?"

"I have no idea. I doubt if the messenger knows, so I didn't bother to ask him. We'll know in a little while."

Brace rounded the buggy, climbed into the seat, and put the horse to a trot. The streets were still a bit wet from the sleet storm the night before, but the sun was shining down from a clear sky, and the puddles were slowly drying up. Thirty minutes later, they drew up in front of the Central Bank and Trust Company. Brace parked the buggy at the curb, hopped out, and tied the reins to a post. He helped Letitia out, and together they walked into the lobby of the bank.

Brace saw a merchant coming from the teller's cages that he knew well. He introduced him to his wife, then they crossed the lobby to a fenced area where several secretaries were busy at their desks. Marla Swenson, who was the president's personal secretary, looked up and greeted the Braces.

"Nice to see you, Marla," said Brace. "Mr. Kottman is expecting us."

"He certainly is," she said, rising from the desk. She opened the small gate near her desk. "Come with me."

Marla approached the door of the president's office, tapped on it, and entered. "I have Mr. and Mrs. Brace here, sir."

Lee Kottman, who was about the same age as Charles Brace,

rose from his desk chair. "Hello, folks! Nice to see you. Please have a seat here in front of the desk." He reached across the desk and shook hands with Brace, did a slight bow to Letitia, then all three sat down.

Charles and Letitia waited for Kottman to speak. "I want to say to both of you that I deeply appreciate the fact that the Children's Aid Society has its general fund and payroll checking accounts with our bank."

Brace smiled. "We're very happy with the service here, Mr. Kottman."

"Good! It's always refreshing to hear such words from our customers." He ran his gaze between them. "No doubt you're wondering why I sent Harold Wiggins to you and asked that both of you come as soon as possible."

"Well, we're a bit curious, yes."

Letitia quietly smiled at him.

"Well, I have something to tell you. I had a meeting with the bank directors yesterday afternoon. As you may know, we have twelve directors, who are all prominent businessmen."

"We do, sir," said Brace.

"I've had something on my mind lately that I wanted to do for the Children's Aid Society. I brought it up to the directors and reminded them of the marvelous work you are doing for the orphans of this city, and together, we have agreed to come up with a gift of fifty thousand dollars for the Society. The money will be deposited in the Society's general fund account this morning."

For a moment, the Braces were stunned into silence. Finally, Charles found his voice, and though it was shaking with emotion, he said, "Mr. Kottman, I don't know how to thank you. This…this is such a pleasant surprise. It was totally unexpected, but so very much needed."

"Yes, Mr. Kottman," said Letitia, hardly able to breathe.

Brace leaned closer to the desk. "As you know, Mr. Kottman, there are literally thousands upon thousands of children who are roaming those streets out there, let alone thousands more who are packed into the orphanages. More children turn up out there in the streets every day. Letitia and I were talking about it just yesterday. We need more funds to care for those we bring in and then send out West. This is going to be a tremendous help to us. Thank you for caring about the children and for leading in this tremendous blessing."

Kottman smiled, letting it spread from ear to ear. "Mr. Brace, you are more than welcome. It always gives me pleasure to help a good cause, as it does our directors. Children are the future of this country, and we must take care of them. I can speak for the directors as well as the staff and employees of this bank. We are deeply grateful for all that you, Mrs. Brace, and your wonderful staff do for this city's orphans and disowned children. We should be thanking you instead of you thanking us."

Charles and Letitia looked at each other, then Charles said, "Our work is a rewarding one, sir. And even more so when we hear comments like that. We just don't know what to say to fully express our appreciation. Of course you and the directors will receive a letter from me, Mrs. Brace, and our directors for your generosity."

This time it was a sly grin on the bank president's face. "Well, I have something else to tell you."

The Braces exchanged glances again, then set their eyes on Kottman, who said, "The directors and I have also agreed that if the Society continues to do the great work you are doing by sending homeless children on your orphan trains and finding homes for them, this fifty-thousand-dollar gift will be an annual thing."

The Braces were in shock again.

Kottman's grin was still on his lips. "I know that many busi-nesses donate money to the Society. That's how you exist. My colleagues and I merely want to have a part in this great work. Well, I know you are busy people, and I won't detain you any longer." The bank president rose to his feet. "God bless you both."

The Braces bid Lee Kottman good-bye for the time being, thanked him again for his generosity, and left the bank.

Outside in the bright sunshine, Charles helped Letitia into the buggy, untied the horse's reins from the post, and climbed in beside her. He took her hand and said, "Honey, let's pray."

They bowed their heads and Charles led them as they gave God the glory for His goodness and mercy toward the Society.

When Charles put the horse into motion and they moved down the street, the Braces talked together, making plans for all that they could accomplish with this unexpected largesse that the Lord had bestowed on the Society.

Still praising their heavenly Father to the sound of clopping hooves and the city sounds around them, they wove their way through the traffic, heading back toward the Children's Aid Society headquarters to share the good news.

Chapter Five

When Charles and Letitia Brace had gone only two blocks from the Central Bank and Trust Company, they were still chattering exuberantly about the unexpected boon that had just come to the Children's Aid Society. Charles pulled rein momentarily to allow a bread wagon to leave the curb, then put the horse into motion once again.

They were approaching a corner, and suddenly they heard loud, angry voices. Their attention was drawn to a group of teenagers on the corner yelling indignantly at two young teenage girls who were both weeping. People were passing by and gawking at the scene, but no one was interfering.

Brace swung the buggy to the curb. "I don't like the looks of this," he said as he started out of the buggy.

Letitia said, "I don't, either," and climbed out her side.

Brace looked at her. "Honey, you don't need to get in on this."

"Yes, I do," she said, moving up to his side and taking hold of his arm. "Those poor girls are being picked on unmercifully."

The shouting went on, and as the Braces drew up they saw that the two girls who were under verbal attack were identical twins. Letitia let go of her husband's arm and stepped between the twins, placing an arm around each of them. They both turned and looked at her through tear-filled eyes.

Charles moved up between the angry group and the twins and ran his gaze over the sour faces. "What's going on here?"

The shouting suddenly faded away.

As with all of the street urchins' groups, this one had a leader. He was a husky boy of fifteen with a sullen look about him. There was intense displeasure in his fiery eyes as he set them on Brace, and his voice was thick when he spoke. "My friends and I live on the street, mister. We have a spot in that alley over there where we sleep. This has been our corner for begging since almost a year ago."

He set his blazing eyes on the auburn-haired twins. "Those two redheads were already on the corner when me and my friends came from the alley to do our daily beggin'. They were gettin' money from people who usually give money to us. This is our corner! They had no business beggin' here!"

"Calm down now, son," said Charles Brace. "What's your name?"

"Darold," came the reply as the boy bolted the twins with a hateful look.

Letitia felt the trembling in the twins' bodies. She gently patted their backs, trying to soothe them.

Darold turned and frowned at Brace. "Why should I calm down? This is our corner, and when I told those intruders I wanted the money they had collected, they refused to give it to me. They said they had as much right to beg on this corner as we do."

Deena Mitchell met Darold's gaze. "We didn't think we were doing anything wrong, and we still don't." She turned to the lady who had an arm around her. "We were just begging like thousands of other children do here so we can stay alive. Then all of a sudden these boys and girls came at us, screaming at us, saying we were in their territory."

"Yeah," spoke up Donna, "they threatened to beat us up if we didn't give them the money we got this morning and leave the corner."

"Beat you up?" Letitia said, acting as if the threat surprised her.

"Yes, ma'am," said Donna.

Letitia set her jaw and looked at the group. "Well, that's not going to happen."

The attention of Charles Brace and the angry group went to Letitia and the twins.

Looking from one twin to the other as she kept her arms around them, Letitia asked, "What are your names?"

"Our last name is Mitchell," said the girl in Letitia's right arm. "My name is Donna and my sister's name is Deena."

"Are you orphans?"

"No, ma'am. Our parents sent us away from home because they can no longer afford to keep us."

Letitia's features pinched. "Oh."

"We've tried to find jobs," said Deena, "but so far we haven't been able to find any. So we turned to begging. We've been sleeping in an alley near here. We didn't know somebody owned this corner."

Darold scowled at her. "Well, we do! You go find another corner to do your beggin'! This one belongs to me and my friends. And before you go, we want the money that belongs to us. You got it on this corner, and that makes it ours!"

Charles Brace shook his head. "No, Darold, it doesn't make the money yours. I'm sorry you have to live on the streets, but you do not own this corner. Nor do you have any right to take the money from Deena and Donna that they begged for and received."

Darold glowered crossly at Brace. His dark curly hair dangled on his forehead. "I know who you are! You're that Charles Brace guy who heads up the Children's Aid Society. I've seen your picture in the newspapers. I'm right, ain't I? You're Charles Loring Brace, ain'tcha?"

"Yes, I am."

Darold sneered. "Well, since you're sendin' so many street kids out West on your orphan trains, how come you don't offer to send any of us?"

"Let me explain something, son. The Society is only allowed to send two coaches of orphans on each train. This limits us on how many children we can send."

Darold pulled his lips tight and made a grunting sound.

Brace fixed him with steady eyes. "When I find street children with a bad attitude like yours and that of your friends, I'm slow to take them in because they usually turn out to be troublemakers while staying at the Society's headquarters or when they're on a train heading west."

Brace felt the heat from all eyes in the group. "Change your attitude, young people. I'll come back by and check on you in a few weeks. If I find you acting civil like you ought to, I'll consider you for a trip west."

With that, Brace turned and set his gaze on his wife and the twins.

Letitia sent a signal to her husband by looking first at him, then turning to look at each girl standing within the circle of her arms.

Having been married to this woman for over twenty years, Charles stepped to Letitia and smiled. "We'll do it, honey. Let's take the girls over to the buggy." Then he turned to the twins. "Would you come with us?"

Darold and his group glared at the Braces as they walked to the buggy. Charles looked over his shoulder at the group. Darold said something to his friends that Charles could not distinguish, but stood with his feet spread apart with a look of defiance. Charles shook his head, then turned back to the twins.

Donna and Deena stood with identical quizzical looks on their faces, casting sidelong glances at the group, who were now grumbling loudly that they wanted their money.

Ignoring them, Charles smiled at Deena and Donna. "Have you girls heard of the Children's Aid Society?"

"We have, sir," said Deena.

Letitia took hold of the girls' hands. "Would you like to come to the Society and stay with us so you'll be warm and have plenty to eat until we can put you on an orphan train and send you out West?"

The voices of Darold and his group were so loud, Donna said, "I'm sorry, Mrs. Brace, I could barely hear you. Did you say we could stay with you and be warm and full?"

Letitia raised her voice. "Yes, dear. We will keep you at the Society's headquarters until we can put you on an orphan train, and you'll have the opportunity to be taken into a foster home out West. Would you want to do that?"

The twins stared at each other in wonderment. "Oh yes!" blurted Deena. "We sure would, wouldn't we, Donna?"

"Very much so."

"Good!" said Letitia. "There are many nice families out West who are taking homeless children into their own homes. That sounds all right?"

"Sounds like a little bit of heaven," said Deena.

Donna took a deep breath. "It sure does! Especially after what we have lived through the past few days."

"Let's be on our way then," said Charles. "Hop in the back seat, girls."

The girls did as they were told while Charles helped Letitia into the front seat, then circled the wagon and climbed in beside her.

Deena took hold of Donna's hand. "Can you believe it, sis? It sounds almost too good to be true!"

"It sure does," said her twin, "but I just pinched myself, and I'm not dreaming!"

The Braces laughed, and Charles put the buggy into motion with a snap of the reins. They drove away with Darold and his group shouting snide remarks at them.

While driving along the street, Charles spoke over his shoulder to the twins. "I was just going over our train schedule in my mind. We'll put you girls on an orphan train that is leaving Grand Central Station on March 30. Until that time, you will be in the girls' dormitory at the Society's headquarters. And as Mrs. Brace said, you will have a warm place to stay and plenty to eat. It looks like you may need some new clothes. We'll take care of that."

Donna said, "We have some clothes in this bag we're carrying, Mr. Brace, but they're sort of worn out. It would be wonderful to have some new ones. And the food and warm place to stay sure sounds good!"

"It does!" Deena said excitedly. "Thank you so much."

"One other thing," said Brace. "Would you tell me your parents' address? I want to go talk to them so they will know that we're sending you out West."

Deena told him the address and apartment number and explained that with their father working two jobs, it would be hard to find him home. Charles said just talking to their mother would be enough.

Soon they arrived at the Society's headquarters. Deena and Donna were taken into Ivy Daniels's office where Charles and Letitia sat down with them. Charles asked the girls to tell their story to Ivy, who made notes as the twins gave her the details.

When they finished, Ivy set compassionate eyes on the girls. "I'm so sorry this has happened to you. But I'm glad Mr. and Mrs. Brace came along when they did." She wrote their names in a notebook. "Well, you're registered with us now, and you are officially scheduled to be on the train that leaves March 30. You'll be staying in room number ten with two other girls."

Charles rose from his chair. "I'll go see your mother right now girls."

Donna said, "Please tell her that we love her."

Deena nodded. "Yes. Please tell her, Mr. Brace."

"I'll do that. Mrs. Brace will take you to your room."

Ivy told the twins how happy she was that they were going west to find a new home, and Letitia walked them down the hall to the girls' dormitory. When they reached room ten, the door was open. The two girls who occupied the room were sitting on chairs talking as sunlight filtered through the windows. They looked up and smiled as Letitia entered with the twins on her heels.

Letitia smiled back. "Betsy, Margie, I have some new room-mates for you. As you can see, they are identical twins. This is Donna and this is Deena. Their last name is Mitchell. They are thirteen years old. Donna, Deena, this young lady with the cast on her arm is Betsy Gilder. She's twelve. This other young lady is Margie Lehman, and she is fourteen."

Donna and Deena noticed that not only was Betsy's left arm in a cast, but there were purple bruises on her face.

Betsy and Margie welcomed the twins, and Letitia could see that their warmth was pleasant to the twins. She showed the twins where to hang the clothes they had in the cloth bag, and while they were placing them in the closet, Letitia surreptitiously glanced at the threadbare clothing. She made a silent guess at their size then excused herself, saying she would let them get acquainted and hurried away.

Margie left her chair and went to where two other chairs stood and dragged them into the center of the room, telling the twins to sit down. As they did so, the twins looked around the room. After living in the cramped, dingy tenement flat, and more recently on the cold streets of Manhattan, the room seemed like a little corner of heaven. There were four single cots in the sun-filled room, each covered with a bright, colorful quilt and a soft pillow.

Margie sat back down next to Betsy and looked into the faces of the twins. "Have you been orphans long?"

"We're really not orphans," Donna said. "Our parents can't afford to keep us any longer, so they sent us out onto the streets."

"I'm sorry it happened to you," said Betsy, adjusting her left arm and the cast.

"It's been hard for us," Deena said. "How did your arm get broken, Betsy? And how did you get those bruises?"

Betsy's eyes filled with tears and she put her free hand to her face.

Deena's jaw slacked. "Oh, I'm sorry, Betsy. I didn't mean to upset you."

Margie put an arm around Betsy. "It's all right, Deena—you *are* Deena, aren't you?"

Deena nodded.

Before Margie could say more, Betsy sniffled and said, "Don't feel bad, Deena. I want you to know." She turned to her friend. "Margie, would you tell them?"

"Sure, honey," said Margie, squeezing her shoulder firmly. "It happened just over three weeks ago. The Gilders lived on the fifth floor of a tenement on Manhattan's north side. Betsy's father, Lyle Gilder, is a heavy drinker. He came home in a drunken stupor late one night. He and Betsy's mother, Elizabeth, got into an argument. They were both very angry, and Betsy saw her father throw her mother off the balcony of the flat. Her mother was killed when she hit the ground."

The twins frowned, then Donna set sympathetic eyes on the battered girl. "Oh, Betsy, how awful!"

Betsy bit down on her lips.

Margie pulled her closer and said, "When the police came, Lyle Gilder told them his wife fell off the balcony, and they believed it. When the police had gone, he warned Betsy that if she ever told anyone what she really saw, he would beat her to death."

The twins shook their heads in silent pity.

Margie went on. "The very next day, when Betsy's father came home from work, he overheard two women who lived in the tenement discussing his wife's death. One woman said to the other one that she had been told that Elizabeth didn't fall, but that Lyle was drunk and threw her off the balcony. Lyle assumed it was Betsy who had told the woman and stormed into the flat. He swore loudly at Betsy and started beating on her. Neighbors heard Lyle's loud profanity and Betsy's cries, and summoned two policemen from the street.

"Lyle was still beating Betsy when the officers burst through the door. They seized him, put him in handcuffs, and placed him under arrest. When they picked Betsy up off the floor, they found that her left arm was broken and her face was severely bruised. Soon everyone in the tenement was aware of what happened and were gathering in the hall outside the Gilder flat. The two women Lyle had overheard talking about Elizabeth's death told the officers that one of the elderly tenants who lived two doors down from the Gilders on the same floor had seen Lyle throw Elizabeth off the balcony, but she was afraid to get involved. She had only told the one woman about it less than ten minutes before Lyle came home."

Deena was shaking her head slowly, tears in her eyes. "Oh, Betsy, I'm so sorry you've had to suffer like this."

"Me too," said Donna. "So what about your father?"

Betsy drew a shuddering breath. Her voice was strained with emotion as she said, "He stood trial for murdering Mother, and he will be executed nine days from now." When those words had come out, Betsy broke down and sobbed incoherently.

Deena left her chair and threw her arms around Betsy. Donna followed and did the same while Margie looked on. Slowly, Betsy's sobbing subsided. The twins still held her in their arms. Deena looked at her sister. "What happened to us with our parents putting us out on the streets was bad enough, but what happened to Betsy is far worse."

Donna nodded. "That's for sure. How were you orphaned, Margie?"

Margie's features pinched. "My parents were both killed in a train wreck up in Massachusetts. I'll tell you more about it sometime. It happened a little over a month ago. I just don't want to talk about it right now."

"I understand. But I'm sorry for your grief and heartache."

Margie managed a smile. "Thank you."

When Letitia Brace left room number ten, she went upstairs to a large walk-in holding closet and chose three dresses for each twin to begin wearing immediately, along with two more expensive dresses each for when they would be traveling on the orphan train. She would explain that when both boys and girls traveled westward, they were dressed especially nice for being examined and questioned by prospective foster parents. None of the dresses were identical, as Deena and Donna were, but Letitia was sure they wouldn't mind.

As she folded the dresses over one arm, a satisfied smile graced Letitia's pleasant face. She looked heavenward. "It's such a joy, Lord, to be able to help these dear young ones, and thank You, again, for the bounty You brought our way today through Mr. Kottman."

With a smile on her face, she left the closet and headed downstairs.

The twins loved the dresses and made an immediate change. They both embraced Letitia, thanking her for all the dresses. Letitia returned to the office, and for the rest of the afternoon, the twins got better acquainted with their roommates. Betsy and Margie took them on a tour of the rest of the building, explaining that it was once the Italian Opera House. While touring, the twins were introduced to both boys and girls who were also waiting to be sent west on orphan trains.

While Betsy and Margie were giving the twins a tour of the grounds, Margie explained that she would be leaving on the orphan train that was going west next week. Betsy said sadly that she was going to miss her.

At that moment, they saw Charles Brace come out of the building and head toward them. When he drew up, smiling, he said to Margie and Betsy, "Giving your new friends a tour of the place, are you?"

"Yes, sir," said Margie.

Brace ran his gaze to the twins. "I talked to your mother and explained that we would be sending you out West on the March 30 orphan train. She shed some tears, saying she misses you, but also said she is glad you will have the opportunity for a good life that would never have come to you here in the city. She said to tell you that she loves you and wishes you the very best."

The twins exchanged glances, blinked at their tears, and thanked him for letting their mother know about them.

On returning to their room, the girls washed their hands and tidied their hair in preparation for going to supper, which was always at six o'clock. Margie helped Betsy with her hair, since Betsy only had one free hand.

At ten minutes before six o'clock, the girls left their room and joined other girls who were heading for the dining hall.

When they drew near it, delicious aromas were wafting toward them. Betsy sniffed and said, "I wonder what we're having tonight."

Donna sniffed, also. "I can't tell what it is, but if it tastes half as good as it smells, it will be wonderful!"

The four girls entered the dining hall and sat down at a table where they joined four other girls. Johnny Smith, Teddy Hansen, Jerry Varnell, and Clint Albright were seated at an adjacent table with some other boys. Margie introduced the twins to the four girls, and the girls welcomed them.

Soon a large bowl of beef stew with potatoes, carrots, and thick dark gravy was placed before them. A basket of hot biscuits was passed around as well as creamy butter and strawberry jelly. A mug of milk was at each place. The twins felt their mouths watering.

Donna could wait no longer. She quickly buttered a biscuit, dabbed some jelly on it and was about to take a bite when she heard a light cough from the front of the room, and looked toward the sound. It had come from Charles Brace, who was looking at her. The biscuit was suspended an inch from her mouth as he said, "Let's pray, children, and thank the Lord for the food."

Embarrassed, Donna lowered the biscuit and bowed her head as the others around her were doing. While Charles Brace was praying, Donna felt her sister squeeze her hand in sympathy with her near mistake.

When Brace said his amen, he smiled at Donna, then ran his gaze over the entire crowd. "Okay, boys and girls, enjoy your supper."

All the children dug in, eagerly complying.

When the meal was finished, Charles Brace stood before the crowd once again and introduced the Mitchell twins to them. Following this, one of the staff men stood before them and gave a Bible lesson, which included the gospel. Before having prayer time, he had two teenage girls come to the front. He announced that last night after the Bible lesson and prayer time, the two girls had received the Lord Jesus Christ into their hearts as their Saviour. They wanted to give their testimonies.

While the girls were telling of their salvation, Deena and Donna looked at each other blankly. This was something totally new to them.

On Tuesday morning of the next week, those children who were scheduled on the March 30 train watched as the others were lining up and being taken to the wagons parked beside the building.

Betsy Gilder clung to Margie Lehman with her good arm, tears running down her face. Margie, also weeping, kissed her friend's cheek. "Good-bye, Betsy. I love you."

As Margie hurried to get in the line, both of the twins put an arm around Betsy. When the wagons pulled away, the departing children waved, and those left behind waved back.

Deena squeezed the weeping girl. "Don't you worry, Betsy. Donna and I will take care of you like Margie did."

"Yes, we will," said Donna. "The three of us will be together on the next orphan train."

Betsy hugged them both individually with her good arm. "I'm glad for that," she said, sniffling and blinking at her tears, "but I'm also dreading the day when at some railroad station, some family will choose you two and take you home."

Donna laid a palm against Betsy's cheek. "It may happen the other way, honey. It could be you who gets chosen first."

Betsy nodded. "It could happen that way, I guess. But whichever way it goes, I'll miss you two something terrible, and I'll never forget you."

During the next few days, Johnny Smith and Teddy Hansen's friendship grew deeper and stronger. Johnny also became closer to Jerry Varnell and Clint Albright. The other boys who had been in their room had been taken on the latest orphan train, but they now had three new boys rooming with them.

On Wednesday night, March 29, when it was close to bedtime, Johnny, Teddy, Jerry, and Clint sat on their bunks and talked about their upcoming train ride and what it was going to be like to have foster parents and live in new homes. The new boys sat quietly and listened.

Teddy looked at Johnny. "You talked the other day about how once you wanted to be a policeman like your father when you grow up, but maybe now you won't do that. Have you thought any more about it?"

Johnny grinned. "Yeah. I still might be a lawman. I'll know more about whether I want to once I get out West and have a chance to see how it is for the men who wear a badge out there. What about you, Teddy? What do you want to be when you grow up?"

Teddy rubbed the back of his neck. "Well, after seeing how nice the people were at the Thirty-second Street Orphanage to Jerry, Clint, and me, I've been thinking that when I grow up, I might like to establish an orphanage and provide a home for children like me."

Clint's eyes lit up. "Hey, Teddy, that's a good idea! Maybe I'll do that, wherever I end up."

Jerry grinned. "You know, I've been thinking the same thing."

Johnny ran his gaze from Teddy to Clint to Jerry. "Hey, guys, I hope all three of you do that. If I don't end up being a lawman, I might just do something like that myself." He yawned. "Well, right now, I think we'd better get to bed. We board that orphan train tomorrow morning."

Chapter Six

The next morning just after breakfast, the children who were going on the train that day were led into the Children's Aid Society's auditorium and seated in the center section. There were thirty-three girls and twenty-nine boys.

They were all dressed in their new clothing and carried their new coats. The boys also had caps and the girls had scarves. Most of the girls had their hair done in pigtails, and every boy had his hair combed neatly.

Though there was some apprehension in the hearts of the children about the trip on the train, they were happy with the prospect of being taken into homes. There was a resonance of chattering voices that filled the auditorium as Charles Loring Brace entered from a side door with three women and four men following. They mounted the steps of the platform.

Some of the children noticed them, while others were busy talking.

Brace moved to the center of the platform, raised his hands and said above the lively voices, "All right, boys and girls, let's get quiet. I want to talk to you."

The chatter faded quickly, and each child settled on his or her seat. Their expectant eyes were fixed on him, and he took just a moment to look at their anxious faces and breathe a silent prayer for God's hand on them, and that eventually each one would come to know Jesus as their Saviour.

Brace motioned for those on the platform with him to step up close. "Children, I want you to meet the staff members who will be going along on the train as your sponsors. Standing next to me are Mr. Dale Radcliff and his wife, Lorinda. Next to them are Mr. Royce Nelson and his wife, Shelley. The men will travel in the boys' coach, and the women will travel in the girls' coach."

He gestured toward the young woman in the white uniform who stood beside Shelley Nelson. "And this lady is Miss Mandy Hillen. She is a certified medical nurse. She will be on the train to take care of any boys or girls who need her."

The sponsors and the nurse ran their eyes over the small crowd and smiled.

Brace went on. "I am usually able to go to the depot and give the children a sendoff with a small speech, but today I have other obligations, so I will make my speech now.

"First, I want to say that when you stand in line in the depots where the prospective foster parents come to talk to you and look you over, I want you to be polite and courteous. You are to answer any questions the people ask you.

"Second, let me caution you not to be discouraged, even if you have not been chosen after many stops out West. Your train is going all the way to Los Angeles and there will be many stops between the Missouri River and the Pacific Ocean where people will be waiting to choose children to take home with them. In our twenty-three years of carrying children out West, there have been very, very few who have had to be returned to New York because they were not chosen by the time they had arrived at the last stop. And let me add that even those children were all chosen when they rode the next orphan train west.

"I also want to mention the Bible lessons you have had while staying here at the Society's headquarters. Although many of you have opened your hearts to Jesus as a result of the Bible lessons, some of you have not. I want to remind those of you who have not been saved that it is the greatest need you have in your lives. You will be having Bible lessons on the train, taught by your sponsors. Mr. and Mrs. Radcliff and Mr. and Mrs. Nelson—as well as Miss Hillen—will always be ready and willing to lead you to Jesus if you will let them. I want to pray for you now, before you leave for Grand Central Station."

After Brace prayed for the children, asking God's protection on them as they embarked on their journey, the children put on their coats, caps, and scarves, and were led by him and the sponsors outside to the wagons that would carry them to the depot.

Before boarding the wagons, many of them—especially the girls—gave Brace hugs, thanking him for what he had done for them. Included in that group were the Mitchell twins and Betsy Gilder.

When the wagons rolled into Grand Central Station's parking lot, the children were unloaded and led into the terminal by the sponsors and Mandy Hillen. They went immediately to the track where the train they would ride westward stood ready for boarding.

Most of the children had never been this close to a train before. They stood in awe at the monstrous engine with billows of black smoke roiling skyward from its smokestack. Steam was hissing from the bowels of the engine.

Dale Radcliff stood before them and explained that the two coaches just ahead of the caboose were reserved for them. The boys' coach was the one next to the caboose. The other three coaches were for the regular passengers, who were now ready to board.

At that moment, the conductor stepped out of the first regular passenger coach. "All aboard! All aboard!"

The young travelers boarded their respective coaches in an orderly manner, with their sponsors standing at both front and back doors of the coaches to give directions and answer questions. The sponsors could tell that the children were apprehensive about this new adventure, but excited about finding homes in the West.

In the girls' coach, Donna and Deena Mitchell chose a seat at the very front, which had them facing the rear of the coach. Betsy Gilder took the next seat, which allowed her to look into their faces.

As Betsy settled on the seat, she said to the twins, "I don't know if I'm more excited or more scared, but it's kinda fun!"

The twins looked at each other and grinned.

Donna chuckled. "It's sure a lot more fun than sleeping in a wooden crate in an alley!"

Deena nodded. "You can say that again, sis!"

Donna shrugged with an impish look in her eyes. "Okay. It's sure a lot more fun than sleeping in a wooden crate in an alley!"

Donna's stab at humor caused both her sister and Betsy to laugh and relax.

In the boys' coach, Dale Radcliff stood at the front and said, "I want to explain that the first stop where prospective foster parents will talk to you and look you over is in Overland Park, Kansas. We have to cross Pennsylvania, Ohio, Indiana, Illinois, and Missouri, first.

"Along the line after we leave Missouri at Kansas City and cross the Missouri River into Kansas, people in the towns where we will be stopping, all the way to the west coast, have been alerted that the orphan train is coming. The local newspapers in all the towns along the line are carrying articles that announce the arrival times of this orphan train so those who are interested in taking in foster children will know when to be at the depots.

"The next stop in Kansas will be Topeka, which is the state capital. And after that, we will stop at Salina. There will be more stops in Kansas, then at points west in Colorado, Utah, Nevada, and California. Just thought you might like to know these things. My wife is giving the same information to the girls in their coach."

Royce Nelson, who was standing beside Dale, said, "So just relax and enjoy the ride, boys. Remember, Mr. Radcliff and I are here to help you in any way we can."

As the days and nights passed while the train traveled westward toward Kansas City, the orphan children watched passengers getting on and off the other three coaches, eagerly anticipating the moment when they would cross the Missouri River into Kansas, where they could begin meeting the prospective foster parents.

The train pulled into Kansas City late in the afternoon on Wednesday, April 5. A cold wind was blowing, but the sky was clear and the lowering sun was casting its long shadows.

The sponsors found the children eager to see the Missouri River, which to them would open up the West and the opportunities that lay before them to find homes and enter into a new life.

In the girls' coach, Betsy Gilder was still seated opposite the Mitchell twins. While waiting for the train to pull out of Kansas City, the girls were talking about their earlier childhood and how much they missed their families.

Betsy set affectionate eyes on Donna and Deena. "I wish you

could be my sisters and we could grow up together."

Donna smiled sweetly. "I would love that, Betsy."

"Me too," said Deena, "but I'm afraid that is next to impossible. I heard Mrs. Radcliff and Mrs. Nelson talking about how it has been for the orphans they have brought west in the past. They said most foster parents only want one child, and some will take two, but only on very few occasions have they ever seen a couple take more than two."

"Well, if someone took you two but not me, I'd sure like to be chosen in the same town where you are. Then at least, we would get to see each other."

"That would make both of us happy, Betsy," said Donna, "but the chances of that happening are pretty slim."

Betsy nodded. "But not impossible, though. I can hope."

Donna smiled. "Well, Deena and I will hope with you, honey."

"We sure will."

Soon the train pulled out of Kansas City, and shortly thereafter, the children in both coaches were gathering at the windows to get a look at the Missouri River in the light of the golden sunset.

In the boys' coach, they all cheered when Dale Radcliff pointed at the wide Missouri. "There's the river, boys! We're about to pass into Kansas!"

A moment later, the train was on the trestle that crossed over the river.

One of the teenage boys was heard to say, "Wow! That river really is wide!"

"It sure is a lot wider than the East River in New York City!" another said.

Teddy Hansen and Johnny Smith were seated together, and after the train had crossed the trestle, the ten-year-old gripped

Johnny's arm. "I wish whoever chooses you will choose me too. I'd really like to be your brother."

Johnny grinned at him. "I'd like that, Teddy. But you will probably be chosen real fast—maybe even in Overland Park."

Teddy shrugged. "Maybe. But you could be too. If the same people took both of us, then we'd be brothers."

Johnny patted the hand that was still gripping his arm. "I guess we'll just have to wait and see."

The western sky was still brilliant, though the sun had now dropped below the horizon, as the train pulled into the Overland Park depot.

The children in both coaches looked out the windows, watching the regular passengers leaving the other coaches. They noted that the departing passengers quickly buttoned up their coats against the cold, penetrating wind that was whistling through the depot as they were greeted by loved ones and friends.

Moments later, the children saw Dale Radcliff move up to a group of people who were obviously prospective foster parents. He talked to them briefly, and they were nodding their heads in agreement with what he was saying to them. They wheeled and went inside the terminal.

Dale turned and went to the girls' coach, and seconds later, entered the boys' coach, telling them that the wind was very cold, so everyone was going inside the terminal for the prospective foster parents to talk to the children and look them over.

The sponsors led the boys and girls from their coaches to the warmth of the terminal, and lined them up, mixing boys and girls in the line.

The prospective foster parents moved along the line and began talking to the children, who nervously but politely answered the questions they were asked.

Two teenage girls and one eight-year-old boy were chosen and taken away after the foster parents signed the official papers for the sponsors.

As the rest of the boys and girls climbed back aboard their respective coaches while night fell, there was disappointment showing on some of the faces. Their sponsors and Nurse Mandy Hillen spoke encouraging words to them, saying there were lots of stops coming up, and eventually they would all be chosen.

The train pulled out of Overland Park and soon was rolling westward at full speed.

In the girls' coach, Donna and Deena Mitchell were on their seat with Betsy Gilder between them. All three girls were showing their disappointment when Lorinda Radcliff came to them. "Girls, don't you remember what Mr. Brace told you that morning we left for Grand Central Station? There are many stops ahead. Come on now. Cheer up. You'll be chosen before this trip is over."

Betsy didn't voice it, but said to herself, I sure hope I can be chosen in the same town as Deena and Donna.

Supper was served to the children in both coaches, and by the time they were finished eating, some of them were covering yawns. The lanterns were dimmed, and not long afterward, they were in dreamland.

The train arrived in Topeka during the night, when most of the passengers were asleep, including those in the orphan coaches. By seven o'clock in the morning, the children had been fed their breakfast. They donned their coats, caps, and scarves, and because the air was chilly, they were taken inside the terminal and lined up. The prospective foster parents were ready, and as soon as they had been interviewed and approved by the sponsors, they began moving along the line, looking the orphans over and asking them questions.

In the line were siblings Katie and Richie Woods. Katie was nine years of age and Richie was two years younger.

A few couples had passed by when a husband and wife in their late twenties stopped at Katie, and introduced themselves as Tom and Vivian Selby. They told her they owned a small farm south of town and began asking questions. While answering the questions, Katie could tell that the Selbys were definitely interested in her.

Vivian bent down to Katie's eye level. "Even though you've always lived in the big city, honey, do you think you'd like living in the country?"

"Oh yes, ma'am. We both would."

Vivian batted her eyes. "Both?"

Tom frowned.

"Yes," said Katie, putting her arm around her little brother. "This is my brother, Richie. He's seven."

Richie smiled at the couple.

Tom cleared his throat gently. "Well, ah…Richie, we would like to be able to take you too, but we just can't afford to take in two children. We'll give the sponsors our address, then when somebody takes you, they can give it to them. Then you and Katie will be able to keep in touch."

It was Katie's turn to frown. She didn't want to be separated from Richie.

Tom turned and motioned to Dale Radcliff, who stood close by with the clipboard in his hand. Dale stepped up and smiled. "Interested, Mr. and Mrs. Selby?"

"Yes," said Tom. "We're going to take Katie."

Dale nodded. "And how about Richie?"

The Selbys looked at each other, then Tom said, "We'd like to, Mr. Radcliff, but we cannot afford to take in two children."

Richie began to cry. He gripped his sister's arm and wailed, "Don't leave me, Katie! Please don't leave me!"

Katie's chest tightened and her voice was strained as she looked at the Selbys and said, "I—I'd better stay with my little brother."

Tom looked down at her with tender eyes. "Katie, we would like to take Richie too, but it just isn't possible."

"But—but—"

Vivian put an arm around her. "Katie, we really do want you. We'll give you a good home."

Katie's eyes were misty. "But I can't leave Richie."

Dale said, "Katie, listen to me. The executive board of the Children's Aid Society has a rule that if only one sibling can be taken by foster parents, they are allowed to do so. This was explained to all the prospective foster parents before they started through the line a few minutes ago. The reasoning behind it is that the executive board feels it is better for brothers and sisters to be separated out here in the West, than to stay together on the streets of New York where so many starve to death or freeze to death in the winter. Since these nice people want to take you, I must allow them to do so."

Tom laid a tender hand on Richie's shoulder and looked at Katie. "We'll do as I said, honey. We'll have Mr. Radcliff give our name and address to whoever takes Richie, so you can keep in touch with each other." Then he said to the boy, "We really wish we could take you too, Richie, but we just don't have the money to take in both of you."

Richie turned to his sister, sobbing, and Vivian let go of her. The boy wrapped his arms around his sister. "Please, Katie! Don't leave me!"

Katie knew there was nothing she could do to change the situation. She must go with the Selbys. Meeting her little brother's tearful gaze, she said, "Richie, it's better this way than living on the streets of New York like we did for almost a year after Mama and Papa died. Like Mr. Selby said, the people who take you into their home will be given Mr. and Mrs. Selby's address. They will write and let us know where you are. If it isn't too far down the line, we may even get to see each other from time to time."

Richie clung to her, begging her not to go. Finally, Dale pulled him loose from her, saying the Selbys needed to be going. Katie kissed her little brother's cheek. "I love you, Richie."

Dale kept a hand on Richie's shoulder as Katie sniffled and walked away with the Selbys. When they passed from view, he said, "Richie, don't cry now. You're going to have a good home farther out West. Why, maybe somebody right here in Topeka will even take you. There are still more people coming along the line."

At that moment, Dale saw a man motioning to him down the line. "Yes, sir?"

"We want to take this little six-year-old girl, Mr. Radcliff."

Dale nodded. "I have to go help those people, Richie. I'll see you later."

Richie watched Dale head toward the couple and the little girl, then turned to see who might be coming toward him. There was a couple talking to a teenage boy next to him. They were showing interest in the boy and concentrating on him. The two girls on Richie's other side were talking to each other. No one was paying attention to him.

Richie took a couple of backward steps, made sure no one was looking at him, and made his way in the direction his sister and the Selbys had gone. It took him a couple of minutes to locate the main door of the terminal building. When he did, he hurried out the door just in time to see the Selby wagon heading south out of town.

Still crying, he ran that direction. "Katie! Katie! Don't leave me!"

The wagon was too far away for Katie or the Selbys to hear him and soon passed from view. Richie kept running. After some ten minutes, he reached the edge of town. He could see a wagon on the road in the distance, but he wasn't sure it was the Selby wagon. One thing he *was* sure of—the Selby farm had to be in that direction. Shoving his hands down in his coat pockets, he maintained a brisk walk southward.

A few minutes had passed when Richie heard the clopping of hooves and the rattle of a wagon. As he turned to look at it, he saw two teenage farm boys in the driver's seat. They were both looking at him. The boy who held the reins pulled the wagon to a halt. "Hey there, little fella. You need a ride?"

Richie looked up at him and nodded. "Some people took my sister for a ride to their farm, but they forgot me."

The other boy asked, "What's the peoples' name?"

"Mr. and Mrs. Selby."

"Oh? Tom and Vivian Selby?"

"Uh-huh."

"We know them. Their farm is about a mile farther down the road than ours. We'll take you to the gate of our place, then you can walk to the Selby farm from there, okay?"

"Sure!"

"Well, come on," said the one with the reins. "Climb in!"

At the depot, Dale Radcliff finished the paperwork with the couple who were taking the six-year-old girl, then headed back up the line. When he drew near the spot where Richie had been, he noticed that he was not there. He looked back and forth along the line, then asked the children who had been flanking Richie if they knew where he went. They replied that they did not. They were busy talking to the adults who were asking them questions.

Dale turned and went to Lorinda, who was busy signing up a couple who were taking a child. She looked at him as he drew up. "Honey, you look worried. What's wrong?"

"Have you seen Richie Woods?"

"No. Didn't those people take him and his sister?"

"They only took Katie. I left Richie in line to go and help another couple, and now I can't find him. The children in the line said they didn't notice him leave."

"Well, somebody must have seen him leave."

"I'll see if Royce and Shelley saw him."

Dale hurried to the Nelsons, who were standing at the head of the line, talking to Mandy Hillen. They had not seen Richie leave, either.

By this time, the prospective foster parents were almost through looking and no one else seemed interested in taking any of the other children.

Dale told the Nelsons and Mandy Hillen he was going to take some of the older boys to help him find Richie. Royce said he would go with him. When they had chosen six boys twelve to sixteen years of age, Dale stopped by Lorinda and informed her that he and Royce were taking the boys to help him find Richie. He asked her to inform the conductor, so he could hold up the train until they returned.

At the Selby farm, Tom and Vivian were with Katie in the bedroom they had prepared for her.

Katie ran her gaze around the bright room and patted the

lovely bedspread. "Oh, this is just wonderful! I've never had my own bedroom before."

"Come over here, dear," said Vivian, and led her to a chest of drawers. She opened one and took out a small bolt of light blue cloth. "We definitely were planning on bringing a girl home, and I bought this material so I could make her a dress. Do you like it?"

"Oh yes! It's beautiful!"

Tom's attention had gone to the window. He took a step closer and said, "Well, look at that, will you?"

Katie and Vivian stepped up beside him and looked out to see Richie coming down the lane toward the house.

In Topeka, the Shawnee County sheriff and his deputies had joined Dale, Royce, and the older orphan boys in their search for Richie Woods. The conductor and the engineer were holding up the departure of the train at the depot while the search was being made.

The town had been covered, and the searchers were standing in the dusty street in front of the sheriff's office as Dale and Royce were thanking the sheriff and his deputies for their help.

Johnny Smith had suggested that Richie might have headed for the Selby farm, but Dale, Royce, and the sheriff agreed that the boy would have no way of knowing where the Selby farm was located.

The sheriff said, "Gentlemen, I know the train has to move on, but my men and I will keep searching. We'll cover every road and every farm until we find him. We'll wire the depots ahead of you and let you know when we have him."

"All right, Sheriff," said Dale. "We'll have you put him on the next train through, and we'll—"

"There he is!" cried Johnny Smith, pointing down the street.

Every eye in the group followed Johnny's finger to see Tom Selby on his saddle horse with Richie Woods riding in front of him. A smile the size of Texas gleamed from Richie's freckled face as Tom drew rein.

Dale and Royce stepped up with the sheriff on their heels.

"Where did you find him, Mr. Selby?" asked Dale.

Tom grinned. "In my front yard. He was walking the direction he saw us go when he hurried out of the terminal. A couple of teenage boys from a farm near mine picked him up and gave him a ride."

Dale frowned at the boy. "Richie, you shouldn't have left the terminal. We've been looking all over town for you. The sheriff and his deputies have been helping us. Come on. We've got to get back to the train so it can leave."

Tom's saddle squeaked as he leaned closer to Dale. "We've decided to take Richie too, Mr. Radcliff. He's really a special boy. We'll just tighten our belts. Even though we don't have another bedroom, Richie has agreed to sleep on the floor in Katie's room."

Dale smiled, as did Royce. "Well, I'm glad for this. It's good to know that Richie and Katie won't be separated."

Tom nodded and placed a hand on the boy's shoulder. "Richie has something to say to you, Mr. Radcliff."

Richie's face crimsoned as he looked down at Dale from the saddle. Tears formed in his eyes. "M-Mr. R-Radcliff, I…I'm sorry I ran away. I'm sorry I caused so much trouble. But…look how good it turned out. I'm gonna have a new home and be with my sister!"

The men and boys all laughed, thankful that the situation had turned out so well.

Dale let a grin curve his lips. "You're forgiven, son. I can imagine how hard it was for you to think of being separated from

Katie. You've got a lot of pluck, I'll say that for you. I hope you have a wonderful life. You be good now and mind the Selbys."

"Oh, I will, sir," said Richie, turning to look up into Tom's eyes.

Tom smiled and tweaked his new foster son's nose.

Richie giggled.

"Let's get back to the depot, Mr. Selby," said Dale. "We'll get your signature on the official papers, and you can take Katie's brother home."

Chapter Seven

In Colorado Springs, Colorado, on that same morning of April 6, El Paso County Sheriff Clay Bostin stood at the kitchen window finishing his final cup of coffee while his wife, Mary, was putting the breakfast dishes in the dishpan.

Bostin looked up at the Rocky Mountains to the west of the house and marveled at God's handiwork. The sun tipped the apex of Pike's Peak rosy red. A deepening rose color reflected on the adjoining mountain tops and this magnificent glow crept down the shadowed slopes. The gray dawn that had been there when the Bostins sat down to breakfast had now changed to a radiant morning with a golden red hue.

Bostin finished the last drop of coffee and placed the cup in the hot, soapy water in the dishpan. He smiled at Mary, who was wiping the table with a wet cloth, and pointed with his chin at yesterday's newspaper, which lay on a small table next to the cupboard. "I meant to ask you last night. Did you get a chance to read the paper yesterday?"

Mary nodded. "Yes, and like you told me, there's a notice that there's another orphan train coming in on Wednesday, April 12."

Clay met her gaze. "Do you want to try again?"

"Yes. Very much so. Though the Lord didn't give either one of us peace about taking an orphan from the last two trains, I really believe He has a special one picked out for us. Maybe he or she will be on next Wednesday's train."

The Bostins, who were in their late twenties, had agreed that whether God had a boy or a girl picked out for them, either would be fine. It was like when a couple had a baby by birth, they must take what comes: boy or girl.

Mary moved back to the cupboard and laid the cloth down.

For a moment, she allowed her mind to reach back to the past, when she was sixteen years old and had to have surgery, which unexpectedly rendered her unable to bear children. She thought of how devastated she was when the doctor gave her the bad news.

Another fragment of memory flashed into her mind: the moment when she told the young man who wanted to marry her that she could never give him children. A warm feeling went through her as she remembered Clay's words. *"Mary, darling, I love you with everything that's in me. If we can't have a child of our own, then we'll adopt one, but I want you for my wife, no matter what."*

A lump rose in Mary's throat as she looked at her husband. "I love you, Clay. More than you will ever know."

He stepped to her and folded her in his arms. "That works two ways, beautiful. You'll never know how much I love you, either."

As was their custom, the Bostins took time to read a chapter of Scripture together and to spend a few minutes in prayer before he went to his office.

They had just finished praying when there was a knock at the front door of the house. As Clay left the kitchen to see who was at the door, Mary picked up her dishcloth, dipped it into the soapy water, and began washing the dishes.

When Clay opened the door, he found Western Union operator Gerald Pearson holding a yellow envelope in his hand.

Clay smiled. "Well, good morning, Gerald. You're at it early, aren't you?"

"You might say that, Sheriff. I have a telegram for you and it's urgent. I'll wait to see if you want to reply." As he spoke, he handed the envelope to the tall, broad-shouldered lawman.

Clay opened it quickly and saw that the telegram was from Warden George Gibson at the Colorado Territorial Prison in Canon City. While reading it, he could hear Mary's footsteps coming down the hall from the kitchen.

When she drew up, drying her hands on a dishtowel, she nodded to Gerald Pearson, noting the grim look on her husband's face. "What is it, honey?"

Clay set his jaw. "Bad news. You remember Shad Gatlin was to be hanged at sunrise this morning."

Mary's brow furrowed. "Yes."

"Well, he escaped from the prison last night without the guards knowing it until dawn. He's on the loose."

The sheriff, Mary, and Gerald Pearson knew that it was Clay's deputy, Art Flynn, who had spotted Gatlin in the nearby town of Widefield two weeks previously, got the drop on him, and put him under arrest. Gatlin, who was from New Mexico, had been convicted of murder there three years ago and escaped before they could hang him. He had murdered at least eleven people in southern Colorado since then, including two children. A week after Deputy Sheriff Art Flynn had brought Gatlin in, he went to trial, was convicted, and was sentenced to hang at sunrise the morning of April 6 at the Territorial Prison.

Clay set concerned eyes on Mary. "Gatlin was carrying a grudge for Art. He just might come after him. I've got to ride like the wind and get to the Flynn house immediately. Gerald, I need to you to go my office for me. When my other two deputies show up—which they will shortly—tell them where I've gone and why, will you?"

"Sure, Sheriff."

"Then wire Warden Gibson and tell him I'm on the alert for Gatlin. Bill my office for the wire charge, okay?"

"Will do," said Pearson. He excused himself to Mary, bounded off the porch, mounted up, and galloped away.

Clay went to the small barn behind the house, saddled and bridled his bay gelding, and led him up to Mary, who was now standing by the back porch. He took her in his arms, kissed her soundly, told her he loved her, and leaped into the saddle.

She watched until her husband was out of sight, then climbed the back porch steps, took the galvanized washtub off the wall, and carried it into the kitchen.

Nearly two hours had passed when Mary Bostin was hanging her wash on the clothesline behind the house. She heard pounding hoofbeats and looked up to see her husband come riding in, his face pale.

Her heart sank as Clay slid from the saddle.

"Honey, don't tell me—"

"Gatlin got to the whole Flynn family, honey."

Mary's hand went to her mouth. "Oh no!"

Clay's voice was strained as he said, "When I arrived at the house, I found Art, Ella, and little four-year-old Ronnie in pools of blood on the kitchen floor. Art and Ronnie were dead. Ella was dying. She lived long enough to tell me that they were just sitting down to breakfast when Gatlin burst into the kitchen. He shot Art first, then Ella, then Ronnie. Art and Ronnie were killed instantly. Gatlin must have thought all three were dead, because

he dashed out of the house immediately and rode away. Ella got that much out, then died."

Tears filled Mary's eyes. "Oh, Clay, this is terrible. Poor Ella. How awful to see her husband and little boy shot to death right before her eyes."

"Yes. That low-down skunk has got to pay, honey. He had to have stolen a horse somewhere near the prison. I found the hoof-prints by the back porch and followed them on the road far enough to be able to tell that he is heading due east. No doubt he wants to get across the Kansas line. I'm going after him."

Mary felt a chill touch her backbone. She had never gotten used to her husband having to hunt down vicious outlaws. "Which deputy are you taking with you?"

"Neither. I'm going after him alone. With Art dead, we're short of deputies. I have to leave Brent and Randy to watch over the town and the county. They both offered to go with me, but understood how it has to be when I explained it."

Mary's lips lost color. "But, darling, I'm afraid for you to go after that beast alone. He's a crafty, heartless killer."

"I have no choice. I can't leave the town and the county with just one deputy to watch over them."

"I—I understand. I just wish it didn't have to be this way. I'll pack food for your saddlebags while you feed and water your horse."

Clay thanked her and asked her to bring his Bible as well, and led the horse toward the small barn.

In the kitchen, while she packed food in paper bags, Mary prayed in her heart for God's protection on her husband as he trailed the killer.

When Clay led his gelding up to the back porch, Mary came out the door with the paper bags in her arms and his Bible in her hand. She handed him the Bible first. He inserted it in the saddlebag

where he always carried it when traveling on horseback.

She then gave him the packed food, and he placed it in the other saddlebag.

He then took Mary in his arms. "Sweetheart, this is one of those times we talked about before you married this lawman. We know this is part of my job. I'm in God's hands, and there is no more perfect place to be. You pray with me that the Lord will deliver that killer into my hands real soon."

"I will, darling, but if you're not back by next Wednesday, I won't go to the depot to look at the orphans. We need to do that together. We'll just have to wait till the next orphan train comes through."

"I hope I will have caught Gatlin and brought him back by then, but if not, you should go ahead and prayerfully look the orphans over. If you feel an attraction toward a certain boy or girl, and the Lord gives you peace about him or her, go ahead and sign the papers for the child and bring him or her home. You have proven over and over on other matters how well you know the mind of the Lord, and I trust your judgment."

Mary smiled. "You flatter me, Clay. You're sure you want me to take this responsibility on myself?"

"Dead positive."

"All right. If you're not back by Wednesday, I'll look the orphans over and follow the Lord's leading."

"Good. Well, I've got to get going."

Clay kissed Mary ardently, and she clung to him, reluctant to let him go.

He sensed her fear and gently pulled away, still keeping his arms around her. He met her tear-dimmed gaze. "Like I said, sweetheart, this is part of my job."

"I know, love, and I send you off in God's care. Please get your job done and hurry home."

"I'll give it my best, honey. Take care of yourself too."

"I'll be fine. Don't worry about me. Just catch that beast and come back to me."

Clay kissed her again, then turned and quickly mounted his horse. As he settled in the saddle, he said softly, "I love you."

"I love you too." Mary's throat tightened with fear.

She watched his beloved form until horse and rider were out of sight, then went into the small white clapboard house and hurried to their bedroom. She fell to her knees with her elbows resting on the bed and her head lowered into her hands, and prayed, asking God's protection on Clay and to help him catch the killer quickly.

She rose from her knees with the peace in her heart that passes all understanding, and busied herself around the house, trying to make the hours pass quickly.

Riding out of Colorado Springs heading due east on the road where he had seen the hoofprints of Shad Gatlin's horse, Sheriff Clay Bostin stopped in small settlements along the road, inquiring if anyone had seen a rider of Gatlin's description. After three stops, he had found no one who had seen the fleeing killer. This did not dissuade him. Gatlin would not ride into New Mexico where he was wanted for murder. The closest territorial border was the one between Colorado and Kansas. Just because he was not noticed by the residents of the small settlements did not mean he wasn't headed for the Kansas border.

It was almost 10:30 when Bostin rode into the town of Ellicott, which was the first town on the road since leaving Colorado Springs. Keeping the gelding to a slow trot, he looked around at the false-fronted buildings that seemed to stare at one another with weather-faded facades across the broad, wheel-rutted swath of earth known as Main Street.

His attention was drawn to two older men who were sitting on a bench in front of the general store. Guiding the gelding up to the boardwalk, he introduced himself and explained that he was in pursuit of a convicted murderer who had escaped the Canon City Prison. He described Shad Gatlin and was pleased to hear that they had seen him ride through town about three hours ago. He was also given a description of the horse Gatlin was riding.

Satisfied that his instincts were right, the sheriff thanked the men for the information and galloped eastward out of town.

As the orphan train rolled westward toward Salina, the sponsors kept the children occupied with games and songs. By noon, however, everyone noticed that dark clouds had filled the sky and were spitting snow. The wind was howling fiercely and driving snowflakes against the windows of the coaches. An early-spring storm had hit the Kansas plains.

The snowfall grew heavier as the hours passed, and by the time night fell, passengers throughout the train noticed high drifts forming alongside the tracks. The conductor moved through the regular coaches, keeping the fires burning in the small woodstoves. In the orphan coaches, this was the job of Dale Radcliff and Royce Nelson.

After supper in the orphan coaches, the children talked about the storm, saying they were glad to be inside the train, rather than on the streets of New York, where they had faced many a snowstorm with little or no shelter.

As the hour grew late with the incessant wind driving snow against the already ice-caked windows, the orphans were cozy in their blankets and heads began to bob as sleep overtook them.

It was near midnight when everyone in the train was jerked

awake with the sound of shrieking brakes as the train shuddered to a stop.

In the coach where Lorinda Radcliff, Shelley Nelson, and Mandy Hillen were riding, they stood quickly, looking at each other quizzically by the light of the few low-burning lanterns that hung over the aisle. Girls were sitting up, rubbing sleep from their eyes and looking frantically around them. Some of the younger ones began to whimper.

Many of the girls pressed their faces to the cold glass of the windows, trying to see outside, but the strong wind continued to buffet the train and the windows were plastered with a thick coat of snow and ice. Inside, the glass was frosted over, making visibility even more difficult.

The three women were standing at the front of the coach. Lorinda Radcliff spoke calmly above the frightened voices. "Girls, don't be afraid. We're safe in here. I'm sure the conductor or someone else will come as soon as they can and let us know why the train stopped."

The whimpering ceased and the girls talked softly among themselves, most of them training their eyes on the front door of the coach.

The women at the front heard a thirteen-year-old girl say to those around her, "I'll bet it's Indians. They're probably gonna jump on the train and scalp us all!"

Some of the girls who heard her began to cry.

"Lottie," said Shelly, "stop that! It's not Indians!"

Lorinda called, "Girls! Girls, please! We don't know why the train stopped, but don't let Lottie scare you. Let's bow our heads and pray. We'll ask the Lord to—"

Suddenly the front door of the coach came open, and they all gasped at the sight of the white apparition that stood in the doorway. No one could tell what this snow-covered thing was, but neither could they pry their eyes from it.

Taking in the frightened faces staring at him—including those of his wife and Shelley and Mandy—Dale Radcliff wiped the snow from his face and said, "Hey, don't be afraid! It's only me!"

The girls began to make sounds of relief as Lorinda said, "Dale Radcliff, I ought to spank you! Do you realize how scary you look? You look like a snowman come to life!"

He removed his hat and shook the snow from it. "I'm sorry. I didn't mean to frighten anybody. I just came to tell you why we're stopped."

Lottie Perkins rose from her seat. "It's Indians, isn't it, Mr. Radcliff? I knew it had to be! It's Indians, isn't it?"

Dale laughed softly. "No, Lottie, it isn't Indians. Nothing that dramatic. We're about to cross the Solomon River. Snowdrifts have piled up on this end of the trestle. When the engine's headlight first shined on the trestle, the engineer had a hard time making out what was wrong with it. This is why he stopped so suddenly. As you can see, I've been out there inspecting the drifts. Everything's all right. We've got men removing the high drifts right now, and we'll be starting up again in about a half hour."

With that, Dale hurried through the coach, exited the rear door, and made his way into the boys' coach.

It was late morning on Friday, April 7, when the orphan train pulled into the railroad station at Salina, Kansas. There was a two-foot depth of snow on the ground, but the sky was clearing and the sun was sending its welcome beams earthward.

In the girls' coach, Betsy Gilder looked at the twins from her seat. "Maybe this is the town where all three of us will be chosen. I sure hope the same family will take all three of us, or at least that we will live close to each other."

"Honey," said Deena, "Donna and I are hoping the same thing, but you must prepare yourself to accept it if it doesn't work out that way."

Betsy nodded. "You're right, Deena. I've been trying to prepare myself, just in case."

When the regular passengers had gotten off the train, the Radcliffs and the Nelsons led the children inside the terminal and lined them up. The couples who had been interviewed and approved by the sponsors began their slow walk along the line.

Deena and Donna Mitchell were standing together with a boy on each side, and Betsy Gilder was on the other side of the boy on their right.

Ahead of the Mitchell twins in the line were Johnny Smith and Teddy Hansen, as well as Jerry Varnell and Clint Albright, with girls between them.

As the adults passed by, Teddy kept glancing past the girl between himself and Johnny. He felt his heart quicken when he saw a couple talking seriously to Johnny and asking him questions. Teddy swallowed hard, unable to keep his eyes off Johnny.

Farther down the line, a couple stopped in front of the Mitchell twins. The man smiled. "Good morning, girls. You look like you're about thirteen or fourteen years old."

"We're thirteen, sir," responded Donna.

The man turned to his wife and nodded. She smiled and nodded in return. He looked back at the girls. "My name is Ralph Dexter and this is my wife, Norma. We have a farm a few miles west of Salina."

"Hello," said Norma. "I can see that you are identical twins. What are your names?"

"I'm Deena Mitchell and this is my sister, Donna."

The Dexters asked questions about the twins' past and how

they became orphans. The twins explained about being sent away from their home in Manhattan because their parents could no longer afford to keep them.

After asking more questions and learning that Deena and Donna had lived on the streets of Manhattan for a brief time, then were taken to the Children's Aid Society headquarters by Charles Brace and his wife, Norma looked at her husband. "Let's do it."

Ralph grinned. "All right. Which one do you want?"

His question struck the twins like a bolt of lightning. They exchanged wide-eyed glances, then Donna said, "Mr. and Mrs. Dexter, Deena and I don't want to be separated."

Ralph's brow furrowed. "Honey, we can't take both of you, but we definitely want one."

Royce Nelson was standing close by and heard what was said. He stepped up and smiled at the Dexters. "Folks, I would really hate to see the twins separated. Isn't there another girl along the line that might interest you?"

Ralph shook his head. "No, sir, there isn't. We wanted a girl exactly their age, and we like these girls. We want one of them. We can't take both of them because we have a sixteen-year-old son at home, and we can only afford to bring home one orphan."

Royce opened his mouth to speak again, but Ralph beat him to it. "I distinctly heard Mr. Radcliff say earlier, sir, that the executive board of the Children's Aid Society had established a policy that if there were siblings on the orphan train, and a family only wanted one of them, they could take the one they wanted. Isn't that right?"

The twins looked on with their hearts pounding as Royce said reluctantly, "Yes, sir. That's right."

"Good! Which one do you want, Norma?"

"Just a minute, sir," cut in Royce. "It is an established fact that it is devastating to separate twins—especially *identical* twins. They are so much a part of each other. As the saying goes, 'If one is cut, the other one bleeds.' Are you sure you can't accommodate both of them? It would really be best for them. And if you can't, there are other girls in the line who are thirteen years of age. For the twins' sake, wouldn't you choose another girl?"

Ralph shook his head. "We can't afford to take them both, Mr.—what was your name?"

"Nelson."

"Mr. Nelson, I wish we could afford to take both girls, but it is simply impossible. But we do want one of them. You *did* say that is the policy?"

Royce gave the twins an apologetic look. "Yes, Mr. Dexter, that is the policy."

"All right," said Ralph, then turned to Norma. "Which one do you want?"

Norma ran her gaze between the twins for a moment, then said, "Let's take Deena."

The twins were stunned. Instantly, they were in each other's arms. Betsy Gilder had been listening to the conversation between Ralph Dexter and Royce Nelson and heard the choice Norma had made. Tears filled her eyes when she saw Deena and Donna cling to each other.

Royce began the paperwork on his clipboard with a heavy heart. *This is the part of my job that I don't enjoy.*

When the papers were signed, Norma turned to the twins—who were still clinging to each other. "Donna, we really wish we could take you too, but as my husband said, it is simply impossible. We'll give you girls a few minutes to say good-bye."

The twins were weeping as they hugged each other, feeling the pain that came with knowing they may never see each other again.

Between sobs Deena said, "Sis, no matter how far apart we may be, our lives and our hearts will still be joined as one. And…and maybe someday we will find each other again."

Donna clung even more tightly to her twin. "The greatest desire in my life will be to see you again. We will be separated physically, but our hearts will always beat as one. I love you, Deena. I hope these people are good to you and that you have a happy life. My thoughts will never be far from you. I am glad that you will have a home. Let's try to make the best of this situation. Grieving for each other will only bring us pain. And we've had enough—" Donna's words cut off as a sob clogged her throat.

"I'll always love you, sis," Deena said with effort, her own throat tight. "I love you, my precious Donna."

Norma touched an arm of each twin. "We need to be going, Deena."

As the girls let go of each other, Betsy rushed up, hugged Deena, told her good-bye, then hurried back to her place in line.

With tears streaming down their cheeks, the twins embraced one more time, then as Deena turned to leave, Donna clung to her fingertips. "I love you."

"I love you too," said Deena as the Dexters hurried her away.

At that moment, Shelley Nelson moved up to Donna and put an arm around her shoulder.

Donna's tear-filled eyes were fixed on her twin as the Dexters ushered her toward the main door of the terminal. When they reached it and Ralph opened the door, Deena paused, looked back, and waved.

Donna waved in return as her twin vanished from view. Her knees buckled, and while Shelley held her up, she sobbed uncontrollably.

Royce waited till Donna regained some control of her emotions. "Honey, I'm sorry this had to happen, but I had no choice but to let the Dexters take Deena."

Donna drew a shuddering breath. "It's not your fault, Mr. Nelson. Thank you for trying like you did, though."

A few children had been taken by the Salina people and the remaining orphans reboarded the train.

Johnny and Teddy were sitting on the same seat as usual. Teddy turned to him and said, "Johnny, I was really scared when I thought that one couple was gonna choose you."

Johnny put an arm around him and smiled.

In the girls' coach, Betsy Gilder sat beside a weeping Donna Mitchell, shedding tears herself while trying to comfort her.

As the train chugged out of the Salina depot, Nurse Mandy Hillen moved to the seat where Betsy and Donna sat together and looked at them with soft eyes. "Betsy, honey, would you let me sit with Donna for a few minutes?"

"Sure."

Mandy sat down and tried to console Donna by saying at least Deena had a home. Deena would be taken care of by her new foster parents and would have a happy life.

Trying to be brave in it all, Donna nodded. "I want her to have a happy life."

Mandy put an arm around Donna's shoulder and pulled her close. "Honey, down the line, there is a family who will want you."

Sniffling, Donna said, "Somehow I will get that family who chooses me to bring me back to Salina once in a while so I can see Deena."

Mandy smiled at her. "Well, Donna, I really hope it works out that way."

Chapter Eight

As the Dexter wagon was moving westward along the well-traveled, snow-crusted road, Norma Dexter engaged Deena Mitchell in conversation about Salina, the surrounding area, and its friendly people, trying to keep Deena's mind off her twin.

They were halfway to the Dexter farm when off to the right, they saw the orphan train rolling westward along the tracks in the distance, with billows of smoke pouring from the engine's smokestack.

Deena looked at the train with a longing in her eyes and tears once again began to slide down her cheeks.

When Norma saw the tears, she patted the girl's hand. "I know this is very difficult for you, dear, but don't you worry. Your sister will find a good home somewhere."

Deena nodded and wiped the tears from her cheeks. "I'm sure she will, but I'll miss her terribly."

"We understand that, little gal," said Ralph, "and we'll do our best to make you so happy that the pain of being separated from Donna will lessen each day."

There was a moment of silence except for the mushy sound of the horses' hooves on the snow and the spinning of the wagon wheels. "Deena, I know you'll love your room," Norma said. "We've got it all fixed up for you."

Thankful to have a home in spite of the absence of her twin, Deena smiled. "Thank you. I'm eager to see it."

Soon Ralph turned the wagon onto the Dexter farm and they headed down the lane toward the house. "Deena, we have a hundred and sixty acres. We're not rich by far, but we do make a decent living. I wish we were well enough off to have taken Donna in too, but we're not."

Deena nodded silently.

Ralph went on. "We have ten milk cows, four draft horses—two of which are pulling this wagon right now—and three saddle horses. We also have sheep, hogs, and chickens."

Deena ran her gaze over the snow-laden land, noted the cows, sheep, and horses in the corral next to the barn, glanced at the hog pen and the other outbuildings, then settled her attention on the farmhouse.

Her thoughts went to Donna, and what she said just before they parted: *"Let's try to make the best of this situation. Grieving for each other will only bring us pain."*

Though Deena's heart was still aching severely over the separation from her twin, she told herself Donna was right. They must not grieve over each other. Deena had ever been an optimist, always seeing the glass half full, rather than half empty. She must employ this optimism.

She took in the farm once again and thought about the crowded city where she was born and raised. Having lived in the dim, dreary apartment, the scene before her was amazing. Being used to the constant noise on the streets of New York, the silence was almost palpable.

Deena's attention went back to the farmhouse as they drew up at the front porch. The gray house with white trim was two-story and had a wraparound porch with a swing.

An audible gasp escaped Deena's lips.

Norma turned to the girl, expecting to see her in tears again. Instead, a sweet smile graced her lovely young features.

"It's all so lovely, Mrs. Dexter, and so totally different from where I have always lived. The quiet may take some getting used to, but I do like it here."

"I'm glad you feel that way, dear. We want you to be happy with us."

"For sure," said Ralph as he climbed down from the seat. He rounded the wagon and helped Norma and Deena down. As they mounted the porch steps, Deena said, "Mr. and Mrs. Dexter, I want to thank you for choosing me. I know I showed my sorrow at being separated from Donna, but I don't want you to think I'm ungrateful. It's just that so much has happened to me and my sister in the past several weeks, and—"

"You don't have to explain, dear," said Norma. "We understand."

Ralph opened the door, let the ladies enter ahead of him, and closed the door.

At the same instant, a blond teenage boy stepped into the hall from the parlor and set dull eyes on the trio.

"Rex!" exclaimed Norma. "Look who we have!"

Rex looked at the girl dismally. "The orphan."

"Yes. Her name is Deena Mitchell. She's thirteen. Deena, this is our son, Rex."

It was obvious that Rex resented her, but Deena was determined to change that. She smiled warmly. "Hello, Rex. I'm glad to meet you."

Rex grunted with a nod, then looked at his father. "Pa, I finished cleaning the chicken shed. Can I go over to Willie's place, now?"

Ralph looked at the grandfather clock that stood in the corner of the foyer. "It's almost two o'clock, son. Just be back by milking time."

Rex took his coat and hat off the coat rack that stood next to the staircase. "See you 'bout four o'clock." With that, he was out the door and gone.

Norma was embarrassed at her son's behavior, but decided to let it go. She turned to Deena. "Well, honey, let's take you upstairs so you can see your room. Lead on, Ralph."

"Okay," he said with a smile. "The tour of the house will begin in Deena's room."

Norma and her new foster daughter followed Ralph up the stairs. When they reached the top and started down the hall, Deena looked around, her eyes darting from side to side. "The house is so bright and clean. Do you always live like this?"

"We do," Ralph said over his shoulder.

In awe, Deena said, "I wish my mother could see this. The tenement where my family lives is so squalid. And their apartment is shoddy and dreary. If she saw this, she would say it's heavenly. Fact is, it seems pretty heavenly to me too."

Ralph and Norma shared a satisfied smile.

They drew up to the last door in the hall. Ralph opened it. "Okay, Deena. Here it is."

Deena moved past Ralph and entered the room. She saw immediately that they indeed had planned to bring a girl home with them. She slowly turned in a circle, taking it all in. Her mouth hung open and her eyes were large in wonderment. "This is my room?"

Norma smiled. "Yes, it is. Do you like it?"

Deena was still turning in a circle in order to take it all in. "It's...it's the most beautiful room I've ever seen. I love it!"

Norma looked at her husband, then back at Deena, who was

now standing still. "Deena, we have saved up some money to buy material so I can make some dresses for you. We're going to buy it tomorrow in town, plus a couple of ready-made dresses, some undies, and some new shoes."

Suddenly Deena thought of the cloth bag that contained clothes belonging to both Donna and herself. It was too late to do anything about those clothes. "Mr. and Mrs. Dexter, I can't tell you how very much I appreciate your kindness to me."

"We're glad we can provide for you," said Ralph. "We want to make everything as good for you as possible."

Deena smiled. "Oh, thank you." She ran her eyes around the room again, then set them on the bed. "And this bed! How beautiful!"

A white and yellow quilt covered the white iron-framed bed. Deena moved to it and ran her hands over the spread. "I've never slept in a bed like this."

From there, she went to the room's two windows. Crisp, lace curtains adorned them. Looking through the windows, she took a deep breath. "I feel like I can see forever out there. There are no tall, dirty buildings to obstruct the view."

She moved toward the white dresser that stood in the corner with a flowered pitcher and washbowl. A large mirror hung above it. "And this! I've never seen anything like this!"

The Dexters looked at each other and smiled.

Deena then went to the opposite corner, where a straight-backed wooden chair with a yellow cushion was pushed up to a small desk. "I've never had a desk before," she said as she rubbed the back of the chair.

Deena looked down at the round rug of multitudinous colors that covered most of the shiny wood floor. "And I've certainly never even seen a rug like this. Oh, Mr. and Mrs. Dexter, how can I ever thank you for letting me live with you? I'll take very good care of everything. And Mrs. Dexter, I'll help you in any way I can."

Norma took hold of her hand. "We're just so glad you're here, honey. Now, let's give you a tour of the rest of the house."

They moved slowly through the rest of the house and stood on the back porch for several minutes to view the barn, corral, and outbuildings. When they returned to the kitchen, Ralph excused himself and headed for the woodshed, which stood a few yards from the back porch.

Norma set her soft eyes on Deena. "Now, dear, I want you to go back up to your room and rest for a while. I know what it's like to travel a great distance on a train. You've got to be tired. Freshen up first, if you like, but do lie down for a while. I'll call you when supper is ready."

"Oh no, ma'am," she said, taking off her coat. "I will help you prepare supper. I know how. Donna and I used to prepare entire meals at home. Quite often Mama had her hands full, taking care of our brothers and sisters. I can help you, really."

Norma shook her head and put an arm around Deena's shoulder. "Not tonight, dear. Just go up there and enjoy your new surroundings. Tomorrow is soon enough for you to start helping with the cooking and housework."

"Well, okay…if you're sure."

"I'm sure. Get some rest, and I'll call you when it's time to eat."

Deena smiled, nodded, and went down the hall, carrying her tattered coat. She bounded up the stairs and made her way to her room. Once again, she looked around at everything in the room and sighed. She noticed the walls, this time—there were yellow and white flowers imprinted in the wallpaper.

She took off her coat, hung it up in the closet, then went to the dresser. She poured water from the pitcher into the washbowl and splashed it on her face. After drying off, she went to the bed and ran her fingers over the bedspread again. She looked around the room and spoke to it. "There must be a God. No one else could have worked out all that has happened today!"

Deena sat down on the bed, testing it out, then removed her dusty high-top shoes. Scooting further up on the bed, she lay down, resting her head on the soft pillow, which was covered with a sweet-smelling pillowcase.

She took a deep breath, sighed, and let her mind drift back over the last several weeks. Tears filled her eyes and flowed down her cheeks. "I miss my mama and my brothers and sisters. I hope someday they can have a home as nice as this. Oh, Donna, how I wish you could be here with me. You would simply love it. I hope you are chosen by people as nice as Mr. and Mrs. Dexter."

Deena brushed the tears from her cheeks and closed her eyes.

The next thing she knew, Norma Dexter was shaking her gently. "Time to wake up, dear. Supper is ready."

That evening after supper, the Dexters took Deena into the parlor with Rex reluctantly following.

They sat down on the overstuffed furniture close to the fireplace, and Norma asked for more details about Deena's past—her childhood in New York City, and what it was like for her and Donna when their parents sent them away.

While Deena told them the story in detail, Rex was bored with it all, but knew he must pay attention and appear to be interested.

As the evening wore on, the emotional strain of the day's events began to wear on Deena. She repeatedly tried to cover her yawns.

It was almost nine-thirty when Ralph said, "It's time we all get to bed. Tomorrow's another day, with much work to be done."

With that declaration, the parlor lanterns were doused, except for the one Ralph held in his hand. With Ralph in the lead, they followed him up the stairs. When they came to the door of Rex's room, he said, "G'night, Ma. G'night, Pa." He opened the door and stepped in.

Just before he closed the door, Norma said, "Son, aren't you going to tell your new little sister good night?"

Rex set emotionless eyes on Deena. "G'night."

The door closed in the middle of Deena's, "Good night, Rex."

Ralph moved on down the hall with Norma and Deena staying close behind him in the circle of light provided by his lantern. When he reached Deena's open door, he set his lantern down on the hall floor, stepped into the room, and lit the lantern on the small table by her bed. It cast a warm glow around the room, and as Deena moved in with Norma at her side, she looked sleepily at the bed.

"Good night, Deena," Ralph said. "You sleep tight now."

"I'm sure I will," replied Deena, stifling another yawn.

Norma hugged the girl and kissed her cheek. "Good night, dear."

"Good night to both of you, and thank you, again, for choosing me."

Norma smiled. "We're glad we did. Sleep well. See you bright and early in the morning. There's a nightgown in the top drawer of the dresser. It's one of mine, but I think you can sleep in it all right."

"Thank you, ma'am."

The Dexters stepped out into the hall, with Ralph closing the door.

Moments later, clad in the nightgown, Deena doused the lantern and snuggled between the sweet-scented sheets. Sleepy as she was, she let her thoughts go to her sister. "Oh, sis, I wish you were here instead of the obstinate Rex. Everything would be perfect then."

She kept her mind on Donna, speaking to her in her thoughts, and soon was asleep.

The orphan train made a few more stops in Kansas, where small numbers of children were chosen, then it crossed the Colorado border. At the moment the sponsors in both coaches told the children they were crossing into Colorado, Donna Mitchell felt her sorrow and loneliness deepen. Somehow crossing the border made her miss Deena even more.

The first stop in Colorado was in Cheyenne Wells, which was seventeen miles from the border. The children were lined up as usual, with the boys and the girls interspersed.

When the prospective foster parents began moving along the line, Donna Mitchell noticed a couple talking to Betsy Gilder, showing definite interest in her. Donna could tell that Betsy liked them very much. Soon the man turned to Shelley Nelson, who was standing close by, and told her they wanted to take Betsy as their foster daughter.

Although Betsy was saddened to leave Donna, she was happy to have such nice people choose her. The girls had a tearful good-bye, and Donna smiled in spite of her tears as Betsy walked away between the man and his wife, looking back and waving.

On Tuesday morning, April 11, Sheriff Clay Bostin rode into the town of Wild Horse, Colorado, which was fifty miles west of the Kansas border.

He knew from people along the way who had reported seeing

the black Appaloosa gelding with the spotted blanket coat on its haunches and the bulky-bodied rider he had described, that he was close on Shad Gatlin's heels.

As he rode slowly down the town's main thoroughfare, he let his eyes drift from side to side. "Lord, please let me catch him today. I know I'm getting close to him, and my instincts tell me that he may very well be in this town."

Suddenly, he saw a black Appaloosa with a spotted blanket coat on its hindquarters tied at the hitch rail in front of the Wild Horse Hotel. The markings were so distinctive, Bostin knew it was the horse stolen by Shad Gatlin.

Moving to the next hitch rail, the sheriff dismounted and tied his horse to it. He glanced at the Appaloosa, and with a keen eye on the front door of the hotel, slipped up beside him. Making sure no one was looking, Bostin loosened the cinch beneath the horse's belly a couple of notches.

As he walked toward the hotel, he loosened the Colt.45 in his holster. *He's in there, Lord. I can feel it in my bones. Please don't let anybody get hurt when I'm in the process of capturing him.*

Moving through the door, the lawman approached the desk where a skinny clerk with carrot red hair looked up at him through a pair of thick spectacles.

The clerk's eyes went first to the badge on Bostin's chest, then met his cool gaze. "May I help you, Sheriff?"

Bostin read the name tag on his shirt. "I think you can, Mr. Kappel. I'm Clay Bostin, sheriff of El Paso County. I've been pursuing a convicted murderer who escaped from the Colorado Territorial Prison at Canon City. His name is Shad Gatlin. Is he registered here?"

"There is no one registered here by that name, Sheriff."

Bostin was concerned about Kappel's edginess. "I've been on Gatlin's trail for several days, Mr. Kappel. His horse is tied at the hitch rail right in front of the hotel. He must have registered under a false name."

Melvin Kappel sensed that the young sheriff was no man to fool with. He must be extremely careful. "Well, uh…Sheriff, can you describe this outlaw for me?"

"He's thirty-four years of age. Stands about five-ten. Weighs about two-forty. Has blunt features. Thick lips. Big ears. Has a mean look in his hazel eyes. His two upper middle teeth are missing."

Kappel's heart was pounding. His scalp felt as though tiny ants were running along the hairs. "Oh, him. He did register under a different name, Sheriff. He's in room twelve on the second floor."

Bostin thanked him and headed for the stairs.

Kappel kept a close eye on him, and when the sheriff topped the stairs and passed from view, he picked up a small sign that read: *Clerk has stepped away for a moment. Will be right back.* Placing it on the counter, Kappel dashed into the hotel's restaurant. He paused just inside the door, running his gaze from table to table. When he spotted the burly outlaw, he rushed up to the table, bent low, and said in a hushed tone, "Mr. Gatlin, Sheriff Clay Bostin from El Paso County just came in looking for you."

Gatlin set his cold hazel eyes on the clerk. "I paid you well to cover for me if any lawmen should come in lookin' for me. What'd you tell him?"

Kappel swallowed with difficulty. "I sent him on a wild goose chase, Mr. Gatlin. I sent him to room twelve upstairs. You'd better get out of here fast."

Gatlin stood up. "You didn't tell him about Bart Caddo, did you?"

"No, sir."

"Good. Thanks, Melvin." With that, he hurried out the back

door of the restaurant into the alley.

"Bostin, huh?" he breathed to himself, and ran around toward the front of the hotel to get on his horse and ride. "He ain't catchin' me!"

At the same time, inside the hotel, Bostin was coming back down the stairs. As he moved past the desk, he looked at the clerk. "Gatlin's not in his room, Mr. Kappel."

Without waiting for any comment Kappel might make, Bostin hurried out the door. At the same time, he spotted the killer about to mount his horse. "Gatlin!" He whipped out his revolver. "Hold it right there!"

His jaw set in determination to get away, Shad Gatlin stepped in the stirrup. The saddle slid downward, dumping him on the ground. The frightened Appaloosa whinnied and stiffened, trying to back away, but the reins held him.

Before Gatlin could gain his senses, Bostin was standing over him with his Colt.45 cocked and aimed at his face.

Defiance came alive in the killer's eyes.

"Don't try whatever you've got in mind, Shad," Bostin said icily. "I'd hate to take you out before they can get the noose around your fat neck."

Gatlin licked his lips and leered menacingly at the sheriff, but did not move.

Bostin leaned over, slipped Gatlin's revolver out of its holster and tossed it toward the boardwalk where people stood gawking wide-eyed. "Roll over on your belly."

The outlaw licked his thick lips again and did as commanded. Bostin holstered his gun, took the handcuffs off his belt, and shackled Gatlin's wrists behind his back.

The crowd was gaining in size.

Bostin jerked Gatlin to his feet and ran his eyes over the faces of the crowd. "Ladies and gentlemen, I'm Clay Bostin, sheriff of

El Paso County. My prisoner is Shad Gatlin. He's a convicted murderer who escaped from the Canon City Prison only hours before he was to be hanged."

At that moment, a man with a badge on his chest rushed up, noting Bostin's badge. "Sheriff, I'm town marshal. My name's Walt Crawshaw. One of the townsmen just came to my office and told me a lawman was capturing a criminal here in front of the hotel."

"Yes, sir. I'm Clay Bostin, sheriff of El Paso County."

"Oh, sure. I've heard much about you from some of the federal marshals who pass through here from time to time. And who is your prisoner?"

"Shad Gatlin."

Crawshaw put narrowed eyes on the outlaw. "I know about him, Sheriff. He's a cold-blooded killer. Wanted in New Mexico too."

"Right," said Bostin. "He broke out of the territorial prison the night before he was to be hanged. He had a grudge toward my deputy who had apprehended him over in Widefield. When he broke out of the prison, he beelined for my deputy's house. Murdered him and his family, then headed east out of Colorado Springs. I've been on his trail ever since."

"Well, I'm glad you caught him, Sheriff. Your plan is to take him to Colorado Springs on horseback?"

"That's it."

"Well, there's a train from the East due to stop here this afternoon. I happen to know it's going through Colorado Springs and will arrive there tomorrow morning. Would you rather make the trip on the train?"

"That would be nice, Marshal, but what would I do with my horse and the one Gatlin stole?"

"There's a cattle car sitting on a sidetrack over by the depot.

I'd be glad to talk to the engineer and the conductor when the train comes in, and get them to transport the two horses to Colorado Springs for you. The cattle car can be returned on the next train coming east from Colorado Springs."

"Hey, I'd appreciate that, Marshal. That way I can see that he is taken back to Canon City and hanged sooner."

Gatlin stared at Bostin with the intensity of a coiled rattler.

Bostin saw it, but ignored him. "So what time is the train due in, Marshal?"

"Three-fifteen."

"Okay. Mr. Gatlin and I will be ready."

Suddenly the day's date came to Bostin's mind. The incoming train was due to arrive in Colorado Springs tomorrow. "Marshal, do you happen to know if this train that's coming in is one of the orphan trains?"

Crawshaw grinned. "Sure is. We've got farmers and ranchers I know of planning to come and look them over. Does it bother you taking your prisoner on a train that's pulling coaches with all those children in them?"

"Oh no. I can keep him in check."

"Well, I'll take care of getting the cattle car hooked onto the train, and if you'll bring the horses over to my office, I'll see to getting them boarded."

"Will do."

"If you want to put this killer in my jail till it's time to go, you're sure welcome to do so."

Bostin grinned. "I'll take you up on that."

There was hatred in Shad Gatlin's eyes when he looked at the sheriff.

Chapter Nine

In his cell at the Wild Horse jail, Shad Gatlin—who was the only prisoner—sat on the bunk and looked at his pocket watch as he heard the sound of the train chugging into the depot with the bell on the engine clanging. It was just after three-thirty.

Rising to his feet, he sighed. "Bart, ol' pal, I'm dependin' on you."

At that moment, he heard the door of the cell block open, and looked to see Sheriff Clay Bostin come in with one of the deputy marshals at his side.

While the deputy lifted the key ring from a hook on the wall next to the door, Bostin drew up to the cell, and pulled the handcuffs from his belt. "Okay, Shad. Time to get on the train."

Gatlin neither spoke nor moved; the defiance in his eyes a silent challenge.

"Don't look at me like that. You chose the path of a killer. I'm taking you back so you can pay for your deeds on the gallows."

At the depot, the children were brought out of the orphan coaches as usual, once the regular passengers who were getting off the train had done so.

While the children were lining up for inspection and questioning by the prospective foster parents, Nurse Mandy Hillen moved up to Donna Mitchell, who was positioning herself between two boys.

"Are you all right, honey?"

Donna tried to smile. "Well, I can't really say I'm all right, Miss Hillen. I'll never really be all right till I see Deena again."

"Well, maybe that day will come, Donna."

"Miss Hillen…"

"Mm-hmm?"

"How far have we come since we left Salina?"

"Well-l-l…about three hundred miles."

Donna's lips pulled into a thin line. "That's a long way. And who knows how much farther I'll go before someone chooses me."

Mandy hugged her, then drew back and looked into her sad eyes. "I know I can't imagine how hard it is for you and Deena to be separated, honey, but just think about this. What if you'd stayed on the streets of New York and one of you froze to death or died from starvation? It could be worse."

Donna bit her lower lip and nodded. "You're right about that."

As Mandy walked away, Donna thought about her twin and about Betsy Gilder, wondering if they were happy in their new homes.

Farther down the line, Teddy Hansen, Johnny Smith, Clint Albright, and Jerry Varnell prepared themselves for the interviews with the adults who were about to approach them.

A few minutes after the prospective foster parents began their inspection and interviews, a young couple in their early thirties stepped up to Donna Mitchell.

"Hello, little lady," said the man. "My name is Ken Talbert, and this is my wife, Molly. We have a cattle ranch about ten miles south of town."

Donna did a polite curtsy. "I'm glad to meet you, Mr. and Mrs. Talbert. My name is Donna Mitchell."

Molly smiled, showing a bright set of even, white teeth. "We noticed a few minutes ago that the nurse was talking to you and you seemed a bit upset. Are you all right, Donna?"

"As well as can be expected in my situation, ma'am. You see, I have an identical twin sister. Her name is Deena. She was chosen by a couple some three hundred miles back, in Salina, Kansas. It's just so hard to be separated from her. The people who chose Deena couldn't afford to take both of us into their home."

"Oh," said Molly. "I know about identical twins, and how close they are. I'm so sorry."

Donna shrugged. "I've just got to make the best of it. Maybe time will help. I'm not sure."

"How old are you, honey?"

"Thirteen."

"Donna," said Ken, "how did you and Deena become orphans? Did your parents both die at the same time?"

"Oh no, sir. They're not dead. They just had to send us away from the apartment in Manhattan because they couldn't afford to keep us any longer. We're the oldest of seven children, and our mother is going to have another baby."

The Talberts looked at each other, both showing the empathy they felt for the girl. They were deeply touched with Donna's sorrows.

Ken nodded at Molly, and she nodded back. She then took hold of Donna's upper arm. "Honey, as Ken and I watched you while you were talking to the nurse, we agreed that if you showed the charm and politeness we expected from you, that we would pick you to come home with us and be our foster daughter. This is what we want to do. We'll do everything we can to make you happy if you will agree to come live with us."

"That's right," said Ken. "We'll give you a good home. We'll provide for you and do everything we can to put happiness and real meaning in your life. We know if we tell the sponsors we want to take you, you will have to go whether you want to or not, but we wouldn't do that to you. What do you say?"

Donna was touched by the offer. She knew they had to be kind people since they were considering her feelings. A far-off look captured her eyes as her mind went back to her home and family, and to the noisy, teeming streets of New York. The prospect of living somewhere so different from the harshness and poverty of where she was born was very appealing. She thought about the three hundred miles that now separated her from Deena, and told herself there might be a slight possibility of see-ing her again. Certainly, the farther west she went, that possibility would grow slighter.

The Talberts waited patiently for Donna's answer, watching the play of emotions on her young face.

A rush of gratitude came over Donna. Here was a fine couple that wanted her. *I need a home and someone who will care for me and give me a promising future. And I also need someone to love and to make happy because they chose to take me into their home.*

Donna set her eyes on the Talberts. A sweet smile curved the corners of her mouth. "Mr. and Mrs. Talbert, I would love to come and live with you. Thank you for wanting me. I will do my best to please you and to be the daughter that you want and deserve."

Molly put her hand to her lips. "Oh, honey, that's what we wanted to hear!" Ken and Molly smiled at each other, then at Donna as they hugged her in a three-way embrace.

When Ken let go of them, he set his eyes on Lorinda Radcliff, who was free at the moment and signaled to her.

As Lorinda drew up, Ken said, "Ma'am, we want to take Donna home with us."

Lorinda noted the smile on Donna's lips and the light in her eyes. "You look pretty excited about this."

"I am!" said Donna.

Moments later, after the official papers had been signed, Ken carried Donna's cloth bag as he and Molly guided Donna out of the depot toward the parking lot where their buckboard awaited them.

At the same time the Talberts and Donna were heading toward the parking lot at the depot, desk clerk Melvin Kappel at the Wild Horse Hotel looked up to see the outlaw who had been rooming with Shad Gatlin come into the lobby from outside.

As Bart Caddo moved toward the staircase, Kappel said, "Mr. Caddo?"

The outlaw stopped and looked at the clerk. "Yeah?"

Kappel motioned with his fingers. "I need to tell you something."

Caddo, who was meaner-looking than Gatlin, moved up to the counter.

"What is it?"

Keeping his voice low, Kappel told Caddo about El Paso County Sheriff Clay Bostin having come into the hotel looking for Gatlin, and that he heard from people who came into the hotel that Bostin had captured Gatlin.

Caddo stiffened, his eyes flaring. "So he's takin' him back to be hanged, huh?"

"Yes, sir. Bostin is gonna take him to Colorado Springs on the train that's at the depot right now. It's leaving in about twenty minutes."

Caddo exposed his gritty, yellow teeth in a wide grin as he

reached into a pocket and pulled out a twenty-dollar gold piece. "Thanks for the information."

Kappel started to reply, but Caddo turned, dashed toward the door, and bolted through it.

As the outlaw hurried toward the depot on foot—already having put his horse in a nearby stable—he thought of how surprised he was to run into his old friend Shad Gatlin there in Wild Horse. He had read in a newspaper a few days previously that Shad was to be hanged at the Territorial Prison on April 6.

Caddo set his jaw. "Hang on, Shad. I'll do whatever it takes to keep that lawman from takin' you back to hang."

Ken and Donna Talbert were driving out of the depot parking lot as Sheriff Clay Bostin and his prisoner were crossing the street from the jail toward the terminal building.

Gatlin's hands were cuffed behind his back as before. He looked at Bostin narrowly. "How come I gotta have my hands cuffed behind me? It's uncomfortable."

Bostin set cold eyes on him. "Oh, isn't that too bad? I'd like to put a lot more discomfort on you for what you did to my deputy, his wife, and their little four-year-old boy, but this badge on my chest keeps me from doing it."

Gatlin spit on the street. "They had it comin' because of what Art Flynn did to me."

Bostin shook his head. "I'll never understand the criminal mind. Deputy Flynn was only doing his job as a lawman when he arrested you. You're a low-down, heartless murderer, Gatlin. You deserve to hang."

They were nearing the door of the terminal.

Gatlin mumbled, "It's a long way to Colorado Springs."

"Yeah, but I'll get you there. You can count on it."

The outlaw gave him a dirty look and a hateful sneer.

When they moved inside the terminal, Marshal Walt Crawshaw was there. "Sheriff, the cattle car has been coupled to the train just ahead of the caboose, and the horses are aboard."

Bostin grinned. "Thank you."

Crawshaw reached in his shirt pocket and pulled out a pair of railroad tickets, wrapped in some currency. "And here are your tickets and your change."

The sheriff took them from Crawshaw and thanked him again, then the marshal said, "I'll walk you to the train. They're boarding now."

Bostin nodded, and neither lawman noticed as they moved to the spot where the train stood that Gatlin was running his eyes back and forth, trying to catch sight of Bart Caddo.

The sheriff glanced at the two orphan coaches and saw the children climbing aboard. His pulse quickened its pace. *Lord, is the child You have for Mary and me among them?*

The marshal's voice intruded into Bostin's thoughts. "Sheriff, the conductor said he'd like for you and your prisoner to ride in the coach just behind the coal car. He's saving a seat for you."

"All right."

As they headed toward the designated coach, Gatlin's eyes were still running back and forth in search of his old friend.

The conductor was just coming out of the front coach. He stepped off the elevated platform of the coach. "Sheriff Bostin, I'm Harvey Wilkins. I guess Marshal Crawshaw told you I was saving a seat for you and—and your prisoner in this car."

"Yes."

"I just wanted to make sure I had a seat for two set aside."

"I appreciate that, sir," said Bostin.

Crawshaw extended his right hand. "Glad to have met you, Sheriff."

Bostin gripped his hand. "You too, Marshal. And thanks again for your help."

"My pleasure, Sheriff."

Bostin nudged his prisoner forward. "Let's go."

The conductor led them into the coach and pointed out a seat midway down the aisle. Passengers were staring at the handcuffed man as the man who wore the badge gestured for him to sit next to the window.

Gatlin scowled at Bostin as he sat down and scooted next to the window. "Can't you see how uncomfortable I am with my hands cuffed behind me?"

Bostin sat down. "Aw, poor boy. He's uncomfortable. Let me tell you something, Shad. I'm not the least bit concerned about your comfort. It's bad enough that you shot Art Flynn and his wife, but you were so cold-blooded that you even shot that little four-year-old boy. I'll do my best to make you as uncomfortable as possible."

"The Flynn kid wasn't the first kid I've killed. I'll kill anybody who gets in the way, resists me, or is related to somebody who does."

"You won't be killing anybody else," Bostin said icily. "Your killing days are over."

At that instant, a man stepped into the coach at the front door.

Gatlin saw who it was. He chuckled. "We'll see, Sheriff."

As Bart Caddo headed down the aisle, searching for a place to sit, he grinned at Gatlin. The killer grinned back, but Bostin was adjusting his position on the seat and did not see it.

Bostin looked at his prisoner. "Yeah. We'll see. You'll have to come back from the grave to do it."

Gatlin's eyes showed nothing but loathing for Bostin. The grin he gave him was filled with malice.

Moments later, the train pulled out of Wild Horse and headed for Colorado Springs.

Passengers around the sheriff and his prisoner were talking about the children in the two coaches just ahead of the caboose, saying this was one of those orphan trains they had heard about.

Shad Gatlin made as if he was trying to get more comfortable in order to sneak a glance toward the rear of the coach to locate Bart Caddo. His friend was seated two rows ahead of the rear door. Caddo nodded and grinned.

Gatlin slouched down on the seat and closed his eyes, telling himself everything was going to be all right.

As the Talbert buckboard rolled southward on the bumpy road, Donna Mitchell rode between Ken and Molly. Her eyes were taking in the vast open farms and ranches around them. Before coming west, she had never seen horses and cattle in pastures.

When they drew up at the gate of the *K-Bar-M Ranch*, Donna marveled at the fancy sign that was attached to thick posts overhead. Metal letters spelled out the name of the ranch and the sign was decorated with old horseshoes, giving it a true western flavor.

As Ken drove the buckboard down the tree-lined lane, the house came into view, with the barn and outbuildings in the background.

Donna was amazed at both the size and the beauty of the place. "How many acres do you have, Mr. Talbert?"

"Two hundred and fifty."

"That's a lot of land. It sure is nice."

"Thank you."

"And you have lots of cattle in your pastures, I see."

"Mm-hmm."

Donna then concentrated on the large yellow two-story house. "Oh my! What a lovely house!"

"I'm glad you like it, honey," said Molly. "You'll like the inside too."

The Talberts smiled at each other. They were pleased to see Donna so enthusiastic about her new home.

Ken pulled rein at the front porch and helped both ladies out of the buckboard. When they entered the house, Donna was even more enthusiastic. "Oh-h-h! I've never seen anything so full of light and so polished! Everything gleams in the sunlight coming through those wonderful big windows!"

Molly smiled at her. "Would you like to see your room now, or after we show you the rest of the house?"

"I'd like to see my room right now!"

Ken was carrying Donna's cloth bag. "Ladies first." He nodded toward the staircase.

Molly took hold of Donna's hand and led her up the stairs. Ken followed.

They topped the stairs and moved down the hall. When Molly led Donna to a room on the east side of the hall where the door stood open, she stopped. "Here it is."

Donna stepped in first, her eyes taking in the bright, colorful room. She had never seen a bedroom so large. White and green ivy wallpaper covered the walls and a ruffled bedspread of the same colors covered a four-poster cherry double bed. A white chiffonier with numerous drawers and a large mirror on the wall above it stood against the wall between the room's two large windows. A cherry dresser with attached mirror stood opposite the bed, and Donna told herself her few garments would have plenty of room in that piece of furniture. A small rolltop desk with a swivel chair completed the room's furniture. The gleaming oak floor had several colorful braided rugs scattered randomly.

The sight of it all took Donna's breath away. Looking at Ken and Molly with tears in her eyes, she said, "Mr. and Mrs. Talbert! All of this is for me?"

Molly hugged her. "Yes, it is, daughter. From now until some fortunate young man comes along, steals your heart, and asks you to marry him."

Donna grinned mischievously. "I'm not sure I'd even let a suitor take me away from here."

"Oh, when the right one comes along and you fall head-over-heels in love with him, you'll be happy to follow him to the ends of the world." She looked at her husband. "And believe me, Donna, I know what I'm talking about."

"Okay, Mrs. Talbert, I'll take your word for it."

Ken took a step closer to the ladies. "Donna, now that you're our foster daughter, we'd like you to call us Mom and Dad, or Mama and Papa, or something like that."

"I'd love to. How about Mama and Papa?"

"Yes!" said Molly.

"Sounds great to me."

Donna hugged them both at the same time. "Thank you, Mama and Papa, for bringing me into your family. I'm so happy here."

The expression on the Talberts' faces displayed how pleased they were to hear these words from Donna. A special joy filled their hearts where up till that day, an emptiness lay.

Ken spoke to the Lord in his heart. *Thank You, Father, for giving us this precious girl.*

Donna drew a deep breath and looked the room over again. "I just love it! In New York I had to share a tiny bedroom with all my sisters. I can't imagine what it will be like to have so much room and real privacy."

"You just enjoy it, honey," said Ken. "Well, I'll leave you

ladies to yourselves, and Molly, you can give our daughter the tour of the rest of the house. I've got some work to do at the barn."

"All right, darling," said Molly. "Just come in at the regular time for supper. We'll have it ready."

"It's a deal!" And with that, Ken went out the door.

"Okay, sweet girl. Let's put your things away." Molly made a mental note of the items of clothing Donna would need, and told herself she would take care of the matter the next time they went to town.

When the clothes were hung in the closet, Donna went to one of the windows, and pulled back the lace curtains. "Oh, Mama, I'm looking forward to all the sunrises I'll see in the mornings from these windows."

Molly smiled. "You'll enjoy them all, honey."

"I'm sure I will." Donna let her eyes roam the room once more. "This room is definitely decorated for a girl. You and Papa must have been planning on choosing a girl before you ever got to the depot."

"That is exactly the case. After much prayer on the matter, we were positive that the Lord wanted us to choose a teenage girl from the orphan train. For both of us, all it took was one look at you as you were standing there talking to that nurse."

"Really?"

"Really. As I told you, we agreed instantly that if you proved to be as polite and charming as you looked and you wanted to come home with us that you were God's choice for us."

Donna's eyes widened. "God's choice?"

"Yes."

"And you said after much prayer, you were positive the Lord wanted you to choose a teenage girl?"

"That's right."

Donna shook her head. "I've never heard anyone talk like that before, Mama. I thought people only prayed when they were in trouble or in danger of some kind."

Molly took her into her arms, kissed her cheek, then held her at arm's length. "This is not so, sweetie. You, yourself, are an answer to prayer."

Amazed at that statement, all Donna could do was smile.

Molly took hold of Donna's hand. "Well, let's take that tour so you can see the rest of the house."

As they left the room and started down the hall, Donna wondered if her twin had a nice place like this for her home.

Chapter Ten

That evening, the lowering sun peeped under the back porch roof and painted the kitchen walls with gold bars, slowly changing to red.

The room was alive with wonderful aromas while Donna Mitchell stood beside her new mother at the stove and stirred the beef stew in its pot as she had been instructed. While Molly was taking hot bread from the oven, Donna said, "Thank you for letting me help with supper, Mama. As I told you, I really don't know much about cooking because even though Deena and I did it for our mother when she wasn't able, the meals were simple and skimpy. But I'm sure willing to learn so I can be of as much help to you as possible."

Molly set the hot bread pan on the cupboard and smiled. "I will love having a daughter that I can teach to cook, honey. I'll teach you how to sew too, so one day you can make a pleasant home for that fortunate young man we talked about and for the children who come along as time passes."

Donna nodded and wiped a hand on the apron that Molly had tied on her earlier. She glanced back at the table, letting her eyes take in the place settings that she had done; of course, only after being instructed by her new mother. Molly had found out the Mitchells were so poor that they only had the bare necessities when it came to eating utensils and dishes. Donna and her twin had never learned how to properly set a table.

While Molly and her new daughter were dishing up the stew and other items from the stove, they were chatting and laughing together. They were so engrossed in each other that they failed to notice that Ken had come in from the barn and was standing just inside the door, a wide grin creasing his face. "Sure smells good in here, ladies."

Donna stopped in the middle of a sentence, and both of them turned and looked at Ken.

Molly smiled at him. "So you like what you smell, eh?"

"Sure do!"

"Well, get washed up and you'll like how it tastes even better. Our daughter really helped me, and it's going to be extra good!"

Ken's eyebrows arched. "So she's a good cook, huh?"

"Excellent cook. She's promised to teach me all she knows."

Donna looked at Molly with a slight frown and a jovial look in her eyes.

Molly laughed and kissed her cheek. "Let's get the rest of this on the table while Papa washes up, sweetheart."

Ken picked up on Molly's humor, laughed, and headed for the washbasin.

Moments later, when the three of them sat down at the table, Ken said, "Let's pray."

As Ken and Molly started to bow their heads, they both noticed the strange look that came over Donna's pretty face.

Ken said, "Is this something you aren't used to, Donna?"

"Ah…I've heard about people who pray before they eat, Papa, but we never did it at our house."

"I see. Well, honey, because it is the Lord in heaven who provides our food for us, we always stop to thank Him before we eat. In the Bible, Jesus taught us by example that it's the right thing to do."

At first there was a blank look on Donna's face, then it vanished as she smiled. "I think it's good to do that."

Ken led in prayer, then they began eating. "Donna, your new Mama and I are born-again Christians. We attend a Bible-believing church in Wild Horse regularly."

"Does your family go to church in Manhattan?" Molly asked.

"No, ma'am. The only time I was ever inside a church was for a funeral when one of my father's friends died. I'll look forward to going to church with you."

The Talberts exchanged glances and smiled at each other.

As they continued eating, Donna said, "I've heard about people being born again, but I don't understand what that means."

Ken grinned. "Well, tell you what, honey. We'll show you all about it in the Bible."

"Okay."

After supper, Molly and Donna did the dishes and cleaned up the kitchen together, then joined Ken in the parlor. They found him reading a sermon in Charles Spurgeon's 1856 edition of the New Park Street Pulpit.

Molly stood over him. "So what's Mr. Spurgeon preaching to you about, honey?"

"It's really a good one. The sermon is called, 'The Beatific Vision.' It's taken from 1 John 3:2, where it speaks of Jesus and says, 'We shall see him as he is.' On this particular page, he is preaching about the awesomeness we are going to feel when we see our precious Saviour on His throne."

Molly nodded. "Oh yes! Awesomeness that can't even be described with mortal tongue."

"For sure," said Ken, closing the book and laying it aside.

Donna noticed three Bibles lying on the small table at one end of the sofa. Molly picked one up and handed it to her. "This is for you, honey. We bought this Bible last week for the girl the Lord was going to send into our home."

Donna accepted the Bible with a reverent look in her eyes. As she opened it and flipped pages, she said, "I've never had a Bible in my hands before."

Ken and Molly looked at each other in amazement.

"Each evening before bedtime, your mama and I read the Bible together and have a time of prayer. We'll start early tonight because we want to show you what the Bible says about being born again."

"All right, Papa. And I want to thank both of you for giving me this Bible."

"You're so welcome, sweetie," said Molly. "We'll sit down here on the sofa. You can sit between us."

When they were settled, each with a Bible in their hand, Ken said, "Let me show you first about Jesus giving us an example in offering thanks to God for our food before we eat."

"All right."

"Let's go to Matthew 15."

Molly helped Donna find the page in her new Bible, then opened her own Bible to the same place.

"Jesus is about to feed a big crowd, Donna," said Ken. "Look in verse 36. See where it says He gave thanks?"

"Uh-huh."

"All right. Let's go to Matthew chapter 26." This time, Donna turned to the chapter on her own.

Ken met the girl's gaze. "In this passage, Jesus is about to eat with His disciples. Look at verse 27. 'And he took the cup, and gave thanks, and gave it to them, saying Drink ye all of it.' See that?"

"Yes."

"There are many other places I could show you where He did the same thing, but I think you can see that Jesus set the example."

"He sure did."

"Good. Well, let's go now to John 3, where we find Jesus talking about being born again."

Molly took Donna's Bible and turned it to the chapter Ken had just mentioned. Donna smiled. "Thank you."

"You're welcome, sweetheart. You'll learn the books of the Bible in short order, I promise."

"I sure want to."

Ken explained to Donna that the man named Nicodemus in the passage was a deeply religious man but lost. Knowing this, Jesus told him what he needed to do to go to heaven when he died. They followed as Ken read it aloud:

> Jesus answered and said unto him, Verily, verily, I say unto thee, Except a man be born again, he cannot see the kingdom of God. Nicodemus saith unto him, How can a man be born when he is old? can he enter the second time into his mother's womb, and be born?
>
> Jesus answered, Verily, verily, I say unto thee, Except a man be born of water and of the Spirit, he cannot enter into the kingdom of God. That which is born of the flesh is flesh; and that which is born of the Spirit is spirit. Marvel not that I said unto thee, Ye must be born again.

Ken looked at Donna, who was obviously perplexed. "You're probably wondering the same thing Nicodemus did. How can a person go back into their mother's womb and be born a second time? Right?"

"Yes, sir."

"Well, it's not as hard to understand as it seems. The key to understanding it is there in verse 6, where Jesus makes it clear that there are two kinds of birth. See? 'That which is born of the flesh is flesh; and that which is born of the Spirit is spirit.' So there is a fleshly birth and there is a spiritual birth. I think you can see that the fleshly birth is your physical birth, when your mother gave birth to you."

"Yes, sir."

"But there is also a spiritual birth, which must come after your physical birth, or you can't go to heaven. And the reason for that is because every human being comes into this world spiritually dead. And God will not allow anything dead into heaven. Let me show you about that. Let's go back to the book of Genesis."

Molly helped Donna find Genesis 1. Ken quickly pointed out the creation work God did in the early part of the chapter, then showed her that the great eternal triune God—Father, Son, and Spirit—said in verse 26: "Let us make man in our image, after our likeness."

He emphasized the "our" to show the three persons in the Godhead, then showed her in 1 Thessalonians 5:23 that man, being made in God's image, began as a triune being: body, soul, and spirit. He then pointed out from John 4:24 that God must be worshiped in spirit and in truth, but if man has no spirit, he cannot know God nor truly worship Him.

Ken then took Donna to Genesis 2:15 where God put Adam in the garden of Eden, and that He said to Adam in the next two verses, "Of every tree of the garden thou mayest freely eat: But of the tree of the knowledge of good and evil, thou shalt not eat of it: for in the day that thou eatest thereof thou shalt surely die."

"Donna," said Ken, "notice God warned Adam that he would die *the very day* he disobeyed and ate of the forbidden fruit. See that?"

"Yes, Papa."

"All right, let's look at another passage."

Ken then took her to Genesis 3 where Satan beguiled Eve and tricked her into eating the forbidden fruit; then Adam came along after Satan had slithered away, and when Eve gave him fruit from the same tree, he ate it too. He then took Donna to verse 24 where God drove Adam and Eve out of the garden, and on into chapter 4 to let her see that Adam and Eve started their family outside of the garden.

"Now, Donna, let me ask you something."

"Yes, Papa?"

"Didn't God say that Adam would die the very day he ate of the forbidden fruit?"

"Yes."

"Did God bury Adam that day?"

"No."

"Adam was physically alive, wasn't he?"

"Mm-hhm."

"But you see, honey, since God means what He says, Adam died that very day—not physically, but spiritually. So he became a depraved being of only body and soul, but no spirit. He was dead spiritually—separated from God, who cannot be known or worshiped except in spirit. Does that make sense to you?"

"Yes, it does."

"Good. Now, the Bible is very clear on exactly what a spiritually dead sinner must do to be born again. Let me show you."

Ken took Donna back to the gospel of John, and this time, showed her in chapter 1 verse 12 that spiritually dead sinners must *become* the children of God. They are not the children of God just because they are born into God's world. They are His creation, but in order to become His children, they must be born again. He pointed out that verse 12 said people are born again by receiving Jesus.

Donna listened intently as Ken read to her from Ephesians 3:17 that she must receive Jesus into her *heart*. He went on to show her Scriptures that said the lost, spiritually dead sinner must repent of his or her sin as they call on Jesus to save them and receive Him into their heart as their personal Saviour.

Then letting her think on that, he took her to passages that dealt with heaven and hell, God's definition of sin, Jesus shedding His blood and dying on the cross of Calvary, and why He had to do that in order to provide salvation for lost sinners.

Donna shook her head in wonderment. "Papa, Mama, I have heard of Jesus Christ, of course, and that He had died on a cross, but I never knew any of the rest of this."

"A lot to think about, isn't it?" said Molly.

"Yes, it is."

Ken and Molly knew it was wise to let the Holy Spirit do His work in Donna's heart for the next few days before they would go any further toward trying to lead her to Jesus.

"Tell you what," said Ken, "you think on all of this for a couple of days or so, and we'll talk about it again. If you have any questions in the meantime, you feel free to ask them, okay?"

"Okay, Papa. Thank you for showing me those things."

"Happy to do so, sweetie. Somebody had to help us once, now we want to help you."

Later, when Ken and Molly were in their own room preparing for bed, they agreed to keep Donna before the Lord in prayer and to continue to direct her daily in reading more Bible passages on salvation.

At the Dexter farm outside of Salina, Kansas, Deena Mitchell stood in the kitchen with her heart pounding and her eyes wide as Rex bolted out the back door and slammed it. Looking at

Ralph and Norma, she said, "Why do you let him talk to me like that? I haven't done anything to him!"

Ralph raised a palm. "Now, take it easy, Deena. Rex didn't really mean what he just said."

"It sounded like it to me! You heard him. He said he wished you had never brought me home with you."

"Rex is just having a hard time sharing us with you, Deena," said Norma. "He'll get used to it."

"I don't think so. He wants to make it so miserable for me that I'll run away. You know what he told me yesterday? He said I'm going to have to learn to milk the cows, and I'm going to have to start working in the barn, cleaning the chicken shed and the pigpen. And he said when he tells me to, I have to do his work—and if I don't do it, he'll beat me up. What about that?"

Ralph shook his head. "That's just talk. He won't beat you up."

"Sounds like he means it to me," said Deena, her voice cracking. "I don't understand what's happened here, Mr. and Mrs. Dexter. Why do you let Rex treat me like he does? And—and you both treated me so nice when I first came here. But every day, you treat me more like a hired hand than a daughter."

Ralph looked at Norma, sighed, and set his steady eyes on Deena. "I might as well tell you, girl: we chose you because you were old enough to do the housework for Norma, as well as the washing and ironing. We've put a roof over your head, haven't we? And we've put clothes on your body, haven't we? And we've put food in your stomach, haven't we?"

Deena's lips quivered. "Yes, but—"

"That's more than your real parents were willing to do for you. Right?"

Deena wiped at the tears that were now brimming her eyes, but did not reply.

Ralph went on. "Let's have an understanding right now, Deena. In your spare time, you're going to help both Rex and me do the work in the barn, the chicken house, and the pigpen. And Rex is right. I do want you to learn to milk the cows, so when I need you to do it, you can handle the job. You'll learn to feed the stock too."

The tears were streaming down Deena's cheeks. "I don't mind hard work, Mr. Dexter, and I'm willing to do my share. I'll gladly do as you ask, but...but why do you let Rex treat me like he does; and why aren't the two of you nice to me like you were when I first came here a few days ago?"

With that, Deena began to sob.

Norma moved up and laid a hand on her shoulder. "You're just upset, Deena. I know everything that happened to you before you came here was enough to do anybody in. You go on up to your room for a while and get a grip on yourself. I'll let you know when I'm ready for you to do the washing."

Deena sniffled again, looked at Norma through her tears, then turned without another word and hurried out of the kitchen.

When she entered her room, she threw herself on the bed face down, and wept like her heart was going to break in two.

"Oh, Donna, I miss you so much! I hope things have worked out better for you than they have for me."

On Wednesday morning, April 12, the train was nearing Colorado Springs and was on a long curve that allowed Sheriff Clay Bostin to look past his prisoner and see snow-capped Pike's Peak glistening in the sun.

Lord, he prayed, *Mary will be waiting for the train, not even knowing I'm on it. She'll have to look the children over by herself, since I've got to take Gatlin to the jail. If the child You have chosen for us is on this train, please guide Mary to him or her.*

Soon the train was pulling into the station. Bostin leaned close to his prisoner. "We'll get off after the other passengers do."

Shad Gatlin nodded grimly, his arms aching for their cramped position behind his back.

When the train stopped and those passengers who were getting off lined up to leave, Gatlin flicked a glance to the rear and saw Bart Caddo in line, facing the rear door. He had no idea what Caddo had in mind to free him, but he knew it was coming.

In the orphan coaches, the children waited patiently on their seats, knowing they would line up on the depot platform immediately after the passengers in the other coaches had gotten off the train. As they looked out their windows, they saw that the prospective foster parents were in full view as they were being questioned by the Children's Aid Society sponsors.

A large number of people were milling about.

Among the prospective foster parents was Mary Bostin. When Lorinda Radcliff had finished questioning her and she had been approved to pass through the line of orphans when they came out, Mary stepped away. "Lord, I wish Clay was back, but since he's not, I'll have to do this alone. Please show me if the child You want us to have is among the orphans."

Moments later, the children were being brought out of the coaches, and were lining up at the same time that Sheriff Clay Bostin and his prisoner were coming out of their coach.

Gatlin let his line of sight stray to the children as he and the sheriff stepped down on the platform.

Bostin looked toward the rear of the train. "Okay, Shad, we'll head for the cattle car and get our horses."

Suddenly Gatlin caught a glimpse of Bart Caddo as he slipped up behind the sheriff, gun in hand. Caddo rammed the muzzle of the revolver tight against Bostin's backbone and snapped back the hammer. "Take the cuffs off Shad, Sheriff, or I'll squeeze the trigger and cut your spine in two!"

A few people close by saw what was happening and looked on in frozen astonishment.

Bostin's mouth went dry. He knew better than to try resisting a friend of Gatlin's with a cocked gun pressed against his back.

"Okay, okay, just take it easy, fella. There are innocent people all around. Don't do anything to hurt them."

"I won't if you'll do as I say."

Reluctantly, Bostin unlocked the handcuffs. Gatlin snatched the sheriff's gun from his holster and looked at the children a few feet away, who were now standing in line, waiting for the procession to begin.

In the line, Teddy Hansen and Johnny Smith were talking to each other past the girl who stood between them.

Gatlin set his jaw and looked at Caddo. "Wait right here and keep your gun on the sheriff." With that, he moved toward the line of children and grabbed Johnny Smith, locking the boy's neck in the crook of his free arm. Quickly, he cocked the gun and pressed the muzzle to Johnny's head.

Bostin's stomach wrenched. All his senses wound tight. Shad Gatlin possessed a menacing quality like no killer the sheriff had ever encountered before. He wouldn't hesitate to kill the boy.

Frozen with fear, Johnny let out a gasp. Teddy and the other children looked on in terror. Men were looking on wide-eyed, women began to scream, and most of the children in the line began to cry.

The sponsors observed helplessly. A few feet away, Mary Bostin looked on, her blood curdling.

"You do what I tell you now, kid," Gatlin said, "or I'll blow your head off."

Johnny's heart was thundering in his chest. His pulse throbbed and his skin tingled. While Gatlin forced him toward the spot where Caddo and the sheriff stood, he repeatedly gasped for breath.

While Gatlin and the boy were moving his way, Clay Bostin caught a glimpse of Mary's white face among the group of prospective foster parents.

With the gun muzzle pressed against Johnny's head, Gatlin growled, "Bostin, I'm takin' this kid as my hostage. If I so much as see you followin', I'll kill 'im. You got that?"

The muscles in Bostin's face tightened and the veins stood out in his temples. "Yeah. I got it."

Johnny put terror-filled eyes on the helpless, unarmed man with the badge on his chest. Bostin's emotions were mixed: wrath toward Gatlin and his accomplice, and empathy for the frightened boy.

The outlaws hurried out of the depot with Gatlin keeping Johnny locked in his arm and the gun muzzle pressed to his head.

As soon as they passed from view, the sheriff rushed up to the stunned sponsors. "What's the boy's name?"

"Johnny Smith, Sheriff," said a dry-tongued Dale Radcliff. "He's twelve years old."

"I want you to know that I am going after those outlaws, and I will rescue Johnny."

At that moment, Clay saw Mary move up beside him, her face still pale. "Honey," she said, her throat somewhat constricted, "you're not going after them by yourself, are you?"

"I must, sweetheart, for the same reason that I went after Gatlin by myself. I can't leave just one deputy to watch over the town and the county. My horse is back there in the cattle car that is hitched to the train. I'll ride to the office, tell Brent and Randy what happened, then go in pursuit of Gatlin and his outlaw friend and rescue the boy."

"I heard what Gatlin said about killing the boy if he sees you following."

"I'll be extremely careful, but I must do it, Mary. Gatlin has already proven that he will indeed murder a child. My going to the office first will give the outlaws time to get out of town and head into the mountains."

"How do you know they'll head into the mountains?"

"Because staying on the flat land north, south, or east would make it too easy to spot them. It's much easier to make an escape in the mountains."

Mary's brown eyes were clouded with concern. "But can't you take at least one of the townsmen who have served in your posses when you've gone after outlaws? I don't like to see you go alone."

"It's much easier for one man to keep himself from being seen than two men. I'll catch those outlaws and rescue the boy. You're aware that I know these mountains like I know the back of my hand, Mary. I was born and raised in them." His keen eyes went to his beloved snow-capped Rockies. "Nobody can hide from me up there when I have a mind to find them."

He looked at her again. "I'll lay my plans well and take no unnecessary risks." He gave her one of those special smiles that always melted her heart. "And besides, I won't be alone. Jesus said He would never leave me nor forsake me. I can't have a better companion than Him, can I?"

Mary managed a smile of her own. "When you put it like that, who am I to argue? Go with God, my love, and my heart and prayers go with you."

Clay took Mary in his arms, kissed her and hugged her tight, told her he loved her, then hurried to the cattle car. He found the conductor, who told him that both horses had been taken to the hitch rail at the front of the terminal.

Ten minutes later, he drew up to his office with the stolen

horse in tow and found Deputies Brent Davis and Randy Ashbrook talking to one of the townsmen, whose name was Edgar Talmadge. When he rushed up to them, he learned that Talmadge had been at the depot, and had hurried to the sheriff's office to alert the deputies so they could give the sheriff some help with the outlaws. The deputies were just about to jump on their horses and ride to the depot.

Bostin thanked Talmadge for his deed and explained that the outlaws had escaped, taking a boy from among the orphans as hostage. He was going after them.

The sheriff then took his deputies inside the office and explained in detail how he caught Shad Gatlin, and what happened when they arrived at the Colorado Springs depot.

"Once I got a good look at Gatlin's accomplice," said Bostin, "I remembered seeing his face on wanted posters. His name is Bart Caddo."

"Oh, sure," said Davis. "I remember seeing posters on him too. He's a cold-blooded killer."

"Sheriff," said Ashbrook, "I'll go with you. I don't want you having to track them down by yourself."

"I can't leave the town and the county with only one deputy, Randy. Besides, I didn't tell you about Gatlin's threat. He said he'd kill Johnny Smith if he so much as saw me following. By myself, I'll have a better chance of staying out of sight, than two of us would. Gatlin *is* a child killer, you know. He wouldn't hesitate to kill that boy. Once I spot them, I'll figure out a way to move around in front of them without being seen and surprise them."

Both deputies nodded.

"All right, Sheriff," said Randy. "I understand. Go rescue that boy."

Bostin nodded. "One of you needs to take that horse Gatlin stole and put it in the stable. When I get back, I'll have to see if we can find its owner, who no doubt lives near Canon City."

"We'll take care of it, Sheriff," said Brent. "You just go rescue that boy."

Returning to the depot with another revolver in his holster, a spare one in a saddlebag, and his rifle in the saddle boot, Sheriff Clay Bostin learned from the townspeople that the outlaws had stolen two saddle horses from the hitch rail outside the terminal and headed toward the mountains. One of them had the boy in the saddle with him.

Leaving the depot, Bostin mounted his gelding and put him to a trot.

Just outside of town on the west side, he talked to people who saw the men with the boy riding into the mountains.

Being an expert tracker, Bostin soon picked up their trail.

As he rode into the high country cautiously, eyes peeled ahead of him, he said, "Lord, please give me wisdom in this pursuit. Help me to catch up to them by surprise somehow, and to save Johnny's life. I know that once Gatlin and Caddo figure they are safe, Gatlin will kill the boy anyhow and ride on."

Chapter Eleven

At the Colorado Springs depot, the orphan children were extremely upset because of what happened to Johnny Smith. Many were saying that Johnny was going to be killed by the bad men.

Two boys and a girl had been chosen by foster parents, and as they were leaving, Dale Radcliff spoke above the loud cries. "Boys and girls, listen to me! I want us all to gather in the girls' coach so I can talk to you."

The Nelsons, Lorinda, and Mandy Hillen quickly ushered the children into the girls' coach, and when all were seated—with some of them bunched up four to a seat—Dale stood before them at the front of the coach while the other sponsors and the nurse were trying to quiet those who were wailing the loudest.

Holding up his hands to get their attention, Dale said loudly, "Please, children, stop crying."

The other adults worked at calming and quieting those who were most disturbed, and after a minute or so, there was almost total silence. Every eye was on Dale. "Boys and girls, I want us to have prayer right now for Johnny. Let's all bow our heads and close our eyes."

Dale led in prayer, asking the Lord to keep His hand on Johnny Smith, and to protect him from harm. He asked that Sheriff Clay Bostin be able to track down the outlaws and subdue them, and to bring Johnny back to Colorado Springs safely.

After the amen, Dale ran his gaze over the faces of the children. "I talked to one of the railroad executives in the terminal a few minutes ago. He told me he would send a telegram to the home office of the Children's Aid Society and let them know about Johnny being taken by those men. He will keep in touch with Mr. Brace by wire and let him know when Sheriff Bostin returns to Colorado Springs with Johnny. He will ask Mr. Brace to wire a message ahead of the train so we can be told the news upon arrival in whatever depot it happens to be. So let's keep praying, okay?"

Heads of the older children were nodding.

The boys were then taken to their coach.

The train pulled out, and as it headed into the mountains on its way to Utah, some of the younger girls began crying again. Lorinda, Shelley, and Mandy went to those who were crying the loudest and tried to comfort them.

Near the rear of the coach, one of the little girls—six-year-old Nellie Thompson—was curled up on a seat alone and unnoticed, trembling and sniffling.

Nellie's once well-ordered life was now in a disordered state. She had lived in a beautiful house on Long Island with her loving parents and had lots of toys, dolls, and games. And now they were all gone. Her parents had been killed suddenly, leaving her all alone.

Nellie's mind went back to that fateful night that changed her life drastically…

It was a cold night in early March, and her crippled mother escorted Nellie to her bedroom as usual, spinning the wheels of her wheelchair.

Nellie pulled back the covers, crawled into her bed, then covered herself. Her mother moved the wheelchair up close, told her a bedtime story, heard her prayers, and kissed her good night. She doused the lantern on the table beside Nellie's bed and turned the wheelchair about.

As she wheeled toward the door, Nellie said, "I love you, Mommy."

Jeanne Thompson paused, adjusted the wheelchair in order to see her daughter, and said with a smile, "I love you, too, honey. With all my heart."

Nellie snuggled down into the warm covers and soon fell asleep.

It seemed like only minutes had passed when suddenly Nellie was aware of being snatched out of her bed. Her next sensation was the acrid smell of smoke, then she opened her eyes to see that she was in her father's arms. The thick smoke she saw was tinged with red flame. Then she saw flames licking up the walls of her room, and as he carried her swiftly into the hall, she heard her mother's voice from the bedroom down the blazing hall. "Hurry, Roy! Get Nellie out! Hurry!"

While running toward the front of the house with Nellie in his arms, Roy Thompson shouted over his shoulder, "I'll be right back to get you, honey!"

Nellie placed her trusting arms around her father's neck. A fit of coughing overtook her, and she pushed her face down into his shoulder, trying to keep from inhaling the smoke.

When they reached the front door, Roy slid back the dead

bolt, opened the door, and plunged out onto the porch. He stumbled as he carried her down the steps and almost fell. Nellie hung on, coughing. At last she felt a blast of cold, smoke-free air and took in a deep gulp.

"It's okay, baby, it's okay," said Roy as he carried her through the flame-tinted night toward a tree stump at the edge of the street.

As her father set her down on the stump, Nellie looked toward the house. It was engulfed in flames. An angry crimson glow brightened the black sky and sparks were falling on the yard.

"It's okay," Roy Thompson said again. "You stay right here, while I go get Mommy."

With that, Roy dashed back to the burning house, bounded across the front porch, and plunged inside.

Nellie was shaking from both the cold air and the terror that had seized her. Tears made tracks down her soot-covered cheeks as she sobbed hysterically.

Before her father could emerge with her crippled mother in his arms, the roof suddenly collapsed with a loud roar. Billows of smoke and flame rose skyward.

Nellie screamed wildly, crying for her parents.

But it was the last time she ever saw them.

Curled up on the coach seat as the train rolled westward, she recalled how the sleepy-eyed neighbors came running from every direction. They all collected at the spot where Nellie sat on the stump, and one of the women gathered her into her arms.

When morning came, Nellie was taken by the police to an orphanage. For several weeks, she hardly uttered a word. Most of the time when the people at the orphanage tried to talk to her, she only stared into space. She ate sparingly of the food that was set before her and cried herself to sleep each night.

Finally, with much loving care from the kind women at the orphanage, Nellie began to talk again and enjoy the children around her. Many nights she woke up when nightmares invaded her sleep and found herself screaming as one of the women attendants took her in her arms, doing everything she could to soothe her.

The staff at the orphanage held many meetings concerning Nellie, and at last they came to an agreement that the best thing for her was a change of atmosphere. They explained to her that she would be going to the Children's Aid Society, who would put her on a train and send her out West, where she would find a new home and new parents.

Nellie recalled how she puckered up at this news. "But I want my real mommy and daddy back. I don't want new ones."

"Darling," the lady had said kindly, "your mommy and daddy can't come back. But a new mommy and daddy out West will love you and give you a nice home. You will be on the train with lots of other boys and girls. Some of them will be ones you already know, right here in the orphanage. It will be lots of fun."

Nellie thought of the wagon ride to the Children's Aid Society headquarters, with four other children from the orphanage. There were two boys and two girls. Both girls had been chosen back in Kansas.

Her thoughts ran to the awful thing that happened at the depot that morning when she saw the bad man put a gun to Johnny Smith's head and heard him say he would kill Johnny if the sheriff followed them.

Tears surfaced again as the terror of that moment came back. "Poor Johnny. Poor Johnny! That bad man will probably kill him anyway."

Through her tears, Nellie saw Lorinda Radcliff coming down the aisle toward her. Mrs. Radcliff had been the one who saw to her needs the most since the trip began. She tried to stop crying, but it only became worse.

Lorinda picked Nellie up and sat down on the seat, placing her on her lap. She held her close. "You don't have to be afraid, Nellie. Those bad men are gone."

"B-but they're gonna kill poor Johnny!" she sobbed.

Lorinda worked at trying to calm the child, but nothing she said could penetrate her fears. Mandy Hillen was administering a sedative to a five-year-old girl a few seats ahead. When Mandy looked Lorinda's way, she motioned to her. Mandy nodded, and when she was finished with the five-year-old, she drew up to Lorinda and Nellie, medical bag and water bottle in hand.

"I think Nellie needs a sedative too, Mandy. She's very distressed over Johnny and this morning's incident."

"Of course." Mandy set her bag down on the empty seat just across the aisle. Leaning close to the weeping child, she said, "Nellie, I'm going to give you something that will help settle your nerves and make you feel better. Will you drink it for me?"

Nellie nodded and sniffed.

Lorinda watched while Mandy mixed some powders in a cup of water. Nellie sipped the mixture until the cup was empty.

"Now, honey," said Mandy, "you just relax as best you can, and pretty soon you'll start to feel sleepy. You'll take a nice nap, and when you wake up, you'll feel better."

Still weeping, Nellie looked up at her and nodded.

"I'll hold you till you fall asleep," said Lorinda, then looked up at Mandy. "Thank you."

"You're welcome," Mandy said softly. "I'm sure the shock of this morning's horrible scene stirred the horror within her that she felt when she lost her parents in the fire. She's so young to have her life so upset. The sleep will be good for her."

As Mandy walked away to tend to a girl whom Shelley was

attempting to calm, Lorinda kissed Nellie's forehead. "You sleep now, sweetheart."

Lorinda held the weeping child close while rocking her in her arms and humming a tune.

Gradually, the sobs became sniffles, and the spent little six-year-old relaxed.

Her eyes closed, Nellie heard Mrs. Nelson and the nurse still working at calming the girls who were crying over Johnny Smith.

She thought about Mr. Radcliff's prayer for Johnny earlier and took comfort that God would answer that prayer and not let the bad men kill him, and also would let the sheriff catch the bad men and bring Johnny back to Colorado Springs unhurt. Then thinking about the promise of a new home and new parents on this trip, she thought, *Well, okay, since Mommy and Daddy can't come back to me, I guess I can be somebody else's little girl.*

The sniffles began to subside, and soon Nellie relaxed against Lorinda's breast and fell asleep.

In the boys' coach, Royce Nelson was walking along the aisle as the train started its climb into the Rockies and was pleased that the boys seemed to be settled down over the Johnny Smith incident.

However, as he approached the seat where Teddy Hansen sat between Jerry Varnell and Clint Albright, he saw that Teddy was crying. Jerry and Clint were attempting to comfort him.

Royce dropped to one knee. "Teddy, are you crying over Johnny?"

"That's part of it, Mr. Nelson," said Clint, "but he's also crying because no one has chosen him. Jerry and I are feeling bad because we haven't been chosen yet, either."

"Boys, don't let that bother you. There are still many stops ahead if us. I'm sure all three of you will be chosen soon."

Teddy wiped tears. "Mr. Nelson, what if we don't get chosen and have to go back to New York?"

Royce gave him an assuring smile. "The chances of that happening are very, very slim, Teddy. It has only happened to five children since the orphan trains started taking boys and girls west twenty-three years ago. And each of those five were chosen on the next trip west."

Jerry grinned. "Well, that's a pretty good record, Mr. Nelson. We haven't told anybody, but we're hoping that all three of us will be chosen by the same family or at least that we will be chosen by people in the same town, so we can be together as we grow up."

"Well, boys, it would be really rare for the same family to take all three of you, but it has been known to happen a couple of times. However, if that doesn't happen, maybe at least you will be chosen by people in the same town or area."

It was a warm spring day in central Kansas, with the sun shining out of a crystal sky and the snow melting on the plains. At the Dexter farm, things were growing worse for Deena Mitchell. Rex was rougher on her every day, and she was worn out from all the work that was put on her by the whole family.

Deena was helping Rex repair fence on the backside of the property. Rex was making her use a heavy iron tamping bar to set a new fencepost while he worked at steadying the post.

Pain was showing on Deena's face as she gripped the bar and pounded the blunt end of it on the dirt in the hole, next to the post.

Rex frowned. "What's the matter, girl? Does it hurt to lift the bar and bring it down hard?"

Deena stopped, leaned the bar against the post, and showed him her blistered hands. "Yes, it hurts. I've got these blisters from using shovels and pitchforks around the barn, and now they're bleeding. See?"

Rex made a mock scowl. "Oh, poor baby."

Her face darkened. She looked at him, eyes laced with disgust. "You have no heart at all, do you?"

"Not for you. Get busy. We need to get this post in so we can do those other two."

"What if I told you to do it yourself?"

For a full five seconds they had a stare down, then finally Rex blinked. "I'd beat you good, and you don't want that. Get busy."

Deena wiped blood on her tattered dress from her broken blisters and began tamping again. After a few minutes, she stopped and wiped sweat from her brow, gritted her teeth and said. "I can't do this anymore. My hands are bleeding too much. Let me steady the post while *you* use the bar."

Rex's eyes honed down like pinpoints. His voice chilled her as he hissed, "If you don't get back to tampin' that bar, I'm gonna beat you to a pulp."

She swallowed hard. "I don't think your parents would like that. Then I couldn't do the work around here that they're used to. They'll be mad at you if you beat me."

"No, they won't. If I report that you were slackin' in your work, and that I beat on you some to make you earn your keep, both my parents will commend me for it."

Rex noticed the tears that surfaced in Deena's eyes and how she stared off into the distance.

He laughed wickedly. "Hey, girl, if you're thinkin' about runnin' away, it's fine with me. But if you do, you'll be in big trouble when my father catches up to you. He'll give you a beatin' you won't forget."

She sighed, wiped her hands on her dress again, and picked up the tamping bar.

Deena was forced to set the other two fence posts while Rex steadied them for her. By the time they headed for the house at sunset, her hands were bleeding profusely. When they entered the house and both Norma and Ralph looked at her bleeding hands, Deena received no sympathy. Norma had her wash her hands in cool water, then she put some salve on the bleeding blisters for her and wrapped them with cloths, cinching them with knots at her wrists.

By the time Deena had the table set and had put supper on, the bleeding had almost stopped.

While they were eating supper, Deena ran her gaze from one foster parent to the other. "Are you going to let me go to school?"

Ralph frowned at her. "There's too much work to do on the farm. You don't have time to go to school."

Her eyes scrunched up with disappointment. A flicker of displeasure skittered across her stony features.

Ralph's face reddened and the veins in his temples stood out. "You're not thinking of showing some kind of rebellion, are you?"

Norma and Rex watched Deena closely as she lowered her head slightly and looked down at the table. "No, sir."

"Good," Ralph said. "You'd wish you hadn't."

Later that night, Deena lay in her bed and wept as she thought of Donna. She had known since she and Donna were very small that identical twins had a special mysterious link between them. Their mother had explained that this link began when they were in her womb, and that the link would grow stronger as they grew older. She gave them examples of other identical twins who had found that even when they were far apart, they sensed how things were going for each other.

Wiping tears on the sheet, Deena felt that Donna was happy,

but she also sensed that Donna missed her very much.

Deena finally cried herself to sleep.

The next morning at the breakfast table, Ralph was giving instructions to Rex about a cleaning job that he and Deena were to do in the barn that morning.

Norma noticed that Deena had tears in her eyes. "Deena, what are you crying about?"

Deena sniffed and wiped tears. "I miss Donna almost more than I can stand. Would you and Mr. Dexter help me to find out where she is? I...I just have to know."

Ralph snapped, "You've got to forget your sister, Deena! I want you to concentrate on fitting into this family."

"But—but, I can't forget Donna. I desperately need to find out where she is so one day soon I can go there and see her. I *must* see her!"

Ralph shook his head vigorously. "Seeing Donna would just make it harder on both of you, especially when you parted again. It's far better just to face the fact that you will never see your twin again and to concentrate on getting on with your life."

Deena wanted to say that she had no life—just a miserable existence—but she refrained.

After Deena did the dishes—in spite of her cloth-wrapped hands—she cleaned up the kitchen. When that was done, she stepped off the back porch and headed for the barn, where she knew Rex was waiting for her.

After her first Sunday in church at Wild Horse and having heard the gospel preached in both morning and evening services, Donna Mitchell was under conviction of her lost condition.

That night, after arriving home, Donna and the Talberts went to the kitchen for a snack. Ken sat down at the table and waited quietly for the ladies to prepare it. While Donna was helping Molly make sandwiches at the cupboard, Molly noticed that the girl seemed upset. She put an arm around her shoulder. "Donna, are you disturbed because you're missing Deena?"

Donna nodded and looked at her. "Yes, Mama, but at the moment something else is bothering me more."

"What is it, honey?"

Tears filled Donna's eyes. "Oh, Mama, I know I'm lost and on the road to hell. I want to be saved."

"Well, you can settle that right now."

"You sure can," said Ken, rising from the chair. "I'll go get my Bible."

When he returned to the kitchen, Ken found both ladies sitting at the table, waiting for him.

He sat down next to Donna, laid his Bible before her, already opened to John 3. He pointed out once more about the necessity of being born again, then went over the Scriptures that showed that a person is born again by receiving Jesus into his or her heart. When Donna assured him she understood this, he took her to three different passages where the Bible says a lost sinner must repent of his or her sin in order to be saved.

"Let me show you one other verse on the subject, honey." As he spoke, he turned to 2 Peter 3. "Look at verse 9. 'The Lord is not slack concerning his promise, as some men count slackness; but is longsuffering to us-ward, not willing that any should perish, but that all should come to repentance.'

"Repentance is simple, Donna. It is acknowledging to God that you have sinned against Him and have been an unbeliever, but that now you believe His gospel, and are turning from your sin and the road that leads to hell *unto Him*. This means a 180-

degree turn from whatever religion or philosophy you've been embracing and that you are putting your trust in the Lord Jesus and Him alone to save your soul and forgive your sins. Now, according to verse 9, here, if you don't come to repentance, you will perish. To perish is to go to hell. Do you understand?"

"Yes, Papa."

"Good. Jesus said in John 6:37, 'him that cometh to me I will in no wise cast out.' So when you turn in repentance from your sin and unbelief and come to Jesus, He will save you." He then flipped more pages. "Look over here in Romans 10:13. 'For whosoever shall call upon the name of the Lord shall be saved.' So what do you have to do to be saved?"

"I have to believe that God's only begotten Son shed His blood and died for me on the cross and turn in repentance to Him, even as the pastor said in both sermons today. I must trust Jesus and Him alone to save me and forgive me of all my sins. I must call on Him, acknowledging that I am a guilty, lost sinner, ask Him to save me, and receive Him into my heart."

Molly had tears in her eyes. "So what are you going to do now, sweetie?"

A smile spread over Donna's face. "I'm going to do what I just said I have to do. Will you help me?"

Together, Ken and Molly had the joy of leading Donna to Jesus. Ken then explained that her first step of obedience now that she was saved was to be baptized, as Jesus commanded. He showed her the Scriptures on the subject.

"I'll walk the aisle next Sunday morning—like that teenage boy did this morning—and tell the pastor I received Jesus as my Saviour tonight, and that I want to obey His first command after salvation and be baptized."

Both Talberts hugged their foster daughter, telling her how glad they were that she was now a child of God.

"I am too," said Donna, wiping happy tears from her cheeks.

Ken looked at Molly, then set misty eyes on Donna. "Honey, your mama and I have been talking about it, and we would like to adopt you. We want to give you our name and make you our daughter by legal adoption. How would that be with you?"

Donna's eyes brightened. "Oh, I would love that! I have come to love you both so very much."

"Wonderful!" Ken said while Molly kissed Donna's cheek. "I'll talk to the judge in town and get things moving toward legal adoption."

After more hugs, Donna said, "Now that I'm saved, I am concerned for Deena. I want her to be saved. I...I sense that Deena is very unhappy. Mama, Papa?"

"Yes, dear?" said Molly.

"Would—would you take me back to Salina so I could find the Dexter farm and see Deena? I want to tell her about my being saved and see if she will open her heart to Jesus. I also just want to have some time with her."

"Honey, we certainly want you to see Deena again," Ken said, "and of course, we'd love to see her saved; but it will be a good while before we'll have the time to do this. I promise you though, that as soon as it is possible, we'll take you to see Deena."

"I understand, Papa, that you are very busy with the ranch. I won't pester you about taking me to see Deena. Whenever you have the time, it will be fine."

"In the meantime," said Molly, "we just need to pray that the Lord will bring Deena to Himself. And we also need to pray that if she is as unhappy as you sense she is that the Lord will take care of the problem."

"Yes, Mama," Donna said.

Chapter Twelve

High in the Rocky Mountains of Colorado, Sheriff Clay Bostin was on the trail of the outlaws who had Johnny Smith as their hostage. With his tracking experience, Bostin was able to stay on their trail, but not until about an hour before sundown on the second day of pursuit did he catch sight of them. One of the horses had part of its iron shoe on the left hind hoof broken off, making it easy to follow.

He was on a lofty road of soft dirt, following the telltale hoofprints along a ridge of blue granite on the side of a mountain, when he spotted them some two hundred yards below. They were getting off their horses beside a creek, where Bostin was sure they would make camp. He was relieved to see that the boy was still with them.

Some three or four hundred feet ahead of him the mountain broke off sharply, offering a magnificent view of the road as it descended into the valley amid towering pines, and numberless deep-shadowed, sunken gorges. Moving the gelding as close to the granite wall as possible, he guided him quickly downward, wanting to stay completely out of sight from Shad Gatlin and Bart Caddo. This was a race with death, for he was sure Gatlin would kill Johnny when he thought he and Caddo were safely out of the law's reach.

Soon he came to a wide spot, where a stand of pines spread out on the mountain side of the road. He was now within a hundred yards of the spot where the outlaws were making camp beside the creek.

Quickly, Bostin dismounted and led the gelding into the stand of pine trees. He tied the reins to one of the trees, rushed back to the edge of the road, and flattened himself on the ground. Peering over the edge, he observed Gatlin and Caddo as they built a fire while the boy stood close by, looking on. Both outlaws were cautiously glancing up toward the road periodically to see if anyone was following them.

Down beside the babbling creek, Johnny Smith stood over the outlaws, who were now kneeling beside the fire. As Shad Gatlin set a full coffeepot on stones over the flames, Johnny said with a shaky voice, "Mr. Gatlin, won't you please let me go? I need to get back to Colorado Springs so I can catch the next orphan train. Like I told you before, I really want to find out where my friends were taken so I can catch up to them."

Gatlin raised his eyes to the boy and gave him a thorny look. "I told you to shut up about askin' me to let you go. I'm not so sure Sheriff Bostin won't come after us. You're my insurance for gettin' away, and I'm keepin' you with us while we're travelin'."

Johnny's face twisted up. "But—but—"

"But *what*?"

"Well…last night when we camped by that lake, and you and Mr. Caddo thought I was asleep, I wasn't. I…I heard you tell him you were gonna kill me when you—when you didn't need me anymore."

The outlaws exchanged glances over the fire.

"Please, Mr. Gatlin," Johnny said, "please don't kill me."

Gatlin jumped to his feet, his face hardened with irritation. "I told you to shut up! Stop that whinin'!"

"But, Mr. Gatlin, I don't want to die! Please! Don't kill me!"

Gatlin's thick hand lashed out, and he slapped Johnny hard, knocking him down.

Up on the road, Clay Bostin felt his blood temperature rise when he saw Shad Gatlin slap the boy and knock him to the ground. Gatlin stood over him, swearing at him, and sent a swift kick to Johnny's ribs. Johnny let out a cry and Gatlin swore at him again, telling him to shut up.

Bostin clenched his teeth and promised himself that Gatlin would pay for that. He considered the possibility of closing in on the campsite in the middle of the night and taking them by surprise, but quickly changed his mind. Those two outlaws were crafty and cautious. They no doubt would trade off keeping watch all night. He dare not try to slip up on them and fail. Johnny's life depended on it.

At that moment, Clay heard his horse whinny. He looked around and saw a large male cougar standing on a towering boulder above the horse, hissing and swishing his tail. The horse knew the mountain lion was about to pounce on him and was straining at the reins, attempting to free himself from the tree.

Instinctively, Clay whipped out his revolver and cocked it. Suddenly he realized if he fired the gun, the outlaws would hear it and know that someone with a gun was up on the road. Gatlin just might kill Johnny even though he couldn't be sure it was the sheriff. He was sure that he and the horse were too far away for the outlaws to have heard the whinny, but they would hear a gunshot.

"Lord," he said, as he eased the hammer down and slid the gun into its holster, "help me to know what to do." Abruptly the idea came to him that possibly he could frighten the cougar away if he threw a rock at him. He knew it was in cougars to instill as much fear into their prey as possible before they attacked. The beast was working this ploy at the moment, watching the horse pulling at the reins in an attempt to escape. But the ploy had almost been played out. He swished his tail faster, hissed louder, and went into a crouch, ready to pounce.

Clay picked up a fist-sized rock and hurled it at the cougar. The rock struck the big cat's right ear. He let out a howl, shaking his head.

Clay threw another rock and hit him in the head again. The cougar howled, pivoted, leaped off the boulder, and disappeared.

Clay rushed to the horse, untied the reins from the tree, and swung into the saddle. He rode down the steep road, keeping out of sight from the campsite beside the creek below. Soon he came to a spot where he could make camp in the dense timber above the road. He guided the gelding up the sharp slope until he was clearly out of sight from the road and dismounted. Just above him to the east was a lofty peak that stood head and shoulders above the others in view.

There was a small stream cascading down the mountain, which Clay figured probably flowed into the creek below. He let the horse take a good drink, then sat down beside the stream and read a chapter from the gospel of John. Returning the Bible to the saddlebag, he sat down again on the bank of the stream, ate cold jerky and hardtack, and drank from his canteen while the sun was lowering from sight behind the massive peaks to the west. All the while, he kept an eye out for the cougar, but the big cat failed to put in an appearance.

By the time Clay had finished his simple meal and removed the saddle from his horse, evening was on the rugged land. Moments after the other peaks had quit reflecting the sunset sky, the towering snow-covered peak to the east continued to glow as if from some internal light, retaining a faint flush as darkness was falling.

Clay lay down in his bedroll and watched the peak until it finally was swallowed by the night, which set in with its dead silence. The only sound at all was the soft breeze that stirred the limbs of the pines and birches about him. The stars were now showing their light against the velvet black sky above.

Suddenly the silence split to the cry of a wolf somewhere a bit higher than where he lay. It rose strange, wild, mournful—not the howl of a prowling beast, but the wail of a male wolf, crying out for his mate.

Clay's thoughts went to Mary. "I love you, sweetheart," he said. "I miss you too."

Then he spoke to his Father above. "Dear Lord, please take care of Mary. Keep her safe from all harm, and bless her as she stands beside me so faithfully. It's no easy task being a lawman's wife. And Lord, give me wisdom as I trail those outlaws. I must find a way to circle around in front of them and take them by surprise. Help me to do it just right, and please protect Johnny Smith in it all."

When he had finished praying, he let his thoughts go to his pursuit of the outlaws once more. He knew he must act quickly. There was the distinct possibility that Shad Gatlin would soon think he was safe, then kill Johnny and ride on with his friend.

He fell asleep praying once more, asking God to help him rescue the boy and take the outlaws into custody.

During breakfast on the Dexter farm, Ralph chomped a biscuit, swallowed it, and took a sip of coffee. "Rex, I want you to give the chicken shed a good cleaning today. And when you're done, make sure you put new straw down."

Rex nodded without comment.

Ralph took another sip of coffee and set his stern eyes on Deena. "And after you're through with the housework, girl, I want you to help Rex at the chicken shed. It's a big shed. Even with two of you, it'll be a full day's job. I've got work to do on the corral fence."

Norma looked at her husband. "Honey, there's quite a bit of housework to be done today. It might be best if Deena not handle a shovel and a pitchfork quite yet."

Ralph frowned. "It isn't going to take all day for her to get the housework done, I hope. Besides, her blisters are just about healed now, aren't they?"

"They're a lot better, yes, but I'm afraid if she works with Rex at the chicken shed, they'll get worse again."

Bothered because Norma was taking Deena's part for the very first time, Ralph shook his head stubbornly. "I want her out there helping Rex no later than right after lunch. No arguments."

Deena thought she detected a mixture of frustration and fear in Norma's eyes. She was amazed that Norma had spoken up in her defense.

Norma set warm eyes on Deena. "I'll help you with the housework, dear, so you'll be ready to pitch in with Rex at the chicken shed this afternoon."

Deena nodded silently.

That evening, as Norma moved about the kitchen, she glanced periodically out the back window. She was expecting Deena to come from her work with Rex at the chicken shed and help her with supper.

While Norma was setting the table, Deena crossed the yard and stepped up onto the back porch, unnoticed by her foster mother.

There was a small table on the back porch that held a plain porcelain pitcher and washbowl. This was where Ralph and Rex washed up before going into the house for a meal.

Deena poured the cool water into the washbowl, then leaned over it and splashed the refreshing water on her face, dousing the left cheek repeatedly. Taking up the towel that hung on a rack above the table, she carefully patted her face dry, taking particular care with the left cheek.

She then dipped her hands into the water. The cool of it felt good. Her blisters had not broken open again, but she had been forced to use a shovel and pitchfork enough to irritate them.

She dried her hands, hung the towel on the rack, took a deep breath, and entered the fragrant kitchen. Norma was busy at the stove, turning over crispy pieces of chicken in the large cast-iron skillet. The movement at the back door caught the corner of her eye. When she turned and looked at Deena, a tiny gasp escaped her lips.

"Oh my, Deena, how did you hurt your cheek?"

With her eyes fixed on the red welt, Norma really didn't want to hear what Deena was about to tell her. She wiped her hands on her checkered apron and stepped closer, examining the bright red bruise.

Deena's emotions were so close to the surface, all it took was Norma's concern to bring tears to her eyes. Her voice broke and she choked on her words. "I…didn't do it…myself, Mrs. Dexter. Your son slapped me because I didn't do the work exactly as he told me. He gave me the hardest job, and it was just too much for a girl, especially one as small as I am."

Norma's face pinched. She wrung her hands, twisting them in

her apron. Her faded blue eyes clouded up. "I…I'm so sorry, Deena. I'm sorry we ever brought you to this place. Believe me, I didn't know that Ralph and my son would treat you this way. I had said many times that I would love to have a daughter, since I'm the only female on this farm, but I wanted a girl that I could be close to. I wanted to teach her how to sew and do the things women do. I wanted to have companionship with her too, so I wouldn't be lonely out here so far from town. But—but—"

"Mrs. Dexter, you're afraid of your husband, aren't you?"

"Well, I—"

"I've seen it in your eyes. You felt you had to be rough with me because he and Rex are, didn't you?"

Norma bit her lip, looked down, then brought her eyes up to meet Deena's gaze. "Yes. Please don't ever let on to Ralph that I told you this, but he frightens me."

"I won't, ma'am."

"Little by little, Deena, I'm going to see that things are better for you here. So you bear with me, all right?"

"Of course."

"I really want a sweet and close relationship with you."

"Me too. That's what I thought it would be like when you chose me at the depot. Everything seemed so good on the ride here, and you had my room all pretty and ready for me. But…but Rex was cold and rude to me to start off with, and then Mr. Dexter seemed to join him in it. Have I done something wrong, Mrs. Dexter? Why do they dislike me so much?"

Norma put an arm around Deena's shoulder and pressed a cheek against her forehead. "No, dear. It's nothing you've done. I hate to have to tell you this, but Ralph has been stern with me at times ever since the day we married and he brought me here to this farm. It's like he feels he has to dominate me and keep me cowering, or he is not the man he should be. And now that Rex is pretty much grown, he is just mimicking his father. Ralph won't ever correct him when he treats me unkindly. I guess he thinks Rex is just practicing up for the way he will treat his own wife someday."

Norma pulled back so she could look into Deena's eyes. "I was so hoping that it would be different when we brought you here. I thought that for your sake, they would go easier on me. And I sure didn't think they would treat you this way. I'm sorry that you must suffer. I wish I knew how to change my plight, but I don't. However, as I said, I'm going to see that you are treated better. It may take a while, but I'm going to do it."

"I appreciate that you want to make things better for me, Mrs. Dexter, but I would like to see them get better for you too. It makes me both sad and mad to know that you are so miserable."

Tears were spilling down Norma's cheeks. She dabbed at the tears with her apron and took a deep breath. "I'm sorry, child. I shouldn't be burdening you with my troubles. I married the man, and I will keep the vows I made. Ralph isn't always so stern and unkind. There's a good side to him too. That's the side I fell in love with and married. I didn't know he had the bad side till it was too late. I will talk to Ralph and try to get him to make Rex treat you better, but I'm not sure it will do any good. They both look out for each other."

"Well, I guess you and I will have to do the same," said Deena, touching Norma's upper arm. "Thank you for sharing your true feelings about this situation with me. Maybe things will get better."

A small glint of light reflected from Norma's eyes. "Maybe so. You are such a dear, Deena, and I will protect you as much as I can." Her attention went to the food on the stove. "Oh my! We'd better get supper on the table. Ralph and Rex will be in soon, and neither one likes to be kept waiting when they're hungry."

At that instant, they heard the heavy footsteps of father and son on the back porch.

Quickly, Norma went to the stove, and Deena began setting the table.

By the time the men had washed up on the back porch and entered the kitchen, Norma and Deena had things looking quite normal.

Ralph set his gaze on Deena, who was pouring coffee into his cup at the table. When she looked up at him, he scrutinized the red welt on her cheek. "Rex told me about your refusal to obey his orders, and that you forced him to apply discipline. Looks like he popped you a good one. I hope this taught you a lesson and next time, you'll do what he tells you without arguing."

Deena put fingertips to her bruise. "Mr. Dexter, he made me shovel the floor of the chicken shed, and it was hurting my sore hands. I told him I just couldn't do it, but he said I had to do it. Then when the wheelbarrow was full, he told me to take it out to the field behind the corral and dump it. My hands were already hurting terribly. I told him the wheelbarrow was too heavy, and I just couldn't push it out there.

"He pinched down hard on my arm and told me if I didn't do it, he would mash my face against the shed wall. I pushed the wheelbarrow out there, but by the time I got there and dumped it, my back was hurting me and my hands were stinging more. Then he made me push the wheelbarrow to the straw pile out behind the shed and load it with straw with a pitchfork. By that time, I was so tired and my hands were hurting so bad, I told him I just couldn't do it. That's when he slapped me. I'm a girl, Mr. Dexter. That kind of work is a man's job. Why do I have to do it?"

Ralph frowned. "Because Rex told you to."

"But why can't he do the heavy work? He just stands there

and grins while I'm doing it. You've got to make him do the heavy work."

Infuriated with her boldness to talk back to him, Ralph blared, "Don't you tell me what I have to do! I'm not puttin' up with your insolence!"

With that, his big hand lashed out, and he slapped the same cheek so hard, she staggered backward, slammed into the cupboard, and fell to the floor.

Rex grinned.

Norma rushed to the girl, helped her to her feet, and examined the cheek. It was redder than ever, and tears were in her eyes. Keeping an arm around Deena's shoulders, she said, "Ralph, hasn't this poor girl been through enough? You and Rex shouldn't strike her. You're both putting too much work on her. She works hard here in the house with me. She shouldn't have to do a man's work on this farm."

A sudden crimson flush crept across Ralph's features. He made a fist and cocked it, taking a step toward Norma.

Deena jumped between them. "No! Don't hit her, you big bully!"

Ralph froze, glanced at Norma, then looked down at the girl with fire in his eyes. His muscular body seemed to swell, and he growled like an angry bear. "You'd better learn to take orders around here, girl! You're the cause of this whole problem. And you'd better keep a civil tongue in your mouth or else!"

Norma's face was pale. She laid a hand on Deena's shoulder and said quietly, "Let's finish getting supper on the table, honey."

Father and son grinned at each other and took their places at the table. The meal was soon on the table and both men started filling their plates before Norma and Deena had even sat down.

During the meal, Deena barely picked at her food, keeping her head bent down.

"Deena!" Ralph said.

Slowly, she lifted her head and looked at him, holding her fork in a trembling hand.

His stare was a fixed pressure against her. "Stop sulkin' and eat your supper! You have to keep up your strength so you can carry your part of the workload around here."

Deena's face was grave and overcast with an unwonted solemnity. She wanted to ask him why her part of the workload was so heavy, but she refrained. Though she was too upset to have an appetite, she ate enough to satisfy Ralph.

When supper was over, Ralph stood up and belched. "Well, Rex, my boy, it's time for a good game of checkers. Ready?"

"Sure, Pa," Rex responded, rising from his chair. "Only this time it's me who's gonna beat your socks off!"

As father and son left the kitchen and headed down the hall toward the parlor, Norma stood up. She bent over Deena and put her arms around her. "I'm sorry, honey. I'll do my best to see that this treatment you are getting comes to a stop."

Deena rose from her chair and hugged her in return. "Please don't get yourself mistreated while trying to help me. I don't want anything to happen to you."

Norma looked at her with admiring eyes. "You proved that when you jumped in front of my husband when you thought he was going to hit me. You're a brave girl, Deena."

Thirty minutes later, when the dishes were done and the kitchen had been cleaned up, Deena looked at her foster mother with weary eyes. "I'm going on up to my room now."

"I know you're tired," said Norma softly, "but if you don't come into the parlor for the rest of the evening, Ralph will be angry."

Deena's features slacked. "But—"

"He will take it that you are shunning us, honey. It will only make things worse."

Deena shrugged. "All right."

Norma doused the lantern in the kitchen, and Deena walked with her to the parlor, where father and son were playing their checker game at a small table. They glanced up, then quickly returned to their game.

Norma headed for the sofa. "Come, dear. Sit with me."

When Deena was seated on the sofa, she watched Norma open the drawer on the small end table and take out a cardboard box. Sitting down, she placed the box at her feet and took out a pair of knitting needles, a roll of yarn, and a partially finished sweater.

Norma met Deena's curious gaze. "Honey, you need to learn to knit. Someday, you'll be a wife and mother, and you'll need to know how. May I teach you?"

"All right."

Norma reached into the box again, took out another pair of knitting needles, along with another roll of yarn, and handed them to Deena. "All right. You watch me, and I'll teach you."

Norma worked on the sweater for several minutes while Deena looked on. "That doesn't look so hard, does it, dear?"

"I…I think I can learn to do it."

"Good. I'll start by having you make a doily. I'll let you use this one on the table as an example. Let's see if you can make one just like it."

Norma showed her how to thread the needles with yarn, and how to hold them properly. When she had mastered this part, she began showing her how to do the actual knitting. Once she had helped her start, she sat back and watched as she followed her instructions.

While Deena worked at making the doily, she was churning inside. *I don't have to live like this. I don't have to put up with the abuse Ralph and Rex are putting on me. I am going to run away.*

When bedtime came, Deena went to her room and closed the door. Instead of getting ready for bed, she sat on the edge of the bed and formed her plan.

There was a forest between the Dexter farm and Salina. She would climb out the window just before dawn and go to the forest. It would be best not to try it in the dark. Once she was deep in the woods, she would decide what to do next. She must go to someone for help.

But who?

She would have to think on it. One thing was settled in her mind...

She was going to get away from this prison labor camp they called a farm.

Chapter Thirteen

Deena Mitchell slid off the bed and went to the closet. She took her worn cloth bag from the shelf and laid it on the bed. She removed her few dresses from their hangers, laid them next to the bag, and folded them. When she had placed them in the bag, she shoved it under the bed.

She doused the lantern that sat on the nightstand and lay down on top of the spread, fully clothed.

Looking out the window at the starry sky, Deena went over her plan again. "Well, it's not much of a plan, but since I'm alone in a strange place and don't have many options for getting away, it's the best I can do. It's just got to work."

She took a deep breath and let it out slowly. "I feel bad about leaving Mrs. Dexter. I hope my running away won't make her life harder. That brutal husband of hers is going to be mad and may be worse to live with than ever. But somehow she seems to have resigned herself to it, and that's her business. But I don't intend to stay here another day."

With that resolved in her mind, Deena closed her eyes, and after a few minutes, sank into a light sleep.

Even her surface slumber was fitful. Less than an hour after she had fallen asleep, she found herself dreaming about Donna, and just being in her twin's presence in a dream was enough to bring her awake.

She sat up with the vision of Donna's face in her dream and pressed her hands to her cheeks. "Oh, Donna, I need you so desperately! Where are you? I need you!"

She lay back down, but sleep eluded her. She wept for her twin, calling to her in a whisper over and over again as the hours passed.

She was awake when the first hint of dawn touched the eastern horizon. Moving quietly, she sat up and threw her legs over the side of the bed. Reaching under the bed, she grasped the cloth bag and made her way to the door. She turned the knob ever so carefully, swung the door open, and stepped out into the hall.

The house was quiet as a tomb.

Tiptoeing down the hall, she descended the stairs, made her way quickly to the kitchen and out the back door. The air was fresh and sweet to her lungs as she moved off the back porch. Glancing nervously behind her, she made sure she was alone and dashed across the yard on the opposite side of the house from where the bedrooms occupied by Ralph, Norma, and Rex were situated.

Some of the cattle and horses in the corral were watching her as she moved through a gate, closed it behind her, and ran across a field. Twice she glanced behind her, making sure all was still at the house. When she was out of sight from the house, she angled toward the road, running hard.

By the time the sun peeked over the eastern horizon, Deena entered the deep shade of the forest, panting. She looked behind her, then leaned against a cottonwood tree, gasping for breath.

When her breathing returned to normal, she glanced behind her once more. There was no sign of Ralph Dexter.

Deena made her way deeper into the woods at a brisk walk. As she threaded her way among the trees, she decided the best thing to do was to find a farm where people were not likely to be acquainted with the Dexters. She had learned quickly that the neighboring farmers all had a great deal of respect for the Dexters. If she told any of them the way she had been treated by Ralph and Rex, they wouldn't believe it. If she was going to get help, it would have to come from people who were not acquainted with the Dexters.

Deena noticed a babbling stream up ahead and just as she sat down on a fallen tree to rest, she saw two men upstream, with fishing poles, standing on the bank, their lines in the water.

Suddenly, above the sound of the stream, she heard pounding hooves behind her. She looked back through the forest and saw two riders coming her direction, weaving among the trees. She could not yet identify the riders, but she recognized the horses. They belonged to Ralph and Rex.

Deena inhaled sharply and jumped to her feet, gripping the cloth bag. She squealed and dashed toward the stream. When she reached the bank, the fishermen were about a hundred feet upstream and had not yet noticed her. She ran along the stream's two-foot-high embankment, gasping for breath. As she drew nearer the fishermen, she looked back over her shoulder to see if Ralph and Rex had spotted her.

She saw quickly that they were galloping straight toward her and she cried out. Suddenly she lost her footing and stumbled over the embankment. The cloth bag left her fingers as she plunged downward, headfirst. Her head struck a rock that protruded from the stream next to the bank, then she fell into the water.

She was now within fifty feet of the fishermen, and the loud splash drew their attention. They both saw the girl just before she went beneath the surface. They looked at each other, dropped their poles, and charged down the bank. When they reached the spot where Deena had gone into the stream, her limp form was surfacing about thirty feet farther down.

They ran to her and jumped in.

One of them grasped the girl's shoulders at the same time the other one seized her by the ankles. As they were carrying her toward the bank, one of them said, "Looks like she cracked her head on one of those rocks. Big bump here on her temple."

Just as they reached the bank and were climbing out with Deena in their arms, they saw the two riders skidding to a stop. Both riders rushed up.

Ralph Dexter saw that the two men were strangers. He put a horrified look on his face. "Is she all right? She's my daughter!"

As the men laid her on the grassy bank, one said, "She's out cold, sir. I think she hit her head on a rock when she was falling into the stream. There's a big purple knot on her left temple. See?"

Ralph gasped. "Oh my!"

Rex put a look on his face to make it appear that he cared.

Because of the cold temperature of the water, Deena was already moving her head and coming around.

Ralph said, "Gentlemen, I really appreciate your pulling Deena out of the stream. My name's Ralph Dexter. I have a farm a few miles from here. This boy is my son, Rex." He forced a dry chuckle. "Rex and his sister had an argument, and she ran away."

One of the men grinned. "I know how it is between brothers and sisters, Mr. Dexter. Especially at this age. I have a teenage son and daughter myself."

Deena moaned and rolled her head back and forth. When she opened her eyes, they were glassy, and she was having a hard time focusing them.

The back window in the kitchen allowed only a limited view of the back porch, but she leaned against the cupboard where the window was located. She heard Ralph grumbling at Deena as he took off his belt, and she heard Rex say, "I told you this would happen if you ran away, Deena. You deserve it!"

Deena let out a loud, high-pitched cry as the beating began. The sound of the belt striking her flesh and the loud shrieks with each blow were too much for Norma. She turned from the window, pressed palms to her ears, and grimaced in sympathy with Deena.

But in spite of her attempt to block out the horrible sounds, she could still hear them. The beating went on and on. Her lips moved as she mouthed, "That's enough, Ralph! Stop! That's enough!"

But the beating continued, and Deena's shrieks were growing weaker. Finally, it was all Norma could stand. The blood was hot in her veins as she bolted out the back door onto the porch and threw her small body against Ralph.

Ralph had not seen her coming, and the sudden impact of her one hundred and ten pounds against him made him stumble sideways. Deena lay facedown on the floor of the porch, her skirt torn and dappled with blood. Skin showed from her knees down, and bloody stripes were clearly visible.

Norma's wrath had been kindled beyond the normal fear she had of her husband. While he was still stumbling, she attacked him with both fists, pummeling his thick chest. "Stop it! Stop it! Stop it! You've done enough to this poor girl! Stop it!"

Ralph's features turned deep red and a bright animal glitter penetrated his eyes as he looked at Norma and showed his teeth in utter contempt. With one swing of his muscular arm, he sent her crashing into the porch wall.

Rex stood frozen in place as he watched his mother hit the

"It's your daddy, sweetheart," said Ralph. "Rex and I came looking for you. These nice men pulled you out of the stream."

Deena tried to speak, but only a tiny moan came out.

Ralph picked her up and said, "Rex, I noticed her cloth bag back there. Will you get it, please?"

"Sure, Pa," said Rex, and ran toward the bag.

Cradling the girl in his arms, Ralph thanked the men again, then carried her to his horse. Rex was running toward them, bag in hand.

The fishermen smiled at each other and headed back toward their fishing poles.

Ralph hoisted Deena into his saddle, then steadying her, mounted up behind her. Rex hung the bag over his saddle horn. He drew up beside his father's horse and looked at Deena. "She's lookin' more awake now, Pa."

Ralph leaned over her shoulder and peered into her eyes. "Hey, girl. You awake?"

Deena turned and looked up at him. Her eyes were losing their glassy look. "I'm awake."

Ralph touched his heels to his horse's side, and headed through the forest with Rex riding beside him. He bent his head close to Deena and said into her ear, "You're gonna be sorry for pullin' this foolish stunt, girl. You've got some punishment comin'."

Deena rode in silence, fearful of what the punishment was going to be.

A few minutes later, they left the forest, pulled onto the road, and headed for home.

Rex moved his horse a step ahead so he could look Deena in the eye. When she saw him, she turned her head the other way.

Rex's voice was cold as he said, "You know what you are, girl? You're an ingrate. You oughtta be ashamed of yourself. My parents took you off that orphan train and gave you a home. They put a roof over your head and food in your stomach. And this is the thanks they get."

Deena kept her face turned away from him and did not comment.

At the Dexter farm, Norma kept herself busy in the kitchen, cleaning the pantry and the cupboards.

While occupying herself, she thought back to earlier that morning when she tapped on Deena's door, telling her it was time she got dressed and was in the kitchen to help prepare breakfast. When there was no response, Norma opened the door, but Deena was not there.

She stood on the front porch half an hour later and watched her angry husband ride away in search of Deena, with Rex at his side.

Norma was secretly glad that Deena had worked up the nerve to escape. She hoped with all of her heart that Deena would elude them. It frightened her some to think of what could happen to a young girl out in the world alone, but she told herself that just maybe Deena would find someone who would take her into their home, and she would have a chance for a happy life.

When Norma could find no more shelves to clean, she made her way to the parlor and sat down in her favorite overstuffed chair. She laid her head back and closed her eyes, her ears alert for the sound of hoofbeats coming into the yard.

Only a few minutes had passed when she heard the clip-clop of hooves, telling her there were horses approaching the house. She hurried to the window, and hiding behind the starched curtains, observed as the two horses drew up to the front porch.

Norma chewed her lower lip and placed her hand over her

mouth. "Oh no. They found her. And Ralph really looks mad. That poor girl."

Her knees feeling watery, Norma left the parlor, went to the front door, and stepped out on the porch. Both men had dismounted, and Ralph was taking Deena out of the saddle. When her feet touched ground, Ralph took hold of her arm and looked up at his wife. The mean look in Ralph's eyes made Norma's skin crawl. Deena was trembling with fright, and Norma bit her lip again when she saw the purple knot on the girl's temple.

Rex stood in silence while his father told his mother where they found Deena: about her falling into the stream after cracking her head on a rock and of the two fishermen pulling her out.

Norma focused on the purple knot. "Come in, Deena. I need to get some cool water on that swollen bruise. I'm sorry you fell and hit your head."

Rex stiffened. "She deserves it, Ma, for runnin' away."

"She deserves more than that," growled Ralph. "She's gonna get a beating for it."

Norma's brow furrowed and she started to speak.

But Ralph beat her to it. Pointing a stiff finger at her, he snapped, "Don't you say a word, woman! She's got it coming!"

Deena sucked in a sharp breath. "Please, Mr. Dexter! Please don't beat me!"

Teeth clenched, the angry man started dragging her toward the side of the house. Norma knew he was taking her to the back porch to administer the beating. It was there that Rex received most of his whippings as a boy.

Rex grabbed the reins of both horses and hurried after his father and Deena. When the three of them and the animals disappeared around the corner of the house, Norma went inside and hurried to the kitchen. She didn't want to watch Deena get her beating, but she would listen from the kitchen.

wall. The back of her head cracked it loudly. She went limp instantly and slid down the wall, landing in a heap on the floor.

Ralph moved back to Deena and raised his belt to strike her again. But he checked himself when he saw that she was almost unconscious. The rage that had gripped him in its relentless claws abated. He glanced at the still form of Norma on the floor by the wall, then looked at the white-faced Rex as he slipped his belt back through the loops of his trousers. "I've got to cool off. Let's take a little ride. They'll both be all right."

In utter silence, Rex mounted his horse and trotted alongside his father as they rounded the house and headed for the road.

Deena heard the sounds of them riding away, and was sluggishly aware of the eerie stillness that seemed to fall over the porch. A strange black vortex was trying to claim her. She struggled to keep it from pulling her into its dark pit…but in her weakness, she succumbed.

Deena had no idea how long she had been unconscious when her senses returned. She also had no idea where she was or what had happened. She was lying flat on a hard surface.

"Donna! Donna! Where are you? I need you! Donna! Donna! I need you!" It was her own voice.

Abruptly she became aware of pain in her backside and in her legs. The breath was sawing in and out of her lungs, and she worked at conquering her labored breathing. After a few minutes, she finally succeeded, and in the quiet, she heard what sounded like a wounded animal whining.

A cat? No.

A dog? Maybe.

The whining continued.

No, it was not an animal. It was a human sound.

Deena raised her head slowly, careful not to put a strain on her throbbing body, and looked in the direction of the sound. She focused her eyes on a crumpled form lying a few feet away from her. It was a woman, and her body shook as she made the piteous, mournful sounds. There was blood matted in her hair on the back of her head.

Deena struggled to rise to her knees, and after several tries, finally made it. Her bruised and battered body vehemently objected to every move. The pain was worse on the backs of her legs. She put a hand to the stinging areas on her legs and felt something sticky. When she looked at her hand, she saw that it was blood; then her eyes focused on the crimson spots on her skirt near the hem.

The woman's whines once again drew her attention. She crawled painfully toward her, and as she reached her, she recognized Norma Dexter.

Suddenly it all came back.

Deena remembered the beating Ralph was giving her, and Norma's futile attempt to stop him.

Still on her knees, she looked into Norma's clouded eyes. "Mrs. Dexter...Mrs. Dexter, can you hear me?"

Norma blinked and tried to focus on the face above her.

"D-Deena?"

"Yes, ma'am."

Gradually Norma gained control of her frantic state. "Deena, are—are you all right?"

"I'm in a lot of pain and I'm bleeding some. You must have hit your head hard when Mr. Dexter knocked you down. There's a lot of blood in your hair on the back of your head. We need to get to the kitchen where there's water. Do you think you can stand up?"

Norma looked around the porch. Whispering for fear of

being overheard, she asked, "Do—do you know where Ralph and Rex are?"

Deena recalled hearing the sounds of father and son riding away before she passed out. "They rode away, ma'am."

Norma nodded.

Deena took a deep breath. "Let's try to stand up. We've got to tend to our cuts."

Norma began a struggle to get herself on her feet.

Being younger and more resilient, Deena crawled to the wall, used it to brace herself, and was soon on her feet. After leaning against the wall for a moment, she took a couple of steps, stood over Norma, and offered her hand. "Here, let me help you."

Norma clasped the hand, and little by little, was soon standing on shaky legs. Deena helped her to the wall, and they both used it for support while letting their breathing return to normal.

Deena took hold of Norma. "All right, let's go. We'll use the wall for support."

It was a long, slow process, but step by careful step, they entered the kitchen. Deena helped Norma to the table and pulled out a chair. When Norma was seated, Deena pulled the next chair from under the table and dropped into it. Pain shot through her backside.

Deena leaned forward and laid her head on her folded arms atop the table. After a few minutes, the cobwebs of pain began to dissipate, and she raised her head. Focusing on Norma, she saw that there was still a dazed look in her eyes.

Deena gingerly rose to her feet. "Ma'am, I'll get some water now and tend to the cut on the back of your head."

Norma followed Deena's movements as the girl held on to the table for support, then moved shakily to the end of the cupboard where the water pitcher and washbasin sat. She poured water into the basin, took two towels from the rack nearby, and set them in front of Norma.

Dipping a towel into the cool water, Deena wrung it out some, and began to wash the blood from the wound and the hair around it. "The bleeding has stopped, ma'am. I'm glad for that. I'll have it cleaned up in a couple of minutes."

While Deena worked to clean the blood from Norma's hair, nothing was said between them. Each was lost in her own thoughts.

When Deena was done, she said, "That's the best I can do for now."

"That's fine, honey. Thank you. Now what about you?"

Deena looked toward the small room just off the kitchen, which was used for bathing. "I'll go in there and wash the blood off my legs. If they're still bleeding, I'll use some of the cloths in there to wrap around them till the bleeding stops, if that's all right."

"Of course, dear."

Some thirty minutes later, when Deena returned to the kitchen, she found Norma at the table where she had left her, staring into space. "Are you all right, ma'am?"

Norma blinked, then focused on the girl. "Oh. Yes. And how about you?"

"I had to wrap up a couple of the stripes, but the rest of them have stopped bleeding. The two I wrapped aren't bleeding much."

"That's good." Her face pinched. "Deena, I'm so sorry...so very sorry for what my husband did to you."

Deena took hold of her hand. "It's not your fault, ma'am. I'll heal. You even got yourself hurt for trying to stop him from beating on me. Thank you for what you did."

"I couldn't just stand there. I had to do what I could to stop him."

Deena smiled. "You're a brave woman." She looked toward the clock that hung on the kitchen wall. "It's almost noon, ma'am. Mr. Dexter and your son will probably come back expecting lunch to be ready. We'd best get it prepared."

Norma nodded and stood up. "You're right."

While Norma and Deena worked at preparing lunch, Deena said, "Mrs. Dexter, I might as well be honest with you. I am going to run away again. Only next time, I'll plan it better. I'm not going to let Mr. Dexter find me." A new resolve filled her young voice. "He's not going to get the chance to beat me again."

Norma set melancholy eyes on her. "I don't want that to ever happen again."

"I will miss you. Thank you for trying to give me a good home. Someday I'm going to find my twin, for I won't be a whole person until I do. I won't let you know anything about my plan to run away. That way, your husband can't blame you or beat it out of you. But one day, I'll be gone."

"I can't blame you, child," said Norma, patting her hand. "And I hope you have a very happy life."

"I will, ma'am. I…I wish you could get away from here too."

Norma patted the hand again. "That isn't possible for me, dear. When I married Ralph, in my mind it was a lifetime commitment. I'll stay by his side and do the best I can. Rex is only sixteen. He still needs me. But you go as soon as the opportunity presents itself for you to make a clean getaway."

"I'll be much more careful next time, ma'am. I'll make it."

The two of them smiled conspiratorially at each other, then returned to preparing lunch.

That night at the *K-Bar-M Ranch* outside of Wild Horse, Molly Talbert woke up in the wee hours. At first, she was puzzled at what had awakened her. Ken was sound asleep at her side.

Then she heard it again. Down the hall in her bedroom, Donna was sobbing.

Molly eased carefully out of the bed so as not to disturb Ken, took her robe from a nearby chair, and slipped it on. By the pale moonlight that was filtering through the curtains into the room, she picked up a candleholder and a match from the dresser. In the hall, she closed the door behind her, struck the match, lit the candle, then hurried to Donna's room.

The door was open a few inches. Molly pushed it wider and moved up to the bed.

Donna looked up at her with tear-filled eyes and opened her arms. Molly set the candleholder on the nightstand, sat down on the edge of the bed, and leaned close as Donna folded her in a tight embrace.

"Honey, what are you crying about?"

Donna sniffed. "Oh, Mama, I was having a dream. I couldn't see Deena, but I heard her calling to me, saying she needed me. She sounded terribly upset. Then I woke up."

Molly hugged her tight. "It was just a dream, honey. Just a bad dream. You need to get back to sleep now."

"But it was so real! It was Deena's voice. It was like she was right here in the room with me."

"Dreams can be like that, Donna," said Molly, easing back to look her in the eye. "But that's all it was. Only a dream."

Donna blinked at her tears. "Oh, Mama, I want to see Deena so badly."

"I know. And Papa and I will take you to Salina as soon as possible. But it will be a while yet. Let's pray for Deena right now, then you need to get back to sleep."

Chapter Fourteen

High in the Colorado Rockies, the sun was setting as outlaws Shad Gatlin and Bart Caddo halted their horses a few yards from the mouth of a cave. Gatlin and Caddo had traded off keeping their hostage in the saddle while they rode.

At the moment, Gatlin had Johnny Smith on his horse with him. Caddo dismounted. "I'll check the cave out, Shad." He pulled out his revolver and drew back the hammer. "Be right back."

Gatlin nodded. "We'll wait right here."

When his partner disappeared into the dark cave, Gatlin gazed around as the boy sat quietly in front of him. The shadows of the deep crags stretched from the west and between them streamed a red-gold light. The sunset was a clear picture of sunshine losing its fire. Fleecy orange clouds rested over the lofty mountain peaks. A sailing eagle dotted the blue sky directly above them, its shrill cry echoing over the high country.

Johnny looked up at the majestic bird and wished he was free like the eagle. Seconds later, it sailed silently out of sight.

The silence around them was unbroken now, and a soft breeze, laden with the incense of pine, touched their faces.

Suddenly the silence was broken by a loud roar inside the cave, followed by three gunshots. A startled Johnny Smith jerked in the saddle, grabbing the pommel. Three more shots came from the cave while Shad Gatlin was swinging out of the saddle, pulling his gun. He headed toward the cave, calling over his shoulder, "You stay put, kid!"

Just as Gatlin reached the cave, Bart Caddo came out, gun in hand. Smoke was drifting upward from the muzzle. "I ran into a black female bear in there, Shad. She was way back at the end of the cave. She's dead now."

Gatlin shoved his gun back in its holster. "Well, let's drag her carcass outta there. I ain't wantin' to sleep in there with a dead bear."

"Me, neither. She ain't terribly big. Won't be hard for the two of us to get her outta there."

Gatlin turned and looked at Johnny. "Okay, kid, get down and come to the cave with us."

There was a fearful look on the boy's face as he slid from the saddle and walked toward the outlaws.

When they moved inside, Gatlin pointed to a spot just inside the cave's mouth. "Siddown right there, kid. And don't you move."

Instantly, Johnny dropped to the floor of the cave and sat with his back against the rugged rock wall. He watched as the two men moved back into the shadows and could barely see them as they grabbed the dead bear by the hind feet and dragged her toward the cave's mouth. Johnny focused on the black ball of fur as they dragged her past him, noting that her eyes were wide open in death. The outlaws dragged the bear outside and left the carcass under a tall spruce tree.

When they returned to the cave, Gatlin was carrying the rope he had used to bind Johnny up each night.

"Okay, kid, lie down right there so's I can tie you up. We've got to go out and find firewood so we can cook supper."

Johnny obeyed by stretching out on the dirt floor, intimidation showing in his eyes.

While Gatlin was cinching up the rope on his wrists and ankles, he said, "If you ever try to escape, kid, I promise I'll kill you for sure. Got that?"

"Yes, sir."

"Good. I'll untie you when we get back, so you can eat."

Twilight was settling over the mountains as the outlaws left the cave and vanished from Johnny's sight. Lying there, he thought of his father. He told himself if his father was a western lawman, he would come to his rescue. Justin Smith would find a way to get the drop on the bad men and free his son.

Tears filled the boy's eyes. His lips quivered. "But this can't happen because Dad lies in a cold, dark grave in the cemetery back in Manhattan." He sniffed and choked on his tears. "Oh, Dad, I miss you so much! I miss you too, Mom. Why did both of you have to die?"

Johnny's tears had dried up by the time he heard the outlaws coming toward the cave. It was now almost totally dark.

Gatlin and Caddo laid half of the broken tree limbs on the ground at the center of the cave's mouth, and laid the rest of it close by for future use. They pulled dried pine needles and cones from their pockets and set them close to the wood. Gatlin pulled out a match, struck it, and put the flame on the needles and cones. Flames flared up instantly, throwing light all around the cave.

Gatlin stood over Johnny and laughed. "Well whattya know! You're still here, eh, kid? I figured while we were gone, that she-bear's mate would find her dead body over there under that tree and come in here ready to rip up whoever was in the cave."

Caddo chuckled. "Yeah, I figured all we'd find of you was your clean bones."

Johnny looked up at both men grimly.

The outlaws had stolen food, tin cups, coffee, coffeepot, and a skillet from a house they had burglarized in the small town of Florissant, just west of Pike's Peak. They went outside to the horses and took the goods from the saddlebags. While Johnny looked on from the floor of the cave, they started cooking supper.

Soon the sound of hot meat was crackling in the skillet while Shad Gatlin leaned over it, stirring the meat around. Bart Caddo was busy with the small coffeepot.

Johnny knew the time planned by Gatlin to kill him had to be drawing near. The fear within him was like a worm crawling through his brain. Gatlin had warned him not to beg for his life anymore, but the twelve-year-old boy could not hold back. He drew a shuddering breath. "Mr. Gatlin?"

Still stirring the crackling meat, Gatlin swung his gaze to Johnny. "Yeah?"

"Won't you please let me go? You and Mr. Caddo are safe now. If there were lawmen on your trail, they would have shown up by now. You don't need me as a hostage anymore."

Gatlin and Caddo exchanged glances by the firelight, then Gatlin grinned at the boy. "You're right, kid. We don't need you as a hostage anymore. Bart and I were talkin' about it when we were gatherin' the firewood. If that lame-brained Sheriff Clay Bostin was on our trail, he'd have been here before now."

Gatlin left the skillet on the fire and rose to his feet. Stepping to where Johnny lay, he looked down at him. "Bostin told me I was through killin'. Well, he was wrong."

Johnny's mouth went dry as Gatlin pulled his gun.

The outlaw chuckled dryly. "We need to get rid of you, all right, kid. You're eatin' food Bart and I need for ourselves. Not only that, but one of us has to have you in our saddle all the time we're ridin'."

Gatlin snapped the hammer back.

Johnny's eyes widened and the firelight cast a gray luminescence on his face.

Gatlin said icily, "I'll just kill you now, and get it over with."

Still holding the coffeepot, Bart Caddo was enjoying the terror he saw in Johnny's eyes as Gatlin aimed the muzzle at the boy's trembling head.

Suddenly a voice from the darkness outside barked, "Drop the gun, Gatlin, or you're dead!"

Both outlaws, as well as a terrified Johnny Smith, looked into the darkness toward the sound of the voice. The owner of the voice took a step into the vague light of the fire, which showed them Sheriff Clay Bostin standing just outside the cave with a cocked Colt.45 in each hand.

In a quick desperate move, Gatlin brought his gun up, swinging the muzzle toward the sheriff. Bostin's right-hand gun spit fire. Gatlin buckled, dropped his gun, and while he was falling, Bart Caddo dropped the coffeepot and whipped out his revolver.

Before he could bring it into play, Bostin's left-hand gun roared, and Caddo went down like a rock, never to move again.

Seeing that Gatlin was still breathing, Bostin kicked his gun deep into the darkness of the cave, then holstered both guns and knelt beside the boy. "Johnny, you all right?"

A relieved Johnny Smith found his voice. "Yes, sir, Sheriff. I'm all right. How'd you know my name?"

"The Children's Aid Society sponsors told me."

"Oh."

Bostin saw the relief displayed on the boy's face as he began untying him. When the knots were loose, Bostin pulled the ropes away. "Can you get up?"

"Yes, sir." And with that, Johnny sprang to his feet, rubbing his wrists and running his gaze to Shad Gatlin.

Bostin took a step toward the outlaw and looked down at him.

Gatlin's face was a twisted mass of pain as he stared up at the sheriff with glassy eyes. He choked, then ejected a vile oath, cursing Bostin. "One…more second…and I would have…killed the…kid."

"I told you that you were through killing."

Gatlin swore at him again, and with that, he breathed out his last breath. His body went limp and his head fell to the side, his eyes frozen open.

Bostin leaned over and forced the eyelids shut. "Bad thing, Gatlin, going out into eternity cursing."

The sheriff turned and looked at the boy. "I'm sorry you had to witness two men being killed, Johnny."

Johnny looked up at the tall lawman and met his gaze. "It's better than what would have happened if you hadn't shown up exactly when you did, sir." At that instant, tears welled up in Johnny's eyes. "Thank you for staying on our trail and for saving my life."

Bostin moved to the boy and folded him in his arms. "I knew Gatlin would kill you once he thought he was safe, Johnny. I had to catch up to him before it was too late. I wanted you to have all your tomorrows."

Bostin's last words touched Johnny deeply. He eased back in the sheriff's arms, wiped tears from his cheeks, and looked up into Bostin's eyes. "All my tomorrows. I never heard it put like that before, Sheriff."

Bostin grinned. "You have a right to live out the life that God gave you. I'm just glad He let me get here in time so I could have a part in making sure it didn't end tonight."

Johnny swallowed hard. "Me too."

Releasing the boy from his arms, the sheriff went to the fire and removed the skillet from the flames. "Johnny, I'm going to remove these corpses from the cave, then you and I can eat supper."

Johnny watched while the sheriff carried the lifeless bodies of the outlaws out of the cave a few yards to the side, where he laid them down and covered them completely with rocks.

He returned, and the two of them sat down on the floor of the cave close to the fire to eat the supper that the outlaws had prepared. Before they began, Clay Bostin said, "Johnny, I always thank the Lord for the food before I eat. I also want to thank Him for letting me get here before those outlaws took your life."

Johnny let a thin smile curve his lips. "Yes, sir."

When Bostin closed his prayer, they began to eat. "Johnny, how did you become an orphan? Did both of your parents die at the same time?"

"No, sir."

Johnny told about his mother's death over a year ago, then explained how his policeman father was killed when he shot it out with two bank robbers. He made sure Bostin knew that the robbers were killed too.

Bostin spoke his condolences in the deaths of both Johnny's parents. "I can tell you carry a great deal of pride in what your father was."

"You're right, Sheriff. Since I was quite small, I wanted to be a policeman when I grew up, but…well, I had thoughts about being something else when Dad was killed in the line of duty." He paused and let another smile curve his lips. "But now that I have seen you in action, I just might become a lawman here in the West when I grow up."

"Johnny, that would be good. The West will be in need of good lawmen when you grow into adulthood even more than it is now, the way the population is increasing."

"That's something to think about, sir." Johnny paused, then said, "Sheriff Bostin, when we get back to Colorado Springs, I need to somehow make contact with the Children's Aid Society in New York so they will know I'm all right, and they can pick me up when the next orphan train comes through. I need to go on until some man and his wife choose me so they can be my foster parents and take me into their home."

"I'll have you back in Colorado Springs in three or four days. I'll help you make contact with the Society by wire."

"That'll really be swell, sir. I appreciate it very much."

"Glad to help."

When supper was over, Bostin added wood to the fire. "Johnny, I'll be right back. I have to go out and get my Bible out of the saddlebags. I always read my Bible before going to bed."

Johnny blinked. "Oh. All right."

The sheriff was back within a short time, and as he sat down beside Johnny, the boy looked at the Bible. "I've only seen the inside of a Bible a few times in my life."

Bostin smiled. "Well, you're welcome to read this one anytime you want. How about right now, though, we read it together?"

"I'd like that, sir. I've always wondered about a lot of things that people have told me are in the Bible."

"Oh, really?"

"Mm-hmm."

"What, for instance?"

"Well, when people die, they don't come back from the dead. But I've been told that in the Bible, God's prophets raised people from the dead, and so did Jesus Christ."

"That's right."

"And they say that Jesus even came back from the dead."

"He sure did."

"How could that be?"

"It was done by the power of God, Johnny. It is God who gives life in the first place. If He wants to give life back to someone who had died, He sure can do it."

Johnny pondered those words for a moment. "Well, that does make sense, sir. I hadn't thought about it like that. I guess God can do anything He wants, huh?"

"He sure can."

Johnny frowned. "Something else, Sheriff."

"Mmm-hmm?"

"I have a hard time believing there's a place called hell where people burn forever."

"God says there is." He opened the Bible. "Let me show you."

Bostin turned to Psalm 9. He angled the Bible toward the fire so Johnny could see it. "Read me verse 17."

Johnny focused on it. "'The wicked shall be turned into hell, and all the nations that forget God.' Who's the wicked, Sheriff?"

"People who never receive the Lord Jesus Christ as their Saviour."

"Oh."

Bostin flipped to Isaiah 14. "Johnny, do you know who Lucifer is?"

"No, sir."

"Do you know who Satan is?"

"The devil."

"Right. Well, when Satan was first created, God gave him the name Lucifer. Here in this passage, Lucifer has sinned against God. Look what God says to him in verse 15. Read it to me."

Johnny licked his lips. "'Yet thou shalt be brought down to hell, to the sides of the pit.'"

"Now keep that in mind," said Bostin, turning to the New Testament. "Look what Jesus said here in Matthew chapter 25,

Johnny. Before I have you read it, let me explain that when Lucifer was cast out of heaven, there was a great number of angels who took his side and went with him."

"Really?"

"Really. In this passage, Jesus is talking about the day of the last judgment. He will have the saved people at His right hand, and the lost people at His left hand. He speaks of Himself in verse 41 and what He is going to say to those who are lost. Read it to me."

"'Then shall he say also unto them on the left hand, Depart from me, ye cursed, into everlasting fire, prepared for the devil and his angels.'"

"You see, Johnny, God didn't create hell for human beings, He created it for the devil and his angels. But when sinners refuse to come to God for salvation His way, He has nowhere else to put them. You see that lost human beings are going to the same hell. And what kind of fire did Jesus say it is?"

Johnny looked back at the verse. "Everlasting fire."

"Mm-hmm. Now look down at verse 46. Jesus says of the lost people, 'And these shall go away into everlasting punishment: but the righteous into life eternal.' What kind of punishment is it?"

"Everlasting, sir."

"What kind of fire is it, according to what Jesus said in verse 41?"

"Everlasting."

"That means both the fire and the punishment will go on forever, doesn't it?"

"Yes, sir."

"There are many other passages of Scripture that tell of the burning hell where people go when they die if they die without Jesus Christ as their Saviour, Johnny, but I think for the moment, this is enough for you to see that there is a burning place called hell that actually exists."

Johnny nodded. "Yes, sir. I believe it."

"Good. The next few days as we travel, I'll show you more on the subject. We'll also look at passages that discuss the wrath of God against sin. Right now, I want to show you some other things."

Before they began to read more, Bostin could see that the Scriptures Johnny had already seen had stamped a deep impression on him. He then took the boy to passages that deal with salvation and what Jesus did on the cross for sinners in His death, burial, and resurrection, and had him read them aloud to him.

Since this was all new to Johnny, Bostin stopped there and told him they would read more tomorrow night. He told Johnny they would have prayer, and while he was praying, the sheriff asked God to help Johnny to understand the gospel that he might be saved. He also prayed that the Lord would place Johnny in the home where He wanted him.

Both those requests touched Johnny's heart.

During the next two days, Clay and Johnny talked much about salvation while Johnny rode the horse Shad Gatlin had stolen. The other stolen horse followed as led by the sheriff from his saddle.

On both nights, the two read Scriptures on the subject of God's wrath against sin, salvation, heaven, and hell. The sheriff discussed them with the boy.

At the end of the third day, they were within less than three hours' ride from Colorado Springs when they stopped and made camp for the night. By this time, the Holy Spirit had done His work in Johnny's heart, and when it was Bible reading time beside the campfire, Johnny told the sheriff he wanted to be saved. Clay Bostin had the joy of leading the boy to Jesus.

After Johnny had gone to sleep in Shad Gatlin's bedroll,

Sheriff Clay Bostin lay awake in his own bedroll, praising the Lord for Johnny's salvation.

As the campfire dwindled, the shadows of the pines closed in darker and darker upon the circle of fading light. A cool wind fanned the embers, whipped up flakes of white ashes, and moaned through the trees. Clay looked up and marveled at the beauty of God's handiwork above him. The sky was a massive black dome spangled with twinkling white stars.

While studying the dazzling heavens, Clay thought about the strange stirring that had been going on in his heart since before he and Johnny had started their trip back to Colorado Springs. The stirring had only grown stronger since then.

He pondered the fact that he and Mary had been married for over four years, and that they learned only recently that she would never be able to bear children. He thought about their attempts at finding a child on the orphan trains, but how the Lord gave them no direction on choosing any of the children.

Clay thought about last Wednesday, and how they had planned again to prayerfully look the children over at the depot, but Johnny Smith was abducted by Shad Gatlin, and Clay had to ride away in pursuit immediately. He and Mary were not able to talk about her looking the children over by herself. He wondered if she had chosen a child.

He thought about the genuine affinity he had felt toward Johnny—coupled with the strange stirring in his heart—even before they began the return trip. Lying there beneath the stars, he looked toward heaven and said in a low whisper, "Lord, I know You have put it in my heart that even if Mary chose another child at the depot last Wednesday, we are also to take Johnny into our home as his foster parents. You have made it so clear. I will talk to him about it in the morning."

After thanking the Lord from the depths of his heart for letting him save Johnny's life and for allowing him to lead the boy to Jesus, Clay fell asleep thinking about the moment he would talk to the boy in the morning about living in the Bostin home as their foster son.

Chapter Fifteen

The next morning as Clay Bostin and Johnny Smith sat down near the fire to eat breakfast, Johnny said, "Sheriff, I want to thank you for caring enough about me to show me that I needed to be saved, and for showing me how to be saved. It's so wonderful to know that I'm not going to that awful place called hell that I thought didn't exist."

Clay smiled. "It was my pleasure, Johnny."

The boy shook his head. "Just think. If that Gatlin guy had killed me before you came along, I would have died lost."

"Yes, but praise the Lord, He kept Gatlin from killing you, and now that you've opened your heart to Jesus, heaven is your eternal home."

The boy's face was beaming. "I'm so glad I'm saved!"

"I am too, Johnny," said the sheriff. "Well, let's thank the Lord for the food and get our breakfast down so we can head for Colorado Springs."

Clay led in the prayer of thanks, expressing his appreciation to the Lord once more for sparing Johnny's life and for drawing the boy to Himself.

As they began to eat, Johnny said, "Sheriff Bostin, I—" Johnny swallowed hard and his eyes misted up.

"You what?" Bostin had a smile on his face.

Johnny blinked at the moisture in his eyes and cleared his throat. "Well, sir, I just want to say that it's going to be very hard to tell you good-bye when I board the next orphan train."

Clay had formed no exact plan for how he would tell the boy his desire to take him into the Bostin home, but this remark gave him the perfect opening.

"Johnny, there's something I want to talk to you about."

"Yes, sir?"

"Let me explain some details first, okay?"

"Sure."

"My wife, Mary, and I have been married for over four years, but we don't have any children."

"Yes, sir."

"You see, Mary is not able to bear children, so we have been trying to find the right child on one of the orphan trains to take into our home. We have prayed hard about it each time before we went to the depot when the orphan trains came in, but the Lord just didn't give us direction concerning any of the children. We only want the child that God wants us to have."

Johnny swallowed the food he was chewing. "Yes, sir."

"You know that Shad Gatlin was my prisoner, and that when I brought him to Colorado Springs last Wednesday, the next move was to have him taken to the Territorial Prison at Canon City so he could be hanged."

"Yes, sir."

"You see, Mary was there at the depot to look the orphans over by herself, because she didn't know when I might be back."

"Uh-huh."

"Well, when Gatlin grabbed you and he and Caddo took off, I only had a moment to let Mary know that I was going to ride out immediately on your trail. We didn't get to talk about the orphans. So, Mary just might have chosen an orphan and taken him or her home."

Johnny nodded, wondering what the conversation was leading to.

Clay set steady eyes on the boy. "What I wanted to talk to you about is this: Johnny, the Lord has spoken to my heart about you."

"What do you mean, sir?"

"Whether Mary chose a child off the train or not, I know beyond the shadow of a doubt that the Lord wants me to take you home so you can live with us. What do you think about that?"

Johnny felt his heart flutter in his chest. "Y-you m-mean—"

"Would you like to be our boy?"

Johnny Smith's eyes brightened. "You really want me to be your boy?"

"I sure do!"

"Well, Sheriff, I would really love to be your boy, but—"

"But what?"

"Well, are you sure Mrs. Bostin will go along with it? Will she want to be my foster mother?"

Clay looked him in the eye. "I guarantee you she'll go along with it. Even if she chose an orphan off that train, she'll still go along with it because Mary and I are of one heart and one mind on this subject. When I tell her the Lord spoke to my heart and told me I was to bring you home, she will be in total agreement. We have that kind of marriage."

The mist in Johnny's eyes became dual rivers instantly. He laid his tin plate down, rose to his knees and threw his arms around Clay's neck. Clay dropped his utensils and hugged him close.

As they clung to each other, Clay said, "I'll tell you this,

Johnny: when Mary has known you for thirty seconds, she will happily say she wants to be your foster mother!"

When Clay and Johnny reached Colorado Springs just before noon, Clay told him they would go to the office first so he could let his deputies Brent Davis and Randy Ashbrook know that he was back, that Johnny was safe and sound, and that the outlaws were dead.

When Clay and Johnny entered the sheriff's office, both deputies were there and rejoiced in the good news. They welcomed Johnny, telling him how glad they were that he had been rescued.

Clay did not reveal the plans he had to take Johnny into their home. He felt Mary should be first to know, although the Western Union agent would know before Mary because a telegram would have to be sent immediately. Clay knew the agent would never divulge the content of a telegram to anyone.

He asked the deputies to find the owners of the stolen horses and to see that they got them back.

"We'll take care of the matter, Sheriff," said Ashbrook. "You'll be happy to know that we were able to get the horse Gatlin stole in Canon City back to its owners."

"Good. Now I have to go to the Western Union office and send a wire to the Children's Aid Society and let them know that Johnny has been rescued. Then I'm taking him home to meet Mary."

"Oh," said Davis. "So you're gonna keep him at your house till the next orphan train comes through, eh?"

Clay grinned. "Something like that."

The deputies watched as sheriff and boy went to the hitch rail outside. Bostin hoisted Johnny up behind the saddle, then mounted his horse. They rode away with Johnny holding on to the sheriff with his arms around his waist.

When they reached the Western Union office, Clay took Johnny inside with him. Johnny observed as the sheriff worded the telegram for the agent, telling of Johnny's rescue, and he added in that he and his wife were taking Johnny into their home as their foster son. He told the Society if they would mail the official papers, he and Mary would sign them and return them quickly.

As they left the Western Union office, Clay said, "Okay, Johnny my boy, let's go home."

At the Bostin home, Mary was keeping herself busy while praying continuously for her husband's safe return, along with Johnny Smith.

On this particular morning, she had been busily cleaning the already clean house. She had washed all the windows until they gleamed in the bright sunlight. She had also washed all the curtains, then ironed them to a stiff crispness. Before hanging the curtains back on the windows, she went to the kitchen and put three loaves of bread in the oven.

It was almost noon when she returned to the kitchen and took the hot bread from the oven. Then, hoping Clay would soon be home to eat it, she placed a pie brimming with succulent apples into the already hot oven.

Mary then sat down and ate a sandwich and drank a cup of coffee. After cleaning up her lunch dishes and utensils, she made her way to the front of the house with a feather duster in hand. She was about to begin dusting the bookshelves when the sound of horse's hooves reached her ears.

She hurried to the parlor window, and when she saw her husband, her heart skipped a beat. She dropped the feather duster and rushed to the front door, thanking the Lord that Clay was home safe and sound.

When she opened the door, Clay was out of the saddle, heading for the porch. Tears flooded Mary's eyes. She bolted from the door, calling his name. Clay met her as she reached the porch's bottom step and folded her in his arms.

"Oh, darling! You're home! You're home!"

Clay kissed her soundly, then held her at arm's length and looked into her eyes. "It's good to be home, sweetheart."

"What about the boy?" she asked, wiping tears from her cheeks.

Clay realized that Mary had not yet spotted Johnny, who was still on the horse. "He's fine, honey. Take a look."

Mary took a step to see past her tall husband, and set her eyes on the boy. "Oh! You brought him home with you!"

A bit nervous, Johnny smiled at her, slid off the horse, and moved toward them. "Hello, Mrs. Bostin."

Clay said, "Honey, meet Johnny Smith."

Mary dashed to him and put her arms around him. "Oh, Johnny, I'm so glad you're all right!"

"Thank you, ma'am. The sheriff rescued me from the bad men."

Mary kept an arm around Johnny and smiled through her tears at her husband. "I want to hear the whole story from beginning to end, but first you two come in and wash up. Let me fix lunch for you."

"Okay," said Clay, laying a hand on the boy's shoulder. "Sounds good to me. How about you, Johnny?"

Johnny looked up at him and grinned. "Yes, sir! I'm mighty hungry, and something sure smells good in the direction of that door."

They entered the house, and while the three of them moved down the hall toward the kitchen, Clay said, "Honey, did you find an orphan for us last Wednesday?"

"No, darling. When you rode away to follow those outlaws, I just didn't feel that the Lord wanted me to look for one at that time. I was too upset over what had happened. My thinking wouldn't have been clear."

Clay felt warmth steal over his heart. "Well, we sure want the Lord to lead us so we pick the orphan He has chosen for us."

Mary smiled up at him. "Right."

While Clay and Johnny were washing up in a small room next to the kitchen, Mary checked on the pie in the oven, then sliced the freshly made bread and cut chunks of cheese and roast beef. She placed butter and a pitcher of milk on the table, with a jar of strawberry jam and butter pickles. She poured Johnny a large glass of milk and filled cups with coffee for Clay and herself.

When they all sat down at the table together, Clay thanked the Lord for the food, then he and Johnny began eating.

Mary said, "Okay, gentlemen, I want to hear all about the pursuit and the rescue."

Clay told her about tracking the outlaws and how the Lord made it possible for him to corner them in the cave. He explained that when he approached the cave, Gatlin had his gun pointed at Johnny's head and was about to pull the trigger. He told her of Gatlin swinging the gun on him and that he was forced to shoot him down; then how Caddo resisted him and how he was forced to shoot him, as well.

Mary closed her eyes and whispered a prayer of thanks to the Lord for sparing Johnny's life and for protecting Clay, then looked at Johnny and asked him to tell her his story.

Johnny told Mary about the deaths of his parents and his subsequent ride on the orphan train. Mary patted his hand. "I'm so sorry about your parents. It must have been horrible for you. Bless your heart."

"Yes, ma'am. It was. But I'm doing better now." He gave Clay a furtive grin, which didn't go unnoticed by Mary. She had felt a certain restrained excitement in her husband since he first kissed her, and it seemed to be growing by the minute.

Abruptly, she shoved her chair back and stood up. "Hold everything. I've got to rescue this apple pie before it burns."

She snatched up two hot pads from a small table beside the stove, opened the oven, lifted the bubbling pie out, and set it on the cupboard to cool.

Johnny looked on, never taking his eyes from the pie until Mary sat back down.

Mary said, "When it has cooled, you can have as big a piece as you want."

A wide smile spread over the boy's face. "I'll look forward to it, ma'am." Then he slipped Clay another sly grin.

Looking from Johnny to her husband, Mary said, "Something curious is going on between you two. What is it?"

Clay finished his cup of coffee, took a deep breath, and set his eyes on his wife. "Mary, darlin'."

She knew by the look in his eyes that he had something important to say. "Yes, sweetheart?"

"From the moment Johnny and I sat down and ate supper in the cave, the Holy Spirit began dealing with me. He continued to speak to my heart as we rode toward home."

"About what?"

"Well, we've prayed hard about His leading us to just the right orphan, haven't we?"

Mary flicked a glance at the boy, then looked back at her husband. "We most certainly have."

"And you agreed a few minutes ago that we sure want the

Lord to lead us so we pick the orphan He has chosen for us."

Mary glanced again at Johnny Smith, who was now smiling at Clay. In her heart, she said, *Lord, please let it be what I think it is. I already love this boy. Is he the one You have for us?* She looked back at Clay. "I sure did. Clay, are you telling me what I think you're telling me?"

A lopsided grin formed on his lips. "I am if you think I'm telling you that the Lord wants us to take Johnny into our home."

Tears bubbled up in Mary's eyes. She looked at the boy, then at her husband. "I can tell by the secret glances you two have been giving each other that you've already talked to him about it."

"He sure has, Mrs. Bostin," piped up Johnny, "and if you want me too, I'd be the happiest boy in the whole world!"

Mary slid her chair back, jumped to her feet, and threw her arms around Johnny's neck. "Oh yes, I want you too! Oh, Johnny, you're an answer to prayer. I can plainly see that the Lord sent you into our lives because we needed a son and you needed a mother and a father."

Johnny was weeping. He wrapped his arms around her neck and said through his tears, "I'm the happiest boy in the whole world! I promise, Mrs. Bostin, I'll always do my best to be what I should be as your foster son."

Clay was wiping tears as he looked on. He wrapped his arms around both Mary and the boy as all three rejoiced together over God's goodness.

When the emotions had settled down, Clay said, "Something else happened on the trail, honey. Johnny wants to tell you about it. Let's sit down."

Mary kissed Johnny's cheek, let go of him, and returned to her chair.

As Clay sat down, he smiled at Johnny. "Go ahead, son. Tell her."

With a beam on his face, Johnny told Mary how on the first night he and her husband were together, the sheriff showed him things in the Bible about Jesus, Calvary, heaven, and hell that he didn't even know were in there. He went on to explain that the next evening on the trail that the sheriff had shown him more Scripture about salvation; and that by the third evening, he clearly understood that he was lost and needed to open his heart to Jesus. And he did so.

A shaft of pure joy hit Mary's heart and radiated in her eyes. She left her chair once more and wrapped her arms around the boy's neck. "Oh, Johnny, how wonderful! I'm so happy for you! What a marvelous God we serve. He has given me a precious husband and now a dear son."

Once again, Clay got up and the three of them embraced each other for a long moment.

Clay tugged playfully at Johnny's ear. "I love you, Johnny."

With Mary still gripping him around the neck, Johnny looked up and smiled. "I love you, too, Sheriff."

Clay sat down again and looked at the pair with praise to God in his heart.

After Mary had hugged the boy a little longer and planted another kiss on his cheek, she returned to her chair, wiping tears. She found Clay's eyes on her and met his gaze.

He let a pleasant grin curve his lips. "Honey, there's something else."

"Well, tell me."

"I haven't talked to Johnny about this yet, but the Lord has impressed me that we should go beyond the foster relationship and adopt him as soon as possible."

While Mary's eyes were lighting up, so were Johnny's. He drew a sharp breath. "Really, Sheriff? You really want to adopt me?"

"I sure do. Is that all right with you? It would mean that your last name would be Bostin."

"Hey, that's all right. I'll be proud to be known as Johnny Bostin!"

"We'll be proud to have you wear our name, honey," said Mary.

Clay smiled. "I'll talk to Judge Ackerson tomorrow and we'll set the adoption wheels in motion. And since it's going to happen, Johnny, no more calling me 'Sheriff.' How about 'Dad'?"

"Okay!"

Mary looked at him with loving eyes. "And I'm 'Mom,' okay?"

"Sure, Mom!"

After Johnny and his new dad had finished off large pieces of pie, the happy couple took him down the hall, past the master bedroom, to the room that would be his.

When Johnny stepped into the room, he told himself the Bostins must have been expecting to take in a boy, for sure. A green, red, and blue plaid quilt covered the dark oak bed, and a small desk and chair of the same wood stood against one wall. A dresser with a mirror stood opposite the bed, and a closet was nearby.

The small table next to the bed held a lantern, and there were paintings of outdoor scenes on the walls, some with horses and cattle in the foreground. Drapes of the same green, red, and blue as the bedspread hung beside the window, with sheer white curtains that were brightened by the afternoon sunlight.

With eyes round as saucers, Johnny breathed out, "Wow! This is really something! I'm really gonna love living here!"

The new parents shared a happy smile, then Clay said, "Honey, I've got to get to the office. I'll be there the rest of the afternoon."

"I'm sure there's a lot of paperwork to catch up on," said Mary.

"For sure." Then to Johnny he said, "On my way to the office, I'll stop at the general store and buy you a Bible."

"Thank you, Sh—I mean, Dad. It'll be great to have my own Bible."

At that moment there was a knock at the front door of the house.

Clay went up the hall toward the front of the house.

Johnny said, "I'll help you do the dishes, Mom."

When Clay opened the door, he found Pastor Dan Wheeler and his wife, Madelyne. He welcomed them. As they moved through the door, Pastor Wheeler said, "I'm glad to see you home, Clay. Mary told us at the service last week about your pursuit of the outlaws who had abducted one of the orphan train boys, and asked us to pray for you and the boy. Madelyne and I have been checking each day with Mary, and that's why we're here. What about the boy?"

Clay smiled. "He's right here in the house."

"Oh, really?"

"Mm-hmm." Clay turned and called toward the rear of the house, "Mary! It's Pastor and Mrs. Wheeler! Bring Johnny, will you?"

Mary and Johnny appeared quickly and made their way up the hall. When they drew up, Clay introduced the Wheelers to Johnny Smith. Clay told them how he rescued the boy, and that he had been able to lead him to the Lord on the way back to Colorado Springs.

The Wheelers thought this was wonderful news.

Clay said, "Mary and I are taking Johnny into our home. I'm going to talk to Judge Ackerson tomorrow and have him draw up the adoption papers."

"Great!" exclaimed the pastor.

"That's really wonderful," said Madelyne. "I understand now

why neither of you had peace about the orphans you've looked at in the past."

Mary nodded. "Right. The Lord had Johnny all picked out for us."

Johnny looked up at the preacher. "Pastor Wheeler?"

"Yes, Johnny?"

"Sheriff Bos—I mean, Dad showed me in the Bible that I need to be baptized, now that I'm saved. He said I would have to talk to you about it. Can I be baptized Sunday?"

"You sure can. I'll be glad to baptize you."

Madelyne smiled at Johnny. "I'm eager for our children to meet you."

"I'd like to meet them. How many do you have?"

"Three. Cliff is fifteen. Eddie is thirteen. And Priscilla is eleven."

"I'll look forward to meeting them on Sunday, ma'am."

That evening when Clay came home, he presented Johnny with a beautiful new Bible. Johnny was thrilled with it and said he would read it every day.

The next morning, Clay Bostin went to Judge Howard Ackerson and told him the story. The judge began the paperwork so the sheriff and his wife could make Johnny Smith their adopted son.

Clay then headed for the Western Union office to send a wire to the Children's Aid Society and let them know that he and Mary were in the process of adopting Johnny. When he entered the office, agent Gerald Pearson greeted him with a smile.

"Hello, Sheriff! I was about to bring a telegram to you. It just came ten minutes ago." He picked the envelope up from the desk and handed it to him. "It's from Charles Loring Brace."

"Oh, good!"

Clay opened the envelope, took out the telegram, and smiled as he read it.

Pearson grinned. "I thought you'd like what he said."

Clay was pleased that Brace said since he was the El Paso County sheriff, he and his wife would not need to sign any papers. The telegram was their official notice that the Children's Aid Society was granting permission for them to become Johnny Smith's foster parents.

Clay looked up. "I sure do like what he said, Gerald. Only now I need to send a wire and inform Mr. Brace that Mary and I are going to adopt Johnny; and that Judge Howard Ackerson is now preparing the official papers."

"I'll get it right on the wire for you, Sheriff," said Pearson.

Two hours later, when Clay was busy at his desk in the sheriff's office, Pearson came in and handed him a telegram from Charles Loring Brace, congratulating the Bostins on the adoption.

Johnny was busy sweeping the back porch of the house for his new mother when the back door opened and he looked up to see his new father.

"Hi, Dad! I didn't realize it was time for you to be home."

Clay grinned. "Well, it's five-thirty. That's when I usually get home."

"Mom told me that, but I guess I've been so busy, I didn't realize how late it was."

"She tells me you've been working hard today."

"Yeah, and I like it."

"Good! We'll always have something for you to do around

here. Of course, we've got to get you enrolled in school. That'll keep you busy too."

Johnny grinned. "Sure will."

Clay pulled the telegrams out of his shirt pocket. "I need you to come inside. I've got some telegrams for you to read. I already showed them to Mom, but she wants to be with you when you read them."

"Okay."

They stepped into the kitchen, where Mary was busy at the stove. She turned and smiled. "Did you tell him who the telegrams are from?"

"No. I wanted you to see his face when I tell him, as well as when he reads them."

Johnny raised quizzical eyes. "Who are they from, Dad?"

"Charles Loring Brace."

Johnny's young features brightened. "Really?"

"Mm-hmm. Here, the first one is on top."

The boy's face beamed even more as he read the first telegram. Clay said, "Go ahead and read the other one."

When he had finished the second one, Johnny's countenance glowed. "Wow! This is great! A few weeks ago, I never would have dreamed that I would be living in the West and about to become the adopted son of a sheriff!"

The Bostins shared a happy smile at Johnny's exuberance.

Suddenly a serious frown puckered the boy's brow. Both Clay and Mary saw it instantly, and Mary's heart skipped a beat. A feeling of dread overtook the happy moment.

Clay put a hand on the boy's shoulder. "What's the matter?"

Johnny looked meekly at Clay, then at Mary, and cast his eyes down to the floor. As he tried to speak, the words caught in his throat.

Clay squeezed the shoulder gently. "Johnny, what is it? You

can talk to us about anything. We're a family now, and your feelings are important to us."

Johnny took a deep breath and cleared his throat. "Well, it's just that I love you both very much already, and I'm so pleased to be your son, but—"

Mary caressed Johnny's head. "What is it, honey?"

Johnny swallowed hard. "I…I still love my real parents too. I will never forget them and the home I had with them. The memories will always be with me." He looked up at both of them hesitantly. "W-would that be okay with you?"

Mary hugged him. "Johnny, dear, we would never want you to forget your real parents. They are the special ones who gave you life. Dad and I will always be grateful to them for raising such a wonderful son."

"Johnny, we would like very much for you to share anything you care to about your real parents. We want to help you keep them alive in your heart."

Johnny's voice cracked as he looked up at Clay. "Really?"

"Really."

"Yes, really," put in Mary. "We will go on from here, making good memories for you, but we also want you to bring along the memories from your life before you came to us."

Johnny sensed a special new bond between himself and the Bostins. Running his gaze between them, he said, "I'll be so proud to have the same last name as you. I'm glad that I have all my tomorrows to be Johnny Bostin."

Mary smiled. "That's a beautiful way to put it, Johnny. *'All my tomorrows.'* Did you make that up?"

"No, ma'am. Those words came from Dad the night he saved my life at the cave. When I thanked him for staying on our trail and for saving my life, he said, 'I wanted you to have all your tomorrows.'"

More tears flooded Mary's eyes. She put an arm around Clay and the other around Johnny. "I'm thankful to the Lord and to my husband, son, that you will indeed have all your tomorrows."

Chapter Sixteen

On Saturday at breakfast, while her two men were wolfing down pancakes and maple syrup, Mary Bostin said, "Clay, dear, I've been thinking. I'd like to have the Wheeler family for Sunday dinner after the morning service tomorrow."

Clay swallowed a mouthful of pancake. "Sure, honey. Be all right with me. Any special reason, or are you just wanting to have them again since it's been a while?"

"Well, it has been a while, but I do have a special reason for doing it tomorrow if they can come. Johnny will meet Cliff, Eddie, and Priscilla at church in the morning, but I would like for him to get to know them better. He'll have a better chance to get acquainted with them over dinner."

"Good idea, sweetheart. That sound all right to you, son?"

Johnny said around a mouthful of pancake, "Sure, Dad. I want to make new friends as soon as I can."

"Good," said Mary. "Honey, will you stop by the parsonage on your way to the office this morning and invite them?"

"Be glad to. And should they already have other plans, I'll swing back home and tell you."

"Fine. If I don't see you by nine o'clock, I'll figure everything is all right, and I can begin making extra bread and such."

When the Bostins arrived at church the next morning, Madelyne Wheeler had her three children with her on the porch, watching for the Bostins and their new son to arrive.

As the trio made their way up the steps, Madelyne and her children moved up to meet them.

"Good morning!" Madelyne said.

"Good morning," came three voices in unison.

"Johnny," said Madelyne, "I want you to meet my children. Cliff, Eddie, Priscilla, this is Johnny Smith, soon to be Johnny Bostin."

Cliff stepped forward first and shook Johnny's hand. "Glad to meet you, Johnny. Welcome to Colorado Springs and to our church."

"Thanks, Cliff. I'm glad to be here."

Eddie was next. As he shook Johnny's hand, he smiled. "Hi, Johnny. Mama said you're twelve, right?"

"Sure am."

"Well, I'm only a year older than you. Cliff thinks he's big stuff, since he's fifteen. Maybe you and I can do some things together, okay?"

"Swell!"

Cliff put on a disgusted look. "Eddie, I'm not too old to do things with you and Johnny. Maybe we can go fishing. Would you like that, Johnny?"

"Sure, Cliff. I've never been fishing before, but it sounds fun."

There was a feminine clearing of throat.

Cliff looked around. "Oh, excuse us. Shall I introduce her, Mama?"

Madelyne nodded. "Go ahead."

Cliff took his sister by the arm and pulled her up to Johnny. "This is Priscilla."

She offered her hand and Johnny took it gently. "Hi, Priscilla. I'm glad to meet you."

"I'm glad to meet you too, Johnny. I'm eleven. Since I'm just a year younger than you, we can be pals, can't we?"

"Of course," said Johnny, releasing her hand. Cliff and Eddie both had blond hair. He was amazed that Priscilla's hair was black like shiny velvet. She had a sweet smile, and she was very pretty. Johnny thought she was the prettiest girl he had ever seen.

As they entered the building, Madelyne told Clay and Mary how much they were looking forward to Sunday dinner.

Johnny was guided to the Sunday school class of twelve- to fourteen-year-old boys by Eddie.

Later in the morning service, Johnny was sitting with the Bostins in their favorite pew, and periodically glanced at Priscilla, who sat with her brothers across the aisle. Their mother was in the choir.

After a few hymns were sung, Pastor Dan Wheeler stepped to the pulpit and made his regular announcements. Before taking the offering, he had Johnny stand up and introduced him to the congregation. He told Johnny's story in brief, then explained that Sheriff Clay Bostin had led him to the Lord after rescuing him, adding that the Bostins were going to adopt him.

There were amens among the crowd, who had prayed earnestly for the boy while the sheriff was riding to the rescue.

There was another hymn sung, then the choir did a special number. The pastor preached the sermon, and when the invitation was given, Johnny walked the aisle and presented himself for baptism. Pastor Wheeler asked him to give his testimony of salvation to the congregation, which he gladly did. He was baptized immediately.

At the Bostin house that afternoon, Johnny had opportunity to get to know the Wheeler children better. He liked the boys very much, and they felt the same about him. Though Priscilla talked less than her brothers, Johnny felt her warmth toward him. He noted that every time he looked at her, she graced him with a smile. He already felt that she was a special pal. He glanced at her often, just to get another smile.

That night when Johnny and the Bostins arrived home after the evening service, they sat down at the kitchen table for a light snack. While they were eating, Clay said, "Hey, son, I noticed something today."

"What's that, Dad?"

"You seem to have eyes for Priscilla. Not only were you looking at her quite often at dinner, but in the service tonight, you kept glancing across the aisle. I don't think you were looking at her brothers."

Johnny's face tinted. "Well, ah…she is a real nice girl. And I have to say that I don't think I've ever seen one so pretty."

Mary smiled. "I think she has eyes for you too, Johnny."

Johnny's face turned a deeper shade of red than before.

In San Bernardino, California, when the choosing had been done by the prospective foster parents, there were two girls and three boys remaining. All five were showing their dejection when Royce Nelson came running from the terminal building with a smile on his face.

The children and the sponsors saw him coming and waited to hear his news.

Drawing up Royce said, "Praise the Lord! The terminal manager just showed me a telegram from Mr. Brace. Johnny Smith has been rescued! It was Sheriff Clay Bostin who rescued him.

And guess what! The sheriff and his wife have taken him into their home and are going to adopt him!"

The three remaining boys were Teddy Hansen, Jerry Varnell, and Clint Albright. Though the boys were feeling dejected because they had not yet been chosen, they rejoiced to learn that their friend had been rescued and was going to be adopted. As the orphans boarded their respective coaches, the girls also showed their relief that Johnny was all right, but their sponsors could easily read the disappointment they were feeling about their own state.

The train pulled out, heading for its last stop—Los Angeles. In the girls' coach, Lorinda Radcliff, Shelley Nelson, and Mandy Hillen did their best to encourage the girls. They pointed out that Los Angeles was a large city, and that there were always a good number of couples at the railroad station seeking orphans to take home. Certainly they would be chosen this time. The girls were encouraged, and their countenances brightened.

In the boys' coach, though they were glad for the good news about Johnny Smith, Teddy, Jerry, and Clint were battling their own dejection.

Dale Radcliff and Royce Nelson were trying hard to encourage them, using the same reasoning the women were using with the girls.

Dale put a big grin on his face. "And, fellas, you ought to be glad that all three of you are still together! At least this way, when you're chosen in Los Angeles, you'll be near to each other and can see each other periodically in the years to come."

Dale's words served to perk up Teddy. Eyes suddenly sparkling, he said, "That's for certain sure, Mr. Radcliff!"

Teddy, like the other two boys, had lived the entire trip in fear that they would be separated. Now it seemed that even if they weren't all chosen by the same family, they would at least live in the same vicinity.

Suddenly an uninvited thought invaded Teddy's mind. His eyes lost their luster and a deep frown creased his brow.

"What is it, Teddy?" Dale said.

The boy cleared his throat. "I just thought of something."

"What?"

Clint, Jerry, and Royce looked on.

"Well, what if one or two of us aren't chosen in Los Angeles? We would be sent back to New York and probably never see each other again." His lower lip quivered as he tried to stop embarrassing himself by crying.

Dale laid a hand on his shoulder. "Teddy, keep this one thing in mind. God is in control of each of our lives, and he already has a plan for all three of you. Don't fret so. God knows what you and Clint and Jerry need, better than you do."

Teddy wiped his sleeve over his eyes and his ever-ready smile replaced the frown. "That's for certain sure! He will take care of us, won't He?"

When the train pulled into the Los Angeles depot, the two girls and the three boys formed their short line and the prospective foster parents began their inspection. Indeed, there was a long line of them.

The first couple to approach the orphans smiled at the boys, and the woman said, "Sorry, boys, we're looking for a girl."

They chose the first girl they came to and took her to Lorinda Radcliff so they could get the paperwork done.

The next couple paused in front of the boys, and the man started asking Clint questions. At the same time, his wife moved to the remaining girl and began talking to her.

After a few minutes, the man called to his wife: "Dear, I like this boy. His name is Clint Albright. Let's take him."

Teddy and Jerry exchanged fearful glances.

The woman shook her head. "No, dear. I want this girl."

They argued for a moment; then the man shrugged. "All right, we'll take the girl." He looked at Clint. "Sorry."

Clint managed a thin smile.

When the man walked away, Teddy let out a big sigh of relief. "Boy, Clint, I sure thought that man was gonna take you. I'm glad he didn't. I mean, unless you really wanted to go with him."

"Naw. I don't want to go anywhere unless both the husband and wife want me. It just wouldn't work. I already lived in a family like that with my real parents. It was my father who didn't want me. I don't want that situation again."

The boys stood close together, trying to look like they were not upset that they were the only ones left. But the hurt caused by the number of rejections was hard to bear.

Two more couples passed by, gave the three boys a glance, and left the depot.

Another couple drew up, but were already agreeing that they wanted a younger child.

The next couple was smiling at each other as they approached the boys. They looked to be in their late forties.

Teddy elbowed both his friends in the ribs. "Maybe these are the ones. They look nice and friendly."

"Yeah." Clint's voice was filled with doubt.

The smiles were then turned on the boys as the man said, "Hello, young men. My name is Marvin Dalby, and this is my wife, Doris. We would like to ask each of you some questions about yourselves."

All three had to give their life stories in brief, then Marvin Dalby looked at his wife, who smiled and said, "Yes!"

The boys looked at each other quizzically.

"Boys," said Dalby, "my wife and I own four large fruit

orchards east of Los Angeles. We came to the depot today, first of all to find three boys about your age whom we could adopt as sons, and secondly, by that adoption, to gain additional workers for our orchards."

Doris warmed all three with a smile. "As far as I'm concerned, you boys are an answer to prayer."

Teddy, Clint, and Jerry stood in mute astonishment.

"I assure you," said Marvin, "you will not be slave labor, as Doris and I know sometimes happens to orphan train children. But we will need your help, as any boys would help their natural parents. What do you say?"

The boys exchanged glances, eyes wide with wonder, and Clint said, "We would love to be your adopted sons, Mr. and Mrs. Dalby! We've been hoping all along that we'd be chosen by the same family. We're best friends, and this is what we've prayed for!"

Doris clapped her hands. "Oh, thank You, Lord!"

She quickly hugged each boy, saying how happy she was, and Marvin followed suit.

Jerry looked at both of them. "We'll be happy to do our share of the work."

Marvin said, "Now, boys, I want you to understand that your work will be done as it fits in with school. We want you to get your education."

The boys thanked him and said they would work hard in school and in the orchards.

Royce Nelson was called over. The Dalbys explained to him that they would sign the papers to become foster parents to the boys, but that they would seek adoption immediately. Royce was happy to hear it and told the boys how glad he was that the Lord made it possible for them to be taken into the same home.

Good-byes were said to all four sponsors and the nurse, and

the Dalbys ushered the boys out of the terminal toward the parking lot.

As they moved that direction, an ecstatic Teddy unleashed his exuberance. "It's happened, Clint! It's happened, Jerry! We're really gonna live together! Can you believe it?"

Clint laughed. "Yes, I believe it! The Lord did it for us, just like Mr. Radcliff said!"

"Yes!" said Jerry, wonder making his voice quiver. "It's like a dream come true! Only the Lord could do this!"

A broad smile captured Teddy's face from ear to ear. "It's a certain sure miracle, that's what it is! Thank You, God! Thank You!"

The Dalbys were thrilled to hear all three boys so maturely giving praise to the Lord.

On the ride toward the Dalby home in the buggy, the boys were full of questions, and the Dalbys took their time answering each one. As the miles slipped by, the boys felt more and more at home. Marvin and Doris smiled at each other as they listened to the boys talk among themselves.

Doris looked toward heaven. *Thank You, Lord. Like always in our lives, You have given above and beyond our greatest expectations!*

At Wild Horse, Colorado, Ken and Molly Talbert left the judge's office that afternoon with Donna walking between them.

Donna's face was beaming. "Oh, this is so wonderful! I am now Donna Rae Talbert!"

She put an arm around each of her new adoptive parents. "Thank you for choosing me at the depot that day. Thank you for leading me to the Lord, and thank you now for adopting me!"

Molly hugged her in return. "Sweetie, we love you as if you were our natural daughter."

"That's for sure!" said Ken.

From the judge's office, the Talberts went to the general store. While Ken was picking up some items from the grocery shelves, Molly took Donna to the spot where several bolts of dress material were on display.

"Okay, Miss Donna Rae Talbert, pick out the material you like for new dresses."

Donna's eyes widened. "But, Mama, you've already made me three new dresses!"

Molly hugged her. "Well, you're about to get three more."

Half an hour later, Ken loaded the groceries into the back of the buckboard, helped the ladies up onto the seat, then climbed up beside Donna, who sat in the middle. A broad smile creased his tanned face as he said, "Well, ladies, now that our shopping is done, let's go celebrate the adoption. We'll have supper at the hotel restaurant. Donna, they have the biggest pieces of chocolate cake you've ever seen."

Donna giggled. "That sounds good to me, Papa. I'm so excited, though. I don't know if I can do a big piece of cake justice, but I'll sure try."

Ken drove the three blocks to the hotel, helped the ladies down from the seat, and ushered them into the restaurant.

Replete with roast beef and mashed potatoes and all the trimmings, topped off with pieces of chocolate cake, the Talbert family left the restaurant in high spirits.

Once again on the buckboard seat with Donna in the middle, Ken put the team to a trot and headed out of town. The rim of the golden sun was barely visible on the western horizon. For a while, they talked together, reminiscing over the events of the day and moving on to the plans for their future.

Soon they grew quiet, with each one lost in their own reverie as twilight settled over the land.

Molly's attention was suddenly drawn to Donna when she felt a shiver go through the girl's body. Thinking the cooler air was getting to her, Molly turned to ask if she was cold and saw the tears cascading down her cheeks.

Molly frowned. "Sweetie, what are you crying about?"

Donna wiped tears. "Deena."

Molly patted her arm. "Of course. I know you miss her terribly."

"That I do, Mama. But it's worse because I know she is very unhappy. I'm sure of it. My heart goes out to her. Here I am, so happy with such wonderful parents. But I just know it isn't the same for Deena."

Molly squeezed her arm. "We must continue to pray earnestly for Deena."

"Yes," said Ken. "It won't be too long now, Donna, until we can make the trip to Salina so you can see her."

Donna wiped away more tears. "I can hardly wait."

At the Dexter farm in Kansas, Deena Mitchell was trying daily to come up with a way to run away without being caught.

One night Deena dreamed that she and Donna were together in a field of green grass and wildflowers. They were holding hands and skipping delightfully across the field. Deena couldn't remember when she had been so happy.

Suddenly in the dream, Donna's hand slipped from Deena's and she disappeared. Deena cried out for her and the sound of her own voice awakened her.

With the dream so fresh in her mind, Deena sat up. "Donna! Oh, Donna! Come back!"

Suddenly her bedroom door swung open and an angry Ralph Dexter stepped in, clad in his nightshirt, holding a lantern.

"I'm sick of you crying about your sister, girl! You woke me up bellowing for her! Now stop it!"

Deena was sobbing. "I dreamed about her. We were together in the dream, then she was gone."

Moving up to the bed, Ralph put a tight pinch on Deena's shoulder and shook her. "You've got to stop this pining for your sister, girl! You hear me? Forget her!"

Norma padded into the room, wiping her eyes as Deena said, "I can't help it, Mr. Dexter. The bond between Donna and me is much stronger than the bond between regular siblings. Please help me find her."

Norma moved close and touched the hand that was pinching Deena's shoulder. Ralph let go and looked at her as she said, "Deena, honey, you can't let this bond between you and Donna tear you to pieces. There is no way we can find Donna. She could be anywhere between Salina and Los Angeles. That's a lot of territory. It would be impossible."

"She's right! Now, you forget that twin of yours. Face it. You're never gonna see her again."

Deena became hysterical. "I can't forget her, you beast! We are part of each other! Donna's missing me as much as I'm missing her! I've got to find her! I've got to find her! I've got to find her-r-r!"

Deena's high-pitched screams infuriated Ralph Dexter. He slapped her face so hard, it knocked her out of the bed. She hit the floor, still screaming at him.

Fear filled Norma as she saw the awful expression on Ralph's red face. Her hand went to her mouth and she bit down on her fingers as Ralph stomped to Deena and stood over her, breathing hotly.

Deena's entire body was trembling and her eyes were wild. She raised up on her knees, her face wet with tears. "How can you be so mean? You're a beast, that's what you are! You're a horrible beast!"

Ralph's beefy features turned thunder black. "Stop screaming at me!"

Deena felt only hatred for the man. "You're a wicked beast! I don't have to obey you!"

He slapped her again, knocking her flat. He headed for the door, saying to Norma over his shoulder, "She's gonna feel my belt again!"

When Ralph vanished through the door and stomped down the hall, Norma knelt beside Deena. "Honey, calm down. You know about his uncontrollable temper."

Deena's eyes were glazed. She stared Norma's direction, but couldn't seem to focus on her face.

"Deena," Norma said softly, "don't scream at him, honey. Don't talk back to him. It only makes him—"

Ralph's heavy footsteps could be heard, growing louder.

"Worse," concluded Norma as the man stomped through the door, belt in hand.

The wrath on Ralph's face was terrible to behold. He rudely shoved Norma aside. "Get outta the way! Go back to bed!"

She fell to the floor and rose quickly, glancing at Deena with pain-filled eyes as she headed toward the door. She knew if she tried to argue with Ralph, it would only make things worse for Deena, as well as herself.

Ralph turned to watch Norma go, and when he turned back, Deena was on her feet but staggering. He grabbed her and threw her on the bed facedown.

When Norma reached the hall, she stopped just out of view from the door and leaned against the wall, throwing her hands to her face. She heard the belt whistling and striking Deena repeatedly as her husband railed at her, saying she had better never disobey him again, and she had better never call him a beast again. With each blow, Deena whined pitifully.

The lashing went on for what seemed an eternity.

Finally, it stopped, and Norma hurried back to their bedroom.

She was sitting on the edge of the bed when Ralph returned and threw his belt on the chair where his trousers were draped. Deena could be heard sobbing.

Ralph stood over his wife. "I suppose you want to go stop her bleeding."

Norma looked up at him, her face pale. "I…I'd better."

"Well, go on. I left the lantern in there. I'm going back to sleep."

When Norma returned to the room, she found a sobbing Deena lying on the bed. She had pulled her nightgown over her legs, but there were blood spots on it. Deena looked up through tear-filled eyes, but said nothing.

Norma said softly, "Would you turn over for me, honey?"

Deena gritted her teeth as she turned over.

Norma lifted Deena's nightgown and saw red welts on her back, buttocks, and the backside of her legs. Some of them were oozing blood.

"Lie still, honey. I'll get some water and cloths. I'll wrap the places where you're still bleeding."

It took Norma about twenty minutes to treat Deena's wounds. After pulling the nightgown back down over the crude bandages, she said, "There you are, Deena. I'm sure the bleeding will stop soon. You try to get some sleep now."

The girl rolled onto her back and pulled up the covers. Through lips that barely moved, she said, "Thank you, ma'am. I appreciate your kindness."

Norma leaned down and kissed her forehead. "I love you, honey. I wish I could keep you, but I can't blame you for wanting to run away. Just be extremely careful when you do it."

"I will. Thank you, again."

Deena awakened several times in the night and the pain lanced through her back and legs. She was awakened by more pain at sunrise and decided to get out of bed. She checked the wounds and found that the bleeding had stopped.

She moved gingerly to the dresser and observed herself in the mirror. There were purple bruises on her cheeks where Ralph had slapped her. While brushing her hair and dressing for the day, she told herself she must find a way of escape soon.

Chapter Seventeen

As Deena Mitchell left her room and headed toward the kitchen, she grimaced from the pain that walking brought to the welts on her body.

There was grim determination within her. *I'll be successful next time. No power on earth will keep me here a day longer than absolutely necessary. That beast will never beat me again.*

Just as Deena was about to pass Rex's room, the door opened. She thought about hurrying to avoid him, but she knew it would intensify her pain.

Rex spotted her instantly and stepped in front of her, blocking her path.

She gave him a bland look and made a step sideways to get around him, but he countered by moving in front of her.

Anger surged through her. "Get out of my way."

Rex sneered. "When Pa and I were doin' chores this mornin', he told me what happened last night. You got pretty sassy, I hear. I hope you've learned your lesson."

Deena burned him with hot eyes. "Will you get out of my way? I'm going to help your mother with breakfast."

"She's got it about done. That's where I'm headed. I'll walk to the kitchen with you."

Deena ignored him as he moved along beside her. When they entered the kitchen, Norma was at the stove. Deena saw that the table had already been set. Leaving Rex behind, she moved to Norma and said, "Mrs. Dexter, I would have helped you with breakfast if you had—"

"It's all right, honey. I figured you needed to rest. I'm sure you didn't sleep well after—well, you know."

At that instant, Ralph came into the kitchen. He gave Deena a cold look, then said to Norma, "Breakfast ready?"

"Yes. Let's all get seated."

When everyone was in their place, Ralph said, "We're all going into town today. We need groceries and supplies."

Later, when they pulled away from the house, Norma was beside Ralph on the driver's seat, and Rex and Deena were sitting in the wagon bed. Norma had provided a folded blanket for Deena to sit on, but as they headed toward town, Deena winced at the times when the wagon hit bumps in the road.

When they had hit an especially hard bump and Deena let out a tiny cry, Rex looked at her with eyes the color of slate. "Maybe the pain you're feelin' will remind you never to talk sassy to Pa again."

Deena gave him a sullen look, but did not reply. She was more determined than ever to get away from the Dexter farm.

While the wagon rocked along, Norma turned around. "Deena, Ralph and I have been talking about this. We want you to stay in the wagon when we get to town. We don't want anyone to see those bruises on your face. Keep your bonnet low over your face and don't talk to anyone."

Deena nodded. "I'll do as you say, ma'am, but if you didn't want anyone to see me, why didn't you just leave me home?"

Ralph looked over his shoulder. "Norma suggested that, girl, but I told her I don't trust you. If we left you alone at the house, you might get the wild idea of running away like you did that day. So you'll just have to stay in the back of the wagon."

Rex was grinning at Deena when his father said, "Rex, I want you to stay with her."

Rex's grin faded. "Why, Pa?"

"Like I said, I don't trust her. She just might decide to hop out of the wagon and run away."

Rex knew better than to argue with his father. "Okay, Pa. I'll stay with her so she don't pull somethin' like that."

Deena continually adjusted herself on the blanket as the wagon bounced along the road. *One way or another, the day will come when my opportunity will present itself. I'll get away from the Dexter prison farm forever!*

Soon they were drawing near Salina. Norma pointed off to the edge of town. "Look! A wagon train!"

The other three looked to see the wagon train, which was parked in a circle just outside of town on the south side.

"Folks from the east heading for a new life out West," Ralph said.

Deena found herself wishing she was traveling in one of the covered wagons.

They drew into town, and moments later Ralph parked the wagon on the street in the business section of Salina. Rex hopped out and helped his mother down from the seat while his father climbed out.

Ralph paused at the tailgate and set firm eyes on Deena. "You stay there, girl, and like you were told, keep your bonnet low over your face and don't talk to anyone, y'hear?"

Deena nodded.

"Rex will be watching you," Ralph said. "If you disobey, he'll tell me. And you'll get another beating like last night. You want that?"

"No."

Ralph stepped up to Norma. "All right, let's go."

As they moved down the street, Rex looked at Deena from where he stood beside the wagon. "I'm gonna sit over here on this bench in front of the hardware store. I'll be watchin' you every minute."

Deena gave him a cool stare.

Rex crossed the boardwalk and sat down on the unoccupied bench.

Moments later, Deena's attention was drawn to a group of people moving together along the boardwalk. She could tell by what they were saying to each other that they were from the wagon train that was parked outside of town.

She heard one woman remind another that the wagon train would be pulling out at eleven-thirty. Deena glanced at the clock in front of the Salina Bank building across the street. It was nine-forty.

The wagon train group moved on down the street and a few minutes later, Deena noticed three teenage girls coming along the boardwalk. One of them spotted the blond boy on the bench in front of the hardware store. "Hey, there's Rex!"

All three hurried toward him, and as Rex saw them coming, he rose from the bench to meet them. His attention was fixed, however, on the pretty redhead in the middle. "Hello, Bonnie." Then he greeted the other two. "Hi, Lulu, Charlene."

All three replied at once, and Rex and Bonnie struck up a conversation while Lulu and Charlene observed. Deena noted that as Rex was occupied talking to Bonnie, he shifted position every few seconds until his back was toward the wagon. As the conversation went on, he remained fixed in that position.

The constant stream of people who passed by on the board-walk was between Rex and the girls and the wagon.

Deena's heart pounded as she told herself her opportunity had come. She would slip out of the wagon on the street side and make her way to the wagon train at the south edge of town. She would find a woman in the wagon train and explain her plight. A glimpse of her welts and stripes would show she was telling the truth. Certainly, that woman and her husband would take her with them in their covered wagon and help her escape the Dexters.

She checked Rex's position. It was the same. He was totally wrapped up in his conversation with the pretty redhead. People were still moving by, and for the most part, blocking the view of the Dexter wagon from where Rex and the girls stood.

The prospect of escape pumped adrenaline throughout Deena's body. She was completely unaware of the pain and stiff-ness as she went over the side of the wagon bed and dropped to the street. Moving in a crouch, she kept the bonnet low over her face and her head tilted down in case someone among the rela-tively few in the Salina area who knew her would recognize her.

Deena quickly moved between the Dexter wagon and the next one behind it and made her way along the boardwalk, filter-ing into the crowd. She paused for a moment and looked back. Rex was still occupied with Bonnie.

Pressing on, she turned the corner and headed down a side street in the direction of the wagon train. Up ahead, she saw some of the wagon train people she had seen before. They were carrying full shopping bags and heading the same direction. Ignoring her pain, she hurried up behind them and followed close, unnoticed.

When the group reached the wagon train and moved inside the circle of wagons, the desperate girl went in as part of the group, still unnoticed.

Deena's mind was spinning. The women were all collected in one spot, talking about items they had bought in town. The men also were caught up in conversation. There were children laughing and playing just outside the circle.

There was no woman at that moment that Deena could single out, but she knew someone would recognize her as a stranger to the wagon train soon if she just stood there. She decided it would be best to climb into one of the covered wagons and wait till whatever woman was attached to it showed up.

She looked around and spotted a covered wagon that appeared to be unoccupied at the moment. She hurried to the wagon. Making sure no one was inside or watching her from within the circle of wagons, she climbed over the tailgate. Dropping quickly to her knees, she noted cardboard boxes placed in a line along one side, clothing piled in one corner, a couple of wooden chairs next to a small round table, and a cot that was against the side opposite the cardboard boxes.

She looked down at one of the boxes and saw lettering on its top. It read:

Mr. and Mrs. Brian Parker
General Delivery
Crown Point, Indiana

So these people are from Indiana, Deena thought. *I sure hope Mrs. Parker has a soft place in her heart for teenage girls...especially one who has been beaten with a belt. Mr. Parker too, for that matter.*

Deena heard voices outside, drawing near. She decided to hide under the cot. Going down on her stomach, she scooted under the cot and lay on her side with her back to the side of the wagon bed.

Holding her breath while her heart pounded in her chest, she heard the people talking as they passed by the wagon. She breathed a sigh of relief and began to come up with a plan as to how she would let the Parkers know they had an uninvited rider in their wagon.

As she thought on it, she decided it would be best to stay concealed until the wagon train had left Salina and had gone several miles further west. Once they had heard her story, it would be more difficult to turn around and take her back to Salina—if they still had a mind to—than to keep her with them at least until they reached their destination out West.

After another hour or so, Deena could tell that the rest of the wagon train people were arriving from town. She figured it had to be getting close to eleven-thirty. She grew tense when she heard the voices of a man and woman as they drew up behind the wagon. They were talking about the bargains they had found at the stores in Salina.

Deena pushed her head toward the edge of the cot to get a glimpse of them, and saw the man drop the tailgate. She guessed that he might be in his late thirties. She pulled back when he picked up two grocery sacks, placed them in the wagon, and shoved them as far forward as he could. They came to rest against the cardboard boxes on that side of the wagon.

Suddenly there was another voice. It was an older woman, who said, "How are you feeling, Valerie? Was the walk into town too much for you?"

"No, Greta, I did all right." She paused. "But I will say that I'm glad I can rest now."

The older woman warned her not to get too tired, and as Deena listened to the conversation, she learned that Valerie Parker had been ill the past several days on the trail and had spent much of her time in the back of the wagon, resting on the cot.

Suddenly the deep voice of the wagon master was calling for the wagons to get ready to roll.

"Okay, sweetheart," said Brian, "let's get you inside. I want you on that cot for the rest of the trip today."

Deena peeked and watched the man lift his wife and place her in the wagon. He then climbed in behind her.

While Deena's nerves felt like they were going to snap, Brian helped Valerie lie down on the cot and put a pillow under her head, making sure she was comfortable. He then hopped out and closed the tailgate. "See if you can get some sleep, sweetheart."

"I'm sure I will," Valerie responded.

Deena heard the man climb into the seat, and less than a minute later, the booming voice of the wagon master filled the air. "Wagons ho-o-o!"

Brian put the team in motion as the wagon train pulled out.

Deena lay under the cot, barely breathing. The rocking and bumping of the wagon shot pain through her wounds and sore muscles. She clenched her teeth at times, but managed not to cry out. After a while, the trail seemed to smooth out some, and she relaxed her stiff body.

She had caught a glimpse of Valerie Parker's face when her husband lifted her into the wagon, and she looked like a kind lady. *Maybe I'll be all right. They seem like nice people. I'll just have to reveal myself at the proper time and hope for the best when they hear my story. My stripes and bruises will certainly back up what I say.*

Deena adjusted her body carefully and found, if not a comfortable position, at least a tolerable one.

As the miles rolled slowly by, Deena found herself tensing up again as she contemplated revealing herself to the Parkers and having to convince them how desperately she needed their help.

She tried to remain calm, but felt a tension growing within her.

I'm frightened, yes, she told herself, *but not as frightened as I would be if I was still with the Dexters. This has just got to turn out all right.*

Back in Salina, Ralph and Norma Dexter were in the general store, carrying some packages from purchases made in other stores when they met up with neighboring farmer Will Dutton and his wife, Althea.

"Howdy, neighbors," said Will Dutton. "Nice to see you."

"You too," said Ralph.

Looking around, Althea asked, "Rex and Deena not with you?"

Norma shook her head. "Ah…no. Deena developed an upset stomach on the way into town. She's lying in the back of the wagon. Rex is with her."

"I'm sorry to hear she's sick. I hope she gets better quickly."

"I'm sure she will. You know how kids are."

"Yes, we sure do, since we have four of our own."

"Well, honey," said Will, "we'd best be on the move. Lots to do while we're in town. See you later, neighbors."

The Duttons moved on.

The Dexters completed picking up what items they needed and headed for the counter. They had just paid the clerk when Norma saw her son come through the door.

Rex rushed up to them. "We've got a problem."

Looking around, Ralph said, "Grab some of these sacks, Rex. You can tell us outside."

As they were passing through the door, all three bearing sacks, Norma said, "Rex, you shouldn't have left Deena."

"Yes," said Ralph as they moved outside. "What did you leave her for?"

"That's the problem, Pa. I didn't leave her. She left me."

Ralph's features darkened. "You mean she's outta the wagon?"

"Yes, and I don't know where she went."

"Oh dear," said Norma.

Ralph glowered at his son. "You were supposed to be watching her!"

"I was, Pa. Bonnie and a couple of her friends came by, and I was talkin' to them right there on the boardwalk. Somehow Deena got away without my seein' her."

They were heading in the direction of the wagon.

Ralph swore under his breath and set angry eyes on Rex. "You were supposed to keep her in that wagon!"

Norma took a deep breath. "Oh, now what are we going to do? What are we going to tell the people who see the bruises on her face?"

"Why not tell them the truth?" said Ralph. "No one would blame me for smacking her for talking back to me like she did. Whoever sees her ain't gonna see the stripes under her dress. We'll put this stuff in the wagon, then split up and find her."

As they moved hurriedly along the boardwalk, Norma looked through the windows of the shops and stores to see if she could catch a glimpse of Deena.

She bit her lower lip. *Oh, what's Ralph going to do this time when he gets his hands on her?*

Suddenly, Norma realized what had happened. Deena had found the opportunity she had been looking for and took it. *I hope this time she's successful.*

Still looking through the shop and store windows, Norma made a pretense of searching for the girl, but secretly she was hoping against hope that Deena had somehow made her escape and that they wouldn't find her.

Rex said, "Pa, maybe Deena will think it over and be waitin' at the wagon."

"I sure hope so. She'll pay if she is. She'll have more bruises than ever when I get through with her."

When they drew up to the wagon, there was no sign of Deena. *Good girl,* thought Norma.

They placed their packages in the wagon, and Ralph gave orders to his wife and son so the family would search in three directions. They would meet back at the wagon.

It was nearly two o'clock when the Dexters met at the wagon, having covered every store and shop without finding Deena or anyone who had seen her. Norma had resolved that if she found the girl, she would encourage her to make good her escape.

Ralph said they would get in the wagon and drive all over town and see if they could spot her. They would ask people in every block if they had seen her.

It was almost four o'clock. The Dexters had covered every street with no sign of Deena.

Trying to appease Ralph, Norma said, "Maybe for some reason she walked home."

Ralph guffawed. "I doubt that, but we'll see."

He galloped the team all the way home, but when they entered the house, Deena was nowhere to be found. Ralph's anger had him breathing heavily as he told his wife and son the only thing they could do now was to go back to the town marshal's office and report her as missing.

They quickly unloaded the goods from the wagon and galloped the wagon back to town.

All three entered the office of Marshal Garth Yeoman. His two deputies, Bud Nolan and Thomas Long, were there with him.

With his wife and son beside him, Ralph reported their foster daughter as missing, explaining that they had searched the town over and could not find her. They also went home to see if she had gone there, but she had not.

Marshal Yeoman said, "Ralph, my daughter Melinda is Deena's age, and in different stores in town, the two of them have had private conversations. On several occasions, Melinda told my wife and me that Deena was very unhappy in her foster home. She has probably run away."

The Dexters were inwardly upset to learn that Deena had been telling people she was unhappy.

Ralph cleared his throat. "Well, Marshal, Deena's been having a difficult time adjusting to farm life. She's a city girl, and it's been pretty tough on her. That's all she's been unhappy about. Can you help us find her?"

Yeoman said, "You didn't knock on every door in town, did you?"

"No. We just covered every store and shop and drove up and down all the streets, asking people if they had seen her."

The marshal rubbed his chin thoughtfully. "Maybe Deena has gone to some family in town, told them a sad story, and asked them to hide her. Since she is so unhappy, she might be able to persuade someone to take her in and shelter her."

Deputy Thomas Long said, "Marshal, I'm thinking about that wagon train that was parked outside of town last night and this morning. It didn't leave till eleven-thirty. Maybe Deena went to the wagon train and was able to persuade one of the families to take her with them."

Yeoman nodded. "Anything's possible. You and Bud get on your horses, catch up to that wagon train, and see if Deena is among them. In the meantime, I'll organize some townsmen to knock on every door in town, and I'll have some others make a circle on horseback within a fifteen-mile radius of the town. I'll have them knock on every farmer and rancher's door."

"Marshal, we really appreciate this," said Ralph.

Yeoman smiled thinly. "We'll do everything we can. Give my deputies and me a description of Deena. I'll pass it on to the two groups of townsmen, since everybody doesn't know her."

Norma set soft eyes on the marshal, knowing she must appear to be siding with Ralph. "Thank you so much, Marshal. And you too, Deputies."

Yeoman nodded. "I just hope we find her, ma'am."

"Marshal," said Ralph, "I'll give you and your deputies Deena's description, then Rex and I will take Norma home. We'll come right back to be in one of those search parties."

Yeoman nodded. "Fine, Ralph. Shake a leg, though. I've got to get this search in motion."

Chapter Eighteen

Ralph Dexter pulled the wagon to a halt in front of the house. Rex hopped out of the wagon bed and helped his mother down from the seat.

When Norma's feet touched ground, she turned and looked up at her husband. "Ralph, if you find Deena, please, please don't beat on her."

A scarlet flush started at Ralph's shirt collar and moved up his thick neck. "She's gonna get what she deserves," he said through his clenched teeth. "C'mon, Rex. Get in."

Rex climbed up onto the seat and looked back at his mother as his father snapped the reins and put the team to a gallop.

A shaky hand went to Norma's mouth as she watched the bouncing wagon move up the lane toward the road. "Oh, Deena, wherever you are, don't let them find you. Go, honey. Go!"

The sun was lowering in the western sky, and it was almost time to put the train in a circle as wagon master Lester Corbin was trotting his horse back along the line of covered wagons. His attention was drawn suddenly to two riders who were coming from the east at a full gallop.

Corbin kept his horse moving toward the rear of the train and had just passed the last wagon when the riders drew up. He instantly saw the badges on their vests.

"Something I can do for you, gentlemen?"

"I believe your name is Les Corbin, sir," said the lawman on his left.

"That's right."

"Mr. Corbin, I'm Deputy Marshal Bud Nolan and this is Deputy Marshal Thomas Long. We're from Salina."

"Yes?"

Nolan told him of the thirteen-year-old girl who was missing and explained in detail why they had come to the wagon train. He then gave the wagon master a description of Deena Mitchell.

Corbin raised his hat and scratched his head. "I haven't seen a girl of that description in the wagon train, but it's about time to stop for the night, anyway. I was plannin' on makin' camp up there by Watson's Creek. I'll put the wagons in their usual circle, then I'll let you gentlemen talk to all the people and ask if any of them have seen the girl."

"We'll appreciate that, Mr. Corbin," said Nolan.

Corbin wheeled his horse and quickly caught up to the train.

He trotted alongside the wagons, giving directions to the drivers to stop at the creek that was about a half mile ahead and form the circle.

Beneath the cot in the back of the Parker wagon, Deena Mitchell heard the wagon master's instructions. Her heart quickened pace. They were going to stop for the night, and she would have to reveal herself to the Parkers.

Soon the train was at the creek and forming the circle.

Valerie rose from the cot as Brian pulled the wagon to a halt. She did not notice that one of the grocery sacks had fallen over and three cantaloupes had rolled out onto the floor. One of them had rolled under the cot and had come to rest just inches from Deena's leg. Deena was not aware of it.

When the circle had been formed, Les Corbin trotted around its perimeter, telling everyone he wanted to meet with them immediately inside the circle. Some of the people saw the two riders closing in from the east, wondering who they were.

While the last of the children and adults were getting out of the wagons, Corbin led the two deputies inside the circle. They stood beside the wagon master while he said loudly, "Everyone gather right here, please."

Underneath the cot in the Parker wagon, Deena could clearly hear every word.

When the group had collected in a half-circle, looking at the lawmen with quizzical eyes, Corbin introduced the two deputies, explaining that they were from Salina. He told the people about the missing thirteen-year-old girl, whose name was Deena Mitchell.

In the Parker wagon, Deena's body stiffened at his words. They would search the wagons, find her, and take her back to Salina—and the wrath of Ralph Dexter! Her heart pounded her rib cage.

Corbin explained that Deena was living in a foster home, having been chosen from an orphan train, and was unhappy. The foster parents, Ralph and Norma Dexter, reported to Salina's Marshal Garth Yeoman early that afternoon that the girl was missing. They thought that she had run away and might have attempted to persuade one of the wagon train families to take her with them.

Beneath the cot, terror was ransacking Deena's mind and body.

Corbin turned to the deputies. "Will one of you gentlemen please give these people a description of Deena Mitchell?"

Bud Nolan took a step forward and ran his gaze over the faces in the crowd. "The foster parents gave us Deena's description. As you have already been told, she is thirteen years of age. She has blue eyes and auburn hair, which is long, reaching halfway down her back. She is five feet one inch in height and weighs ninety-two pounds. When she disappeared, she was wearing a blue-and-white–checked calico dress with a white collar and a white bonnet. Has anybody here seen her, and if so, are you hiding her in your wagon?"

Dead silence.

Deputy Thomas Long moved up beside his partner. "Folks, it is important for the Dexters to get their foster daughter back."

"I ask again, has anybody here seen her?" When there was total silence in the crowd, Deputy Bud Nolan said, "Thank you, folks. I appreciate your kind attention." Then he turned to his partner. "Well, Thomas, it's evident that Deena isn't here."

In her secret place, Deena heaved a sigh of relief.

The deputies thanked the wagon master for allowing them to talk to the people. They mounted up and rode away.

From just outside the Parker wagon, Deena heard Brian and Valerie talking with another couple about their stop back in Salina and about the missing girl.

Valerie said, "I sure hope they find her. Well, honey, if you'll lift me up into the wagon, I'll take the food for tonight's supper out of the grocery sacks."

The other woman said, "How about you two eating supper with us? We bought two extra beefsteaks in town so we could feed you tonight. Those steaks will spoil on us if you don't eat them."

Valerie said, "Okay, Louise, we'll eat supper with you if you'll let me help you cook it."

"It's a deal."

Deena heard both couples walk away and sighed with relief again. Silence seemed to fill the wagon. Soon a rumble of muffled voices could be heard from the fire in the middle of the circle, where the wagon train women were doing their cooking. There was a mixture of other sounds while the men did jobs around the wagons.

Slowly releasing her pent-up breath, Deena slightly changed her position, giving her cramped muscles some relief. Fresh pain arose from her wounds.

Soon she heard the happy chatter of adults and children who were sitting down to enjoy their evening meal.

After a while, a welcome breeze floated through the wagon, and once again, she searched for a more comfortable position, knowing it would not be long until the Parkers returned to their wagon.

Running her dry tongue over equally dry lips, she longed for a drink of water. *Might as well think of something else to take my mind off my thirst. At least for the moment, I'm safe.*

Breathing deeply again, Deena relaxed as much as possible in her hiding place. Her eyes grew heavy with fatigue, but she forced them to stay open, telling herself she could not have the luxury of sleep until she had revealed her presence and they had all settled down for the night. But how was she going to do this? She still must come up with the best plan.

When Deputies Bud Nolan and Thomas Long arrived back in town, it was almost dark. They drew up to the hitch rail in front of the marshal's office, noting that a lantern was burning inside. They dismounted, entered the office, and found elderly Buck Patterson sitting at the marshal's desk. He gave them a toothless smile. "Howdy, boys. Marshal Yeoman and his search groups are still out lookin' fer that girl. The marshal asked me to stay here in the office and tell you that if you have her with you, to wait right here till he comes back."

Nolan shook his head. "She wasn't on the wagon train, Buck, nor had anyone seen her. You can go on home now. We're gonna stay right here till the marshal returns."

Buck had been gone only minutes when both search teams came riding up in front of the marshal's office. The deputies went to the door in time to hear Yeoman say they would take up the search at sunrise tomorrow morning.

The deputies looked at each other by the light of a nearby street lamp.

"They haven't found her," said Long.

Nolan shook his head. "I was sure hopin' they had."

All but three riders trotted away, leaving Marshal Garth Yeoman and Ralph and Rex Dexter. They dismounted and the three walked up to them. They knew by the look on the deputies' faces that they had been unsuccessful.

"She wasn't on the wagon train, I guess," said the marshal.

"No, sir," responded Nolan. "The wagon master let us talk to the whole crowd. Nobody's seen her."

Ralph Dexter shook his head. "I don't understand it. Where could she be? She couldn't just vanish into thin air."

Marshal Yeoman rubbed his chin. "She has to be somewhere near here, Ralph. She couldn't possibly have walked any further than the wide circle we made. As I said, we'll resume the search at sunrise in the morning."

"Well, Rex and I will be here. C'mon, son. Let's get home and let your mother know that Deena's still missing."

Darkness crept into the Parker wagon. Deena Mitchell lay under the cot, listening to the people talk while eating supper. The aroma of the hot food made her mouth water and her stomach growl. She lay there, trying to figure out how to introduce herself to Brian and Valerie Parker, but as yet had not come up with a solution.

Abruptly, she heard someone tuning up a fiddle. Then the sound of a mouth organ met her ears. The soft, pleasant music filled the night air.

The small children in the wagon train had grown weary, and some were asleep in their mothers' arms.

After a while, the last strains of music faded into the night, and soon the people were leaving the campfire, heading for their wagons.

Inside the Parker wagon, Deena's pulse quickened as she heard Brian's and Valerie's voices while they moved up to the tailgate.

Brian dropped the tailgate, picked up a lantern, lit it, and placed it on the floor. He kissed Valerie, then lifted her into the wagon. "Good night, honey. You go ahead and get on your cot. I'll be back after I feed and water the horses. You get a good night's sleep, okay?"

"I'll do my best."

He raised the tailgate, locked it in place, and walked away.

As Valerie stood up and turned around, she saw by the light of the lantern that the one grocery sack had fallen over and two cantaloupes were lying on the floor. She stood the grocery sack upright, and dropped the two cantaloupes back where they belonged. She frowned, wondering where the third cantaloupe had gone, and dropped to her knees.

Beneath the cot, Deena tensed up. A chill slithered down her spine.

When Valerie knelt down in search of the missing cantaloupe, she was startled to see two wide, fear-filled eyes looking at her. She gasped. "Wh-who are you?"

Deena's mouth seemed frozen shut.

Valerie slid the lantern closer, noted the white bonnet lying on the floor, and peered at the girl with the long auburn hair. "I know who you are! You're Deena Mitchell, the girl the deputies are looking for!"

Deena's heart was pounding so fast she could hardly breathe. The moment of her discovery had come, and in a way she had never imagined. She gulped and managed to squeak out, "Yes, ma'am."

"Honey, come out of there. You must be terribly uncomfortable. Come on."

Trembling, Deena scooted herself toward Valerie. When she was almost out, Valerie saw the dark, purple bruises on her cheeks. She took hold of her arms and helped her out the rest of the way. When Deena sat up on the floor, wincing, Valerie moved the lantern so she could get a better look at her.

Valerie's compassionate spirit went out to the girl, who looked more like a trapped animal than a human being. "Honey, how did you get those bruises on your face?"

"My foster father, Ralph Dexter, did it."

"Your foster father."

"Yes. Do you remember that the deputies told all of you I had been chosen from an orphan train, and that I was unhappy in my foster home?"

"I remember. Why were you so unhappy there?"

Deena told her of the heavy work she was forced to do on the Dexter farm, of how Rex was so mean to her, and of the frequent beatings she received at the hands of Ralph Dexter.

"Oh, I'm so sorry, Deena. Since you're an orphan, you've undoubtedly had many sorrows, haven't you?"

"Yes, ma'am."

"Want to tell me about it?"

Deena told her story in brief: how she and her identical twin, Donna, were sent out of their home in Manhattan because their parents could not afford to keep them, and of being taken in by the Children's Aid Society, and finally put on the orphan train. She wept as she told Valerie that she had no idea where Donna might be by now.

Deeply touched by Deena's story, Valerie examined the bruises. "We must wash these, honey, and get some salve on them right away." As she spoke, she rose to her feet, her emotions shaken from the unexpected guest she found in her wagon.

Deena sensed that she had found a friend. "Mrs. Parker?"

"Yes, honey?"

"I have many more bruises that need salve. I got a beating with a belt by Mr. Dexter last night."

Valerie frowned. "Where are these bruises?"

Deena glanced at the rear of the wagon. "If you will drop the canvas flaps at the opening back there, I'll show you."

When the flaps were down, Deena showed Valerie the purple stripes on her back, buttocks, and the back sides of her legs.

Valerie was shocked at the sight before her. "This is an outrage! No human being should ever be treated with such brutality and disrespect!"

The humiliation of her situation coupled with the pain of her wounds overcame Deena. Huge scalding tears suddenly coursed down her pathetic discolored cheeks.

Although she was not a mother, this brought Valerie's motherly instincts to the surface. She took Deena in her arms, careful not to inflict any more pain on her. "Deena, I can't understand why anyone would take you into their home and treat you like this."

Deena clung to the compassionate woman who was holding her. "Please don't let them take me back! He'll beat me even worse.

I'm afraid he might even beat me to death! He abuses his wife as well, and his son, Rex, is almost as hateful and mean as he is."

Valerie felt bile rise in her throat. At the same time, a resolve filled her heart. She knew her husband well enough to be assured that he would feel exactly as she did when he heard Deena's story, and she told him about the stripes on her body and legs. She swallowed the bitter bile and said, "Deena, I promise you—you will never again feel the sting of Ralph Dexter's belt, or have to live with the indignity of this kind of treatment. I don't know how I am going to keep this from happening, but I will. Don't you doubt it. You deserve a far better life than you've had so far, and I will do everything in my power to see that you get it."

Valerie put Deena on the cot, picked up some washcloths, and poured water into a small pan. She took salve from a small canvas bag and went to work on the stripes and bruises.

By the time she finished, Deena's tears were dried, and she was wearing a tiny smile. She sat up on the cot, and Valerie eased down beside her. "Feel better now, honey?"

Deena took hold of her hand. "Yes, much better. Thank you, Mrs. Parker. I really appreciate your caring for me like this. It's been a long time since—"

From outside, Brian's voice penetrated the canvas. "Valerie, who are you talking to in there?"

Chapter Nineteen

Valerie Parker turned and pulled back the flaps. She smiled at her husband. "Climb up here, darling. There's somebody I want you to meet."

Brian was up and over the tailgate. When he set his eyes on the girl, a perplexed look etched itself on his face. "Who are you? I don't recall seeing you in the wagon train before." His voice was a bit tight.

Deena shrunk back in fear, her eyes darting to Valerie.

Valerie moved to Deena and laid a comforting hand on her shoulder. "Brian, this is Deena Mitchell, the girl the deputies were looking for."

Brian's brow furrowed. "Oh yes. She fits the description perfectly that Deputy Nolan gave." He hunkered down before Deena, noting the stark fear on her face, and softened his voice. "I'm sorry, little lady, I didn't mean to frighten you. You…well, you were such a complete surprise to me."

Deena's emotions were on the surface. Tears filled her eyes and began to spill down her cheeks. The lump in her throat kept her from being able to speak.

Brian said again, "I didn't mean to frighten you." He looked at Valerie, raising his eyebrows in question.

Valerie gently squeezed Deena's shoulder. "It's okay, honey. My husband will understand when he knows the full story. My promise to you still holds, and I know he will feel the same way."

Deena looked deeply into the woman's soft caring eyes. She blinked to clear away the tears still lingering on her lashes and slowly nodded her head.

Valerie pulled a clean, pressed handkerchief from her dress pocket and carefully dabbed at the tears on Deena's bruised and battered cheeks. "It will be okay, Deena. I promise. Is it all right if I tell him your situation?"

Deena looked at Brian, who smiled at her encouragingly, then looked back at Valerie. Sighing deeply, she lowered her head. "Yes, ma'am."

Brian asked, "Valerie, where has she been hiding? How did you find her?"

"She's been right there under the cot since we pulled out of Salina. The grocery sack that contained the cantaloupes had fallen over, and I picked up two of them, but the third was nowhere in sight. When I knelt down to look for it under the cot, I found her."

Brian nodded, then focused on Deena's purple cheeks. "How did you get those bruises?"

Valerie answered for her by first telling him it was Deena's foster father, Ralph Dexter, who had bruised her face, then told him of the horrible treatment she had received in the Dexter home from Ralph and their sixteen-year-old son, Rex. She went on to tell him of the stripes and bruises she had just seen on the girl's body, put there by Ralph Dexter with a leather belt.

Brian shook his head in disgust, trying to absorb the despicable information that Valerie was giving him about the girl's tragic life. He studied the bruises on Deena's young face again. "How could any man beat on a child like that?"

"Brian, Deena begged me not to let anyone take her back to Salina. She said Ralph Dexter would beat her even worse. She's afraid he might even beat her to death. I promised her I wouldn't let anyone take her back."

Brian nodded, his heart aching over Deena's plight. "I agree. We can't let her go back to that kind of abuse. I'll talk to Les Corbin, advise him that she's been hiding in our wagon, and tell him what she's been suffering in that foster home." He looked at Deena. "Honey, I assume since you were on the orphan train that you have no one back where you came from to provide a home for you—relatives, or anybody like that."

"No, sir." Then gaining courage, she said, "Mr. Parker, I was so happy when the Dexters chose me. Ralph seemed so kind and caring, but it all changed when they took me home. Rex was mean to me. Mrs. Dexter did her best to protect me, but she is frightened of her husband and mistreated herself. I did the only thing I could do. I ran away."

"Of course, honey. They left you no choice. I can see that."

Deena took a deep breath; then looked first at Valerie, then at Brian. "Maybe—maybe there is some family in the wagon train who would take me in. I'm a good worker. I can cook and care for babies and little children. My twin sister and I did a lot of that."

Brian's eyebrows arched. "Your twin sister?"

"Yes, sir. I told Mrs. Parker about Donna."

"Where is she?"

"I don't know. She was still on the train when it pulled out of Salina."

"Oh, I'm sorry. Is she your identical twin?"

"Yes, sir. We look exactly alike, and we're exactly alike in every way. I sure hope she gets a good home."

"I do too. But right now, I'm concerned that *you* are placed in a good home."

"Me too," put in Valerie. "Deena's got to have a good home. I—I—"

Brian turned and looked at her. He read the look in her eyes and grinned. "Valerie, darlin', you don't have to say it. I can see it in your eyes. You want to keep Deena with us."

Valerie's eyes misted. She put an arm around Deena's shoulder. "Yes, I do. Very much so. And how about you?"

Deena's eyes were wide as she ran her gaze hopefully between the two of them.

A smile spread over Brian's rugged features. "I very much want to take her too."

Valerie hugged Deena close. "Is this all right with you, honey?"

Deena's heart was pounding. "Do you mean for keeps, or just till you get to wherever you are going?"

Brian spoke before Valerie could reply. "We mean for keeps, Deena. Let me tell you something. Valerie and I have talked a lot this past year about adopting a child. We'll be your foster parents now, and later, if you're happy with us, we'll see about legally adopting you."

Deena burst into tears and hugged them both. It was a precious moment for all three of them. Valerie and Brian had been longing for a child. They had so much love to give and were grateful to have found the child upon whom they could pour out that love.

Deena could hardly believe what was happening. This couple really wanted her.

Suddenly, an unwelcome thought entered her mind. *Can this really be, or is it all pretend like it was with the Dexters?*

Her teary eyes, which only seconds before had been shining with tears of joy, reflected the unbidden thought.

Valerie caught the change in her expression and took hold of

Deena's hand. "What's wrong, sweetie? You're frightened about something. Tell us what it is."

Deena swallowed hard, trying to gather her wits about her. If these people were sincere, she didn't want to reveal her doubts about them and hurt their feelings. *They may think I'm ungrateful and change their minds about wanting me.*

Sensing what he thought was a feeling of insecurity, Brian took hold of her shoulders. "Deena, in our hearts, you are already part of this family. Family members should always share whatever is troubling them with each other."

She looked up at him and saw only kindness in his eyes. Her words came out weakly. "You—you won't get mad at me if I tell you?"

"No. I promise."

"Well…" she began, a quiver in her voice, "I w-was remembering back to the day when the Dexters chose me. Ralph—Ralph really seemed nice, and like he really wanted me, then…" Her voice trailed off, and she looked at the rough wagon floor.

Valerie and Brian exchanged an understanding glance, then Valerie bent down, putting her face level with Deena's. Taking the girl's lowered head in both hands, she gently raised it until their eyes met.

"Deena, we understand your troubled thoughts and why you are skeptical about our sincerity in this. But you, my dear one, are an answer to our prayers. Brian and I want a child with whom we can share our love and our lives and the new home we're going to have out West. We know with all our hearts that you are that child. Won't you please trust us? I can speak for both Brian and me. We promise—you'll never regret becoming our daughter."

Valerie paused, giving time for her words to sink in.

Deena searched the kind woman's eyes and saw nothing but goodness there. Tears of joy pooled in her eyes and spilled down her battered cheeks. "Yes, I will trust you," she said, her voice choking on her tears. She ran her eyes between man and wife. "Thank you for wanting me to be your daughter. There is nothing in the world that feels as good as knowing you are wanted, and that you belong to someone who cares. Even my own parents—" She choked on a sudden sob and put a fist to her mouth.

Brian frowned, looked at Valerie, then back to Deena. "Are you saying that before they died, your parents didn't want you?"

Deena sniffed and blinked at her tears. She tried to speak, but her throat was constricted.

"Her parents aren't dead," said Valerie. "The twins are the oldest of seven children, with another one on the way. Deena told me all about it. Their parents sent them out of the home in Manhattan saying they could no longer afford to keep them. Deena and her twin sister joined the thousands of other children who live on the streets of New York City."

Brian was stunned. He scrubbed a palm over his mouth. "That's awful! No wonder you have a problem trusting anyone. Add what happened with the Dexters and it's a wonder you can ever trust anyone when they say they love you and want you."

Deena wiped tears. "Thank you for understanding."

"I sure thought you were an actual orphan. So it was the Children's Aid Society who put you on the train, then. I've read about Charles Loring Brace and his great work. Somehow I got it in my head that he only took care of children whose parents were both dead…you know, actual orphans."

"Now that I think of it," said Valerie, "I remember reading once in the *Crown Point Sentinel* about the Children's Aid Society. The article stated that quite often they put children on their orphan trains who are not actually orphans, but their parents had put them out of their homes because they could no longer afford to feed and clothe them. Most of the time, though, it was mothers who had been widowed and were in financial straits."

Brian nodded. "Seems like you mentioned that to me. I had forgotten it. Deena, how did it happen that the Children's Aid Society took you and your sister off the streets?"

"Well, with Donna and me, it was Mr. Brace and his wife who came along and saw that we were being treated bad by some of the other street children. They put us in their buggy and took us to the Society's headquarters, and the next time there was an orphan train going that had room for us, they put us on it."

Brian's brow furrowed. "Honey, I know a lot about identical twins. When I was a boy in Indiana, we had neighbors who had identical twin boys. I grew up with them and had the opportunity to observe the strong bond between them. It must have been horrible for you to be separated from Donna."

Deena's face pinched. "There are no words to describe it, Mr. Parker. I thought my heart was going to tear right out of my chest."

"I can't imagine that the Society would allow any siblings to be separated—especially twins, and more especially, *identical* twins."

"They have a rule, sir. If any couple wants just one sibling, they are allowed to take them. They say that it is better for them to be separated and taken into different homes anywhere out West than to starve or freeze to death as thousands of street children have done in New York."

Valerie said, "It has to be terrible for you, not knowing whether or not Donna has been chosen by foster parents, and if so, where she is."

"Yes, ma'am. It is terrible. I miss her so much, and I know she misses me so much too, wherever she is. Often at night, before falling asleep, it seems I can hear Donna calling to me. Sometimes it happens in dreams, and I wake up with her voice still in my ears."

"I believe that, honey," said Valerie. "I know there is a special bond between twins that ordinary siblings don't have. Brian read a book about that a few months ago, didn't you, darling?"

"I did. I happened upon it when I was in Crown Point's public library looking for a good book to check out and take home. It covered several fascinating medical subjects. Just glancing inside it caught my interest, so I checked it out and took it home. I was especially interested in the chapter on twins because of those neighbor boys. It was written by a medical doctor named Anthony Harmon. Dr. Harmon pointed out that there are two kinds of twins—the one-egg kind, which produces identical twins of the same sex; and the two-egg type, which produces twins who are not necessarily of the same sex, and who do not necessarily resemble each other. He was emphatic that the one-egg type has a bond between them that often amazes medical science.

"Dr. Harmon spent a great deal of time on the subject in that chapter. He said identical twins so often know what the other one is thinking, that even when they are apart they can discern if the other twin is under emotional strain, experiencing emotional elation, or is in some kind of physical pain."

Deena nodded, a thin smile on her lips. "Dr. Harmon knows what he is talking about."

Valerie cleared her throat gently. "Deena, how long has it been since you had something to eat and drink?"

"This morning, ma'am, when I had breakfast at the Dexter house."

"That's a long time. I'll fix you something to eat while Brian goes and talks to the wagon master."

"Good idea," said Brian. "I'll be back shortly."

"Honey," said Valerie, reaching for a large mug that sat on the small table in the corner, "will you fill this for me from the water barrel on the side of the wagon, please? This girl has got to be terribly thirsty."

Brian took the mug. "She has to be." He hopped out of the wagon and returned to the tailgate a moment later. Handing it to Valerie, he said, "If she needs more, I'll get it for her when I get back."

Valerie gave the mug to Deena. "Drink all you want, dear. I can get more for you before he gets back if you need it."

Deena accepted the mug and began to drink while Valerie prepared her something to eat—including a thick slice of cantaloupe.

While Deena was eating cantaloupe for dessert and Valerie was talking to her about traveling in the wagon train, Brian appeared at the tailgate with the wagon master at his side. "Deena, this is our wagon master, Mr. Lester Corbin. I told him your story, and he wants to meet you. Okay?"

Deena swallowed a mouthful of cantaloupe. "Yes, sir."

Both men climbed over the tailgate. The girl sat at the small table and Valerie was seated on the cot.

Smiling down at Deena, Corbin said, "Mr. Parker told me your whole story. I can see the bruises on your face for myself. I'm sorry that you have had such a hard time in your young life, and I'm sorry that you have been separated from your twin sister. I can only imagine how horrible that is."

She nodded solemnly. "Yes, sir."

"I want to say, also, that my heart goes out to you for what your real parents did to you and your sister and for the awful treatment you received at the hands of Ralph Dexter and his son. I need to ask you something."

"Yes, sir?"

"Is it your desire to go on west with the Parkers and live with them?"

A smile broke over Deena's pretty features. "Oh yes, sir!"

"All right. You seem pretty excited about it."

"I am, Mr. Corbin. Mr. and Mrs. Parker have been so kind to me. I already love them very much."

Valerie's eyes were sparkling. "And we already love you very much, sweetheart."

"Yes, we do," said Brian, his own face beaming. "It's like you've been ours all your life."

Deena's heart was throbbing. "Thank you."

Corbin set his eyes on Deena once again. "The deputies from Salina made it clear that you were the Dexters' foster child. Since the Dexters did not adopt you, they have no legal claim on you. I feel no obligation to report your whereabouts to the law. You are free to live with the Parkers, who according to Mr. Parker, want to be your foster parents and are planning to adopt you once they settle out West. It is my sincere hope that the three of you will be very, very happy together."

Deena smiled joyfully as Valerie stood up and moved toward her. Brian followed. Deena rose to her feet and the Parkers folded her into their arms.

Les Corbin smiled. "I'll tell Deena's story to everyone in the wagon train after breakfast so they will all understand why you folks have her in your wagon. If you'll excuse me, I need to get back to my lead wagon."

Brian let go of his foster daughter and shook Corbin's hand. "Thank you for being so understanding. I know you have a moral obligation to make sure no laws are broken by the people in your wagon trains, or to report them to the authorities if they do so."

"No laws are being broken here. Like I said, the Salina

deputies made it plain that the Dexters had Deena in their home as a foster daughter. They have no legal claim on her. Everybody sleep well, now. Good night."

When Corbin was gone, Deena wrapped her arms around the Parkers' waists. "Thank you for taking me in. Can I call you Mama and Papa now?"

"You sure can, sweetheart!" said Brian.

"Yes! I've wanted to be a mama for so long!"

Brian kissed Deena's forehead. "Now it's time for all of us to get to bed. I usually sleep on the floor here inside the wagon on those thick blankets that are piled at the foot of the cot. That's where you'll sleep. I have a bedroll, so I'll sleep in it out here on the ground beside the wagon."

"But Papa," protested Deena, "I shouldn't take your sleeping spot. I could sleep under the cot, where I hid till Mama found me."

Brian hugged her. "No daughter of mine is going to sleep under the cot. I'm very glad to give you my bed. Okay, ladies, I'll leave so you can get ready for bed."

"I have a nightgown you can use, honey," said Valerie.

Overwhelmed at the way things had worked out for her, Deena hugged both of them again. "Oh, I'm so happy!"

Deena lay in the darkness of the covered wagon, nestled in the bedroll provided by the Parkers. Valerie's even breathing on the cot gave sign that she was fast asleep.

A happy Deena Mitchell looked up at the stars through the opening at the back of the wagon, which was left with the flaps back. The stars seemed to wink at her, telling her how glad they were for this wonderful turn of events in her life.

Her mind went to her family back in New York. She wondered if they ever thought of her. For as long as she could remember, she had never felt as loved and wanted as she did at that moment. Nor had she ever felt so protected as she felt now with the Parkers.

She remembered some happy times in Manhattan, but the poverty and unrest in the home far overshadowed them. *Donna and I have had to work and care for the little ones since we were barely more than toddlers, ourselves. Seems like almost every year there was a new baby born. We never minded working and helping out, but there was never any tenderness shown by our father and very little by our mother. Mama was sick so much and with child and Papa had such a bitter outlook on life. The Parkers are so different. I'm such a fortunate girl. I hope Donna is as happy as I am. I don't understand why I had to go through that awful experience in the Dexter home with Ralph and Rex, but it sure makes me appreciate the home I have with my new Mama and Papa, even though right now it is a covered wagon.*

She pictured the sour faces of Ralph and Rex on the screen of her mind, and felt the joy of her freedom from them.

Her thoughts ran to Donna again, and because she sensed happiness in Donna's life, she relaxed and fell asleep, wondering just where her twin might be.

At the *K-Bar-M Ranch* near Wild Horse, Colorado, the Talbert family arrived home late in the evening after a rousing revival service at their church.

They had their prayer time together, and after the last amen, Ken and Molly noticed a beam on Donna's face.

Ken smiled at her. "What are you so happy about, honey?"

"Well, Papa, while we were praying for Deena, a sweet calm came over me. I sense that she is no longer unhappy and disturbed like she has been almost since the day she was chosen by the Dexter family at Salina."

Molly put an arm around her and kissed her cheek. "God does indeed answer prayer, sweetheart. I'm sure what you are sensing is real and true, and that things are better for Deena now."

Donna looked at Ken, then Molly. "I still want to go back to Salina and find her, though."

"Of course," said Ken. "This obvious answer to prayer doesn't change your need to see Deena. It won't be too long. We'll be able to go in just a few days."

Donna's face flushed, and tears moistened her eyes. "Oh, Papa, Mama, it will be so wonderful to see her again!"

Lying in her bed in the darkness that night, Donna said in a low voice, "Thank You, Lord Jesus, that I know things are better for Deena. And thank You for working in Papa's and Mama's hearts so they are willing to take me back to Salina so I can see my sweet sister. I so desperately want to talk to her about being saved. Please, Lord, give me the wisdom and power to win Deena to You. I want my precious Deena in heaven with me."

At the Bostin home in Colorado Springs on the same night, Johnny Bostin lay in his bed. "Thank You, Lord, for bringing me together with the wonderful people who have adopted me as their son. Help me, dear Lord, to be the kind of son my parents deserve. I want them to always be glad they adopted me. And dear Jesus, help me to be the servant to You that I should be."

When Johnny had finished praying, his thoughts went to Priscilla Wheeler. Every time he was in her presence, she became dearer to him. He pictured her in his mind, marveling at how pretty she was and how much he liked her long, velvet black hair.

Priscilla and I are too young to really fall in love, he thought, *but Johnny Bostin, when you are old enough to fall in love, you most certainly will fall in love with Priscilla. She is everything a Christian young lady should be, and there is no doubt that she likes you very much.*

He smiled to himself in the darkness and whispered, "And Priscilla, I am going to do everything I can to make you fall in love with me when we're both old enough."

Chapter Twenty

The next morning at the wagon train, Deena Mitchell sat at the Parker table beside their covered wagon. She was quite aware of many covert glances being sent her way from the curious crowd inside the circle. To the Parkers she said, "Looks like everybody's wondering who I am and where I came from."

Brian gave her a pleasant look. "They'll all know in a few minutes. You're not afraid anymore, are you?"

Sporting a grin from ear to ear, Deena replied, "No, Papa. I'm not at all afraid. I trust you and Mama, and I feel very safe with you. No one has ever been so good to me."

Brian and Valerie smiled at each other.

At that moment, wagon master Les Corbin moved to the cook fire in the center of the circle, lifted his hat, and smoothed his hair back. "All right, listen up everybody. We are now nearing Comanche Indian territory as we dip into the southwest corner of Kansas. You will remember that before we crossed the Missouri River at Independence I warned you about the Indian threat all across the West. I asked all of you to keep your eyes peeled for any sign of the hostiles.

"Now, you need to double your watchfulness. Let me explain

about the Comanche leader, Quanah Parker. He surrendered to the United States government last year and began taking his people onto the reservation provided for them, which is partly in Kansas and partly in the territory known as Oklahoma. However, there are some rebel groups among the Comanches who have not agreed with the surrender. They're showing their hatred for white men by attacking farms, ranches, villages, stagecoaches, and wagon trains. They are short on guns and ammunition, so they also use bows and arrows.

"They only have small groups, and when they attack, they shoot as many bullets and arrows as they can, then gallop away, satisfied that they have killed or wounded some white people, and frightened the rest.

"Remember that if we sight any of the hostiles, I will immediately call for the wagons to make a circle. In Missouri, you men encouraged me by letting me know that so many of you are crack shots with guns. This is good. And remember that all the women and children are to get inside the wagons and lie flat on the floor till you are told it is safe to come out. These Comanches are savages to the core, so keep your eyes peeled and give a shout if you see any sign of them."

Corbin sensed the pall of apprehension that came over the group.

"Folks, I know the prospect of Indian attack is frightening, but let me tell you something. Usually on a wagon train the people begin to form sort of a family feeling for each other. This is good because the family bond is the strongest bond on earth. When we are threatened, we must depend on each other in order to survive. Genuine friendships are developed on these journeys too, and there's an unwritten law that what hurts or affects one, has an impact on all. Let's determine to unite ourselves if attacks come, and we'll make it together."

Some of the men waved their hats and sent up a cheer. Women and children joined them.

Corbin smiled. "Good! Now, I have something else to do." He looked toward the Parker table. "Mr. and Mrs. Parker, will you come here and bring that lovely young lady with you?"

The Parkers put Deena between them and headed for the spot where Corbin stood near the fire.

"I'm scared now," Deena whispered.

"No need to be, honey," said Brian.

Valerie squeezed her arm. "That's right, Deena. These fine people will understand and welcome you when Mr. Corbin tells them your story."

As they drew up beside him facing the crowd, the wagon master smiled at Deena, then looked at the crowd. "Yesterday we pulled put of Salina and two sheriff's deputies caught up to us and told us about a thirteen-year-old girl named Deena Mitchell who was missing from a farm just outside of town. The deputies told us Deena was unhappy in her foster home and possibly had run away.

"Well, none of us knew it, but at the very time the deputies were talking to us, Deena was hiding under the cot in the back of the Parker wagon. Even the Parkers were unaware of it. Deena had climbed in there and hid herself while we were still parked outside of Salina."

All eyes were on the girl with the long auburn hair.

Corbin gestured toward her. "Ladies and gentlemen, boys and girls, this is Deena Mitchell. I'm going to tell you her story."

The wagon master had everyone's attention as he told them Deena's story. At times he turned to her to corroborate a certain point, or to expand on it, which she did.

The group was having a hard time absorbing the unthinkable information that was coming from Corbin's lips. They were stunned, first of all to hear of Deena and her twin being sent away from their Manhattan home by their real parents, and second to hear of the abuse she had suffered at the hands of her foster father and his son. Corbin also dwelt on the mental anguish Deena had suffered in being separated from Donna, with the strong possibility that she would never see her again. The obvious astonishment they felt showed on their faces. They stood in absolute silence.

Deena thought that they did not believe her story. She looked up at Brian and Valerie, seeking some kind of assurance.

Noting the trepidation that showed on her face, the Parkers each put a protective arm around her.

Deena stood rigid, staring at the ground. *If just one person turns against me,* she thought, *they might report this to the authorities. Maybe there really is a way I could be sent back to the Dexters.* Her heart was pounding in her ears and her breathing was rapid and shallow.

It was Les Corbin who broke the silence. "Remember what I said about people on a wagon train treating each other like family? Mr. and Mrs. Parker are going to keep her and give her a home. They plan to adopt her when they settle at their destination further west. She could also use some warmth and welcome from the rest of you."

Suddenly, children and adults alike rushed to Deena and welcomed her into the wagon train. This touched her deeply, and she responded with warm words and a bright smile.

The meeting soon broke up and the people went to their wagons to prepare to move out for another day's travel.

At the Parker wagon, Deena was doing what she could to help Valerie while Brian was tending to the horses. As they worked side by side, Valerie noticed tears on the girl's cheeks. She put an arm around her.

"Honey, did Mr. Corbin's speech about the Comanches frighten you?"

"It made me real uneasy, Mama, but that's not why I'm crying."

"Then what is it, sweetie?"

Deena sniffed. "I—well, I'm crying because when Mr. Corbin told the people of the strong possibility that I may never see Donna again, it just hit me even harder. He's right, I know, but it hurts so much to think about it. I can hardly stand the thought that I may never see her again."

Valerie wrapped her arms around her. "Honey, I wish I could offer hope to you in the matter. Where was the orphan train headed?"

"Los Angeles was its final stop. Of course it had many stops scheduled all along the way where the orphans would be looked over and chosen by those who wanted to be their foster parents. Donna could be anywhere between Salina and Los Angeles. That's a lot of territory."

"Indeed it is. I'm so sorry it has turned out this way, and I really can't understand how it feels to you. I'm not a twin. And like you just said, that's a lot of territory. There is no way we could ever find Donna. I know that people who are interested in becoming foster parents often travel for days to a town where the trains are going to stop. Donna could be living a long way from whatever town where she might have been chosen."

Deena sniffed again. "You're right, Mama. I simply must face the fact that I will never see my sweet sister again."

Valerie and Deena finished their task, and Brian showed up just as the voice of the wagon master was heard, calling for everyone to get in the wagons.

Brian said, "Valerie, I'll take Deena up on the driver's seat with me. You'd better lie down on the cot."

"Not right now, honey. Maybe later. I'd like to sit up front too."

"Okay, but if you start getting tired, I'll signal Mr. Corbin that we have to stop long enough for me to help you into the rear of the wagon so you can lie down on the cot. If we didn't have so much stuff piled up behind the seat, you could crawl back without us having to stop. But that's where you're going if I see you getting tired."

Valerie chuckled and gave him a military salute. "Yes, sir, General Parker, sir!"

Deena laughed.

Brian tweaked her nose. "It's good to hear you laugh, sweet stuff. You look like you've been crying."

Valerie nodded. "When Mr. Corbin mentioned in his story that Deena was facing the possibility that she may never see Donna again, it hit her afresh. I wish I could give her some hope in the matter, but I can't. She told me the orphan train was going all the way to Los Angeles with many stops in between. It would be impossible to find Donna, no matter how hard we searched. There's a lot of territory out there."

Brian nodded and tweaked Deena's nose again. "Let's get aboard."

Brian helped both of them up onto the driver's seat, putting Deena up first so she could sit between them. When he settled onto the seat beside Deena, placing his rifle on his lap, he picked up the reins. "Well, here we go."

Deena looked at the rifle and nervously ran her tongue over her lips.

"Just in case those Comanches show up, honey. I want this gun where I can get a hold of it in a hurry."

A moment later, Les Corbin was on his horse and calling for the wagons to move out.

As the train rolled along the vast rolling prairie, Deena looked up at Brian. "Mr. Corbin said that Comanche leader who took his people onto the reservation is named Quanah Parker. I don't know much about Indians, Papa, but those I've studied about in school never had a white man's last name. How come he has the same last name as you?"

"Well, I've done a little studying about him. His last name is Parker because he is a half-breed. You know what that is."

"That's when one parent is white and the other is Indian."

"Correct. Quanah's father was a Comanche, and his mother was a white woman named Cynthia Ann Parker. As a young girl, she was captured by the Comanches. They raised her, and she married a young chief named Peta Nocona. The Noconas were one of the main bands of Comanches. A year or so after they married, Cynthia Ann gave birth to their firstborn son. They named him Quanah, which means 'fragrant' in Comanche. He grew up and became a fearless warrior chief. It was the Texans who first began to call him Quanah Parker to mark him as a half-breed."

"I see."

Valerie looked past Deena at her husband. "I didn't realize you knew all of this about that Indian."

Brian chuckled. "I learned it when I checked out a book on the history of the American Indian from the library in Crown Point. I was especially interested in Quanah because his last name is the same as mine."

"Interesting, to say the least."

"I agree."

They rode along in silence for a while, then Deena said, "Papa, Mama, with all that's been going on, you haven't told me where you are planning to go to make your new home. I know by listening to conversations among the people who walked past the wagon while I was hiding under the cot, that most of them are going all the way to southern California. I've heard some say they are stopping in New Mexico or Arizona, though. Where are we going?"

Brian and Valerie exchanged smiling glances, and Valerie was about to tell her when suddenly they heard the whoops of wild Indians. Rifles began to fire from the wagons while Les Corbin shouted for the wagons to make a circle. The war-painted Comanches were galloping out of a nearby gully where they had been hiding.

Hurriedly, Brian handed Valerie the reins, telling her to follow the other wagons as they formed a circle. He shouldered his rifle and fired off a shot at a warrior who came riding close. The warrior let out a scream and fell from his horse, hitting the ground like a broken doll.

Deena clung to the seat with an icy coldness in her chest while her new father took a bead on another Indian and her new mother guided the wagon into the circle.

Men were firing their rifles while the women and the children were making their way into the back side of the wagons. It was bedlam outside the circle with Indians screeching, guns roaring like a string of firecrackers, and arrows hissing through the air.

Brian fired off another shot, and while levering another cartridge into the chamber, looked over his shoulder to see Valerie on the ground, raising her arms to Deena. "That's it, honey! Hurry! Get inside fast! Can you make it without me?"

"Yes! You keep shooting! Come on, Deena!"

Deena rose up on her feet and leaned down toward Valerie.

Abruptly, two Comanches galloped up close. One was shouldering a rifle, and the other was bringing a bow and arrow into play. Brian's shot dropped the one with the rifle, and at the same instant the arrow from the other one hissed past him, followed by the sound of the arrow striking flesh. Deena let out a high-pitched cry.

Brian quickly levered another cartridge into the chamber and fired, dropping the second Indian. He whipped around on the seat to see Deena fall into Valerie's arms with the arrow protruding from her back.

Valerie gripped the limp form. "Deena-a-a-a! Brian, she's hit!"

At the *K-Bar-M Ranch* near Wild Horse, Colorado, the family sat down for lunch.

Ken looked at the hot onion soup. "Mmm! Sure smells good, ladies."

Molly grinned. "Donna made this soup all by herself."

"Well, honey, if it's as good as it smells, I'll hire you as the chief soup maker around here!"

Everybody laughed, then Ken reached across the table and took their hands into his. "Let's pray."

Ken had hardly said the amen when suddenly Donna put her hands to her mouth, eyes wide. "Something's wrong! I'm sure something's wrong!"

Ken's brow furrowed. "What do you mean, Donna?"

Molly took hold of her arm. "You mean something's wrong with Deena?"

"Yes! Terribly wrong! I know it! Oh, I've got to go to her!"

Brow still furrowed, Ken said, "Well, honey, we weren't going to Salina till next week, but since you feel this strong about it, I'll ride into town after lunch and make reservations for the next train east."

Half an hour later, Molly and Donna stood on the front porch of the ranch house and watched Ken gallop away.

When horse and rider vanished from view, Molly said, "Well,

honey, let's get the dishes done, then we'll pack a couple small bags so we'll be ready to go in case there's an east-bound train coming through right away."

Donna drew a shuddering breath. "I hope there is, Mama. I've got to get to Deena as soon as possible. Something is terribly wrong."

Ken was back shortly and told Molly and Donna that he booked the three of them on a train that was scheduled to arrive in Wild Horse in three hours. It would have them to Salina by nine o'clock tomorrow morning.

In less than an hour, they were in the buckboard on their way to town.

Donna was seated between them, and Molly had an arm around her as she said, "Oh, Mama, Papa, I keep getting this horrible feeling! Whatever it is, it's bad!"

At Wild Horse, Ken left his team and buckboard with the local livery stable, and the Talberts walked the short distance to the depot.

At nine o'clock the next morning, the train pulled into the Salina railroad station. As the Talbert family left the coach, carrying their small pieces of luggage, Ken said, "We'll rent a horse and buggy at the nearest livery stable, and I'll see if the stable people know the location of the Dexter farm."

When they reached the street, Ken moved up to a hired buggy and said to the driver, "Excuse me, sir. Can you tell me where the nearest livery stable is? We need to rent a horse and buggy."

"It's the *only* livery stable in Salina, sir. 'Bout four blocks north. Only cost you fifty cents if I take you to it."

"All right. Let's go."

While the buggy was rolling along Main Street, Donna's hands were shaking. Molly took hold of them. "Just hold on, sweetheart. We'll be there in a little while."

Ken leaned up close to the driver. "You wouldn't happen to know where the Ralph Dexter farm is, would you?"

The driver angled his face toward him while keeping an eye on the street. "No, sir. I think I've heard that name, but I have no idea where his farm might be. Charlie Dodd—that's the owner of the livery stable—might know."

"Fine. I'll ask him. Thank you."

When the buggy came to a halt in front of the livery stable, Ken helped the ladies out, then dropped a dollar into the driver's hand. When they moved up to the office door, a silver-haired man was just coming out. He smiled. "May I help you, folks?"

"Are you Charlie Dodd?" inquired Ken.

"Sure am."

"The buggy driver told me your name. We need to rent a horse and buggy."

Charlie grinned. "Well, that's what I'm here for."

"He also said you might be able to tell me how to find the Ralph Dexter farm."

"Oh, sure. North of town about six, seven miles. I'll draw you a little map."

Less than an hour later, the Talberts turned off the road on to the Dexter place and headed down the lane toward the house.

Donna Talbert gripped her mother's hand. "Oh, we're almost to Deena. My heart feels like it's going to flutter right through the wall of my chest."

Ken smiled at her. "Just hang on, sweet stuff. You're about to hold that precious sister of yours in your arms."

Drawing to a halt at the front porch, Ken stepped out, and helped Molly and Donna from the buggy. They walked up the porch steps together, noticing that the front door was standing open behind the screen door.

Ken knocked on the door, and instantly, they heard the sound of heavy footsteps coming that way. Seconds later, a big, muscular man appeared. He looked through the screen at Donna and his face went purple with rage. He flung the screen door open. "Oh, so you've come crawling back, eh? And who are these people?"

Donna knew something indeed was wrong. She looked at her parents to see their reaction to the big man's nasty attitude. They seemed as shocked as she was. "I'm not Deena, Mr. Dexter. I'm her twin, Donna. Remember? Wh-where is my s-sister?"

Ralph looked at her in mute shock.

Aware of Donna's distress, Ken's fatherly protectiveness took over.

He stepped closer, pushing Donna behind him. "Mr. Dexter, my wife and I have adopted Donna. We brought her here to see her twin sister. Where is sh—"

"Deena!" came a shrill female voice as Norma drew up, looking past Ken at the girl.

Donna moved up beside Ken. "I'm not Deena, Mrs. Dexter. I'm her twin sister, Donna. You saw me at the depot the day you chose Deena."

A stunned Norma could only stand there, eyes bulging, mouth open.

Ken squared his shoulders. "Our name is Talbert. My name is Ken, and my wife's name is Molly. We chose Donna at the depot in Wild Horse, Colorado, and we've adopted her. We have a ranch near there. Donna has missed her twin something awful, and she has sensed that Deena is in some kind of trouble. We brought Donna here so she could see her. Do I understand by your words, Mr. Dexter, that Deena has left you?"

Ralph found his voice. "Uh…well, Deena had been missing her twin. She was very unhappy in our home. It seems the change was too much for her, coming from life in the big city to this farm. It became so difficult for her that she ran away. The town marshal and his deputies formed search teams from among the townsmen and tried to find her, but were unsuccessful. She is no doubt gone for good and won't be back."

Donna's heart sank, and her shoulders drooped.

Molly put an arm around her, noting the profound look of sadness on the face of Ralph Dexter's wife. A closer look showed her what appeared to be faded purple bruises on the woman's face. Fearful of what Deena may have been forced to endure and not wanting Donna to become aware of this, Molly placed a hand on her husband's arm. "Ken, I think it's time to go. Since these people have no idea where Deena is, nothing more can be done here."

Ken nodded. "Mr. and Mrs. Dexter, may I leave you our address, so if Deena should surprise you and return, she could write to Donna?"

Ralph set his jaw. "You can leave it, but Deena isn't coming back."

As the Talberts were driving back toward Salina, Donna sobbed as if her heart would break in pieces. "I'll never see Deena again! Oh, what has happened to her? Whatever it is, it's got to be dreadful. I know it! I know it!"

Molly held her in her arms. "I'm so sorry we weren't able to find Deena, honey, but maybe what you're feeling isn't as bad as it seems."

"It's bad, Mama! Deena needs me, and I can't get to her! Oh, this is awful!" The sobs grew heavier. "I should have come sooner, while she was still here! She needed me! Oh-h-h! I'll never see her again!"

Ken put the reins in his left hand and took hold of Donna's hand with his right. "Sweetheart, we came as soon as we could. I know it looks hopeless now, but we have a big, powerful God, and there are no impossibilities with Him."

"That's right, Donna," said Molly. "God knows where Deena is. We'll pray that He will bring you and Deena together in His own way and His own time."

Donna ran her gaze between her parents. "I'll pray that way every day of my life until the Lord brings Deena back to me."

At the Marvin Dalby home east of Los Angeles, Teddy Hansen, Jerry Varnell, and Clint Albright were superbly happy with their foster parents. Marvin and Doris had given each of them his own room in the spacious house, and the boys loved their school.

The three orphan boys had become as close as any brothers could be. They loved their parents and their new life and found each day filled with joy.

One common thread held the boys together in a special way—their deep desire to someday found and direct an orphanage themselves. They talked about their dream, formulating ideas, and sometimes after discussion, discarding some of them. They realized it would be years before they could actually realize the big dream, but they knew that each passing day drew them closer to it.

One Saturday, while working in one of the orchards by themselves, they got on the subject once more.

Jerry climbed up a stepladder, and as he began clipping dead ends from the limbs of a pear tree, he said, "Hey, guys, I have some good news for you."

Teddy and Clint looked up at him.

"I can always use good news, Jerry," said Clint. "Let's hear it."

Teddy nodded. "Yeah. Me too."

"Well, you know, we've discussed many times that the biggest problem was going to be how to finance the orphanage."

Clint grinned. "We're listening."

"Remember this morning when Papa Marvin took me over there by the orange trees to help him?"

Both boys nodded.

"Well, while we were working together, he brought up the subject of our future orphanage."

"Yeah?" the boys said in unison.

"He told me then that he and Mama Doris have talked about it. They are putting money aside every month so they can finance it for us."

"Wow!" exclaimed Teddy. "That's great!"

"Sure is," said Clint. "Praise the Lord!"

Chapter Twenty-one

TEN YEARS LATER

On a Monday morning in September 1866, Pastor Dan Wheeler sat at his desk in the church office, his attention on his open Bible. A smile broke across his face. "Yes, Lord! That's it! That will make a great sermon. You know how I love to preach on the cross."

There was a knock at the door.

Wheeler closed the Bible. "Come in, Johnny!"

The door opened and twenty-two-year-old Johnny Bostin stepped in and moved toward the desk. Johnny was handsome in a rugged way, with angular features. He was tall, with broad shoulders, and presented a lithe, erect figure with a carefree walk. On his vest was a silver star, and he wore a pearl-handled Colt.45 on his right hip.

Wheeler glanced at the deputy U.S. marshal's badge and smiled as he rose from his chair, shaking Johnny's hand. He gestured toward the chair in front of the desk. "Sit down, Johnny."

As they both sat down, Johnny said, "Pastor, thank you for giving me this appointment today, since I have to ride out of town tomorrow."

"Glad to. So what do you need to talk to me about?"

Johnny's nerves were stretched tight, and he felt as if a wad of chill, wet leaves was pressed to his spine. He cleared his throat nervously. "W-well, sir, l-let me remind y-you that Priscilla and I have been dating each other exclusively for some four years now, and I think she is the most wonderful girl in the whole world. I'm deeply in love with your daughter, Pastor, and—and I w-want your permission to ask her to marry me."

Wheeler chuckled. "Johnny, I knew exactly what you wanted to talk to me about when you asked for this appointment yesterday at church."

Johnny swallowed with difficulty. "Y-you did?"

"Yes, and let me tell you—Madelyne and I know how very much Priscilla loves you too. She is completely open with us about it, and even if she weren't, it's written on her face every day of her life."

Johnny grinned. "Really?"

"Really. And we couldn't have picked out a better man for a son-in-law. You're a dedicated Christian. You love the Lord and serve Him faithfully. On top of that, like your dad, you're an excellent lawman. We're very proud of you, Johnny, and it is a great pleasure to grant you permission to ask Priscilla to marry you."

Johnny sighed. "Thank you, Pastor. I will be so proud to have Priscilla for my wife and you and Mrs. Wheeler for my in-laws."

"I'm glad you feel that way. What time frame do you have in mind about the wedding?"

"I was thinking of suggesting to Priscilla that we have a June wedding next year."

The preacher smiled. "That's excellent. An engagement of nine months will be good. It will give both of you sufficient time to prepare for married life."

"That's what I was thinking, sir."

A slight shadow crossed the pastor's face. "There is one thing that concerns me, though."

Johnny grinned. "My job, right?"

"Right. It concerns me that as a deputy U.S. marshal, you have to spend so much time traveling in pursuit of outlaws. I understand this is what the job demands, but I'm thinking about how much Priscilla misses you now, when you're gone sometimes weeks on end. It's going to be even harder for her when you're married."

"Pastor, Priscilla and I have discussed this subject extensively. She, of course, is aware of the danger I'm in just wearing the badge of a lawman. And second, she is aware of the demands that fall on a federal deputy to be away from home weeks on end. She's quite a girl, sir. She insists she can handle it."

Wheeler smiled. "You've got that right. She is quite a girl. I know she's got the fortitude to handle the badge part, but I just hate to see her having to be without her husband so much of the time."

"Well, let me tell you, Pastor, I've been giving that a lot of thought myself. I want to be fair to her. Marriage is a partnership, I know, and it can't be all just one mate's desires. So let me tell you what I've been considering. One of my father's four deputies—Randy Ashbrook—is talking about retiring."

"Oh? Does this have to do with the wound he sustained in his leg in the shootout with the stagecoach robbers a year or so ago?"

"Yes. As you may know, the bone in his thigh was shattered."

"I recall reading that in the newspaper."

"Randy has to use a cane, and he walks with a definite limp. Dad gave him a desk job, but this has cut the force to three deputies who are fit physically to do a deputy's job. Dad needs another deputy, but the county can't afford the extra salary.

Randy knows this, and I'm sure that's why he is planning to retire. He has been offered a desk job at the Pike's Peak Bank."

"Oh, good."

"So, I'm going to talk to Dad today about the possibility of hiring me in Randy's place when he actually retires. I don't doubt at all that he will hire me. I haven't spoken to Priscilla about it yet, but I will do so tonight after I've talked to Dad."

"Sounds good to me. It's difficult enough for a lawman's wife to live with the constant danger her husband faces daily. Your mother has talked to Madelyne about it many times. But at least if you are home most of the time, it will help Priscilla."

"Yes, sir. And the Lord is going to see that it happens, I am sure."

"So when you leave town tomorrow, who are you going after?"

"You're aware of the infamous outlaw gang led by Dolph Widner?"

"Oh yes. Like everyone else in these parts, I'm well-acquainted with the wicked deeds of the Widner gang. They've robbed banks, stores, and stagecoaches, and have killed many innocent people in cold blood."

"Right. Have you ever met my boss, Chief U.S. Marshal Max Carew?"

"Yes. We've met on a couple of occasions."

"Well, Chief Carew has assigned another deputy marshal named Jack Caldwell and me to go on the trail of the Widner gang. They're holed up somewhere on the plains of eastern Colorado. You probably read about the big bank job they pulled in Pueblo on Friday."

"I did."

"The robbery netted them over a hundred thousand dollars. You also know then that they killed three bank employees, and in the shootout with Pueblo's town marshal, they wounded him seriously."

Wheeler nodded solemnly.

"Two of Widner's men were shot and killed in the shootout."

"Yes."

"This leaves Widner with only four men besides himself. Chief Carew wasn't sure just which direction the rest of the gang had fled until he got a tip from a farmer east of Pueblo yesterday afternoon."

"I see."

"The farmer told Chief Carew that Widner and his gang stopped at his place to fill up their canteens at his well. They didn't see him. He recognized Widner from his picture being in the newspapers, and was hiding nearby. He heard them say they were going to hole up somewhere close and take it easy for a while. Chief Carew is waiting for Jack Caldwell to get back from taking a convicted outlaw to the Canon City prison. He's due back this afternoon. He and I will head east and go after the Widner gang."

"But there are five of them, Johnny. Shouldn't Chief Carew send more than two of you?"

"Like Dad, he's short on deputies too. Jack and I will just have to find a way to surprise them and get the drop on them."

"Well, I'll be praying for you. Let's have prayer together right now."

The pastor led as they prayed, asking God to guide and direct Johnny and Priscilla as they became engaged that evening, and to protect Johnny and Deputy Jack Caldwell as they went in pursuit of the gang tomorrow.

When the amen was said, both men rose to their feet and Wheeler rounded the desk. He shook Johnny's hand again. "I'm excited for you and Priscilla. May the Lord bless you, son, as you propose."

"Thank you, Pastor. I like that 'son' part."

Wheeler grinned. "Figure I might as well get used to calling you that."

"Sure sounds good, sir. Makes me mighty proud, too."

Deputy Randy Ashbrook was at the front desk in the sheriff's office when he looked up and saw Johnny Bostin come in. "Hey, look who's here! Hello, Deputy U.S. Marshal Bostin."

Johnny moved up to the desk. "Hello yourself, Deputy Sheriff Ashbrook."

"So how are things in the federal lawman business?"

Johnny chuckled. "Busy—just like the county sheriff business. Lots of bad guys to bring to justice."

At that moment, Sheriff Clay Bostin opened his office door and came out with official-looking papers in his hand. A smile spread over his face. "Hello, son."

"Hi, Dad."

"You need to see me?"

"If you have time."

"Is this about—"

"Mm-hmm."

"I have time, all right." He handed the papers to Randy. "Get these in the mail for me, okay?"

"Yes, sir."

Clay turned and put an arm around his son, and as they headed for the private office, he said, "Johnny, I sure don't get to see you as much since you moved to your apartment."

"Right, Dad, but a guy my age shouldn't be living with his parents."

"Yeah, I know. But his parents would keep him if he wanted to stay. Your mother feels the same way."

They moved into the office and Clay closed the door behind them.

"Sit down, son." As they sat down and faced each other over the desk, Clay said, "So, how did your meeting with the pastor go?"

"Just fine. He gave me permission to ask Priscilla to marry me without a moment's hesitation."

"Just like I told you he would."

"There was one thing he brought up, though, Dad. I've been thinking about it for some time."

"And that is?"

"As I've pondered the prospect of marrying Priscilla, I've thought it would be better if I didn't have this federal deputy job that keeps me away from home weeks on end."

Clay smiled. "I've thought about it too, son. As you know, just being married to a man who wears a badge is rough on a woman. You've seen how it affects your mother."

"Yes. But she's handled it well."

"Mm-hmm. But it hasn't been an easy road for her. You know that being any kind of a lawman is dangerous and demanding work. It isn't like being a carpenter or a merchant. It requires you to be on call literally twenty-four hours a day, seven days a week. You can have the best of plans for any occasion, and they suddenly have to be changed. The only certainty in a lawman's job is its uncertainty. You know all of this because you've lived with it all of your life; first with your natural father, and then with me."

"I know, Dad, but Priscilla and I have talked about my wearing the badge, with all of the pressures that it will put on our married life, but she is completely willing to spend the rest of her life as a lawman's wife. You and Mom have been married all of these years, and she has coped with the pressures quite well."

"That she has, but like I said, it hasn't been an easy road for her." Clay paused, looking at Johnny with his brow creased. "You said it would be better for you and Priscilla if you didn't have this federal deputy job that keeps you away from home weeks on end. In spite of what you have just said, are you considering another profession?"

"Oh no. I was born to wear a badge."

"I'm sure Priscilla and your mother would both welcome a change in profession for you."

"I understand that, but *you* understand what it's like to be born to wear both badge and gun, in spite of the danger."

"What can I say?"

"Dad, I look at it the same as you do. My wonderful God can protect me as a lawman, just as He could if I were a carpenter or a merchant. He isn't limited to just protecting His children who don't wear badges."

Clay smiled and shrugged. "A point well made, son."

A crooked grin came into play on Johnny's handsome face. "Now to what I came to talk to you about. Randy is going to retire from this job and go to work at the bank, right?"

"Yes. It's going to happen within a few weeks. I have to find another deputy and train him."

"Okay, this is just what I wanted to discuss with you. Would you consider hiring me in Randy's place? You wouldn't have to train me."

Clay's eyes brightened. "You mean it?"

"I sure do."

"Well, if you want the job, it's yours. Randy told me when he came in this morning that they want him to start his new job at the bank on Monday, November 1. He needs the pay from the county until then, so I told him he would have his job here until that time. His last day will be Saturday, October 30."

Johnny's face beamed. "All right! I'll tell Chief Carew today, so he'll have time to find another man to take my place."

Clay stood up and Johnny did the same.

"All right, son," said Clay, "I'll plan on you starting as my deputy on Monday, November 1, unless you happen to be chasing some outlaws at the time. If that's the case, you will start here when you come back to Colorado Springs."

"It's a deal, boss!"

Clay moved around the desk and opened his arms. As father and son hugged each other, Clay said, "This makes me very happy. I'll tell your mother about it this evening."

"If you don't mind, Dad, I'll go by the house and tell Mom after I give my notice to Chief Carew."

Clay chuckled. "Of course I don't mind. That's fine. I'm sure when you tell Priscilla tonight, she's going to be very happy about it too."

"She sure will!"

At the Colorado Springs United States Marshal's office, Chief Max Carew sat down with his young deputy. Johnny explained the situation to him and informed him that potentially his first day as an El Paso County deputy sheriff would be November 1.

"I understand your situation, Johnny," Carew said. "I can't say that I blame you at all. I hate to lose such a fine deputy, but for Priscilla's sake, it most certainly is the thing to do. But don't forget to invite Clara and me to the wedding."

"I will not forget, sir. I want both of you there."

"Johnny, I appreciate your giving me this much notice. You're going to be hard to replace. It will take some time. Sheriff Bostin is a very fortunate man."

Johnny's face flushed. "Thank you, sir."

"Let's talk about your Dolph Widner gang assignment with

Jack Caldwell. I want both of you fellas to keep in mind how cold-blooded and vicious that bunch are. Be extra careful. I wish I had more men to send with you, but as you know, all the other deputies are already out on assignments. I want you and Jack to come back alive and unharmed. I also want Widner and his bunch brought back in handcuffs or draped over their saddles, whichever it has to be. The ones in handcuffs will hang."

"We'll do our best, sir."

"I'm sure of that."

Mary Bostin was in the kitchen when she saw her son ride past the side window. She went to the back door, opened it, and watched him dismount at the porch. When he saw her, she laughed. "Well, lookee here, Mrs. Bostin's wayward son has come home!"

Johnny bounded across the back porch and folded her into his arms. "Wayward son, eh?"

"Exactly! He took that apartment, and even when he comes home from chasing all those outlaws, he sleeps in a strange bed."

"A guy has to grow up sometime, Mom." Johnny kissed her rosy cheek.

When they moved into the kitchen, Johnny found the room fragrant. He sniffed, a pleasant look coming into his eyes. "Mmmmm! Smells like oatmeal cookies baking!"

Mary laughed again. "Well, what brings you here other than the fact that you probably smelled those cookies baking all the way from downtown?"

Johnny felt her soft eyes admiring him.

Mary was thinking how much she loved her adopted son. God had only given her this one child—and him by adoption—but he had fulfilled her every dream. She and Clay were both grateful that he had never disappointed them. They had every reason to be proud of him.

"Sit down, son," she said. "I'll let you eat a cookie or two."

Johnny took his place at the table where he had been fed all those years in the Bostin home. Mary poured two cups of steaming black coffee, set a plate of warm cookies on the table, and settled in her own chair. As he chewed a cookie, she said, "Johnny, dear, you look like the proverbial cat that swallowed the canary. Tell me what Pastor said."

Johnny told her the meeting in detail how it went with Pastor Wheeler.

Mary set her cup down and smiled from ear to ear. "I knew it would go well, honey. The Wheelers have known you and loved you as long as we have, and I know they've been praying for the right mate for Priscilla, just as we have for you. I'm sure they have felt confident for the last four or five years that the Lord had chosen you and Priscilla for each other. She's a very special girl, and we love her as if she were our own daughter. I know she will be the perfect wife for you. It's been quite obvious for some time that the Wheelers wanted you for their son-in-law."

"I sort of felt that, Mom, but it was good to have Pastor treat me so well about it. Anyway, tonight, Priscilla gets her engagement ring."

"I wish I could be a fly on the wall when you pop the question."

Johnny chuckled. "Won't be a wall, Mom. I'm taking her for a ride out of town after we eat at the restaurant."

"I know, silly. It's just a figure of speech."

"Just thought I'd tease you a little bit." He paused, then said, "Mom, I have more to tell you."

"Oh? Well, I'm all ears."

Johnny told her about having talked to his father about

Randy Ashbrook, and that he had asked his father if he could be hired. His father had said yes, and he told her how Chief Carew took it and gave her the date that he would go to work as a deputy marshal of El Paso County.

Mary sighed. "Oh, honey, that's good news! I'm so glad to see the Lord working to make things better for you and Priscilla. Your mom will be plenty glad to see you at home more, too."

He reached across the table and patted her hand. "I was sure you would be."

Mary's face pinched. "Honey, I'm nervous about this assignment that you and Jack Caldwell are undertaking. That vicious gang won't be easy to capture."

"I know, Mom. But it has to be done."

"Well, I'll be praying hard, asking God to take care of both of you."

Johnny took a deep breath and let it out slowly. "Right now, my mind is on tonight." He reached into his shirt pocket. "Would you like to see the ring?"

Her face brightened. "Oh yes!"

Pulling out the ring, Johnny placed it in his mother's hand.

"Oh, Johnny, it's beautiful! She's going to love it."

He took another deep breath. "Mom, I'm so nervous. I've never done this before. What if she says no?"

Mary laughed. "Oh yes, I can imagine that! You know as well as I do that Priscilla has been infatuated with you since she first met you. Your father and I have watched that infatuation turn into young love in your teen years, and now it is mature love. There is no way under heaven she is going to turn you down!"

Johnny smiled. "I know that. I was just kidding. But I'm still nervous."

"It's only natural, Johnny, but you'll settle down once you've put this ring on her finger."

❧❧❧

That evening, Johnny stood before the mirror in his apartment and looked at himself. He had taken extra care with his appearance because of the special occasion that was about to take place.

His nerves had been on edge all day. Even though he knew what Priscilla's answer would be, their definite plan to marry would be a life-changing decision.

While recombing his hair, he paused with the comb in midair and thought of the day he first met little Priscilla. *It was really love at first sight, wasn't it, Johnny? That sweet girl wasn't even aware of it, but she crawled right down into your heart.*

A tender smile played across his face. *And she's been there ever since.*

Suddenly becoming aware of the time, he gave himself a mental shake and finished the combing job. He checked himself one last time in the mirror, laid the comb down, and walked to the bed. He picked up his jacket and put it on. Making sure the treasured engagement ring was secure in his shirt pocket, he then buttoned it and headed for the door, whistling a happy tune, his eyes alive with anticipation.

Johnny Bostin was not the only one with jumpy nerves. Anticipating her dinner date with the man she loved, Priscilla Wheeler dressed with particular care in her room on the second floor of the parsonage. All day long, her woman's intuition had told her that tonight was *the* night. Her parents had been behaving a bit peculiar since lunch, and her inner heart just knew it was coming.

Standing before the mirror, Priscilla looked at her reflection. She wore a royal blue wool dress, trimmed with a soft black velvet ribbon around the mandarin collar and down the placket of the bodice. Small velvet covered buttons marched in a row from the collar to the waist, and a gathered skirt fell gracefully to the tips of her shiny black shoes.

Priscilla knew that Johnny liked her hair down. She had brought the sides up and secured them with an ornate round gold-colored barrette. Fluffing out a fringe of bangs, she stepped closer to the mirror for one final inspection. She pinched her cheeks until they glowed with a pinkish tint, took a deep breath in an attempt to settle her nerves, and left the room.

Just as she reached the staircase that led down to the vestibule, she heard a knock at the door. She paused at the top of the stairs and watched as her father went to the door and opened it.

"Hello, Johnny," said the pastor. "I believe Priscilla's about ready."

"All right, sir."

Johnny's gaze trailed up to the top of the stairs. The look in his eyes made Priscilla's heart jump.

From where Johnny stood, Priscilla looked like a princess about to gracefully descend the stairs. As she smiled at him and started down, his heart did flip-flops in his chest.

Chapter Twenty-two

The faces of Dan and Madelyne Wheeler beamed as they stood at the door and watched Priscilla and Johnny step off the porch by the last glow of twilight that was settling over the land. Johnny helped the beautiful brunette into the buggy, walked around to the other side, and hopped in beside her. He took up the reins and put the horse in motion. As Johnny and Priscilla waved, the Wheelers waved in return.

Dan said, "Honey, somehow I get the feeling that our little girl already knows what's going to happen tonight."

Madelyne nodded as they turned and headed for the door. "She does, honey. Take it from me. She knows."

After dinner at the town's nicest restaurant, Johnny Bostin drove the buggy down Main Street, heading south. Priscilla was commenting on the delicious dinner when she noticed that he passed the street that would have taken them to the church and parsonage. Brow puckered, she smiled at him. "Where are we going?"

He put an arm around her shoulders. "Oh, just for a little ride in the moonlight."

The moon was full and bright as they left the town behind and kept moving southward along the road.

Priscilla—especially lovely in the moonlight—looked up at the man she loved. "Johnny, where are we going?"

"You'll see."

The night was crystal clear and on the cool side, but the love flowing between them generated a warmth all its own.

Priscilla told herself she was right. This was going to be the night. She tried to calm her rapidly beating heart while clutching her hands together in anticipation.

Soon Johnny pulled the buggy off the road and drew rein beside a gurgling brook. Priscilla glanced at the brook with moonlight glistening off its active surface and sighed. "Oh, Johnny, it's beautiful."

He stepped out of the buggy and his white teeth glistened as he smiled. "Not as beautiful as you, my sweet."

Her heart was pounding as he rounded the buggy and drew up on her side. He helped her down and led her to the bank of the brook. They sat down on a large rock, and he looked into her eyes. "Sweetheart, I have good news for you."

She felt like a large butterfly was in her chest, fluttering its wings. "What is it?"

Johnny told her about being hired by his father starting November 1 to take Randy Ashbrook's place, and that he had already given notice to Chief Carew.

Priscilla was thrilled. "Oh, Johnny, I'll be so happy having you in town most of the time!"

He let a crooked grin curve his mouth. "Well, I had another reason for wanting to quit my U.S. marshal's job. It's one thing to be in town most of the time, but it's another thing to be in town most of the time and being able to go home each night to my loving wife."

The fluttering in Priscilla's chest grew more rapid as she saw him reach into his shirt pocket and pull out a ring bearing a single diamond that glinted as it reflected the light of the moon. Even though she had felt sure this would be the night he formally asked her to marry him, the actual deed had her speechless.

Johnny held the ring in front of her, his eyes full of love. "Priscilla, darling, we've talked a lot about one day becoming husband and wife, but right now I want to make it more than talk. I have your father's permission and blessing to ask this question. Will you marry me?"

Tears filled Priscilla's eyes. "Oh yes, Johnny. I will marry you!"

Johnny smiled and slowly slipped the ring on the third finger of her left hand. "Then with this ring, I do engage thee to become my lawfully wedded wife at a date we will discuss in a moment."

"Oh, you wonderful darling!"

Johnny folded her in his strong arms and they sealed it with a sweet, tender kiss.

When he released her, she held her left hand out so she could get a good look at the ring. He took hold of her other hand. "How about a June wedding next year?"

She looked at him with love light shining in her tear-filled eyes. "Sounds perfect to me."

"Your father liked it too. He said this would give us time to prepare ourselves for married life."

They sealed that with a kiss, then held hands as they watched the moonlight dance on the gurgling water. Their hands stayed locked together as they made plans for their future as countless other couples before them on earth had done. Gazing deeply into one another's eyes, they pledged their endless love and devotion to each other.

On the ride back to town, they talked more about their

future, and soon Johnny was pulling the buggy up in front of the parsonage. The lantern on the porch was glowing. He helped Priscilla out and held her arm as he guided her up the porch steps. Lantern light showed against the curtains in the parlor, indicating that her parents were still up.

When they stopped at the door, a sudden shiver ran through Priscilla.

Johnny frowned. "Are you cold?"

"No. Your love is keeping me warm, but—"

"But what?"

"With all the joy and happiness we've shared this evening, I hadn't thought of it till now."

"What?"

"Daddy talked about it when he came into the house for lunch today. Tomorrow you and Jack Caldwell will be going after that awful Dolph Widner gang."

"Oh. That."

"Yes. That."

"Honey, it's a job that has to be done. I may have other such assignments before I go to work for Dad. But come November 1, my work will involve this town and the county. We must keep our minds fixed on that."

A whimper escaped her tightly-pressed lips. Her eyes lifted to meet his, filled with dread. "But...but that Widner bunch are so cold-blooded, Johnny. Shouldn't Chief Carew send more than just you and Jack?"

"He can't spare any more men, sweetheart."

She drew a shuddering breath and wiped at her tears.

Johnny folded her into his arms. She laid her head against his chest, wrapped her own arms around him, and held him tight. They clung to each other in silence for a long moment.

Feeling Priscilla's trembling body next to his, Johnny silently asked the Lord to comfort Priscilla and give her peace about his Widner assignment.

At last, Priscilla's trembling ceased. She drew back in his arms just enough to look into his eyes. "I'm sorry, Johnny. Since the day you pinned that badge on, I've never been able to get used to the danger your job entails. I promise that with God's help, I'll do better."

"Sweetheart, I know the life I'm asking you to live is not an easy one. But as I told Dad today, God is as able to protect and care for me as He is a carpenter or a merchant. Please don't be afraid for me."

Priscilla let a smile curve her lips. She reached up and caressed his cheek lovingly. "You're right, my love. I have to learn better how to let the Lord keep me from being afraid. God says in His Word, 'Perfect love casteth out fear.' And we know God's love is perfect. I will strive to always trust you into His mighty hands, and let Him cast out my fears with His perfect love. My heart and my prayers will follow you wherever you go, and whatever the dangers you face, my confidence will be in the one who promised never to leave us nor forsake us."

She rose up on her tiptoes and placed a kiss on his lips.

Johnny smiled. "That's my girl. We must trust everything, every day, into His perfect care and plan for our lives."

He kissed her again, then opened the door for her. "Good night, sweetheart. I'll drive away the happiest man in the whole world. I'll see you just as soon as I get back. Stay busy making plans for our wedding. It will occupy a lot of my thoughts as well. Remember that I love you with all of my heart, and I *will* be home soon."

Priscilla warmed him with a smile. "I love you too, my darling. Hurry back. I'll be waiting and praying."

She watched Johnny move to the buggy, climb in, and shake the reins.

As it rolled away, he waved. She waved back, then stepped in, closed the door, and leaned her back against it. A lantern burned on a small table next to the door. She lifted her left hand and gazed at the ring that sparkled on her finger. With a happy heart, she headed toward the parlor door, eager to show her parents the ring and let them know that all was well concerning her future with the handsome young lawman.

The next morning, Johnny Bostin dismounted in front of the U.S. Marshal's office, his heart throbbing with joy from the night before. When his feet touched ground and he headed toward the door, he put his thoughts on the business at hand.

As he stepped into the office, he saw Deputy Jack Caldwell sitting on a chair by the deputy at the front desk. He greeted both men, noting that Caldwell looked a bit pale. "Jack, are you not feeling well?"

"I've had a sour stomach since I got back from Canon City last night. I'll be okay, though. Chief's waiting for us in his office."

The two deputies had a few minutes with Chief Max Carew, who cautioned them to be very careful, but assured them he had the utmost confidence that they would bring the gang to justice. He handed Johnny a slip of paper bearing the name of the farmer who had reported seeing the gang in his yard at the well, and a description of how to find the farm.

The pair mounted up and trotted their horses due south. When they rode past the spot where Johnny had proposed to Priscilla the night before, a warm feeling washed over his heart.

They arrived in Pueblo two hours later, and turned east. Just under an hour after that, they rode through the gate of the farm some twelve miles from Pueblo. Farmer Bill Farley was walking between the house and the barn when he saw the two riders heading straight toward him. Their badges glinted in the sun.

He was smiling as they drew up. The younger one said, "Mr. Farley, I'm Deputy United States Marshal John Bostin, and this is Deputy United States Marshal Jack Caldwell. We're on the trail of the Widner gang, and Chief Carew asked us to come by and talk to you."

Farley nodded. "Sure. Slip outta those saddles and we'll go sit down on the back porch of the house."

When they were climbing the porch steps, the deputies noticed the face of a woman at the kitchen window. She smiled and disappeared.

After talking a few minutes, the deputies were assured that there were five gang members who took water from the well, and that they rode out headed due east. Farley reminded them that he heard the gang members say they were going to hole up nearby for a while and rest.

While they talked, Johnny noticed that Jack was rubbing his stomach and there was less color in his face. When they were ready to go, Jack gritted his teeth as he stood up and his hand went to his midsection.

Johnny frowned. "Jack, are you all right?"

Jack bent over. "I…I'm in a lot of pain and I'm getting nauseated. But it'll probably pass. We need to get going."

Johnny shook his head. "You're in no shape to go on. I'll go after the gang alone."

"But it's gonna be tough enough for two of us. You can't go up against them alone."

Johnny turned to the farmer. "Mr. Farley, could I get you to take this stubborn mule to the doctor in Pueblo?"

"Sure. Be glad to. I'll take him in my wagon. You go on, Deputy."

Johnny rode off the Farley farm. By asking questions of farmers and villagers along the way, he learned that they had seen five men riding together, a couple of days before, heading due east.

Later that afternoon, as he trotted his horse along the road, he caught sight of a group of men riding southward through a field about a quarter-mile from the road. He slowed his horse, squinted, and was able to count five riders. A moment later, they passed over a rise and disappeared.

Johnny felt sure the five riders were the ones he was pursuing. They must be holed up somewhere over the rise. He put his horse to a gallop until he reached the crest, then slowed to a walk. He saw that the riders were heading toward a small farmhouse in a grove of cottonwood trees.

He followed at a distance, making sure if they looked back, they would think he was just a rider heading across the fields, minding his own business. Drawing rein in the shade of a clump of trees about a hundred yards away, he watched them ride up to the aging old farmhouse and dismount. The place looked deserted, which made Johnny relieved. There wouldn't be a farm family involved.

When the riders put their horses in the dilapidated old barn a few yards from the side of the house, they gathered on the front porch and sat down.

Leaving his horse in the shade of the trees, Johnny made a circle and drew up close to the farmhouse by crawling on the ground and hiding behind a large boulder that was imbedded in the soft soil. He noted that the area was cluttered with similar boulders, each rising two to three feet above the ground.

Johnny peered around the edge of the boulder and immediately recognized Dolph Widner. It was the gang for sure!

Pondering the situation for a few minutes, Johnny had an idea. He thought on it a few more minutes and decided he had the solution. Quickly, he went back to his horse, mounted up, and galloped toward Pueblo.

When he reached Pueblo, the young lawman went into a clothing store and purchased eight hats, all with wide brims. Some were black, some were brown, and some were white.

At dawn, Deputy U.S. Marshal Johnny Bostin hunkered behind a boulder some sixty feet from the front porch of the old farmhouse where the Dolph Widner gang was holed up. He looked toward the barn, which he knew was now unoccupied. Under cover of darkness, he had gone into the barn and led all five horses to the clump of trees where he was yesterday, and tied them along with his own horse, where they couldn't be seen from the hideout.

Johnny ran his gaze over the eight western-style hats that he had placed at different spots in a large half-circle around the front of the house. They were positioned strategically on boulders—which were large enough to hide a man—and would appear to be deputy marshals, ready to cut them down if they resisted arrest. Heavy rocks on the back sides of the hats would keep them from being blown off by the morning breeze.

Rifle in hand, Johnny had his head high enough so he could see the house, and a few feet from his head was one of the hats, making it look like two armed men behind his particular boulder.

At sunup, all five of the gang members came out onto the front porch, obviously intending to make their way to the adjacent barn.

Johnny prayed for help, waited for all five to step off the porch, then raised his head a little higher and aimed his rifle at them. "Everybody freeze right where you are! Get those hands high in the air!"

The outlaws' heads swung around, and their eyes bulged as they saw the numerous hats, thinking they were cornered and outnumbered by a band of lawmen.

"Dolph, there are nine of 'em!" one of the gang said. "We ain't got a chance!"

"You're right about that, mister!" shouted the lone lawman. "My men and I are not going to play games! If you don't drop your gun belts instantly, we'll shoot you down like dogs and save the hangman from having to put ropes around your necks!"

Late that afternoon, Sheriff Clay Bostin was in his office when Deputy Randy Ashbrook limped through the door in a hurry, using his cane. "Sheriff! Come outside! You gotta see this!"

When the sheriff reached the boardwalk with Randy at his side, he was overjoyed to see his son dismounting with all five members of the Widner gang on their horses with their hands tied behind their backs, their faces grim and sullen.

Johnny grinned at his father. "Got room enough for Dolph and his boys in your jail, Dad?"

Clay's mouth hung open. "How…how did you—"

"I'll explain later, Dad. Let's get them locked up first."

"Where's Jack, son?"

Johnny explained about Jack's stomach giving him trouble yesterday morning, and that farmer Bill Farley had taken him into Pueblo to the doctor. "I stopped in Pueblo this morning and found out that Jack had to have his appendix out. He won't be home for a week to ten days."

By this time, a crowd was gathering around the front of the sheriff's office.

They looked on in amazement as the sheriff said, "Son, you're telling me that you did this all by yourself?"

Johnny grinned. "No, Dad. Not by myself. The Lord helped me."

Johnny then went to the U. S. Marshal's office and told the story to Chief Max Carew.

Priscilla Wheeler ran into Johnny's arms as soon as she opened the parsonage door in response to the knock. She explained that her parents were making a visit to one of the church members on the other side of town.

They went to the Bostin home, and Mary was happy to see her son and to hear that the Widner gang was behind bars. Johnny told her that they would be transported to the Canon City prison tomorrow, where they would face the hangman.

Johnny explained to his mother about Jack Caldwell, then took Priscilla back to the parsonage and spent a few minutes telling the story to the pastor and Madelyne, who were home by then. The Lord was praised, and Johnny was invited back for dinner that evening.

When Johnny returned to the U. S. Marshal's office, Chief Carew was standing in the front office, telling the story of the gang's capture to two deputies who had just returned from an assignment. The deputies congratulated the young deputy, then Carew took Johnny into his office and closed the door. "Sit down, Johnny."

Carew sat down behind his desk and leaned his elbows on the top. "I knew that President Grover Cleveland was to be up in Denver for a couple of days this week for a special meeting with the Indian agents in this part of the West. I wired Chief U.S. Marshal John Brockman in Denver an hour ago about your single-handed capture of the Widner gang, since his office has jurisdiction over this office, as you know."

"Yes, sir. Like you and my dad, I admire Chief Brockman very much. Dad knows him personally, but I have never met him. So the president is in Denver right now?"

"Yes, and listen to this. Brockman wired me back five minutes ago. He said he went to President Cleveland and told him about your accomplishment. The president had heard about the bloody Widner gang back in Washington, D.C. Brockman's wire informed me that President Cleveland is making a special trip down here by train tomorrow to honor you for what you did. Chief Brockman is coming with him."

Johnny put a shaky hand to his mouth. "Chief...I...I'm scared."

Carew laughed. "You single-handedly captured the most notorious gang of killers in these parts, and you're scared to face the president?"

Johnny swallowed hard. "Yeah."

The next afternoon, the bulk of Colorado Springs' population was on hand at the railroad station, where on the rear platform of the presidential coach, Chief Max Carew stood between the president and the tall, dark chief U.S. marshal from the Denver office. A nervous Johnny Bostin stood on the ground, ready to mount the steps of the platform when it was time. Carew introduced President Cleveland first and the crowd gave him a rousing welcome. Cleveland then took a step back, allowing Chief Carew opportunity to make his next introduction.

Carew then introduced Chief U.S. Marshal John Brockman, and because the people of Colorado Springs knew Brockman's outstanding record as a federal lawman, they also gave him a rousing welcome.

Cleveland gestured for Brockman to step forward and speak

first. Sheriff Clay Bostin and his wife, Mary, stood at the forefront of the crowd. Close by the Bostins were their pastor and his wife, and standing next to Madelyne was a bright-faced Priscilla.

Brockman smiled as he looked at the sheriff and said, "Ladies and gentlemen, your sheriff and I have met on several occasions over these past few years, and I very much admire him. I'm sure that with his open and bold testimony, all of you know he is a dedicated Christian."

Heads in the crowd were nodding.

Brockman smiled. "I also happen to know that his wife is also a dedicated Christian, as is their son, whom we are honoring today." He looked down and smiled at Johnny, whose face was a bit pale. Johnny managed to return the smile.

Brockman continued. "I will not infringe on the president's time, but I want to say to you, Deputy Marshal Johnny Bostin, I am impressed with your courage and adeptness as a lawman. God bless you."

There was applause, then as the president stepped forward, he motioned for Johnny to mount the steps of the platform and stand beside him. Carew stepped back, giving Johnny room.

The crowd listened intently as President Grover Cleveland presented Deputy U. S. Marshal Johnny Bostin with a special written letter of commendation signed by himself, commending him for his courageous and resourceful capture of the infamous Dolph Widner gang.

The crowd applauded. Johnny noticed that Priscilla had tears running down her cheeks, as did her mother and his own mother. Sheriff Clay Bostin's buttons were about to pop off his shirt. He and Brockman exchanged smiles.

Cleveland said, "Deputy Bostin, I'm sure these people would like to hear a few words from you."

Holding the letter, Johnny swallowed hard, ran his gaze over the faces of the crowd, then turned to Cleveland. "Mr. President, I want to thank you for this honor. I…I don't feel that I deserve it, but I will always cherish this letter. The reason I don't feel I deserve it is because I was not alone in capturing the Widner gang. I had help."

Surprise showed on the president's face, as well as the faces of most people in the crowd. Some, however—including the Bostins and the Wheelers—knew what was coming.

Feeling more relaxed, now, Johnny said so all could hear, "The one who helped me capture the killers is the same one who went to Calvary's cross for me, shed His precious blood, and died to provide this sinner forgiveness for his sins and salvation for his lost soul—my Lord and Saviour, Jesus Christ. He promised in His Word that He would never leave me nor forsake me. Yesterday, I called on Him to help me capture the gang because I knew I couldn't do it by myself. All the praise and glory goes to Him."

While the crowd was applauding, Johnny motioned for Priscilla to come to him. Blinking in astonishment, she left her parents and made her way to the steps of the platform. John Brockman moved down, gave her his hand, and helped her mount the steps. She gave him a smile that expressed her thanks.

Johnny took Priscilla's hand, then looked out at the crowd. Smiles were spreading on faces.

"Ladies and gentlemen," said Johnny, "since the Lord has allowed me this moment in the limelight, I want to make use of it. I would like to announce that this lovely young lady, Miss Priscilla Wheeler, has consented to become my bride. We plan to be united in holy matrimony next June. I don't deserve her, either, but the Lord gave her to me, and I'm going to keep her!"

There was applause mingled with cheers.

A proud Clay Bostin applauded with tears in his eyes, as did Mary and the Wheelers.

When the applause and cheering faded, President Grover Cleveland congratulated the young couple, and the whole crowd cheered and applauded again.

Chapter Twenty-three

It was a clear April morning in 1887 on the Arizona desert. At Fort Apache, Colonel James Strasburg—commandant of the fort—stood outside the stockade gate and watched as his four patrol units rode away for their daily security tour.

A flood of golden sunshine was on the desert, and a dry, fragrant breeze drifted across the wide-open spaces, carrying the sweet scent of the wildflowers that blossomed in every direction.

Strasburg gave the patrol units one last glance as they spread out in four directions, then turned and walked back inside the fort. The corporal who stood at the gate said, "I hope all is quiet out there on the desert today, Colonel."

"Me too," said Strasburg, "but you never know about those Apaches."

As the colonel headed toward his house inside the fort, the corporal closed the gate and returned to his partner in the tower.

Strasburg smiled when he saw his guest come out of the officers' barracks on the other side of the compound and head toward the house, where Della was preparing a special breakfast.

His guest was Colonel Fred Howell, who was on his way from where he had served as a major at Fort Laramie, Wyoming, to serve as commandant at Fort Thomas in southern Arizona on the Gila River.

At that moment, Howell's escort of twelve cavalrymen was eating breakfast in the mess hall.

Strasburg had been pleasantly surprised upon meeting Colonel Howell yesterday to learn that he was a born-again man and was dedicated to the Lord. It had made the evening they had spent together a special blessing.

Others expected at the Strasburg house any minute were Fort Apache's chaplain Ben Locke, his wife, Tina, and missionaries Cody and Donna Rogers.

As he met up with Colonel Howell at the front porch, he noticed both the other couples coming toward the house.

"Good morning, Colonel," said Strasburg. "Sleep well?"

"Sure did, Colonel. I wish I could take that bed to Fort Thomas with me."

Strasburg laughed. "Well, maybe they'll have one that good."

"I sure hope so."

The other two couples drew up. Strasburg introduced the Lockes to his guest, both of whom were showing their seventy-plus years. The Rogerses were in their mid-twenties.

Strasburg said, "I want you folks to know that Colonel Howell knows and loves our Lord Jesus."

Instant smiles spread over four faces, and each one told Howell how happy they were to know he was their brother in Christ.

Howell set smiling eyes on Donna. "Mrs. Rogers, my wife Sarah has auburn hair just like yours."

Donna smiled. "Oh?"

"Mm-hmm. Well, not exactly like yours. We are in our fifties now. So her hair has some gray creeping in." He chuckled. "Like mine."

"Well, Colonel, if the Lord lets me live to see my fifties, I'm sure there'll be some gray creeping into my hair too."

"But I'll love you just the same," said Cody.

Donna clipped his chin playfully. "You'd better!"

Everybody laughed, then Colonel Strasburg said, "We'd best get inside. I'm sure Della has breakfast about ready."

Della was inside the door to greet her guests and the aroma of hot breakfast filled the house.

They sat down at the dining room table and James Strasburg led in prayer. He thanked God for the food and asked His blessing on the Rogerses as they were about to begin another missionary tour among the Apache villages. He thanked the Lord for the precious blood that was shed by the Lamb of God at Calvary and for the salvation He provided.

As they began eating, Donna said, "Colonel Howell, you mentioned your wife. Is she joining you at Fort Thomas soon?"

"Yes. She had surgery just a few weeks ago, and she isn't up to traveling yet. She'll be coming sometime in June, the Lord willing."

"So she is recovering from the surgery all right?"

"Yes, thank the Lord."

Howell worked at devouring his pancakes for a minute or so, then set his gaze on Ben Locke. "How long have you been an army chaplain?"

Ben grinned. "Almost thirty years. I was a pastor in Indiana before that."

Strasburg shook his head. "We're losing the Lockes, though, Colonel Howell. Chaplain Locke is retiring, and he and Tina will be leaving for Indianapolis in two weeks so they can live close to their children and grandchildren."

"Oh? Well, you will miss them, I'm sure."

"Very much so."

Howell nodded. "Has a new chaplain been assigned to the fort?"

"Yes. The army brass in Washington, D.C., has assigned a young chaplain named Donald Vaughn in Chaplain Locke's place. Vaughn has been serving as assistant chaplain at Fort McDowell, Arizona, for the past two years."

"Let's see, Fort McDowell. Where is Fort McDowell?"

"It's a hundred miles west of here. Near Phoenix."

"Oh. And when will Chaplain Vaughn be coming?"

"He and his wife are scheduled to arrive here a day or two after the Lockes leave for Indiana."

"That's good. You won't be without a chaplain very long, then." Howell then glanced at Cody and Donna. "I'm amazed to hear that you are able to go into the Apache villages and preach the gospel."

"Well, sir," said Cody, "it's a relative few villages where the chiefs will let us in. But thank God for those few. Fourteen, to be exact. We have seen some of the chiefs come to the Lord, and we've had a good number of their people saved."

"You're both so young. How long have you been doing this work among the Apaches?"

"Three years, sir. We started when I was twenty-three and Donna was twenty-one."

"Cody and Donna live in a cabin inside the fort here, Colonel," said Strasburg. "As commandant, I have provided the cabin for them since they came to this area. It's only by the hand of Almighty God that they are able to get into those fourteen villages. They are gone from the fort on their missionary tours three to four weeks at a time. When traveling, they live in their covered wagon, which was given to them by Donna's parents Ken and Molly Talbert, who live in Safford, Arizona."

Howell touched his temple. "Safford. That's south of here, isn't it?"

"Yes. About eighty miles. Cody's parents also live in Safford.

His father is president of the Bank of Safford."

"I see."

As breakfast continued, the Rogerses told the Strasburgs they would be looking forward to meeting the new chaplain and his wife when they returned from their next missionary tour of the Apache villages.

"When will you begin the next tour?" asked Howell.

"Today, sir," replied Cody. "We'll be pulling out right after breakfast. We'll be back sometime the second week of May, three weeks from now."

When breakfast was over, Cody and Donna told the Lockes and Colonel Howell good-bye, climbed into their covered wagon, and drove away.

On Tuesday, May 3, Colonel James Strasburg was in his office at Fort Apache when there was a knock at the door. Looking up from the papers on his desk, he called, "Yes?"

The door came open and his adjutant corporal said, "Colonel, the new chaplain and his wife have arrived."

The colonel smiled, rising from his desk. "Bring them in, Wally, and—" Strasburg noticed a strange look on the face of the corporal. "Is something wrong?"

"Well, sir, not really wrong. It's just something out of the ordinary."

Strasburg's brow furrowed. "What do you mean?"

"Have you ever met the Vaughns, sir?"

"No. Why do you ask?"

Wally Benton wiped a palm over his mouth. "I'll...ah...bring them in, sir. You can see for yourself."

The furrows deepened on Strasburg's brow as Wally stepped out of view and he heard him say, "Colonel Strasburg is waiting for you, folks."

Strasburg's attention remained riveted on the open door. His eyes bulged and his jaw slacked when Chaplain Donald Vaughn and his lovely auburn-haired wife stepped into the office. He looked at the woman and said, "D-Donna, is th-this a j-joke?"

The chaplain frowned as his twenty-four-year-old wife looked at Strasburg, her own eyes wide. "Excuse me, Colonel. Did—did you call me *Donna?*"

Strasburg blinked. "Of course. Donna Rogers, what are you doing posing as the chaplain's wife?"

Suddenly the woman's mouth was working loosely as though she had lost the power of speech.

Her husband took hold of her hand. "Honey, are you all right?"

She drew a shaky breath. "Don, can this really be happening? You know I've waited and wondered about Donna for eleven years. Colonel Strasburg just called me by her name!"

The colonel took a step closer. "I'm sorry, ma'am. I didn't mean to upset you. But—but you are the exact image of a young woman I know well. Her name is Donna Rogers."

A hand went to her mouth. "Colonel, I have an identical twin sister named Donna. I lost track of her eleven years ago. My name is Deena. Donna and I were separated, and neither one of us knew what happened to the other. She didn't know where I was, and I didn't know where she was." Her eyes suddenly filled with tears. "Colonel, the woman you know as Donna Rogers is my identical twin sister! You have nothing to apologize about. No wonder you were taken aback when you saw me. You thought I was Donna!"

Strasburg pointed to the sofa and chair in the corner of his office. "Let's sit down." The colonel led them to the sofa. Before they sat down, he shook hands with Donald Vaughn. "Chaplain, I'm so glad you're here."

"Me too, sir."

Deena offered her hand. "Colonel, this has been quite a moment. I'm glad to meet you."

When Strasburg had shaken Deena's hand, he waited until the Vaughns were seated on the sofa, then sat down in the overstuffed chair, facing them.

Deena's eager eyes were fastened on the colonel. "Tell me about Donna!"

Strasburg talked slowly as he explained to the Vaughns that Cody and Donna Rogers were missionaries to the Apache Indians in that part of Arizona. He explained that they had a log cabin there in the fort, which he provided for them when they first came there three years ago.

The colonel went on to tell them that he and his wife Della were born-again Christians, which brought big smiles to the faces of the Vaughns, along with warm comments. He then told them about Cody and Donna's covered wagon, and that they were usually out three to four weeks at a time, giving the gospel to the Apaches. He explained that they were doing that at the moment, and would be back sometime the second week of May.

Deena got so excited she could hardly contain herself. She bounced up and down on the sofa, eyes glistening, and took hold of her husband's hand. "Oh, Don! God is so good! I'm going to see my sister and hold her in my arms again!"

"Yes, sweetheart. Praise the Lord!"

Don slipped an arm around her and looked at the colonel. "Deena and I have been praying ever since we got married four years ago that the Lord would bring the twins together one day."

Deena wiped tears. "Colonel, if you have time, I'll tell you the whole story, so you'll be all filled in when Donna and her husband return."

Strasburg smiled. "Right now, I don't want to do anything but hear this story."

While Don kept an arm around her, Deena told the colonel the whole story, starting back when the twins' parents sent them to the streets of Manhattan because they could no longer afford to keep them. She told him of the orphan train, and how she was chosen by Ralph and Norma Dexter in Salina, Kansas, and of the horror she experienced knowing that her twin would head further west on the train without her.

She explained how Ralph and his son Rex mistreated her, and how she ran away and hid herself in a covered wagon that was part of a wagon train that was headed west. The owners of the wagon, Brian and Valerie Parker, heard her story and took her with them.

"So you see, Colonel, I had no way of knowing what had happened to Donna. It's a long way from Salina, Kansas, to the West Coast. The possibilities of where she might have been chosen were endless. Since I've been saved, I've prayed every day that the Lord would unite me with my twin. There have been so many times when I've been filled with anxiety over her, and many nights my sleep was disturbed because I knew Donna was in some sort of pain or distress. Identical twins usually know when one is agitated or troubled or in physical pain. I don't understand how it works, but I know it does."

"I've heard that, Deena," said the colonel.

Deena sighed. "God has given me peace about my separation from Donna, or I would never have been able to stand it. I never stopped praying and hoping that someday He would bring us back together. The Bible says for us to pray without ceasing, and believe me that was easy to do in this situation."

Strasburg smiled. "I can believe that."

Deena stared off into space for a moment, remembering the last time she saw her beloved sister, and the pain that tore at her heart as they were forced apart. "When Donna and I were separated, I felt that half of me was missing, and I've felt that way every day since."

She looked at Don. They smiled at each other, then she looked back at Strasburg. "Colonel, you have no idea how much joy you have given me."

Strasburg smiled again. "I'm glad I could help heal your broken heart, Deena. And I've been thinking…"

"Yes, sir?"

"I'm going to call the entire population of the fort together, introduce both of you, and tell them the story. I want them all to know about it, so when Cody and Donna get back here, they won't spill the beans. I want you to surprise them in your own way on that day."

"That's good thinking, Colonel," Don said. "That will be one glorious day, indeed."

Deena looked at the colonel again. "Sir, I should really tell you the rest of the story, about how the Parkers adopted me, and we got saved, and all that."

"I'm all ears!"

Deena told him about the day the wagon train was entering Comanche territory in southwest Kansas, and how a small band of Comanches attacked them and she was shot in the back with an arrow. The Parkers thought at first that she was dead, but moments later, when the Indians who were not shot down by the men of the wagon train were gone, they found that she was still alive. The wagon master knew of a doctor in nearby Missler, Kansas. They took her there and the doctor removed the arrow.

She went on to tell Strasburg that the Parkers were headed for Phoenix. Brian had a close friend from his hometown back in Indiana who owned a hardware store in Phoenix. The friend had offered him a job in the store if they moved out there. A short time after they got settled in Phoenix, the Parkers legally adopted her. Not long after that, they were visited in their home by the pastor of a Bible-believing church in Phoenix who led them to the Lord. It was in that church where she met Don and they fell in love.

Colonel Strasburg rubbed his jaw. "Donna never told Della and me about you, Deena. And I'm sure I know why. It had to have been because she was carrying such a burden, wondering what had happened to you. The subject had to have been too painful for her to bring up."

"You're right, sir. I can understand that completely. I know exactly what that pain is like. Oh, I'm so thrilled to know that Donna is saved and is in missionary work with her husband. I can hardly wait to see them!"

Don pulled her tight against his side. "Sweetheart, this is wonderful! Isn't God good to us? Even though it's taken years, and His answer to your prayers was 'wait,' now it's His time to say the waiting is over!"

Tears were spilling down Deena's cheeks. "Oh yes, He is good to us! I'm so excited, I can hardly stand it!"

In the days that followed, Chaplain Don Vaughn settled in on his job at the fort and Deena busied herself fixing up the cabin to give it her own personal touch. The Rogers cabin was right next to it, and often Deena found herself looking at it and picturing in her mind how it would be when her sister and husband returned.

As was to be expected at a lonely outpost in the Arizona desert, the Vaughn cabin was rustic, and Deena immediately met the challenge of making it into a cozy, comfortable home for the two of them. A thorough scrubbing of the walls and floor did much to improve its appearance. Deena washed, starched, and ironed the curtains until they were white enough and crisp enough to suit her. The grime of winter was cleaned off the windows, and they sparkled in the spring sunlight. She polished the furniture until it gleamed.

One day she had Don take her to the nearby town of Whiteriver, and they purchased some things she very much needed. Upon returning home, she made up the bed in a colorful new quilt and placed a matching braided rug on the rough planks of the floor. A bright checked cloth adorned the round table, and her treasured knickknacks filled the shelves. Her prized china filled the cupboards.

When all was done, Deena took her scissors and a basket and went outside to cut some wildflowers that she had noticed growing beside the cabin. She put them in a jar and placed them in the center of the table, then stepped back to survey her handiwork.

Turning in a slow circle, she viewed the small cabin. A bright smile of satisfaction lit up her face and her eyes sparkled. "There now," she said with a sigh. "My husband has a restful, comfy place to come home to."

Deena continued to stay busy every day with household chores, wishing away the hours in anticipation of her sister's return to the fort. One picture after another flitted across her mind as to what it would be like when at last she and Donna would be together again.

Every day, Deena walked close to the Rogers cabin and wept for joy, thanking the Lord for bringing Donna to Himself and putting her in His service. Just being near the structure where her twin lived sent tingles down her spine.

On Tuesday, May 10, Cody and Donna Rogers were about to leave their last Apache village before heading back to Fort

Apache, which was twenty-three miles away. Women and children were looking on as the Rogerses stood beside their covered wagon, talking to the chief and his wife.

The men moved about, sending pleasant glances that direction, their sharp-featured bronzed faces shining in the morning sun.

Chief Mizno and his squaw, Aratena, whom Cody and Donna had led to the Lord six months earlier, thanked them for coming once again. They and the Rogerses talked about the five souls who were saved during that particular visit, and Chief Mizno and Aratena told them they were looking forward to the next time they would come back.

Donna embraced Aratena, saying she loved her, and Aratena spoke words of love in return. Cody helped Donna onto the seat, climbed up beside her, and they both waved as they drove away. The Apaches waved back.

While the wagon rolled along the desert trail, Donna said, "Honey, I'm getting sensations from Deena again."

"Bad or good?"

"Good. *Very* good. She has happy emotions."

They talked about how Donna had sensed Deena's happy times and her sorrowful times over the years, and how Donna had prayed so long that the Lord would bring them together. Cody had prayed that way with Donna since before they were married.

The subject turned to the new chaplain and his wife, whom they knew were to arrive before they returned to Fort Apache.

They hoped Chaplain Donald Vaughn would be liked as well as Chaplain Ben Locke was.

Soon the fort came into view, and twenty minutes later, Cody pulled the covered wagon up to the gate. One of the guards hurried down from the tower and opened the gate, welcoming them home.

Cody headed the wagon toward the commandant's office. It was the custom that the missionaries always stopped to tell Colonel Strasburg how things went on their tour.

When they pulled up in front of the office, the colonel was standing on the porch, talking to two officers. The officers welcomed the Rogerses home, and the colonel invited the missionaries into his office. When they told him that thirty-four people had come to the Lord, the colonel praised the Lord.

"Well, sir," said Cody, "did our new chaplain and his wife arrive?"

A thrill ran through Strasburg. "They sure did. I really like Chaplain Vaughn and his wife, and so does Della and everyone else in the fort. He's a great preacher too. The chaplain is in his office next door. I'll take you over right now and introduce you to him. He's been excited about meeting you."

"Swell!" said Cody.

With his heart pounding, Colonel James Strasburg took them to the chaplain's office. They liked Don Vaughn immediately, and Vaughn liked them. The chaplain asked about the tour, and was happy to hear of the thirty-four souls that had been saved. He then talked about how much he and his wife already loved Fort Apache—without ever mentioning his wife's name.

Across the compound, Deena was coming out the front door of her cabin with three officers' wives when one of them saw the covered wagon parked in front of the offices. She pointed to it and said, "Deena! That's the Rogers wagon, right there!"

Another said, "Ladies, let's make ourselves scarce real quick. Deena needs this moment to herself."

The women hurried away, and Deena's heart went to her throat when she saw movement at the door of her husband's office, and a couple come out, talking to both Don and the colonel.

She instantly recognized her twin.

Her heart was pounding as she dashed inside the cabin and moved up to one of the windows beside the door. Through the lace curtains she had a perfect view of the Rogerses as they came that direction with Cody leading the team.

All over the compound, soldiers looked on furtively, as did the officers and their wives. They were excited, knowing Donna was about to get the surprise of her life.

Deena's pulse was pounding as she watched Donna and Cody draw up in front of their cabin some forty feet away. Donna followed Cody to the rear of the wagon and watched him climb over the tailgate. Deena could hear him as he looked back at Donna and said, "Sweetie, I'll hand you down some of the light things, then I'll carry the heavier items into the cabin."

She saw Donna smile as she giggled and said, "Well, Mister Muscles, I can carry anything you can!"

Cody laughed, shaking his head.

Inside the cabin, Donna's twin was drinking in the scene and could endure the waiting no longer.

She headed for the door.

At the covered wagon, Donna giggled again. "What are you laughing about, big man? Just hand me down one of those heavy boxes, and I'll show you."

Inside the wagon, Cody froze as he saw the auburn-haired young woman come out of the adjacent cabin, and suddenly Donna heard a trembling female voice from behind her call out, "Donna! Donna!"

Chapter Twenty-four

When Donna Rogers heard her name called, it seemed as though it was her own voice falling on her ears. From where Cody stood inside the covered wagon, he saw her stiffen and stand still. His spine tingled as he anticipated what was about to happen.

It can't be, Donna's mind told her, but in that electrifying moment, her racing heart told her it was so.

She spun around, and a startled expression claimed her face when her eyes beheld the wondrous sight. "Deena!" she cried as her twin stood ten feet away with tears streaming down her cheeks.

The twins bolted into each other's arms. Both of them were crying as Donna choked out, "Oh, Deena! My precious Deena! How can this be? I've waited an eternity for this day! Though I've prayed for it for so long, deep down, I was afraid it would never happen!"

Deena eased back, wiping tears in an attempt to clear her vision. "Let me look at you, honey! Oh, this is wonderful! We still look exactly alike, just grown up." She ran trembling fingers over Donna's tear-stained cheeks. "God made us wait eleven years, but He didn't forget us! All the time, He has been preparing us for this special moment! I...I just can't take my eyes off you. I'm afraid if I do, you might disappear. This all seems like a dream."

Donna hugged her again, kissed her cheek, then drew back to look at her. "I know what you mean, sis, but believe me, I'm not going anywhere! We've so much catching up to do. You have to tell me what brought you here. Oh, I still can't believe it's happening! It's going to take time for reality to set in."

They embraced again, tears flowing.

At that moment, Don arrived, and Cody jumped down from the wagon. Don shook hands with Cody. "Cody, I'm Don Vaughn. Deena's husband."

Cody's eyes widened. "You're the new chaplain!"

"That's right."

"Well, praise the Lord! This is unbelievable!"

Don chuckled. "With God, all things are possible."

The twins turned to their husbands, keeping an arm round each other. Donna said, "Oh, Cody, isn't this marvelous?"

"It sure is, honey! All your prayers about Deena have now been answered!"

"And vice versa, Deena!" said Don.

"Yes!" Deena squealed. "Donna, this is my husband, Don Vaughn."

Not having heard the words exchanged a moment ago between the two men, Donna gasped. "Vaughn? He's—he's—"

"The new chaplain," Cody finished for her.

"Oh, praise the Lord! Deena, this is my husband, Cody Rogers."

"We already know all about your missionary work," said Deena. "And we both think it's wonderful."

The brothers-in-law embraced the sisters-in-law, and by that time, nearly everyone who was in the fort at that time joined them and shared the happy moment. Colonel Strasburg and Della were especially elated to be in on the occasion. After a while, the people drifted off to their own quarters and various duties, a happy glow filling each heart over the reunion of the twins.

Holding her sister's hand, Deena said, "We have a lot to talk about. How about you and Cody coming into our cabin? I'll heat up some coffee."

Don said, "Honey, you two go get the coffee hot while I help Cody unload the wagon."

"Okay, but hurry. We want you in on all the catching up. You're both big parts of all this, you know."

"We'll be there shortly," Cody said.

The twins entered the Vaughn cabin, and Donna stopped just inside the door, her eyes roving from side to side. A smile beamed. "Deena, you're not going to believe this, but our cabin is decorated almost identically to what I see."

Deena smiled back. "Oh, I believe it. Our taste in everything always was pretty much the same."

Donna followed her sister to the kitchen. As Deena stoked up the fire that was still smoldering from breakfast, Donna said, "Can I do something to help?"

"Not much to do at this point, honey. I'll get the coffee heating here in a moment. Why don't we just plan on you and Cody eating lunch with us? It's almost ten o'clock. We'll need the next two hours just to begin catching up."

"Sounds good to me."

The twins hugged each other again and were chatting happily when their husbands came in a short time later. They sat down at the table together with the coffee mugs steaming, and the next two hours were spent with Deena and Donna telling each other their stories. There was much joy as they told how and when they came to know the Lord, how they met their husbands, and how they ended up at Fort Apache.

All the while, both husbands and wives were shedding happy tears and rejoicing in the Lord and praising Him that the twins were together again.

In Los Angeles, twenty-one-year-old Ted Hansen, twenty-four-year-old Jerry Varnell, and twenty-year-old Clint Albright were preparing to found the orphanage of their dreams and construct a building.

The Dalbys were leading in the financing of the project, but also wanted to let the people of the community have a financial part in it.

In the first week of June, the Dalbys sponsored a large banquet in the Los Angeles city auditorium and hundreds of people were in attendance.

When the meal was finished, Marvin Dalby stood at the head table and introduced his three foster sons. He asked Ted, Jerry, and Clint to step up front and tell everyone of their desire to found the orphanage and when this desire began.

Jerry said, "Dad, Clint and I both feel that Teddy—ah, Ted—is the one with words. We'll let him tell the story."

Marvin smiled. "Well, I can't argue with that. Ted, the floor is yours."

Jerry and Clint took a step back and looked on as Ted began by pointing out that with the growth of Los Angeles and the surrounding southern California towns and cities, more and more children were ending up on the streets.

Ted then engaged Jerry and Clint in conversation in front of the crowd, and together they spoke of their fond memories of the Thirty-second Street Orphanage, which cared for them until they were placed on the orphan train.

Ted smiled. "Ladies and gentlemen, it was while we were traveling westward on the train that we began to talk about it, and we found that we each had a desire to one day provide a home for children with the same needs as ours. Our common desire molded us together in a special way, and from that moment on, we began to hope that the three of us would be chosen by families in the same area, so we could grow up together and realize our dream together. And what a blessing it was when the Dalbys chose all three of us and took us to their home."

The crowd applauded.

Smiling, Ted went on. "There is no orphan train here, but we will do our best to care for the unfortunate children in southern California until they are adopted into good homes or until they grow up and are able to care for themselves."

When Ted finished his speech, there was a standing ovation, and when he turned the floor back to his adoptive father, Marvin soon had the crowd taking out their checkbooks.

On Saturday morning, June 11, in Colorado Springs, rain was falling from heavy clouds as Priscilla Wheeler stood in her bedroom at the parsonage before breakfast and looked at her lovely chantilly-lace wedding gown, hanging ready and waiting in the closet.

"Oh, well," she said while caressing the gown, "rain or shine, this is my wedding day, and nothing is going to spoil it." She took a deep breath. "But it sure would help, Lord, if You would send the storm away."

Shortly after noon, the rain stopped falling as the dark clouds lifted and began breaking up. Soon the Colorado sun shone down from a cobalt blue sky and only a few puffy clouds remained.

Priscilla thanked the Lord for the sunshine, and with her mother's help, began preparing herself for that most special day.

At three o'clock that afternoon, the church auditorium was redolent with the sweet scent of lavender and white lilacs, and a soft gentle breeze wafted its way through the open windows.

Everyone stood when the pump organ began the wedding march and Pastor Dan Wheeler walked his lovely daughter down the aisle. Johnny Bostin waited at the foot of the platform, a nervous smile on his face. For a brief moment, he took his eyes off his approaching bride to look at his parents, who stood at the second pew on the right side of the aisle.

Sheriff Clay Bostin winked at him, and Mary blinked at her tears, giving him a smile. Standing on the other side of the aisle, Madelyne dabbed at her eyes and smiled at Johnny.

The pastor and his daughter drew up to Johnny, and after placing her hand in the hand of the groom, the pastor bent down and kissed her cheek. "I love you, princess."

Priscilla's eyes were misty. "I love you too, Daddy. You will always have your special place in my heart."

Taking a deep breath to control his emotions, Pastor Dan Wheeler moved up onto the platform and turned around facing a smiling audience. He nodded to the bride and groom. Johnny helped Priscilla up the steps, and reaching the platform, they stood before the preacher, ready to take their vows.

A few days later, Sheriff Clay Bostin was walking down Main Street alone when he heard a loud argument going on inside the Rusty Gun Saloon. Suddenly shots were fired.

Tensing, the sheriff whipped out his gun and started toward

the saloon, but halted when two men with guns bolted out the door. Cocking the gun, he raised it and said sharply, "Stop right there! Drop those guns!"

One of them swung his revolver on the sheriff and dropped the hammer. The gun roared, and the bullet hissed past his ear. Clay fired, hitting the man dead-center in the chest. The second man swung his weapon on Bostin. Both of them squeezed their triggers at the same time. Flame blossomed from both muzzles.

Clay felt like a red-hot claw ripped at his upper right arm, and as the jolt knocked the gun from his hand, he saw the other man go down like a dead tree in a high wind. The thunder of the gunshots echoed along the street, where wagons, buggies, and men on horseback were moving at a slow pace. People in the street and on the boardwalks looked on in shock.

Johnny and a deputy named Cade Gilman were half a block away and were running that direction full speed.

The sheriff gripped his wounded arm, and the whole world seemed to be spinning around him as his legs gave way, and he dropped into the dust of the street. He was vaguely aware of people crowding around him when he heard the voice of his son calling for someone to go get Dr. Hornsby. Johnny knelt beside him. "Dad! It's me. Doc Hornsby will be here in a minute!"

Clay was barely conscious when the doctor arrived and knelt beside him. He took one look at the bleeding arm. "Johnny, you and Cade carry him down to my office. I've got to tend to this wound quickly."

The lawman heard his son call to someone in the crowd named Jim and ask him to go to the Bostin house and advise his mother that his father had been shot.

While Johnny and Cade were carefully picking the sheriff up, the doctor went to the two men who lay in the dust and pronounced them dead, telling someone to go get the undertaker.

At his office, Dr. J. C. Hornsby quickly examined the sheriff's wound as one of his nurses stood across the examining table from him. Johnny stood close by, his heart in his throat.

Hornsby turned to Johnny. "The slug severed several nerves and a main artery. There are bone chips here, too. I'll operate at once and do what I can to save the arm, but it's gonna be touch and go."

"Do what you can, Doctor. I'll be out here in the waiting room. Mom should be here soon."

Johnny had been in the waiting room less than ten minutes when his mother came through the door, her face sheet white. "Oh, Johnny! What—how's he—"

He folded her into his arms. "It's his right arm, Mom. Dr. Hornsby is doing surgery right now. It's not life-threatening."

"That's what Jim said, honey. I guess I'm so worried about what it could have been, and that's certainly not trusting the Lord, is it? Shame on me."

Johnny squeezed her tight. "Mom, it's okay. God understands that we're mortals. He knows we don't always react to emergencies like we should."

Mary eased back in his arms and looked up at him. "You're a good son, Johnny Bostin. I'm so thankful God gave you to us."

"Me too, Mom," Johnny replied softly.

Deputy Cade Gilman had gone to the sheriff's office to advise the other deputies that the sheriff had been shot. Johnny and his mother were just sitting down when they came in. Johnny advised them that his father was in surgery, but he didn't know the extent of the damage. Realizing they had to be busy at their jobs, Johnny told them he'd let them know how it turned out.

Almost two hours later, the doctor entered the waiting room, where Mary and her son had been praying, and they both noted the frown on his brow.

Both of them rose to their feet. Mary swallowed hard. "What's wrong, Doctor?"

Johnny's strong arm gripped her shoulders in support.

Dr. Hornsby rubbed the back of his neck. "Clay's all right, Mary. I was able to save the arm, but—well, he'll never be able to use a gun again. I'm sorry. I did everything I could."

Johnny licked his lips. "You mean Dad will have to resign as sheriff."

"Right. There's no way he can use that gun arm again."

There was dead silence for a moment, then Mary sniffed as she tried in vain to stem the tears. Johnny held her tight against him. "I hate to hear this too, Mom, but it could have been a lot worse."

"Of course, son. He could have been killed. Is he awake yet, Doctor?"

"He's coming out of it."

"May I see him?"

"Let's give it an hour, then he'll be able to talk to you."

An hour later, Johnny guided his mother into the small room where Clay had been placed on a bed. He rolled his head and even managed a weak smile. The doctor was standing beside the bed.

Johnny moved up to the bed on the opposite side, staying at his mother's side.

Mary bent down and kissed her husband's cheek. "Dr. Hornsby said he told you about the arm...that you'd never—"

"Yes. It's all right, darlin'. The Lord has given me peace about it. I've had many good years doing the job I loved, now God must have something else for me to do. He'll show us."

Mary and Johnny talked to him for a few minutes, then the

doctor advised that they leave and let him rest.

Clay was getting drowsy from the laudanum Dr. Hornsby had given him. He took hold of Mary's hand. "Don't you worry. Everything will be all right."

Johnny told his father he would check on him later. Mary kissed his cheek again, and the doctor walked out of the room with them.

In the hall, Dr. Hornsby said, "Mary, he's quite a man, that husband of yours."

"Indeed he is, Doctor. I don't know what the future holds, but I know *who* holds the future, and we can't be in better hands."

A week later, an election was held, and the people of El Paso County—having the utmost confidence in Johnny Bostin—elected him as their sheriff.

He was sworn in the next day in a public ceremony. Priscilla was at his side, her face glowing with pride for her husband. Clay was close by, with Mary at his side. The parents were feeling the same kind of pride as their daughter-in-law.

Johnny Bostin had been sheriff of El Paso County for nearly three weeks when one day a lone rider came into Colorado Springs and dismounted where he saw a pair of older men sitting on a bench in front of the general store.

He approached them, smiled, and said, "I wonder if you gentlemen could give me some information."

Neither one liked the looks of the man, but one of them asked, "What is it, stranger?"

"I'm an old friend of a fella named Johnny Bostin. I understand he's no longer a federal deputy marshal, but has become a deputy sheriff."

"Well, he was, but that's changed too."

"Oh? What do you mean?"

"Johnny's our sheriff, now."

"Oh, really? And where would I find his office?"

The old man pointed down the street. "Next block. On the far corner."

"Thanks."

They watched the man mount up and ride slowly down the street.

The stranger set his jaw as he guided his horse in the direction of the sheriff's office.

As a deputy U.S. marshal, Johnny Bostin had made many enemies among the outlaws. One of those enemies was Duke Finch. He harbored a powerful hatred toward the young lawman, who had killed his brother Jake in Raton, New Mexico. Jake, who was wanted on two murder charges, had resisted Bostin violently when he put him under arrest.

Duke had a grudge against Johnny Bostin that had been eating at him like a cancer since the incident, which had happened almost three years ago. He told himself the grudge would never be satisfied until he had gunned him down.

As he drew near the sheriff's office, he dismounted, tied his horse at a hitch rail, and positioned himself a few doors from the sheriff's office. He would wait patiently, keeping out of sight between two buildings, until Bostin came out of his office, then he would have his vengeance.

Finch was not aware that Johnny was walking down the boardwalk toward the office with his father, who had his arm in a sling.

Father and son were talking about matters concerning the

sheriff's department as they drew near the office.

Duke Finch was keeping a close watch on the door of the sheriff's office when he spotted Johnny and the man with his arm in a sling. He set his jaw, pulled his gun, and thumbed back the hammer. "This is the date they'll put on your tombstone, Bostin."

Up the boardwalk, Johnny's head was turned toward his father as they talked, and suddenly Clay saw Duke Finch step out from between the two buildings, gun in hand, aiming at his son.

In a lightning-fast move, the unarmed Clay Bostin jumped in front of Johnny, using his body as a shield.

Finch's gun roared, and Clay went down. Before Finch could cock his gun again, Johnny fired, putting a bullet in his heart.

Finch fell dead on the boardwalk, flat on his back.

People were gathering around as Johnny called for someone to get Dr. Hornsby, then knelt beside his father, who had been hit in the chest. Johnny lifted him by the shoulders and held him in his arms.

Clay was breathing hard. He looked up at Johnny and said in a strained voice, "Son, that day…when I saved…your life by taking out…Shad Gatlin and Bart Caddo, I told you…I wanted you to…have all your tomorrows."

Johnny's heart felt like it was shattering. He nodded, tears in his eyes. "I remember, Dad. I could never forget those words."

Clay coughed and said weakly, "Make those tomorrows count for Jesus and for the people of this county, son."

"Dad, I—"

Clay coughed again and breathed out his last breath.

Two days later at the funeral service in the church auditorium, Pastor Dan Wheeler finished his brief sermon, then said, "Johnny has asked to say a few words before I draw this service to a close."

Johnny was sitting on a nearby pew between his mother and his wife. Madelyne Wheeler sat on Mary's other side. He gave them both a squeeze, rose from the pew, and mounted the steps. Priscilla moved next to Mary, and both women put their arms around the new widow.

The pastor stepped back from the pulpit and patted Johnny's arm as he moved in.

Praying in his heart that the Lord would help him to say what he wanted to without breaking down, Johnny ran his gaze over the somber faces in the audience. "Friends, what Pastor Wheeler just said in his message is as true as true can be. The Bostin family and all our Christian friends will have a glorious reunion in heaven one day with my dad, in the presence of our Lord Jesus Christ, the angels, and the saints of God."

Johnny swallowed with difficulty, trying to stem the flow of his tears, and looked down at his mother, her own eyes glistening with tears. She smiled through the mist, revealing a wonderful peace that only the Father in heaven could give to His own children in their time of grief and heartache.

Before he got another word out, Johnny remembered something his father had told him once, not long ago. *"Son, always remember that God's grace can make our peace greater than our pain."*

With those words echoing in his mind, Johnny felt God's unfathomable peace flood his heart.

He went on to tell the people before him how his adoptive father had saved his life high in the Rocky Mountains when he had been taken hostage as an orphan at the Colorado Springs depot by killer outlaws when he was twelve years old, and that when he thanked him for it, Sheriff Clay Bostin had said he wanted Johnny to have all his tomorrows.

Johnny blinked at his tears. "Since Dad is in heaven and looking into the bright face of the Saviour, I can't wish him back. This world would be too dark a place for him now."

Heads nodded and tears flowed, including those of Mary and Priscilla Bostin. In spite of their sorrow, there was joy in their hearts that only the Lord could give to born-again people when one of their saved loved ones had gone home to heaven.

Johnny pulled out his handkerchief and wiped the tears from his face. "Friends, as you all know, my hero dad jumped in front of me to take the bullet that outlaw meant for me. He gave up all his tomorrows so that I might have all my tomorrows."

The publisher and author would love to hear your comments about this book. *Please contact us at:* www.allacy.com

Discussion Guide

1. Have you ever wondered what your tomorrows might bring? Give an example.

2. Were you under stress at the time? How did the Lord work in your life to relieve that stress?

3. Which character in this book did you relate to the most, and why?

4. Have you ever had an association with a child who was orphaned? Was your heart moved with compassion toward that person?

5. Were you ever abused as a child, or have you known someone that was? How did this affect the rest of your tomorrows?

6. In this book there are Christians who have compassion for lost souls, witness to them, and lead them to Christ. As a Christian, how do you compare in your compassion and witnessing?

7. How has this book helped you not to fret over your future in this earthly life, but helped you to trust God with the keeping of your tomorrows?

The Orphan Trains Trilogy #1

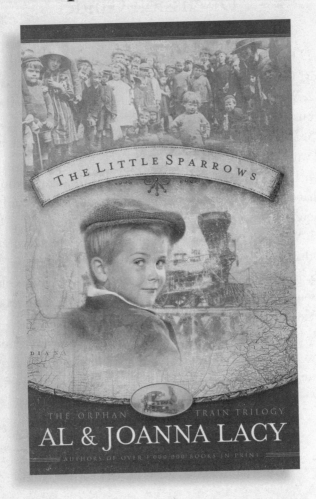

Kearney, Cheyenne, Rawlins. Reno, Sacramento, San Francisco. At each train station, a few lucky orphans from the crowded streets of New York City receive the fulfillment of their dreams: a home and family. This "orphan train" is the vision of Charles Loring Brace, founder of the Children's Aid Society, who cannot bear to see innocent children abandoned in the overpopulated cities of the mid-nineteenth century. Yet it is not just the orphans whose lives need mending—follow the train along and watch God's hand restore love and laughter to the right family at the right time!

ISBN 1-59052-063-7

Mail Order Bride Series

Desperate men who settled the West resorted to unconventional measures in their quest for companionship, advertising for and marrying women they'd never even met! Read about a unique and adventurous period in the history of romance.

#1	Secrets of the Heart	ISBN 1-57673-278-9
#2	A Time to Love	ISBN 1-57673-284-3
#3	The Tender Flame	ISBN 1-57673-399-8
#4	Blessed are the Merciful	ISBN 1-57673-417-X
#5	Ransom of Love	ISBN 1-57673-609-1
#6	Until the Daybreak	ISBN 1-57673-624-5
#7	Sincerely Yours	ISBN 1-57673-572-9
#8	A Measure of Grace	ISBN 1-57673-808-6
#9	So Little Time	ISBN 1-57673-898-1
#10	Let There Be Light	ISBN 1-59052-042-4

Shadow of Liberty Series

Let Freedom Ring

BOOK ONE

It is January 1886 in Russia. Vladimir Petrovna, a Christian husband and father of three, faces bankruptcy, persecution for his beliefs, and despair. The solutions lie across a perilous sea.

ISBN 1-57673-756-X

The Secret Place

BOOK TWO

Popular authors Al and JoAnna Lacy offer a compelling question: As two young people cope with love's longings on opposite shores, can they find the serenity of God's covering in *The Secret Place*?

ISBN 1-57673-800-0

A Prince Among Them

BOOK THREE

A bitter enemy of Queen Victoria kidnaps her favorite great-grandson. Emigrants Jeremy and Cecelia Barlow book passage on the same ship to America, facing a complex dilemma that only all-knowing God can set right.

ISBN 1-57673-880-9

Undying Love

BOOK FOUR

Nineteen-year-old Stephan Varda flees his own guilt and his father's rage in Hungary, finding undying love from his heavenly Father—and a beautiful girl—across the ocean in America.

ISBN 1-57673-930-9